CARNIVAL OF SAINTS

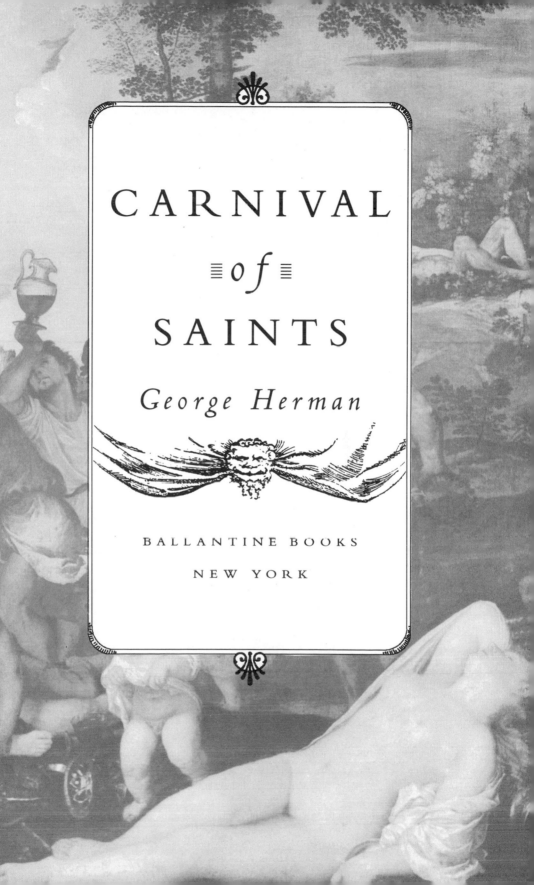

CARNIVAL

≡ *of* ≡

SAINTS

George Herman

BALLANTINE BOOKS

NEW YORK

Library of Congress Catalog Card Number: 92-54989

ISBN: 0-345-38150-5

Interior art: Titian, *Bacchanal*, Prado, Madrid
(Giraudon/Art Resources, NY)

Text design by Beth Tondreau Design
Manufactured in the United States of America
First Edition: February 1994

10 9 8 7 6 5 4 3 2 1

For Kurt, Erik, Karl, Lisa, Katherine,
Christopher, Jena, Amanda, Lizette, Kirk, Paul,
Laura, Crystal, Joey, Cory, Nicholas George,
and especially
Victoria Piper Herman

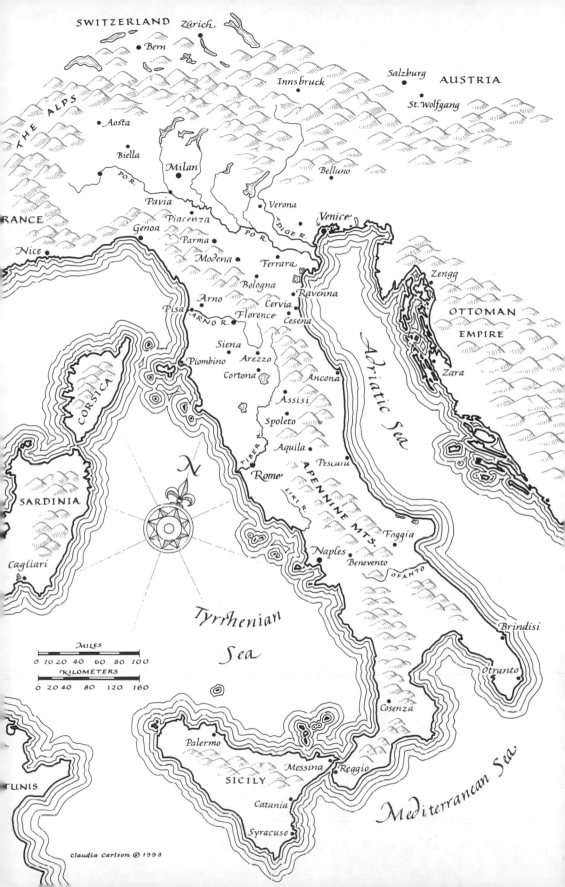

Supporting Players

For the French: Yves d'Alegre (commander), Captain Antoine de Baissey

For the good guys: Annamarie Masaccio, Gentile Zappachio (painter of Venice), Vitellozzo Vitelli, the Baglioni brothers, Cardinal Orsini and his brothers, Pandolfo Petrucci, Hermes Bentivoglio, Oliveretto of Fermo, Piero Varano, Oliveretto Eufreducci, Giovanni Sforza, Duke Guidobaldo da Montefeltro, Duke Francesco da Gonzaga

For the bad guys: Cardinal d'Albret, Cardinal d'Amboise, Gaspare Torrella (Cesare's physician), Sancia of Aragon (Jofre's wife, Cesare's concubine), Poli and Blackbeard (assassins), Cardinal da Corneto

Uncommitted: Filippo Masaccio (Grand Master of the Clothmakers Guild and Annamarie's husband), Gasparo the Wainwright, Angelo the Mole

Whores: Fiammetta, Cursetta

Horses: Giuliano (deceased), Piccolo, Zephyr, Salvation

Mules: Death and Destruction

with

Leonardo da Vinci..as himself

PART ONE

The Company

IN THE MOUNTAINS OF
NORTHERN ITALY, A
RAGGED VAGABOND AND AN
AGING WHORE SET FORTH
ON AN ODYSSEY THAT
SOON ATTRACTS A SMALL
ARMY OF MALCONTENTS
AND REFUGEES FLEEING FROM
MILITARY, ECCLESIASTICAL,
AND SOCIAL
AUTHORITIES.

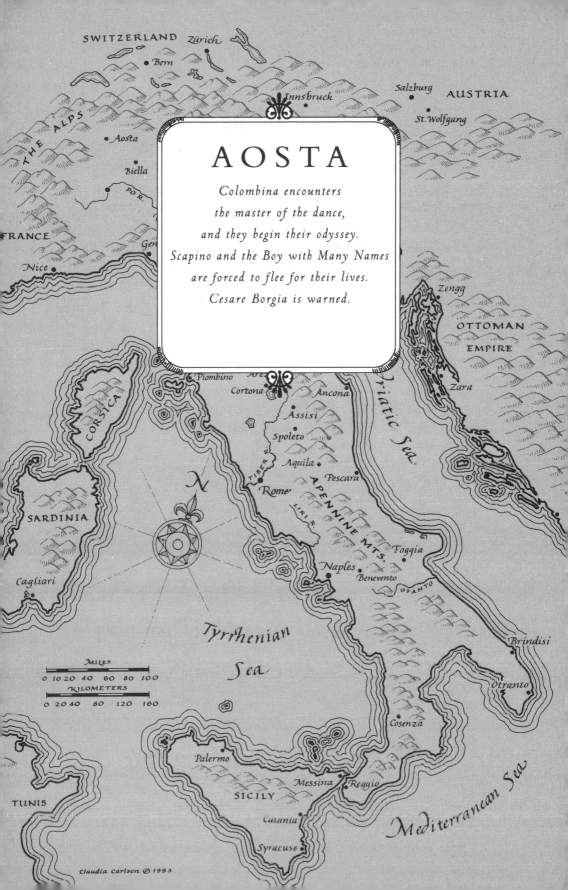

AOSTA

*Colombina encounters
the master of the dance,
and they begin their odyssey.
Scapino and the Boy with Many Names
are forced to flee for their lives.
Cesare Borgia is warned.*

Claudia Carlson © 1993

Through the drifting mists of dust reflecting the golden fires of the footlights, the pale skin of the tambourine circles the head of the dancing girl like a small moon. A rainbow of ribbons spills from the frame of her instrument and reflects those ribbons woven into her dark hair. The golden bracelets and bangles on her arms keep a jingled rhythm to the *saltarello*, and her bare feet dart lightly over the highly polished, wooden floor of the *theatrum*. As she turns, the scarlet petticoats flare from her hips like a blossoming, inverted rose and reveal the young, tapered legs that are her pride and power.

Then she sees the man standing in the back of the *theatrum* watching her.

He is dressed in the fashion of the noble families of Savoy or Monferrato. The emblem of a white stag in full flight hangs from his shoulders on a massive gold chain, and his dark beard is trimmed short, laced with silver. There is a small jeweled dagger at his waist and a sword and scabbard suspended from a scarlet sash.

She pauses in her dancing to study him for a moment—as he is examining her—and then she begins to dance again.

The rhythm this time is slower, more sensuous and enticing, and she covers her dark eyes with her tambourine as she makes slow, circling motions with her hips.

Silently the watcher moves, walks slowly, slowly down the narrow aisle. He comes to the small steps that lead to the platform stage and ascends them. She stops dancing to face him. She feels his gloved hands at her waist, and she permits him to lower her to the shining floor. The weight of the watcher is upon her, and she turns her head from side to side with the tolling of the distant church bells.

Pealing bells.

Chiming bells.

Damned insistent bells.

We can do without the goddamned bells.

Then she sees herself, the ribbons in her hair uncoiling like tiny snakes against the wooden floor. The smooth firm line of her chin becomes shadowed and soft. She watches the small creases form at the corners of her eyes, the deeper furrows plow across her fore-head. One cheek becomes smeared with grime, and her blouse is stained with sweat.

And through it all, the demanding, nagging conscience of the bells monotonously toll the truth of her age.

Thirty-five.

Thirty-five!

She sat upright then, in the dark interior of her small wagon, reeking of the hanging garlands of garlic and the stench of soiled clothing demanding to be washed, among the crates, barrels, bolts, and sacks. And she realized who and where she was.

"Goddamn whoreson of a bell ringer!" was her early-morning prayer.

*T*HE VAGABOND, mantled from head to knee in a blanket of many-colored rags and patches, swept down the Vialle della Pace like a striding brushfire. The face of a middle-aged satyr appeared from time to time from the shadows of his large, soft hat with its brim of an exotic bird's beak. Everything about him seemed to suggest that he was offering himself for the amusement of the towns-people, and his efforts were not totally wasted. Laughter and catcalls followed after him like the army of children who dogged his heels and threatened him with paving stones.

He stopped abruptly at the end of the tree-lined street and wheeled on them, roaring like an enraged lion.

"Aegroto, dum anima est, spes est!"

The urchins scattered in their surprise and fright, retreating up the street and falling over the stalls of the merchants.

The Vagabond laughed, and his small thunder was no less impres-sive, frightening, and loud than the Latin proclamation that was his personal credo. He turned into the narrow side road that he knew entered the Via San Giocondo and the piazza of the cathedral and glanced to see if he was followed. The women and the children in the piazza seemed to have lost interest in him, and he felt relieved and better than he had in some time. He rubbed his elbow against the left side of his body and felt the reassuring bulk of the packet sewn within the lining of his tunic.

He remembered, then, that it had been a day and a half since he had tasted food, and his unmatched boots were so worn that he could describe in minutest detail every contour and texture of the cobblestones beneath his feet.

Still, he reasoned hopefully, *life is full of possibilities. Perhaps today I will meet a saintly benefactor who will lend me a horse to ride south.*

Today, his experienced and practical nature replied, *you will probably be beaten and robbed.*

"Be quick, you understand? And move as soon as the cut is made!" The young, dirty-faced, and ragged boy nodded and fingered the handle of the knife sheathed at his waist. "You must be faster than you were in Vercelli, and never, never hold the purses. When you have one or two, throw them on the rooftop that I pointed out to you. Is that clear, Piero?"

"Salvatore," the boy corrected him.

Scapino clenched his teeth and hissed. "Is that clear, *Piero?*"

Piero glanced at the man and said, "Yes. I can do that."

Scapino straightened up and took one more searching look around the piazza. He reflected on the fact that he was uncertain of his directions although this was his fifth visit to Aosta since the French invaded three years earlier. He reviewed the escape route one last time.

"Now remember," he cautioned the boy, "if there is any trouble, we head for that narrow passageway just across the piazza. It is too confining for more than two men to move along it at any one time. Near the top of the lane I will put you on my shoulders, and you will swing yourself up to the rooftops as I showed you. Then you will recover the purses, and wait for me to come back for you."

Piero nodded again. "I can do that," he said.

"I will continue up the passage to lead any pursuers away from you, swing myself over the sign of the puller-of-teeth to the balcony above the door. Then I will leap for the edge of the adjoining roof, run across the tops of the buildings, and work my way back to you. Then together we will drop back into the street, head for the Piazza del Mercato, then up the wide road, past the Roman arch, and across the bridge over the Baltea. Clear?"

Piero nodded and scratched his behind.

"Bravo!" Scapino snarled. "Now, the piazza is beginning to fill with merchants and guildsmen. Remember what I told you!" The boy nodded again, and the man allowed himself the luxury of feeling relatively confident. *Maybe the boy isn't an imbecile.*

Suddenly Scapino wheeled and raced across the square toward the small communal fountain where the wives were filling their water jars. With a great leap his left foot landed nimbly and lightly on the fountain wall like a bird settling to roost. Unfortunately the right foot poised momentarily on the surface of the water as if testing its strength, and then the entire leg plunged into the fountain. The women screamed and backed away until they noticed that the incompetent acrobat was handsome under his mantle of dirt, and suggestively virile, so they expressed their admiration by attacking him with laughing curses and an occasional friendly slap to his bare legs.

"Behold!" the rooster crowed to the clucking hens. "Hands swifter than the wings of hummingbirds! Fingers faster than the lightning's flash!" He shook one wet leg and began to juggle.

On the edge of the piazza, Piero tried desperately to remember which roof was the one designated to receive the purses. Then he spied the beautiful young woman on the arm of the passing merchant, and the entire question seemed irrelevant.

*A*T THAT MOMENT, far to the south, a scarlet-and-gold carriage-and-six rolled past the papal guards at the western gate of the castle and raced toward the Via Flaminia. On the doors of the carriage were the crossed keys and the figure of a bull encircled by tongues of flame that indicated its owner to be the Roman pontiff Rodrigo Borgia.

From the dim interior came the bright laughter of women, and as the carriage rolled over the Ponte di Sant'Angelo, a silk kerchief fluttered from a window and floated lazily down to the dark waters of the Tiber.

At the Palazzo di Venezia, the vehicle veered sharply north, passed the Pantheon and under the archway in the Aurelian Wall toward the borders of the papal state.

*I*N THE BED of her ancient, worn wagon in Aosta, Colombina turned to the fat carcass wedged against her thighs and attempted to move the huge mountain of flesh.

"Damn your eyes to fourteen kinds of hell, wake up!" She raked her fingers down the soft, pale expanse of the mountain, and it quivered and shook as though an earthquake had erupted somewhere within that gluttonous interior. In a moment the mountain grew a head, and the head grew a beard and a shining bald pate and red-rimmed eyes.

"Wh-where am I?" he asked in the thick patois of the southern French.

She answered him in Italian. "In my wagon. In the Piazza Sant'Orso. Aosta. Savoy. Morning. The last day of June. Monday."

Colombina yanked at her skirt and petticoats to cover the most obvious portions of her nakedness, and she tried to free herself from both the mountain and the rubble of her wagon. She worked herself to her knees and crawled to the back of the ancient vehicle and then exited into the cool spring air. The annoying bells from the Collegiata di Sant'Orso across the piazza had ceased its welcome to the day, but now, from inside the church, an unmatched chorus of male voices began a sonorous intoning of a Latin requiem. Colombina sniffed the cool air of the morning and looked at the snow-topped mountains beyond the town where the Little Saint

Bernard Pass opened to France. *It would be no different over there*, she thought, *since I'm surrounded by the French now.*

She remembered the chaos and hard times when the French invaded Italy through the Alpine passes for the second time in six years, of the arrogant French and Swiss troops that poured through Aosta on their way to take Milan in revenge for their ignominious retreat at the end of the previous war, and she thought, *Perhaps if I went south, I would fare better with the Italian mercenaries.*

Her client stuck his bald head into the morning sunshine. "Have I paid you?" he asked.

"No," she lied.

"I'm sorry," he mumbled. "We—ah—we *did* it? I mean—didn't we?"

"How could you forget?" She forced a crooked smile upon him.

"Sorry. Had a lot to drink." He made a small leather pouch appear from somewhere and began to open the drawstrings. "How much?"

"We agreed last night, didn't we? Two *soldi.*"

The client growled. "I thought we said one."

"I remember now! We said three."

"Two!" he snapped with an air of finality.

Colombina raised her hands in a gesture of surrender. "My generosity will be my death." She sighed.

He handed her the coins and disappeared back inside the wagon. When he did not reappear immediately, Colombina called to him.

"What's the matter, soldier?"

"I seem—to have lost—my knife," the client muttered. He stuck his head out of the wagon again. "My long knife," he repeated.

"How long?"

The fat man separated his hands about the width of his stomach, and Colombina laughed. "You add a meter to everything, don't you?" She turned back to face the mountains. "I haven't seen it."

He was visibly distressed. "It was given to me by my captain, who received it at the hand of the Marquis of Monferrato himself. Have you any idea what I might have done with it?"

"I might have suggested something amusing last night, but you fell asleep." She pinched his fleshy cheek.

The chanting of the monks grew louder, and her client worked his massive bulk out of the wagon and down the three wooden steps to the piazza, tucking, gathering, and adjusting his uniform as he descended.

"My God! Is that matins?" he whined.

Colombina shrugged. "It's Latin. Do I look like I'd know Latin?"

"I have to get back to my company!"

Now that the man was cloaked once more in the handsome raiment of a French mercenary, Colombina remembered why she selected him in the first place: the magnificent uniform, and the fact that he was already reeling with drink and had only an hour of consciousness left to him. She drew an apple from a small sack hanging from the frame of her wagon and bit into it. "Will you be here tonight?" he asked.

"Will you? I thought you French were preparing to march on Naples—again."

He grinned. "Not yet, dumpling. The king is still in Milan with this Italian duke of yours." He leered at her. "So perhaps we can—I mean—later perhaps?" Then he frowned. "Well—who *are* you?"

Colombina groaned. "Do you always christen your mattresses?"

He shrugged. "Well—anyway—it was my pleasure."

"You won't get an argument there."

The mercenary gave a small laugh, turned as smartly as he could, and crossed the piazza at a rapid march. Colombina waited until he was out of sight as she mentally computed her profits: the two *soldi* paid her, the two paid her last night, the two she stole while the client was asleep, and the knife, which she now drew from under her skirt and examined.

No gold. No silver. No jewels.

From the hand of the Marquis of Monferrato indeed! Enough to get me to Milan, she reasoned. *And there is a little Giuliano left, and the morning is still young. When the monks stop chanting, I'll try dancing a little.* She smiled. *The worst that could happen,* she reflected, *is that I'll break my leg again.*

*I*N THE PIAZZA MANZETTI, Scapino was in the process of keeping five colored balls, which circled his head like a scarlet halo, in the air. One or two small coins landed with a pleasing clink at the base of the fountain.

He had attained that degree of proficiency in his art where he could juggle, count the people watching, and keep his eye on Piero, who was now elbowing and insinuating himself next to a well-dressed merchant who had a pretty young girl clinging to his arm. Suddenly the young woman flinched and turned angrily to Piero—only to be treated to the boy's imitation of an idiot: mouth agape, eyes wide open and staring at the juggler. Scapino saw the confusion on her face, and she turned again to watch his routine as a great smile slowly emblazoned Piero's ridiculous face.

Get to work! Scapino commanded silently, and Piero did. Scapino could not even detect the cutting of the thongs that held the merchant's purse, but Piero was moving away, and there was a bulge in his blouse that indicated he had performed his mission with skill and alacrity.

Once beyond the scattered groups that were watching Scapino, Piero tried again to determine which of the narrow side streets contained the specific house whose roof had been chosen as their depository. He selected one of the narrow lanes, entered it, and saw to his right a one-story building that he seemed dimly to remember. With a wide, looping movement he hurled the two leather pouches high in the air. They arched cleanly and fell on the rooftop. He turned then to see a number of half-dressed women watching him from the windows, and he realized that this was the area Scapino had called the Court of the Saluzzo Whores—the territory of the camp followers to the French. In the interval between invasions, their ranks had been replenished with camp followers to Swiss, Gascon, Castile, and Flemish mercenaries in the city-state disputes.

His eyes rested on one especially beautiful, dark-eyed girl watching him from a second-floor window across the narrow passageway. Her lecherous smile warmed him, and he hopefully blew her a kiss.

She returned the gesture, and Piero found himself indulging his perpetual fantasy: bedding a genuine, experienced woman of pleasure. To date, his passions had driven him to an occasional, willing farm girl, while the older boys in Vercelli had regaled him with lurid tales of the incredible pleasures that could be experienced only with a professional woman of the night. So now Piero struggled to determine how much time he could spare for his sexual education.

None. There was only the trick with the cups, and then he and Scapino were to leave—rapidly and together. He shrugged to the girl in the window, who pretended to pout. Her moist lower lip immediately raised in him visions of illicit and immoral diversions. He thanked God then that the older boys had shaken his belief in God and freed him to indulge himself. But at this time and place there was business to be transacted; and business always came first. At least with Scapino. The juggler had impressed this upon the boy many times. Occasionally with one of the huge sausages from Genoa that were their principal source of sustenance and a handy club for discipline.

So he turned from the girl in the window and proceeded back into the piazza and the people watching the performance on the fountain's rim. *The sacrifices one must suffer for one's art,* he thought.

*T*HE VAGABOND FOUND HIMSELF in the Piazza Sant'Orso, where a long line of brown-mantled monks snaked their way out of the *collegiata*. He instinctively drew back a little so he would not be seen, and then, remembering who and where he was and the appearance he now assumed, he crossed the square.

His attention was caught momentarily by an unkempt, weary, but not unattractive woman apparently having a seizure near a small wagon. She weaved and wobbled and puffed and pranced, managing now and again to lift one foot a centimeter above the ground. She seemed to be dancing—if that term could be applied to the movements she was attempting—appearing to the Vagabond as though she were bearing an invisible mountain on her shoulders or

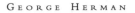
about to deliver an infant wildcat. Her arms looked as if they had been fabricated entirely of elbows, and when she turned, her hair blew into her eyes and blinded her. Twice she nearly fell over the wooden steps of her wagon.

Nevertheless she had attracted a mildly amused audience of three: a well-dressed young man who was obviously the son of a merchant, and two avaricious whores who clung to either arm. Although they laughed at Colombina's efforts, after a moment the young man threw a few *soldi* at her feet. He then projected his two companions across the piazza by a hand to the backside of each, and they disappeared around the cathedral.

As they moved away, the Vagabond moved closer. He watched with open amazement at Colombina's incredible display of ineptitude; but then, sensing her only audience was this multicolored stranger with the beaked hat, she stopped.

"Too many hands," murmured the Vagabond in Latin. Then, sensing from her reaction that she could not understand him, he repeated the admonition in the language of the commoners—Italian.

Colombina looked at him and then at her hands. "I have only two," she replied.

"I mean you use them too much. You're not selling your hands."

Colombina sniffed. "I'm not selling anything." She studied him for a minute. "Are you a dancing master?"

The Vagabond whipped off his grotesque hat and bowed elaborately to her. "I am," he said, "a simple man." He replaced his hat. "So I know what men like."

"I know what men like, too," snapped Colombina, "especially simple men, and it has nothing to do with my hands or my dancing." She started for the wagon, and he followed her.

"It's the men who throw money to you, right? The women have nothing to spend. So why not give the men what they want?"

She wheeled to face him. "I dance so I don't *have* to give the men what they want!"

The Vagabond shrugged and started off. "I apologize," he said.

She looked after him for a moment. "I'm a dancer, not a whore!" she shouted.

He turned back to face her. "You are most certainly not a dancer"—he smiled—"so you are very likely—"

She raced toward him, and he caught the full brunt of the blow on his forearm. He quickly grabbed both of her wrists in a strong grip and shouted, "How else could you live?" She delivered a hard, sharp kick to his right leg that made him release his hold on her, and then, apparently satisfied, she smiled and turned toward the wagon.

"Besides," she said over her shoulder, "I don't dance just for men. Or for money. I'm an artist. I dance only to please myself."

"Then you are certainly not an artist." The Vagabond smiled as he bent to pick up one of the *soldi*. "And you have no need for this money!"

She moved with a grace and agility not evidenced in her earlier maneuvers. She was behind him; the knife taken from the mercenary was against his throat. "It's mine," she growled.

He slowly placed the coin in her outstretched hand.

She backed away from him then, depositing the *soldi* in the shadowy vault between her breasts, but kept the knife pointed at him. He turned slowly to face her.

"Who are you?" she asked.

"I told you." He shrugged. "A simple man."

"Have you a name, simple man?" she asked. He nodded. "And it is?" she asked.

He shrugged and grinned at her. "Forgotten," he said. "And yours, signora?"

She hesitated at first. It seemed like a long time since she had actually voiced it, and she barely whispered, "Colombina Fortini. Widow."

"Like a dove." She lashed out once again to deliver a kick to his legs, but he held her at arm's length and added quickly, "Colombina. From the Greek. It means 'dovelike.'"

She backed away. "Greek? Are you Greek?"

"No."

She circled him once to see if there was anything about him that might identify him with one place or one people. "Why do you wear those rags? You look like a walking brushfire."

He smiled at her. "People avoid brushfires."

She returned his smile. "You don't talk like a vagabond."

"Talking is not my art." He smiled. "If it were, Signora Fortini, words would flow from me like rivers white with rage and inundate you."

She backed farther away from him cautiously. "In-un-date? That's a fancy word for a ragged thief."

"Don't diminish me," he protested. "It's a fancy word for ermined kings, too."

Colombina studied him more intently for a moment, then she crossed to her wagon, recovered her half-eaten apple, brushed aside the more obvious portion of the dirt, and resumed her morning meal.

"You know Greek, heh? And you speak Latin. Can you read and write? Are you educated?"

"Oh yes." He smiled. "The more I was taught, the less I knew. The more I learned, the less I understood."

"You *do* like to hear yourself talk, don't you?" Colombina smiled. "Are you some knight—traveling in disguise maybe?"

His attention was riveted on the apple, and it was a moment before he replied. "If you intend to kiss me and turn me from a frog prince into something more socially acceptable, forget it," he said. "What you see is all I am."

She noticed his interest in the apple. "Are you hungry?"

"Yes!" he roared.

Colombina smiled. "Well, *that's* a straight answer anyway! You *can* talk sense sometimes."

"Talking sense is not my art." He grinned.

She stood up. "Godsblood, what *is* your art?"

It was *the* question. And, as always, it made him stop and reflect. After a moment he made a gesture of futility. "I don't know." Then he quickly added, "But I'll know it when I find it."

Colombina laughed and started into the wagon. "Come on!" she commanded him.

He approached the wagon uncertainly. "Why?" he asked.

She turned to look at him. "So I can feed you! Godsblood, I'm not going to rape you!"

"Good!" He grinned and followed her into the wagon. "I have had a long and tiring journey, so I can satisfy only one appetite at a time."

THE MONFERRATO CONDOTTIERE FELT the tug at his waist and instinctively his gloved hand reached down to fasten itself around the boy's wrist. He glanced down quickly to see the blade flash in the sunlight and his purse dangling from a single thong.

Piero caught the full weight of the captain's hand on his nose, and he felt the warm and salty blood begin to flood his mouth as he was hurled across the piazza. It was instinct, too, that made him bring the blade up without thinking, and he watched with some astonishment as it entered the small opening between the heavy belt and the breastplate of the charging officer.

The mercenary who had been standing beside his captain drew his sword and started for the boy crouched on the cobblestones. He did not see the blur that leaped from the fountain's rim or the cartwheel that ended with both of Scapino's feet firmly in his back, but he felt the sharp pain that left him breathless and hurled him beyond the fallen condottiere. He hit the piazza and instinctively rolled himself over to defend against any further attack. What he saw then was the juggler from the fountain as he grabbed the boy by the wrist and pulled him across the square.

The mercenary was on his feet in a moment, but in his desperate attempt to leap after the fugitives, he inadvertently collided with another mercenary who wore the uniform of a French regular. The Frenchman naturally drew his sword and turned on the man who had insulted him.

*B*Y THE TIME Scapino and Piero had reached the edge of the piazza, the entire area had become a battlefield, with guildsmen, servants, mercenaries, monks, washerwomen, and even small children throwing rocks, crossing swords, kicking, gouging, and rolling on the cobbles. The wounded captain, however, had located two of his command, and these three raced across the piazza after the juggler and the thief.

Scapino relied on Piero to pick the right street, and after a few strides into the shadowy area, he quietly and unceremoniously hoisted the boy to his shoulders so he could lift himself to the rooftop in keeping with their master plan. But even with that extension, Piero realized the roof was still far above him, and he realized at the same time that he had inadvertently led them both back to the Court of the Saluzzo Whores.

Scapino discovered the error as he turned and stepped deeper into the shadows and suddenly felt his burden lifted from him. He looked up to see Piero with the supporting arm of a guildsman's sign tucked under his chin, dangling between earth and sky. At the same moment he saw the condottiere and his men struggling together in the narrow confines of the passageway. He pulled Piero down to a cradle made of his hands and expertly catapulted him over his shoulder. Then he took a moment to roll a cask from a merchant's stall down the passage.

He turned to gather up Piero, but the boy had magically disappeared.

Now, how the hell did he do that? Scapino asked himself. A bolt from one of the pursuer's crossbows reminded him that he had his own skin to look after; and with a few long bounds, he, too, disappeared in the shadows of the street.

*P*IERO FOUND HIMSELF pressed tightly against the firm feminine body of the girl who had watched him earlier from the window. He deduced that she was the one who had grabbed him by the collar and pulled him through the open doorway into this entrance to the house. She smiled at him as they heard the condottiere and his men curse and clatter their way past the door.

Well, Piero told himself, *it is plain that fate has provided me with the opportunity to experience a professional.* She interrupted his thought by seizing his crotch, and his eyes widened, and his breath stopped. *How much will this cost me?* was his second thought.

*T*HE VAGABOND SAT in the wagon and gnawed happily on a great bone buried under folds of fat and cold meat. "This is delicious. What do you call it?" he asked.

She shrugged. "Giuliano."

"It's magnificent!"

Colombina smiled and studied him as he ate. "Where are you going?" she asked.

With his mouth stuffed with the cold meat, he mumbled, "South."

"I know that," she snapped. "Only a fool would go north now with more French preparing to pour through the mountain passes, pillaging and raping."

"How do you know they will pillage and rape?" asked the Vagabond.

She shrugged. "They're French, aren't they? They raped Naples, and that's how they got the French pox!" Then she made her proposal. "Now listen to me," she ordered. "You want to go south, you tell me, but you have no food, no horse, and no money."

He ignored her and attacked the meat.

"So," she continued, "I will take you south in my wagon and feed you, and you will teach me to read and write."

The Vagabond paused in midbite.

"I'd sooner teach a dog to bay the Angelus."

"Good!" cackled Colombina. "People would pay a fortune to see *that*!" Then she added, "But *first* you will teach me to read and write."

"It would be less of a miracle to teach the dog to sing," he said.

She ignored him and rambled on. "I need to make a place for myself while I still have time. If I could write and work figures, I could better myself."

The Vagabond shook his head. "You'd be better situated to earn your daily bread, but it may or may not be a better position. Despite what you may have been led to believe, wealth does not assure happiness."

"Well, it doesn't guarantee misery either."

"Ah," he sighed. "That's—interesting. Usually women don't look upon education as a benefit."

Colombina smiled too sweetly. "*Men* don't look upon education as a benefit for women." She drew closer. "But a condottiere told me once that in the courts at Mantua and Urbino, they are educating the daughters as well as the sons! And not just the Bible or church history, either, but Greek and Latin and even what they call the 'vulgar tongue'—Italian. The girls even learn riding and fencing and—"

The Vagabond nodded. "It's true, signora. Before his death Vittorino da Feltre established a school that includes women. It is called *la casa giocosa*—the happy house. And there is another such school at Padua."

Colombina's excitement was evident. "Wonderful!" she exclaimed. "Then teach me to read and write—and how to dance—since you are expert at everything."

The Vagabond paused, studied her for a moment, and then said as kindly as he could, "You have no discernible talent, signora, and I am not a dancing master."

She persisted. "I was good once, but I seem to have forgotten how. Now, when I tell my body to turn, it takes longer. Sometimes it never gets the message at all."

He took another bite of the meat and looked at her. "Signora," he began, "I would like nothing better than to oblige you, but you move like a camel in labor. When you leap, your feet seem reluctant to say farewell to the earth. You flail your arms like a reaper with six scythes in each hand, and you have absolutely no sense of rhythm."

She glared at him. "How about the color of my eyes? Are *they* right?" Then she snapped, "Of course I'm a poor dancer! That's why I need a teacher, idiot!"

The Vagabond stared at her in disbelief. "Why should I teach you?"

"I told you. Because I can provide you with food and drink and transportation." Then she studied him for a moment. "And—maybe—sometimes—other things."

His eyes widened in amazement at the indecent proposal, but his devotion to honesty warred with his appetite, and he said discreetly, "I have gone a long time without—other things."

She nodded. "With your manners, I'm not surprised."

"Signora," he said, "I can sympathize with you, but I travel alone—like a rhinoceros."

"I can see how you would identify with wild and horny creatures," she said dryly, "but you have no money or food. You'd starve before you reached Bologna."

"The Lord will provide."

"In Italy, the lords collect taxes," she said. Then she began to enumerate them on her fingers. "The tax on oil is now fifteen *soldi* per *orcio*. Imagine! The tax on salt has increased twenty times from what it had been last year, and the egg tax has increased twelve times. In Florence there is a new tax apart from their *estimo* taxes on the rich and the *gabelle* duties on food. Some say Genoa has stopped their *avaria* tax, but I'll believe it when I see it. And new levies are due here next week to replenish the treasury of the Duke of Milan, who has fled to Austria, leaving the coffers empty. That's another good reason to head south."

The Vagabond sighed and decided on a more direct approach. "Signora, I will teach you to read and write," he said, "when the devil sings high mass."

Her hand whipped out faster than a thought and tore the meat from him. He noted that the smile was gone, and then the unsatisfied ache in his stomach became even more insistent. "Well," he said in surrender, "most monks sound like the devil."

Colombina slipped the meat back into his hand and smiled again.

"But," he added, "we travel together only as long as it takes me to teach you to read and write. Dancing is optional. Then I go on by myself."

"Where?"

"Farther."

"Why?"

"Because," he said slowly and deliberately as if he were taking an oath or educating an idiot, "the stars circle. The rivers run. Birds soar, and mountains crumble, and the wind carries both toward the sea. It is, in short, a moving universe, so it is reasonable to assume that I will be happiest when I move with it. Free—and alone."

She smiled and nodded. "The hunger for freedom I can understand, but the rest is just so much oil." She headed for the front of the wagon. "I'll hitch Piccolo to the wagon."

"Piccolo?"

"My last horse," she explained.

He looked up from his eating, his mouth full. "Your *last* horse? How many did you have?"

"One other," she said.

"What happened to it?"

"He broke his leg and had to be destroyed." She smiled. Then, as she stepped from the wagon, she said, "But he was a good horse, that Giuliano."

SCAPINO FELT as if he had personally examined every corner of every rooftop in Aosta. There was no sign of the boy or the purses. *The boy,* he told himself, *I can do without. But, damn his eyes, I have a right to half of the spoils.* He had often felt that some malevolent divinity had decreed that he work out his purgatory on this earth by yoking him to this impossible apprentice thief who even refused to acknowledge his own name.

He stood now on a rooftop of a low house within view of the piazza. There was nothing visible that would indicate whether the boy had been there before him. No purses, certainly, but no arrows or bolts or marks of a fight either. *The bastard just took the purses and ran,* he decided. *Not that it isn't a relief to be free of him.*

As he turned to leave, his attention was caught by a flash of something near the window directly opposite his rooftop position. He stared and saw a pair of beautiful, nude, female breasts, their insolent nipples at attention. Then he saw two hands enter the frame of the window and stroke the breasts. *I'm glad someone is having a better day than I am,* he thought, and he turned to leave.

Then something else about the picture flashed across his mind. That ring. That ring on the middle finger of the hand that was stroking the breasts. That gold-and-silver ring that was part of the contents of a purse liberated from a wizened guildsman in Vercelli. That ring that had so fascinated the boy that he agreed to trade Scapino a ducat from his share of the spoils to keep it.

"Piero! You bastard son of a whoring gypsy!" he screamed. And with that war cry, he ran at full speed toward the edge of the rooftop and hurled himself headfirst across the narrow passage toward the open window.

And at precisely that moment, seeing winged death approaching, Piero wisely and abruptly slammed the shutters closed.

*P*ICCOLO STRAINED against the weight of the wagon, its contents, and the two riders perched on the driver's bench. The pitiful vehicle managed to crawl down the Via Torino toward the Porta Pretoria at a rate slightly faster than a snail beneath it. The ancient bell tower that had been erected three centuries earlier loomed ahead of them.

The wagon passed a score of bustling masons and carpenters erecting a new priory. A large glass window depicting St. George and the dragon was about to be set in place into the stone wall beside the octagonal tower, which was nearly complete.

"That's a wonderful story," said Colombina, "St. George and the dragon."

The Vagabond laughed lightly. "Indeed. But just once I would like to hear it from the dragon's point of view."

Colombina could not resist laughing, but she quickly added, "You have a strange way of looking at things, signore—" She paused. "I have to call you *something*," she snapped.

Her fellow traveler closed his eyes. . . .

*T*HE TWO HOODED TORTURERS *towered over him once again. They looked without interest or compassion on his bloody and swollen face. He tried to see them clearly through eyes caked with blood and sweat, but they appeared only as shadowy waves of black, like dark flames. He felt the cold, damp floor of the chamber against his bare skin. His tormentors backed away, and he heard once again the cold recitation of his crimes from the Examiner seated in the dimly lit corner. He tried to concentrate on his words.*

"Why do you wish to change your life? Have you forgotten your commission? Your contract signed before God? You agreed to accept your position forever—forever—according to the Order of Melchizedek. You remember that, don't you? You were aware of the nature and the gravity of that oath, weren't you? You knew what was meant by the Order of Melchizedek?"

He knew he could die there. Others had before him. But somehow—by some recollection of the conditions that had brought him to this place—he felt they would not kill him. Not now. And not for this. And it was that assurance that prompted him to answer.

"Do—as—you're—told?"

He was lifted from the cold floor by a rough hand clutching his throat, and the shorter of the two torturers hissed at him. "You are driven by evil forces. Your name hereafter shall be Helquin. Demon. And you shall be the consort of whores and harlots."

*H*E REMEMBERED NOW the harlot beside him as Colombina snapped the reins to urge on poor Piccolo a little faster. "You may call me—" He pressed the words into one. Harlot. Helquin. There was a pause as he considered it and sounded the new name to himself. Then he pronounced it aloud.

"Harlequin."

*S*CAPINO LANDED A KICK squarely to the seat of the boy's worn pants as he half chased, half dragged him toward the Via Torino. He had the young man at a disadvantage, because Piero was still struggling to fasten his trousers. The boy tried to keep ahold of the purses and one of his boots, hop on his successfully shod left foot, and dodge the kicks and slaps simultaneously; but what was really annoying him was the fact that he had had no time to experience the arts of the professional whore before Scapino had thundered his way into the house.

"Spawn of a pig's behind!" Scapino cursed at him and aimed another kick that missed by a fraction of an inch.

"Why are you so angry? I have the purses, don't I? I had to do something while I waited for you, didn't I? I never gave the girl a single coin! Not a *soldi*! And she *did* save my life, didn't she?"

"You're right!" Scapino growled. "I should be kicking *her*."

By the time they had reached the wide street that led from the city, Piero had managed to don both boots and tuck the purses in the sack he looped over one shoulder. Meanwhile Scapino's attention had been diverted from his errant apprentice to the number and location of every mercenary within sight. He groaned as he looked east toward the old Roman structure, the Porta Pretoria.

"What's the matter?" Piero asked.

"Damn your eyes! Can't you see?" He turned the boy's head to force him to look.

"Mercenaries. So? Italy is full of mercenaries."

"If your eyes were as quick as your prick, you whoreson, you'd see that they wear the same crest as that unfortunate captain you stabbed in the piazza. They are in service to the marquis. They're checking all the transients leaving the city."

At that precise moment Scapino looked west and saw an old horse-drawn wagon plodding its weary way toward them. He pulled Piero's head around to face it. "Now listen to me, you sperm of a jackass! This wagon coming toward us, you see it?" Piero nodded as best he could with Scapino's iron grip on his neck. "When it passes," Scapino said, "you are to move as though the devil himself had a pitchfork up your behind. Throw yourself as quietly and as fast as you can inside the wagon and, once inside, burrow under anything you can use to hide yourself. I'll be right behind you. Clear?"

Piero nodded, and Scapino released his hold.

As the horse and wagon passed by them Scapino examined the strangely garbed man and the rotund woman on the driver's bench. *Well,* he thought, *beggars cannot choose.*

Within seconds both thieves were inside the wagon and hidden under the sacks, bolts of fabric, and assorted other cargo. Harlequin and Colombina felt nothing, although Piccolo was aware of an added burden and nearly stumbled.

*A*s COLOMBINA'S HUMBLE WAGON descended from Aosta to the south and east, a gilded carriage-and-six rolled through the Piazza Rinascimento in the city of Urbino and stopped before the great doors of the palazzo. Two servants hurried down the stairs to open the carriage door and lower its step.

In a moment a short dark man garbed in black from head to toe descended and lifted a hand to help the cardinal, in his scarlet cap and cape, to step down. Both men then turned to assist their companions, two courtesans in elegant ruffled gowns.

As the visitors approached the doors a servant was dispatched to inform the duke that his brother-in-law, Cardinal Amanieu d'Albret, and Father Francesco Troches, personal secretary to the Pontiff of Rome, had arrived with two—friends.

The four guests entered and passed through the arcaded *cortile d'onore*, the walls of which were lined with huge frescoes. Here the women were separated from the secretary and the cardinal and escorted by servants up the broad staircase. The gentlemen and four guards continued down the long corridor to the anteroom, where two large doors decorated with blue-and-white reliefs depicting Greek and Roman gods were quickly opened to them.

The dark-bearded and elegantly dressed young duke sat behind a wide and polished mahogany table placed before a huge banner with his personal coat of arms, a combination of the Borgia bull with the blue bands of the Oms family and the fleur-de-lis of France, a reminder to everyone that the former Italian cardinal was now a prince of France, the Duke of Valentinois. Cesare Borgia, who wore the Order of St. Michael on a thick silver chain over his customary black velvet doublet, turned to face his two visitors with neither warmth nor disdain. He rose slowly, came around the table, and half genuflected to kiss the cardinal's ring. "Eminence," he said softly, "and how is your daughter?"

"Your wife is well," the cardinal replied.

"Well," repeated the duke without further comment. Then he turned to Troches. "And?" he asked.

"Your father has sent me to tell you that Louis is angry that Vitelli and Baglioni have attacked Florence, despite the fact that that city is under pledge of the French king."

Cesare shrugged and came back around the table. "Is he? Well . . . what can I do? They are good soldiers." He sat down and gestured the visitors to red plush chairs opposite him. "What does my father want of me?"

"He says you should ride at once to Milan and personally assure the king that you were not violating his commands," said Troches.

"Does he?" Cesare rose and crossed to the great windows that looked down on the hanging gardens. "Then I suppose—I must." He turned slowly and smiled at the cardinal. "I understand your traveling companion is an old friend, Eminence."

The cardinal returned the smile. "Signorina Fiammetta has done me the honor."

"She does it well." Cesare smiled. "But—as a precaution—you both might be examined by my physician, Gaspare Torrella, while you are here. He has developed a cure for the French pox that is surprisingly effective."

The cardinal nodded and said softly, "I hope you do not name it so to the king. The French refer to it as the Neapolitan curse. They say *they* caught it in Naples."

Cesare smiled briefly. "*I* caught it in Lyons," he said, and turned to the giant, black-bearded condottiere by the door. "Michelotto, prepare orders for Vitelli and Baglioni to leave Arezzo and Tuscany. Have the gray saddled for me, and choose two others to ride with us. We are going to Milan—as knights of St. John of Jerusalem. We shall change horses at Forli and at my sister's palazzo in Ferrara."

Michelotto nodded and silently disappeared as Cesare turned to his guests. "I regret I cannot join you for the meal, but Milan is a long way, and apparently my father wants me there before the French king leaves for Genoa." He turned to face the cardinal. "The ladies are in adjoining apartments in the Iole wing. I'm sure you will have no trouble finding them. Signorina Fiammetta's scent will permeate the corridors."

He smiled, and as quickly the smile—and he—vanished.

"THAT IS THE LEPER'S TOWER," Harlequin said. He gestured to one of the structures along the old Roman wall. "There, according to an old legend, some strange and mysterious leper of high rank was held until he died."

"Have you been here before?" asked Colombina.

"I've been everywhere before," replied Harlequin. Then he pointed to the huge Arch of Augustus that spanned the road. "That is the arch built to honor Caesar Augustus despite the fact that the Roman Emperor, understandably, avoided this pitiful town all his life." He pointed then to a huge crucifix that was suspended beneath the arch. "That great crucifix," he said, "was supposedly erected on order of Sant'Anselmo himself, who later became Arch-bishop of Canterbury and who held the dangerous theory that the kings of England should be subservient to the popes of Rome."

As they approached the bridge and the river they passed the ruins of an old Roman amphitheater.

"A *theatrum!*" Colombina exclaimed with obvious pleasure.

"Not just any old Roman amphitheater," said Harlequin. "Look at the size of that stage wall still standing. Over twenty meters high. Imagine the vast productions that could be played upon *that* stage!"

Colombina smiled. "I dream sometimes of dancing in a *theatrum.*"

The Vagabond looked at her, and then turned away. "I—dream sometimes," he said softly.

He became silent and absorbed in his own thoughts after that, and Colombina encouraged Piccolo onward and did not press con-versation upon her ragged companion. She nodded, in passing, to the mercenaries in green standing by the Porta Pretoria, and the wagon crossed the bridge and left the city.

BIELLA

Pantalone receives a new name.
Piccolo dies.
Scapino is introduced to a fulcrum,
and the capitano explains the
city-state wars in northern Italy.

SWITZERLAND   Zürich

Bern

Innsbruck   Salzburg   AUSTRIA

St.Wolfgang

THE ALPS

Aosta

Biella

POR.

FRANCE

Nice   Gen

Zengg

OTTOMAN
EMPIRE

Zara

Piombino   Are   Adriatic Sea

Cortona   Ancona

CORSICA   Assisi

Spoleto

TIBER R.   Aquila

Rome   Pescara

APENNINE MTS.

LIRI R.

SARDINIA   Foggia

Naples   Benevento

Cagliari   OFANTO

Brindisi

Tyrrhenian

Sea   Otranto

Cosenza

MILES

0 10 20 40 60 80 100

KILOMETERS   Palermo

0 20 40 80 120 160   Messina   Reggio

SICILY

TUNIS   Catania

Syracuse   *Mediterranean Sea*

Claudia Carlson © 1993

The road south and east from Aosta was a steep grade descending past iron mines, the abandoned strongholds of Nus, Bard, and Issogne, and the vineyards of the Piedmont set down on vast, terraced land resembling a giant's staircase. The ancient wagon traced the river to Ivrea, rattled and creaked past the four towers of the castello that gave a name to the stone fortress, and then through the Piazza Marsala and past the ruined remains of the Roman amphitheater. As they continued along the downgrade west they eventually came to the fork in the road: north to Biella, south to Vercelli.

Hidden in the back, Scapino and Piero breathed a sigh of relief as they felt the wagon turn north and not south to Vercelli, from which they were fugitives from Savoy justice.

The problem now facing Colombina was no longer trying to urge Piccolo to pull a loaded wagon a few more miles as he was forced to do on the plateau of Aosta. The road to Biella was so steep, and the construction of Colombina's wagon so peculiar, that Piccolo found he could lift his feet from the ground, hang between the traces, and ride down the mountains along with everyone else—which posed the new difficulty of steering the vehicle around the winding roadway without turning over.

Colombina and Harlequin struggled to brake the wheels and keep the wagon from flying down the Val d'Aosta and straight into the waters of the Dora Baltea. The problem was partially solved when the wagon—and Piccolo—abruptly left the road, continuing the descent over the rocks through the scrub pines, raking the sides of the wagon against the firs and larches and the birch trees, and occasionally leaping over the stone-and-log shelters erected in the pastures for the grazing animals.

During this mad journey, the old wagon creaked and protested and lurched from side to side like a drunken sailor. Colombina heard the crash and clang of her goods tumbling around behind her, and occasionally she thought she heard a sudden explosion of air, a curse, and soft moaning. But navigation demanded all her attention.

The vehicle—and the wildly triumphant Piccolo, who thought

the speed was a product of his rejuvenation—came to an abrupt stop under a great birch at the very edge of the river.

"Shall we pause and eat a little something?" asked Harlequin dryly.

Colombina struggled to regain her breath and strength and nodded weakly. She dismounted on liquid legs. "I'll unhitch that crazy horse and let him have some of this sweet grass and water," she said. "There's a sack of apples near the back of the wagon. Have one or two of them until I see what else we have to eat."

She began to tug at the harness, and the ragged man went to the back of the wagon and began to rummage through the shifted cargo. "Apples, apples," Harlequin muttered to himself as he fingered the sacks, trying to determine the contents. "Onions." And then without thinking, "With fingers." Suddenly he snapped his arm like a whip, and Piero was ejected from the wagon as though he had been hurled from a siege catapult.

Harlequin had the boy's right hand gripped in his own, and as the youth struck the ground the ragged vagabond pivoted quickly, still keeping hold, and planted one foot firmly on his chest. The boy's scream of pain was echoed by the war cry of rage that erupted from Scapino, who suddenly appeared on the top step of the wagon. The juggler seemed to have been ejected from a giant, uncoiling spring as he leaped, hands and arms outstretched, like an angry bear, straight for the bizarre figure standing on his apprentice. The force of that lunge was enough to hurl Harlequin back from the boy.

If Harlequin had been there when the flying Scapino arrived.

Instead he stepped lightly to his right, and Scapino sailed past and landed with a depressing thump at the base of an umbrella pine.

Instinctively Scapino rolled on his back and brought his legs up to defend himself, but the ragged man in the strange hat just stood there, one foot still restraining Piero, and smiled at the juggler. Scapino arched himself up and on his feet in a single dazzling move, and cartwheeled toward his smiling opponent.

It was while the juggler was suspended between earth and sky that Harlequin momentarily abandoned Piero, squatted on one leg, and swept the other around in a wide arc that snapped both of Scapino's hands out from under him. The juggler entered the gentle and grassy earth nose first.

Piero watched the movement with admiration. *I can do that,* he thought.

Seizing his opportunity, the boy lowered his head and raced toward Harlequin's back, but at the last moment the vagabond stepped to one side, whipped off his grotesque cap, and caught Piero's head in it. He released the cap and the charging boy at the same time, and the blinded youth collided with the trunk of another umbrella pine and fell immobile beside Scapino.

"Friends?" Colombina inquired of Harlequin.

"They are *now*," he said, and stepped to Scapino to examine his bleeding nose. "I think we'll need a wet cloth for this."

"I'll get one," Colombina volunteered as she headed for the river.

Scapino clamped his hand under his nose to stop the flow of blood temporarily. "How did you do that?" he muttered in admiration through his fingers.

"Leverage." Harlequin smiled.

"What?"

"I was a fulcrum. You were an unbalanced weight."

Scapino studied him for a moment. "Show me again."

"Certainly," said Harlequin. "Have you another nose or shall we just break this one in a different place?"

Piero was squatting on the grass, trying to work the knots from his neck by slowly rotating his head in small circles. "You didn't have to beat us," he said. "We didn't steal anything."

Harlequin turned his attention to the boy. "Who are you?" he asked.

"His name is Piero," said Scapino.

"My name is Rodrigo," said the boy.

"Piero!" snarled Scapino.

"Giovanni!" the boy snapped back.

"The little bastard only does that to annoy me," muttered Scapino into his bloody hand.

"What were you doing in the back of that wagon?" asked Harlequin.

"Setting out to see some of the world," said the boy.

"What about your parents?" asked Colombina as she returned with a wet cloth that she handed to Scapino.

"They've already seen too much of the world," said the boy.

"Were you apprenticed?" she asked.

The boy glared at Scapino, who was too engrossed with his repairs to notice him.

"I was," he said, "but I didn't like the work."

"What kind of work was it?"

"Hard work."

"I see your point." Harlequin smiled.

Colombina turned her attention to Scapino. "If you weren't stealing anything, what were you doing in the back of my wagon?"

Scapino sighed. "The boy and I had to depart from Aosta—quietly but quickly. We saw your wagon pass, and we took the opportunity."

"A theological mistake," said Harlequin as he seated himself on the wagon steps and munched the apple he had located in one of the sacks. "Seek, and you shall find. Ask, and it shall be opened to you. Take, and you run the risk of having your head broken."

Scapino rose uncertainly to his feet, smiling. "Not if I know how to be a fulcrum," he said. "Teach me!"

Harlequin paused in astonishment. "What is there about me that makes everyone take me for an instructor?"

"He's going to teach *me* to read and write," said Colombina.

"And that will be my miracle for this year." Harlequin resumed eating his apple.

"Why did you have to leave Aosta—how did you put it?—quietly but quickly?" Colombina asked.

Scapino exchanged a glance with the boy. "Mercenaries. We had a slight misunderstanding with a condottiere whose purse suddenly appeared in the hands of this little bastard here."

Harlequin studied the two for a moment. "What is this boy to you?"

"I just told you."

"He's your *son!*"

Scapino shrugged and said softly, "I suppose."

Harlequin grinned and threw away the apple core. "How can he be your son when you don't even know his name?"

Scapino stormed to the boy's side. "*I* know his name," he roared. "*He* doesn't know his name!"

"It's Luigi," the boy muttered.

Scapino delivered a sharp blow to the boy's head, and almost at once the boy sank his teeth into the juggler's right leg. They rolled together in combat, cursing and swearing and swinging wildly at one another.

Harlequin had started on another apple, and Colombina leaned against the side of the wagon and watched silently as the two continued their battle. Scapino's nose was bleeding again, and he was apparently trying to twist the boy's head into a position that would enable him to look permanently over his right shoulder.

"They're family," said Colombina after a moment. "Strangers don't fight that well."

The combatants had managed to get to their feet, and it was then that Harlequin, having devoured the second apple, stepped between them and grabbed a wrist of each with his own hands. He rotated his arms in such a way that the father and the son completed a cartwheel and landed on their backs in the grass.

Scapino looked at Harlequin in unbridled admiration. "You've *got* to teach me how to be a fulcrum!" he demanded.

Harlequin squatted between the prostrate juggler and his son. "Why does he refuse your name?" he asked Scapino.

"That's the bastard's way of telling me I have no right to name him!" snapped the juggler.

The boy was on his feet, angry. "Because I was named long before I was sent to you! My mother named me!"

"Then damn it! What name did she give you?!" Scapino roared at him as he climbed to his feet.

"I forgot!" the boy screamed. "But when I hear it again, I'll remember!"

Harlequin stood and drew Scapino to one side. "Where is the boy's mother?"

"Who knows?" the juggler shrugged. "One day there was a knock on my door, and when I opened it, there was this boy. He said he was about eleven or twelve. He had a piece of sheepskin in his grubby hand with strange markings on it. I took it to a friend who could read, and he said the only words on it were, 'He's yours.' So I suppose he is."

Harlequin stared at him in amazement. "You did badly." He sighed. "You are supposed to seduce the girl and leave the baby with *her*."

"You see how ignorant I am?" Scapino grinned. "Teach me!"

Harlequin backed away, but Scapino pursued him, arguing, "Look, I'm a juggler and a thief. But there are only so many tricks a juggler can do, and I'm a terrible thief. One day someone will catch me thieving, and I'll have to fight. Only—because I am no better at fighting than I am at thieving—I'll have to use a knife to defend myself. And when I do, it's only a matter of time before I accidentally kill someone. And then they'll hang and quarter me, and my poor wife will have to sell herself to feed our starving children, who, having no father to guide them, will grow up to be thieves and murderers. Except my daughters, of course, who will become whores like their mother. And all these wasted lives will be on *your* head, because you didn't teach me how to be a fulcrum so I could defend myself!"

Harlequin shook his head to recover his reason after this verbal assault, and then he muttered, "Your wife? What wife?"

"I must have a wife somewhere!" Scapino roared. Then he pointed to Piero. "*That* was not an immaculate conception!"

"And children? Other than this nameless bastard?"

Scapino shrugged. "Who can be sure in these confusing times?"

Colombina took Harlequin by the arm then and led him to one side of the wagon, away from the juggler and his son. "We have a small problem," she whispered.

"So does this gentleman." Harlequin laughed lightly.

"Piccolo is dead."

He backed away from her. "The horse? The horse is dead? How is that possible?"

Colombina scratched her head. "I guess the trip down from Aosta was too much for him." Then she added with a smile. "He was a good old horse. He died happy, I'm sure."

Harlequin sighed. "I'm delighted he achieved that goal of all good Catholics, but how do you propose we move the wagon?"

She smiled at him. "It could be pulled—if we had someone to pull it."

He looked at her then, and she turned her head in the direction of the two thieves. Harlequin smiled. "I underestimated you. You have the mind of a Sicilian." He glanced in the direction of the two thieves. "How far is it to Biella?" he asked.

"About ten kilometers more." She grinned. "And downhill all the way."

Harlequin smiled again and shook his head in quiet resignation. He started around to the other side of the wagon.

"By the by." Colombina stopped him. "Giuliano is almost gone. Shall we . . . ?"

"No!" he snapped.

*I*N SAVONA, south of Biella, the papal carriage raced away from the Palazzo della Rovere at breakneck speed, causing the four occupants to ricochet and bounce off one another with pleasurable abandon.

"What did the cardinal say?" asked Fiammetta as the papal secretary attempted to steady himself by grasping both her breasts.

"He said thank you." Troches winked.

"Not much reward for passing on information about the duke."

Cardinal d'Albret laughed as the other courtesan's shapely and cotton-stockinged legs whipped around his face. "It may prove profitable—later."

Fiammetta patted his cheek and assisted her friend in smoothing her skirts and recovering her seat beside the cardinal. "It may also prove fatal—should the duke find out."

"But who would tell him?" Troches smirked. Then, at the sight of the flashing eyes and crooked smile of his companion, his expression faded as he turned to the cardinal. "Well, there goes the profit." He sighed.

ᴀᴛ ᴛʜᴇ ᴍᴏᴍᴇɴᴛ when Harlequin and Colombina stepped behind the wagon, Scapino had moved quickly to the side of his son.

"Now listen, Piero!"

"Cesare," the boy whispered.

"Listen!" Scapino pulled him closer. "We have to get as far from Aosta as we can, and these strangers are going south. If we stay with them, we're less likely to attract attention, and—what's more important—we won't have to walk."

The boy pondered for a moment. "I don't know. We have the purses from Aosta, and I still have the gold ring. We could probably buy horses in Biella, or find someplace here in the countryside where we could hide for a while, and—"

His father released him. "All right. Have it your way," he said. "But it wasn't the juggler who put a knife in the belly of a condottiere. The mercenaries won't be after me. They want you."

"You wouldn't let them take me!" the boy said. "Not your loving son! Not your little boy!"

"What could I do?" Scapino sighed. "I'm not a fulcrum!"

At that moment Harlequin reappeared from the opposite side of the wagon. He walked slowly toward Scapino and slipped his arm around his shoulders.

"I like you, signore—" he began.

"Scapino," the juggler coached him. "Scapino Petrucci." He paused. "Or Scapino Biondo." Then he shrugged. "Or Torrigiano. There was some—confusion about—"

"Signore," the Vagabond repeated. "This is the widow Fortini, and you may call me Harlequin. I can see where learning my arts would benefit you, so I've reconsidered, and I've decided to teach you how to be a fulcrum." They stopped, and Harlequin turned to face him. "Now, what do you think is the most essential element to becoming a fulcrum?"

"Money." Scapino sighed.

"Not at all!" corrected Harlequin. "But you must have strength! A strong and muscular body!"

Relieved that he was not expected to pay tuition, Scapino smiled and nodded in understanding.

"Now I have noticed," Harlequin continued, "that your ellipsoidal muscles are completely locked by your trapezoids."

Scapino examined his arms. "They are?"

"Indeed yes!" assured Harlequin as he began to fasten the harness belts around Scapino's chest and shoulders. "And the square of your triangles are not always equal to the sum of your other two sides."

Scapino frowned as Harlequin tightened the leather harness. "What does that mean?"

"It means you need work, my friend! Hard work to correct your problems and build your confidence!"

"What kind of hard work?" Scapino asked cautiously.

"Never mind," said Harlequin. "God in His providence has provided the means, dear Scapino. In His infinite mercy He has taken the life of poor Piccolo, our last dear departed horse, and in so doing, He has granted *you* the opportunity to become strong and powerful and an aide to your fellowmen."

Scapino backed away, but he couldn't go far, because Harlequin now had the reins in his hands. "You don't mean you want me to . . . ?"

By this time Colombina had appeared with an additional set of harness. "It's only ten kilometers further and downhill all the way," she cheerfully informed him.

Scapino stared openmouthed at Harlequin and Colombina. "You want me to *pull* this wagon to Biella?"

Harlequin smiled. "Why, not alone, of course!" And he turned to face the boy, who began to back away.

"Oh no," said the youth. "I'm not replacing a horse!"

Colombina scolded, "You're not going to let your poor father pull this wagon by himself? The man who gave you life? The man who sheltered and protected you and loved you?"

"I don't know any such person," snapped Piero.

"Now, listen, Ludovico. . . ." Harlequin began.

"Rudolfo!"

Harlequin turned to Scapino. "The boy's an ingrate." He sneered. "Why didn't you drown him in infancy like an unwanted kitten?"

Scapino sighed. "I tried. Four times. He has the natural buoyancy of a dead tree! I pushed him off a high cliff, and the bastard was so thin, the wind kept him aloft for an hour and a half! Believe me, I've tried everything! The brat has only one gift: he survives."

Harlequin turned on the boy. "Then I'm giving you a new name, boy, and it will be yours forever, and you will answer to it!" He started walking toward the hapless youth, who began once more to back away. "I am going to name you after St. Pantaleon the Greek."

"Who?"

"A saint. He was sentenced to die for his faith, but his executioners had a hard time of it. He survived molten lead. The wheel. The sword. Burning. Drowning. Wild beasts. He just refused to die." Piero, in retreating, suddenly tripped over a rock and landed squarely on his back. Instantly Harlequin put his foot on his chest again. "Your name now is Pantalone," he announced as he bent over the boy and dropped the second set of harness on him. Then he seized him by his hair. "In Greek it means 'the lion,' and you will answer to it or go through life as bald as your backside."

"I like it! I like it!" the boy screamed.

"Of course you do." Harlequin grinned. "And you will help your loving father to pull this wagon into Biella, where, if God is generous, we can acquire another horse." He took his foot away from the boy and lifted him to his feet. "Because if you don't assist your loving father, the first Savoy mercenary I see is going to know exactly where to find you."

Pantalone swallowed and sighed. "Naturally," he said, taking the harness and starting for the front of the wagon, where Scapino was being hooked to the traces by Colombina. "No one explained it to me so clearly before." Reaching his father, he snarled, "We won't attract attention and have to walk, eh?"

Harlequin took Colombina by the arm and whispered, "Don't use the whip unless we come to mountains."

*I*N THE OUTSKIRTS of the mountain town of Biella, in a bedroom of a house on the Via Candelo, the portly frame of Capitano Francesco Benevelli had stripped away armor and sword, boots and helmet, and now reposed silently beside the buxom and equally naked, young, and beautiful daughter of the armorer Niccolo. He smiled to see her auburn hair trailing over his arm as she lay tightly on her side and stroked his beardless chin with a delicate, tapering finger.

I wonder, he thought to himself, *if she knows how much she reminds me of Annamarie. Annamarie, the lost love. Annamarie the faithful. Annamarie the married.*

"Must you leave soon?" she asked him.

"I must," he replied. "I meet in Milan in two days with Yves d'Alegre, the French condottiere assigned to the duke, and then I have an—appointment—in Piacenza." He thought again of Annamarie.

Annamarie the fiery. Annamarie the ideal.

"Besides, your father may return at any time."

"It takes three days to get to Genoa and three back, and he left only yesterday."

"I once had an arrow completely pierce my shield and prick my chest," he growled. "Since that day I do not trust armorers."

She smiled and rolled over on her back. "*He* says he does not trust mercenaries."

"Understandable," he said. "We are in related businesses, and we seek the same goal: large profits with a minimum of effort."

She sat upright then, the sheet falling to reveal her beautiful, full breasts. "How can you say that?" she scolded. "You risk your life!"

He laughed at her. "Nonsense! I sell my strength and agility and my instincts. But there aren't enough ducats in all of Italy to buy my life."

She threw herself over him, and he felt her nipples against his own. "But *you* could be killed! Nobody wants to kill my father. They need his arms."

He kissed her lightly. "I'm a professional. My job is to kill, not to be killed."

He lifted her from his chest, and she rolled away from him. "You enjoy killing!"

"Not at all! What do you take me for? But I enjoy the gaming, the move and countermove, matching strength against cunning, and cunning against power."

"I think you're brave."

"I am!" he boomed. "Don't I find myself in bed with the daughter of one of the richest and most powerful men in Biella!"

She laughed at him then and drew the sheet to her chin. "You're not really afraid of my poor father?"

He sat up and looked at her. "Of course I am! That's the secret of my survival! I'm afraid of everybody!"

She frowned. *Was he serious?* "But Papa Niccolo is old! You know that! He is very old! And he is short and fat! Enormously fat!"

He laid himself beside her again. "And he supplies weapons and armor to my lord, Cesare Borgia, the Duke of Valentinois! Don't think the duke wouldn't offer me up to the hangman if it meant the preservation of his amiable relationship with his armorer."

She laughed lightly. "Then it's the duke you're afraid of!"

He nodded vigorously. "Everyone in Italy is afraid of Cesare Borgia. That's only sensible."

She pouted a little and turned her back to him. "All this fighting is stupid. And confusing. I don't understand these wars at all."

He sat up again and gently turned her on her back. "The prize, my little vixen, is the same with all wars: power and wealth. And the single rule of the game is: Make treaties when it is expedient to make treaties, break them when they frustrate your greed and personal interests. This quality is called *virtù*, and Cesare is a master." He began to roll the sheet down from her chin. "Let me see if I can make it clearer for you. Ah!" He rolled the top of the sheet to just below her breasts. "Here we have the high northern hills of Italy. Lovely, aren't they?"

She laughed lightly at this and placed her arms by her sides, where they would not impede the lesson.

"Now," he said. "This is Milan." He touched her right breast lightly with the tip of one finger. "And this is Cesare Borgia." His finger brushed against the nipple. "The duke has replaced a Sforza who was married to an Este and ruling for a Visconti. The deposed duke, known as the Moor, had murdered his nephew to get the duchy, and now, to keep it, Cesare must also keep an eye on his own many enemies, including the Orsini and the della Rovere families."

She laughed again. "Has he no friends?"

"A few, but powerful," said the capitano. "They include the French, and his father, the pope." He touched her left breast, and a little shiver went through her body. "Now this," he continued, "is Venice."

"Venice is very sensitive."

"Indeed." He smiled. "It is the doorway to the trade routes of Europe and the East. It is ruled by a mean-spirited and narrow-minded doge and an assembly of nobles who have elevated lying, hypocrisy, and deception to the level of an art form." His finger tapped the nipple. "This is the doge."

She laughed again. "The doge stands tall."

He nodded and smiled. "Doesn't he?" He tapped the doge again. "Well, these are exciting times, and he's easily aroused. Venice was once allied to the French and friend to Cesare, but there are rumors that the serene Republic's love affair with the duke is crumbling. If they abandon him, their armies could well be the deciding factor in the Romagna."

His hands rolled the sheet further down her body. "This is Florence." He touched a small birthmark about three inches below her breasts. "Ruled, at one time, by the de' Medici, and briefly under the influence of a mad monk named Savonarola, who convinced the Grand Council to kick out Piero de' Medici and proclaim Christ as the real king of the Florentines."

She lifted her head a little to look at the birthmark. "I can't see Savonarola," she said, and her head fell back on the pillow.

"No one could," he said. "He hid in the dark shadow of a Dominican cowl—until the pope had him hanged and his body burned." He rolled the sheet lower. "Now let me see," he said, pondering. "The navel—ah, the navel is Rome." He gently ran his finger around the edge of it. "And that small button resting snugly within the folds of the belly is the pope—Alexander the Sixth." He began to roll the sheet lower. "He is a Borgia, so never trust him below your navel. He has at least five children by Vannozza Cattanei, and at least one by Giulia Farnese, although Pope Sixtus declared one of the bastards—my lord, Cesare Borgia—legitimate."

She felt the cool breeze from the window between her legs.

"Now, here, my honey pot," he continued, "is Naples. As you may imagine, at least three European monarchs want to plunge into Naples." She squealed at this prospect. "Most recently it was controlled by the French, who invaded two years ago and took it—for six months. The Hapsburgs covet it, but the Borgias have forged a link with the Aragonese dynasty, and they have claim to it. So right now Cesare Borgia is with the French king, and you may be certain that Naples is one of the topics of discussion." His fingers brushed the soft hair aside with precise authority. "And that little creature sticking his head out now and again is Federigo, the new King of Naples."

She moved involuntarily as he touched her. "You have to be gentle with Federigo," she whispered.

"And everyone *has* honored the Ferrantes," he agreed, "until the pope seemed to change sides and now supports the French claim, and they are planning to march on Naples with their *chriemhilde*." He touched Federigo then, and she gave a small shriek.

"What—was—that!" she gasped. "Cream—what?"

"*Chriemhilde.* Long, thick cannon modeled after the German original."

"Long—thick?"

"We'll go into that later," he promised. His hand reached up and lightly brushed her breasts again. "Now, you see," he said softly, "Milan and Venice are, for the time being, friendly but suspicious of one another."

"But they are both beautiful," she said. "Aren't they?"

"Magnificent," he agreed, "and firm—in their convictions." He tapped lightly on the birthmark and the soft hair between her thighs. "And Rome and Naples are—friends." He touched her navel. "And Florence is friends only with themselves."

"I see!" she cried. "The Italian cities will fight the French invaders!"

He laughed. "No, no, no, no. Much too simple. Italy isn't a nation, my sweet. It is an assortment of powerful city-states each ruled by one or more of the noble families. It is an arena for all these cynical, rich, and powerful groups, and the rules of the game are lies, vendetta, and murder. Take the della Rovere, for example. Cardinal Domenico della Rovere sides with the pope, because the holy father paid off an election debt with a fief and several abbeys. But Cardinal Giuliano della Rovere is a sworn enemy to the Borgian holiness, because *he* wants to be pope. It is all," he said menacingly, "a ticklish situation."

With that his fingers flew over her body, and the woman erupted with uncontrolled laughter. She swung her delicate arms at him with little effect until finally he stopped as she gasped for air.

"Now," he continued, "as you can see, the key to it all is my lord, Cesare Borgia." He held up his right hand and wiggled his fingers. "This is Cesare."

She took his hand and kissed it. "I like Cesare," she said.

"Then you would be very foolish." She released his hand. He waved it around in a small semicircle over her head. "Though much of Italy shares your admiration of the Borgian duke. He has the quality Italian men understand and appreciate. *Terrabilita.* He will do what he must do without scruple or hesitation," he said, "and, at this moment, he is in Milan, which he took from Duke Ludovico." He cupped her right breast in the palm of his hand. "He is allied to the new French king, who has ancestral claims against both Milan and Naples."

She had closed her eyes as he caressed her breast. "That's nice," she whispered. "Attention should be paid to Milan." He gently brushed the open palm over her nipple, which hardened under his touch. "I can see why Milan likes Cesare." She sighed.

"But that makes the doge in Venice stiff with fright," he said.

She opened her eyes to see and smiled. "He *is!*"

He moved his hand away from her breast and placed the open palm flat against the birthmark. "You can see that Florence stands between Milan and Naples. Florence is a fortified city with an armed militia that can be summoned by the ringing of the church bells. Still, with just a little pressure from the pope, and with French approval, Florence would be no problem."

She closed her eyes again and lightly touched her left breast with her own hand. "What about Venice?" she asked. "Won't Cesare take Venice, too?"

He removed her hand. "Cesare is, at present, friends with Venice."

She pouted a little. "Well, then why doesn't he visit the doge once in a while?"

He laughed at her again, lowered his mouth to her ear, and whispered, "I think Cesare will probably visit Venice very soon."

"Fine!" She grinned at him.

He moved his body then to position himself a little lower in relation to hers, and lightly traced a pattern around her navel with his finger. "Cesare has one little problem with the pope in Rome, his father, because the pope wants—everything. And he has another with the French, who have promised to protect Florence, which Cesare needs to command the Romagna. So"—he smiled— "Cesare will promise, negotiate, and prod a little here and poke a little there." He matched his actions to his words, which had the lady alternately squealing and sighing. "In the end, Cesare will probably do what he wishes—while he still bows and kisses the papal ring."

He lowered his mouth to her navel, and his tongue flicked the small fold of flesh. She groaned beneath the touch and trembled. He drew back a little, cupping his left hand in the small of her back while his right moved down her body and brushed the light hair between her legs. "Then the French king will move on and prepare his major assault on his personal goal, Naples!" He moved quickly and roughly, inserting a finger and withdrawing it again.

She gasped for air as he repeated the maneuver. And again. And again. "Naples—surrenders," she said.

He surprised her then by slipping his hand completely between her legs. "Ah," he whispered, "but suppose the French king doesn't want Naples alone, but sees it as an ideal location to wage a crusade against—the Turks!" And with that he plunged a finger between her buttocks, and she screamed in shock and twisted her body away from him.

"The French king," she said, "is a very rude man, and I do not enjoy crusades."

He laughed again. "True," he said, "and that is an additional complication." He lowered his voice to a small whisper. "You see, the pope accepted a monthly stipend of forty thousand ducats from the Turkish sultan Bajazet to keep his brother, Prince Djem, a prisoner guest in the Vatican. But the pope turned the prince over to the French during the last invasion, and soon after, the Turkish prince died. Some say it was a special poison made of beetles and much favored by the Borgias. But for a period we had the unique situation with a Catholic pontiff protecting a heretic Muslim prince against a virtuous Catholic monarch."

She groaned, "Oh, forget all that. It's too confusing." Then she smiled a crooked, knowing smile and rolled her body back toward him. "Now," she whispered, "show me how the French use that long, thick creamy cannon."

*T*O THE EAST, four horsemen wearing masks and the white mantles of the Knights of St. John of Jerusalem thundered across the wooden causeway that spanned the dark moat of the Castello

Estense. In the inner courtyard servants rushed to calm the horses, which were breathing heavily and flecked with foam and sweat.

Minutes later Cesare Borgia, mask removed and slipped into his belt, strode into the bedchamber of his sister, Lucrezia. Candlelight bathed the room in golden warmth, and the blond, gray-eyed lady of the manor greeted her brother in a violet dress trimmed with golden scales. A gold belt encircled her waist and from it hung a rosary whose beads emitted a heavy perfume of musk. She did not move from her chair before the fire, but Cesare crossed to her and kissed her lightly on both cheeks.

"I'm sorry I cannot rise to greet you," the blond lady said softly in Latin. "The—the baby was—stillborn."

"I know," Cesare murmured. "Sit still."

"It's so good to see you," Lucrezia said. "Can you stay awhile?"

"No," he replied. "Father wants me in Milan to apologize to the French king."

She laughed. "Why? What have you done now?"

"Nothing. Louis is nervous and upset that one of my officers stirred up Arezzo against the Florentines—which the French king feels is his own protectorate. My captain was in the right, of course. He was avenging the execution of his brother by the Florentines. What else could a man of *virtù* do? Family is the one bond that cannot be severed. Now the French king thinks I was responsible, although I sent no troops and did not order the invasion of the Florentine lands."

"Then how can Louis blame you?" asked Lucrezia. She reached down to a carafe of wine resting on a silver plate beside her chair and poured some into a gold chalice, which she handed to her brother.

"The Florentines were intimidated, which, of course, was my aim, and to prove their loyalty and friendship, they flew my standard from the Palazzo Vecchio." Cesare drained the chalice.

She gestured her brother to another chair beside her own. "And what news of Rome?"

"Nothing changes. Father forbid the cardinals to hire young boys as personal servants and then reversed his decision. The mistresses of the cardinals still sit in the front row at high mass in Santo Agostino. Catamites are everywhere. The prostitute Cursetta was arrested and led through Rome in the company of a black transvestite who had his skirt tucked around his waist and his genitals fully exposed. He was eventually strangled and burned."

"And the prostitute?"

"She was Father's guest at a party in the Vatican, where she gave the Cardinal of Segorbe the French pox, and Father had to dispense the gentleman from bowing during the Easter services." Lucrezia clapped her hands and Cesare marveled at the way the flames of the candles seemed to sparkle in and be reflected by his sister's long golden hair.

"And how is Father?" she asked.

Cesare took the carafe and poured some more wine into his chalice. "What can I tell you? Every day he gets worse. He trembles at every shadow and hides when lightning flashes."

"He *is* seventy-one."

"His weakness is not physical, it's spiritual. He has never forgotten the night the lightning struck the statue of St. Michael on the Castel Sant'Angelo, and he saw the ghostly lights in the Vatican corridors."

"I don't want to talk of that." Lucrezia shivered. She took the carafe from Cesare and poured some wine into her own jeweled chalice.

"Nevertheless it is not forgotten," Cesare said solemnly and softly. "And I'm afraid they have been—chronicled. That's one of the things that has Father afraid of night's shadows." He drew his chair closer to his sister's. "There is a letter. Allegedly written by someone known to us and now serving with the Spanish army. Addressed to Silvio Savelli in the Austrian court. The letter advises Savelli not to seek reparations for damages inflicted on his estates by our armies, because justice is alien to the pope."

"What!"

"Worse. It apparently details some of Father's more 'entertaining' diversions. To be specific, it describes in detail the feast of the fifty courtesans I gave for Father in my apartments at the Vatican. . . ."

Lucrezia gasped and whispered, "Everything? The chestnuts? The naked *saltarello*?"

Cesare nodded. "And the coupling competition."

She quickly raised a hand to stop him. "I don't want to hear this. If you remember, I retired before the competition."

"I remember," he assured her. "But who would believe it?" He drew his chair still closer. "But it also describes the night you and Father released the stallions and the mares in the courtyard and watched them fight and mate."

"My God!"

"It is all recorded and documented. Juan. The *infans Romanus*. Perotto. All of it."

Lucrezia raised a hand again. "Stop!"

Cesare smiled and stood up. He took a long swallow of the wine and looked at his sister intently. "The letter even includes that doggerel of Sannazar where he refers to you as 'the daughter, wife, and daughter-in-law of Alexander.' "

"This is intolerable! How do you know what it contains?"

He shrugged and finished the wine. "Cardinal Ferrari got his hands on a copy and showed it to Father."

His sister picked up the carafe and filled her chalice again. "Where is this letter now?"

"Ah," sighed Cesare, returning to his chair. "That is the mystery. My agents report that Maximilian of Austria read the letter, was horrified, and prepared a reply in which he promises what he will do—what support in men and money he will give—if the Romans and the cardinals rise up against Father. My agents say both the original letter and Maximilian's reply are on their way to Savelli, who is said to be now safely tucked into the castle of Giangiordano Orsini. I can't touch him, because Giangiordano is servitor to Louis of France."

Lucrezia took a swallow of the warm wine. "But of what use is this—documentation? What purpose will it serve?"

"It seems that the intent of the letter is to drive a wedge between the French and Father. The letter was allegedly written in the camp of the Spanish condottiere, remember? If the Catholic monarchs of

Spain receive a copy, they might unite with the French and the Austrians to overthrow him."

"Overthrow the pontiff of Rome! Ridiculous."

"Highly probable. It wasn't so long ago that the French had their own popes at Avignon." He emptied his chalice and rose. "In any case, I am to go to Milan, calm the French king, and see if I can find any trace of the Savelli letters and intercept them."

Lucrezia snapped, "You *must!*"

Cesare kissed his sister lightly on the cheek. "And so I will." He came into the center of the room and consulted the great clock that stood in the corner. "But I have only an hour and a half remaining to be with you." He went and knelt before her and took her hands in his. He lowered his voice. "Now tell me all the gossip of the Este and the Gonzaga. Have Isabella and Elizabetta forgiven you for stealing the attention of everyone at your wedding festivals?"

Lucrezia's eyes twinkled and then she whispered softly into her brother's ear.

*T*HE WAGON RESTED in the shade of the trees outside Biella, and Scapino sat on the banks of the river with both of his feet in the cold running water. From somewhere deep inside the wagon Colombina could be heard rummaging for food. After a moment she stuck her head out into the afternoon sun. "Would you like a carrot?" she called to Scapino.

"Why not?" he grumbled. "What else would you feed a beast of burden?"

The bushes that bordered the campsite suddenly shook violently, and Harlequin appeared, fighting off the branches and twigs as though in mortal combat with them. "Well," Colombina asked as she stepped down from the wagon, "where are we?"

He straightened and brushed off his rags with great vigorous sweeps of his gloves. "We are," he explained, "somewhere between Biella—and eternity."

Colombina crossed to Scapino, handed him his food, and sat down beside him. "We're lost," she said.

"We are not lost," growled Harlequin. "We are simply between indeterminate points." He sat beside them and motioned for a carrot.

"Any sign of my son?" asked Scapino.

"No."

He sighed. "Well, the remaining horse would greatly appreciate it if you would find something resembling a road."

Harlequin munched his carrot. "I ran into a friar a little way off there." He gestured in the general direction of the bushes. "I said, 'Good friar, can you tell me how to reach Biella?' He looked at me from the shadows of his great hood and said sweetly, 'Follow the road, my son.' 'Fine,' I said, 'but where is the road, good friar?' And just before he disappeared into some patch of woods, he yelled back to me, 'You can't miss it. It runs from Aosta to Biella.' "

"That was a friar all right," said Colombina.

"We're lost," echoed Scapino.

"We are not lost," insisted Harlequin. "We are simply wayward saints cast out from paradise and struggling to return." He climbed to his feet and headed for the wagon. "But what is paradise for *me* may be *your* hell. So the question is: Where is that place of refreshment and peace that is the same for every man?"

"What does that mean?" whispered Scapino to Colombina.

"We're lost," she said.

Scapino drew his feet from the water and examined them. "You said it was only ten kilometers to Biella. I must have pulled that wagon twenty by now."

Colombina shrugged and ate another carrot. "It could be worse. It is a lovely spring, and I still remember two winters ago when the harvests were spoiled, so we had shortages of food and high prices. Remember? The rivers overflowed and carried off cattle and houses; and they found the monster on the banks of the Tiber."

"They found what?" asked Harlequin.

"A monster. It was an omen. Scared the hell out of the pope."

"Nonsense," snapped Harlequin. "It was probably some unfortunate sea creature left stranded and decomposing after the flood."

Colombina glared. "It had the shape of a woman. Mostly. One arm was like an elephant's trunk, and—and she had a bearded backside—and a serpent's tail. And her right foot had claws, but her left was cloven—like a bull. That's what scared the pope, because he's a Borgia, and the bull is his symbol."

"Sounds like a woman I knew in Vercelli," said Scapino. He sighed again. "I don't blame my bastard son for running off. If I could have gotten the harness off in time, I would have run, too."

Colombina handed him another carrot. "He's only been gone a short time. Maybe he's trying to find out where we are."

Harlequin exploded. "The boy is a parasite! An ingrate! After all we have done for him, to run off the moment we unhook him from the traces! It's unforgivable!"

They turned as the bushes began to shake again, and a cry like a doomed soul wailed from the foliage.

"It's demons!" yelled Colombina.

Instantly all three were huddled together, trembling, in the wagon. There was a pause, and then the flushed, smiling face of the boy emerged from the brambles followed by two strong, young burros, who hawed and picked at the earth in annoyance.

"They followed me back." Pantalone grinned. "Can we keep them?"

MILAN

*Giacomo proves he is a master
of the black arts and is
entrusted with a mission.
Cesare mends his fences.
Harlequin composes a hymn.*

Colombina's wagon rattled north of Biella to the crossroads. Then it turned south and entered the duchy of Milan, nearly colliding with Capitano Francesco Benevelli on a great black war-horse who raced around and beyond them and into the village of Novara. The wagon followed, much more slowly and with a great deal more noise, creaking past the Palazzo Fossati, where a small industrious army of carpenters and masons swarmed about the new wing of the Casa della Porta. The vehicle crawled through the Broletto, the square formed by four ancient buildings, and finally crossed the Ticino River into Milan from the west.

*H*IGH ON THE TOP FLOOR of the Castello Sforzesco in Milan, Giacomo Martinelli inventoried the strange wooden device half-hidden in the shadowed corner of a huge studio that was as large as three ordinary rooms. Light poured from the windows that lined one wall, which looked down on the great park and the gardens of the Corte Ducale, but the sun did not penetrate very far into the room.

Now, what did Leonardo call this machine?

The gaunt, tall man studied the contraption. *Let me see. It has gears. And that thing there is a—what was the word? Oh yes! A pinion. And this is a windlass. This is a pulley.* He paused and reflected. *Or is this a pinion and that a pulley?*

He mentally cataloged the items positioned around the edges of the studio, hoping to define the machine by simple elimination. He stepped back to better survey the entire room that was dominated by many sets of great dragon wings mounted from the ceiling and an unusual saucer-shaped invention.

According to the maestro, a man could sit in that saucer, pedal with both his hands and feet, and—if he pedaled fast enough and long enough—the saucer would fly. Giacomo laughed to himself. *Imagine what the good people of Milan would think if they looked up and saw a flying saucer! They would probably be frightened to death and think it came from somewhere beyond the stars!*

Then Leonardo had designed four supporting legs that could be withdrawn inside the saucer while in flight. This, the maestro felt, would help the contrivance soar into the clouds. Giacomo had to point out that the rider of the machine would have to stop pedaling to retract the supports and would, presumably, plummet to his death.

Giacomo chuckled at the memory and continued his inventory.

That mechanical hammer in the opposite corner utilized a counterweight system in opposition to a second system so it could drive a metal rod with great force. Once activated, and with no further assistance, it worked and worked and worked.

Which reminded him of his position in the court. He was not a seneschal to the duke. That position carried the weight of prestige and some respect. Nor was he an apprentice to Leonardo da Vinci. That position was held by a beautiful and spoiled boy. Giacomo's title was "assistant," meaning he prepared the stone for the maestro's sculpture and cleaned the painter's brushes.

And yet he was approximately the same age as Leonardo. They had both been apprenticed to Verrocchio. Giacomo could read and write in both Italian and Latin and was noted for his ability to memorize large portions of the books in the ducal library with only a single reading. He could do magic tricks and had mastered the art of mimicry. *So,* he demanded of his Creator, *why is Leonardo da Vinci a maestro, and I am only a lowly assistant?*

He shrugged and sighed and continued his work.

Over there was a wheeled war machine that the maestro had made for the Moor. He recognized the two long traces and the gear system that was the key to the weapon. The machine was designed to be pulled by a horse and rider placed between those traces. The wheels would rotate and the sharp, curved sword blades mounted on the outer rims of the wheels would cut down the enemy. Which was not new. Such war chariots were common in biblical days. But in this arrangement, the wheels also activated a third axle, which in turn rotated four, huge, curving scythe blades in front of the horse and rider, and still another set of such blades behind them. Such a device, the maestro had told the Moor, would cut a path through the most heavily armed knights and protect the flanks and the rear of the mounted mercenaries.

He laughed to remember that the Moor had pointed out that the device would also cut down his *own* mercenaries and everyone else in proximity to it. So the project had been abandoned. That, of course, had been the maestro's intention all along. It was the principles employed to make the machine work that interested Leonardo, not the practicality of the device itself. But both the Moor and the new duke, Cesare Borgia, believed that Leonardo could develop new and magnificent military devices—which were sorely needed now in the Romagna—so Cesare would continue to indulge the maestro's other, more visionary projects.

That's a strange idea, thought Giacomo, *to use the creation of war machines to finance the creation of art—that would probably, in turn, be destroyed by war machines.*

He shrugged again and attributed the matter to the insanities of the world—like his position to Leonardo.

Giacomo decided that the machine in the center of the room was the new winepress that could receive grapes in that large bowl, crush the fruit by rotating the handle on top, permit the juice to flow through those small troughs into receptacles, and then tilt to discard the pulp.

He also knew that strange device by the door with the upraised blade and the counterweight system was a file maker. As the weight fell it dropped a sharp cutting tool against the blank metal bar mounted on that moving wagon, and that engraved a cut in it. Then the counterweight was lifted by a winch. The weight would fall. The tool would descend, and the moving wagon advance one turn along the grooved cylinder. That way the hammer would create another cut in the metal with each groove exactly the same distance from each preceding groove.

Or something like that.

He remembered with amusement that, for all the maestro's work, the machine had made only one file. Still, that had been enough. Once Leonardo knew something worked—or was capable of working—he lost interest in it and would turn his attention to something new. In that respect, Giacomo was ahead of Leonardo.

He didn't care about *any* of the maestro's mad machines.

That triggered another memory, and Giacomo trembled. He recalled all too clearly the day that the maestro had fitted him with dragon's wings and commanded him to leap from the studio window. Leonardo had argued that if Giacomo would only wave his arms fast enough, he would soar out over the gardens and land gently in the grass. Giacomo had whined and argued with the maestro at least to let him attempt the flight from the quarters of Signorina Gallerani on the second floor. Finally the maestro had agreed to the condition.

It was that difference of a single floor, Giacomo felt, that had saved his life and resulted in only a broken arm, a bloody nose, and the twelve minor lacerations.

Of course, da Vinci had argued it was the difference in launching heights—in addition to Giacomo having become terrified and having stopped waving his arms an instant after the maestro had shoved him from the window—that made the test end unsatisfactorily.

Giacomo, on the other hand, had argued that the test had ended quite satisfactorily. He was still alive.

Or was that what the maestro meant?

Giacomo stroked the strange machine in the corner and silently cursed Leonardo's inventions, but then he remembered the kindness shown him by Signorina Gallerani after the flight, and his mood mellowed somewhat. He crossed to the large easel by the windows where the maestro was completing his portrait of the young girl, and he pulled back the covering, gazing with open admiration and devotion on the ivory skin and the delicate features of the Moor's mistress. The maestro depicted her in three-quarter profile holding an ermine, the symbol of both the House of Sforza and the quality of innocence. He marveled at the lights and shades of the portrait, the beauty and innocence and gentility of the girl that Leonardo had somehow captured and preserved. *How does he paint like that?*

Giacomo wondered. *Didn't I and the maestro study with the same teacher, Andrea del Verrocchio? What did Verrocchio teach Leonardo that he failed to teach me?*

"There is a secret," he complained aloud to himself, "that Verrochio did not share with me. And it has something to do with the light."

He noticed that Leonardo only painted his portraits by twilight. *That,* thought Giacomo, *must be the difference.* No. It couldn't be the light. Hadn't he started painting Marie the goat girl by twilight and nearly gone blind in the process? *Maybe,* he thought, *the secret is in the pigment!*

He jumped at the sound of the door behind him opening, and he quickly replaced the cloth over the portrait. He turned abruptly with his arms behind his back and his eyes lowered—an attitude befitting a humble servant.

No matter who it is, he reasoned, *he is certain to be of superior station to me.*

He was surprised, therefore, to hear a familiar voice from another time and place. "Giacomo! Giacomo Martinelli, is that you?!"

He looked up to see the short, rotund figure of Gentile Zappachio coming toward him. "Gentile!" he called, and held out his arms to embrace the little man with the flaming red hair and beard. "Gentile! I thought you were dead!"

The little man's eyes twinkled as he responded with the classic line that was ancient even when they were boys. "I was too sick to die."

They laughed together at the old joke and pounded each other on the back and the arms and squeezed each other's head in the crook of their elbows and prodded each other's bellies and politely completed all the rituals demanded of old friends reunited.

Giacomo said, "Listen! Do you remember this?" And he quickly ran to a crate near the door and extracted two or three bent pieces of metal, which he discarded impatiently as he searched.

Gentile picked up one of the pieces. "What are these?"

Giacomo looked up briefly. "Horseshoes," he said, dolefully adding, "Leonardo bends them with his bare hands. It amuses the duke." He resumed his search. "Ah!"

What he brought up was a beautiful, silver lyre shaped like a horse's head. He stroked it quickly to see if it had been tuned recently, and then he began to sing in a raucous, guttural voice.

> "Gentile Zappachio paints
> what Master Verrocchio sees.
> Gentile does all of the painting.
> Andrea collects all the fees!"

They laughed at the old song. "Sweet God in paradise," murmured Gentile through his tears of pleasure, "I haven't heard that in such a long time."

Giacomo strummed the instrument one more time and then returned it to the crate. "The maestro made the lyre. He makes a great many things." He gestured around the studio.

Gentile seated himself in one of the three chairs in the studio. "But what are you doing here, Giacomo?"

Giacomo sighed. "Well, when Leonardo told Maestro Verrocchio that he was leaving his studio, Verrocchio took me aside." He began to mimic the voice and posture of the old master. " 'Martinelli, you have absolutely no talent for painting, and you are even worse at sculpture. Your grasp of even the simplest principles of architecture is minimal. So I worry about you, Giacomo. I would like to see you in a secure position where you can be comfortable and happy.' "

Gentile relished this performance. "That's the old master!"

Giacomo smiled and said, "There was more."

Then he resumed the mimicry. " 'Now, Giacomo, you do clean a good brush well, and you only burned yourself twice while assisting me in casting the Colleoni monument. And you nicked only one thumb while performing the preliminary cutting of the stone for my *David*. So I have asked Leonardo to take you into his service, and since he admitted a debt to me, he has agreed.' " Giacomo straightened his posture and shrugged. "So," he concluded, "here I am."

"You clean brushes? You prepare stone?"

"Yes. But you see, I knew that Verrocchio was jealous of my talent. So I agreed to serve Leonardo while really learning the secret Verrocchio taught him and no one else."

Gentile was surprised. "Secret? What secret?"

"How else can you explain Leonardo's success and my failure? We studied together! We used the same paint!" He leaned closer to his chubby friend. "Verrocchio passed on—the *secret*."

Gentile looked over the tall, thin figure who had been so close to him as a fellow apprentice. "This change has proven of some benefit to you nonetheless?"

"I am well fed," replied Giacomo. "I have access to the duke's library and Leonardo's devices and tricks."

"Devices and tricks?"

Giacomo gestured to the rows of dragon's wings suspended from the ceiling. "The maestro wants to fly," he whispered.

Gentile looked at his friend in amazement. "To fly?"

Giacomo nodded. "He already walks on water."

Gentile's mouth dropped in his astonishment. "Really?"

Giacomo nodded again. "He puts two large, white things on his feet—like giant's slippers—and then he takes two poles, one in each hand, and he—glides as it were—over the surface of the water, extending one pole at a time before him. He walked clear across the small lake in the garden and back again." He read the wonder in Gentile's face. "I tried it myself," he said, and then, remembering, he whispered, "and almost drowned." Then he exploded. "I didn't know the damned secret, you see!"

"Why does Leonardo want to fly?" asked Gentile.

"Who knows?" Giacomo remembered another of his master's habits: "Why does he have a special room back there where they bring him an occasional dead body of a mercenary?" Gentile gasped. "It's true!" said Giacomo. "I've seen them!" He looked around cautiously, then he added, "He cuts them open and then draws pictures of what he sees."

"Holy Mother of God," Gentile moaned. "Why?"

Giacomo tapped his forehead. "I think he's working to become

God," he said softly. "He feels he can fly and walk on water already. Now I think he's trying to raise the dead."

He noted the dismay on Gentile's face at this announcement. "It's only a matter of time," said Giacomo, "until I come in here one day and find he's nailed himself to a cross."

"A man can't nail himself to a cross," said Gentile.

"No," conceded Giacomo, "he'll invent a machine to do it for him." Then he added as an afterthought, "And then test it on me."

Gentile began to pace anxiously back and forth, rubbing his hands together, and now and again stroking his beard. "But enough of Leonardo. What brings you here?" Giacomo asked.

"Ah," said Gentile, "that is the question. I—ah—I thought perhaps—the maestro might be of some—assistance."

"He is probably at the refectory of Santa Maria delle Grazie, where they have him painting a wall or something, and this afternoon he leaves for Cesena. I am being left behind to inventory the maestro's devices, and then the whole lot will be moved to Cesare's palazzo."

"Cesena? Why?"

Giacomo drew his portly friend aside. "Well, it all began with the party given by Vannozza Cattanei in the Vincoli."

"Vannozza Cattanei?"

Giacomo looked surprised. "The pope's first mistress! She is the mother of Juan and Cesare and Lucrezia, and God knows how many others."

"Yes, I know," said Gentile. "Well, what of her?"

Giacomo seated his friend by the window. "Well," he said, "Vannozza decided to give a party for her sons and daughters at her home on the Esquiline Hill."

Gentile squirmed in his chair. "Fine, fine. But what has this to do with Leonardo going to Cesena?"

Giacomo lowered his voice. "I'm getting to that." He glanced around to make certain no one was eavesdropping. "Well, after the party, the brothers Cesare and Juan left together, but Juan never reached his home. He was murdered. Assassinated. They found his body in the Tiber with nineteen knife wounds in him."

"My God, who did such a thing?"

"Well, that is the question," whispered Giacomo. "Some said it was a Mirandola whose daughter had been seduced and abandoned by Juan."

"I see."

"But some say it was the younger brother, Jofre Borgia, because Juan had also been sleeping with Jofre's wife, Sancia."

"Ah," sighed Gentile.

"But that didn't make sense, because Cesare had also been sleeping with Sancia and with his own sister, Lucrezia, and nobody murdered him!"

"Lucrezia Borgia has been sleeping with her brother?"

"Oh, that's old news," said Giacomo. "Everyone knows that. Why, Lucrezia is rumored to have been sleeping with her own father, the pope!" Gentile gasped. "But I personally doubt that," he added, "because everyone knows the pope has been sleeping with a former nun from Valencia, and a married Castilian lady, and a young girl of sixteen, in addition to his own mistress, Giulia Farnese."

"Lucrezia has been sleeping with her father, the pope, and with her brother Cesare?"

"They are a very close family." Giacomo nodded. "When Lucrezia tired of her former husband, Giovanni Sforza, and complained to Cesare, the duke promptly gave orders to have Giovanni murdered. But Giovanni raced out of Rome to his own castle in Pesaro and then here to Milan, to his brother's court, for protection."

"But—"

"So the pope simply had the marriage annulled on the basis that Giovanni was impotent, and Lucrezia, in keeping with custom, retreated to the Convent of San Sisto near the Appian Way—where she was rumored to be sleeping with the Spanish envoy, a man called Perrotto."

"But again, I ask you—"

"Cesare found out, of course, and stabbed Perrotto right in the Vatican—at the feet of the pontiff."

"But what has all this—"

"He recovered, but a few days later they found him floating in the Tiber, and the pope, forced to do something about all these murders, banned masquerades at carnival."

"I don't see how that—"

"He said disguises promote assassination."

"That's incredible!"

"But back to the murder of Juan," Giacomo persisted. "Some said it was the Orsini who murdered Juan, seeking revenge for the murder of their own leader, Virginio."

"I see!" whispered Gentile. "Then it *was* the Orsini who killed Juan Borgia!"

"Never." Giacomo smiled. "For one thing, Orso Orsini was ordered by the pope to go to Bassanello and stay there so the pope could have access to his wife, Giulia, so Orso couldn't have done it; and the rest of the Orsinis were at war with the Colonnas, so they had other things on their mind."

"Then who killed Juan Borgia?!" pleaded Gentile.

"Cesare, of course," Giacomo explained patiently. "He was jealous of the honors Juan had received, and he was tired of sharing Sancia, Jofre's wife, with both his brothers."

Gentile shook his head in confusion. "But—a moment—please! What has all this to do with Leonardo going to Cesena?"

"Ah!" said Giacomo. "But someone has to be blamed for Juan's death, and the pope decided on the Orsini. Now Cesare is waging war against the Orsini and their friends. He has commissioned the maestro to design and build new war machines for him, and his headquarters happen to be in Cesena."

Gentile rose to his feet. "I see!"

Pausing for breath, Giacomo remembered his friend's recent commissions. "I have heard you are very successful in Venice—how the entire city paraded your cartoon of the Crucifixion along every canal for the admiration of the people. Bravo, Gentile!"

Gentile grimaced. "Yes. My work *is* popular, and the doge himself has commissioned a Pietà and two Annunciations for next year.

Venice is very fond of Pietàs and Crucifixions." The portly gentleman resumed his pacing. "But this is terrible," he repeated again and again. "This ruins everything."

"What's terrible?" Giacomo asked.

"I came to Milan for the maestro's help, but now you tell me he's gone mad, that he's leaving the city and making war machines for the Borgias!" He made a gesture of futility.

"What kind of help?"

Gentile studied him for a moment, and then he moved quickly to the chair in which he had been seated. He picked up the roll of canvas that he had there, and then he crossed to a table by the window. "Come here!" he commanded as he untied the thongs around the roll. He spread the canvas out on the table, removed two wrapped items that he placed to one side, and then placed weights at the corners of the fabric. "Look."

Giacomo looked, and he felt his breath stop. The canvas was a painting of a buxom, naked woman under a tree. On her lap was a great white bird that seemed to be nibbling at one of her breasts as the bird's huge wings embraced her. To the left of the tree two more naked, beautiful women watched with what Giacomo took to be amusement; and on the other side of the tree, another naked woman was in the process of being attacked by a man with the horns and legs of a goat.

"I call it *Leda and the Swan*," Gentile whispered.

Giacomo felt his heart pound. "Of course," he said. "What else could you call it?" He studied the painting further.

They won't run this painting along the canals.

Gentile unwrapped the other two items that had been rolled in the canvas. "Look at these!" he commanded.

They were statues. The first, about eight inches tall, was of a naked young boy with long hair and his arms bound behind him. He was also lashed to a tree and seemed delicate and almost feminine.

"It's St. Sebastian," said Gentile proudly.

Giacomo noticed the small shaft of an arrow that protruded from the youth's chest. "Naturally," he mumbled.

The other statue was of a naked young woman, her hair loose

and flowing over her shoulders, reaching nearly to her waist. One delicate hand held a mirror away from her body, and she seemed to be examining her own beauty in it. The other hand was held out from her side. One leg was thrust forward, bent slightly at the knee, and revealing her inner thigh. Giacomo suddenly felt warm and uncomfortable looking at it.

"I call it *Lady with Mirror*," Gentile explained.

Giacomo was speechless.

"Aren't they beautiful?" Gentile smiled as he looked fondly at his work. "Aren't they magnificent?"

Giacomo finally recovered his voice enough to say, "Yes. Yes. But I noticed—that is—well—they aren't wearing any clothes."

Gentile nodded, his eyes still fixed on the figures. "Yes," he whispered. "Aren't they lovely? Look how their flesh curves and flows."

"Yes, yes. It flows. But—well—they're *naked*!"

Gentile looked at him then, shook his head, and began to rewrap the pieces. "I know," he said softly. "That's the problem. About four years ago I had the good fortune to be invited to the court of Bajazet, the Sultan of Constantinople. While I was there, painting portraits of the sultan's wives and concubines, I saw statues and paintings done by other artists—in far parts of the world. Their themes were not ours. While we labored over Annunciations, they painted birds in flight. While we struggled to inspire devotion to the saints, they were revealing God's beauty in everything we take for granted: sunrise, flowers, running water."

"And naked ladies," added Giacomo.

"Yes." Gentile returned the rolled canvas to the chair. "I discovered that my imagination had been freed and my eyes opened. I looked at things with different eyes. I became fascinated with the effect of light on different surfaces, with the fluid motion of breasts."

"On naked ladies," added Giacomo.

"Yes! On naked ladies! And the muscled chests of naked men! The human form in all dimensions! Natural! Not enveloped in meters of heavy cloth!" He turned his eyes on Giacomo intently. "In that large painting didn't you see what I was able to do with light and shadow to suggest dimension in the body of the little deer?"

"I noticed the little dear had no clothes on."

Gentile sighed and sat down. "I understand. You see the naked-ness, exactly what the doge would see. And the churchmen. My paintings . . ."

"Paintings! You have more?"

Gentile nodded. "Thirty-three," he said. "And fourteen pieces of statuary."

Giacomo sat down beside his friend. "Then why did you leave Constantinople?" he asked. "These paintings wouldn't be consid-ered scandalous there!"

"It is a strange city," mused Gentile. "In some ways remarkably civilized. And in others remarkably brutal. It is a city without logic, without reason. A man could go mad there."

"I can well imagine—with all those naked concubines." Giaco-mo sighed.

"The concubines weren't naked," snapped Gentile. "And besides, they were always accompanied by the sultan's eunuchs."

Giacomo understood. "When the maestro was preparing to paint Signorina Gallerani, the Moor didn't like the idea of his mistress spending so much time with Leonardo. But someone reminded him that the maestro had been tried twice in Florence for seducing boys, so the duke consented."

"Those charges were never proven," said Gentile. "I think Leonardo practices celibacy to conserve his energy and focus his at-tention on his work."

My God! thought Giacomo. *Suppose* celibacy *is the secret!*

Gentile sat back in his chair.

"You were telling me why you left the sultan," Giacomo re-minded him.

"As I said, it is occasionally brutal. The sultan asked me to paint a scene of his father in battle. I found it difficult to imagine a man dying of wounds, so the sultan had a servant brought before me and mutilated so I could see the effect."

Giacomo felt cold. "And I thought I was ill-used when the mae-stro pushed me out the window."

Gentile started. "The maestro pushed you from a window?"

"It's not important," said Giacomo. He watched his old friend clutching the rolled canvas to his breast. "What are you going to do with all those paintings and statues?"

"That's why I came to see the maestro," explained Gentile. He rose and began to pace again. "Such works would be burned in Venice. I would be accused of great sins, and my reputation would be shattered completely. But you can see for yourself that they are fine works! Great perhaps! But the times are not right for them. Not yet. They must be preserved until such time as others begin to see and paint as I do." He sat down again unhappily.

"Then you shouldn't have brought them here," Giacomo said. "Milan itself isn't safe. The French are barbarians, and even the maestro feels some of his own works might be destroyed."

"But Venice is no safer. I have no choice. I must send my work with Isabella to Mantua. We have friends there."

"Isabella?"

"My—ah—my daughter. Young. Beautiful. Brilliant. Obstinate. While I was in the Constantinople, she was being educated in the courts of Venice and Urbino."

"Urbino? With the Montefeltro?"

"She was a—protégée. But the Montefeltro have their own problems these days, so I would feel better if she were in Mantua. The Gonzaga family would protect her."

Giacomo interrupted, "Good. That's fine."

"But I was hoping Leonardo might use his association with the duke to request three or four mercenaries to accompany my daughter to Mantua. I must return to Venice at once on command of the doge. But if the duke's troops are preparing for another engagement in the Romagna, and if Leonardo has gone mad . . . !"

Giacomo slapped his forehead with the palm of his hand. "Sending a beautiful young girl to Mantua with mercenaries! What are you thinking of?"

"They wouldn't touch her," argued Gentile. "The duke would kill them if they did."

"I'm not thinking of the duke's mercenaries. I'm thinking of the brigands and cutthroats who would realize at once that the girl is of some importance, traveling as she is with armed knights."

Gentile collapsed against the back of the chair. "What should I do, then? I cannot accompany her myself. I must return to Venice."

Giacomo leaned over the rotund artist. "*I* will accompany her," he said, "and we will go in disguise. No one will even notice us."

Gentile frowned. "You? But you're not a warrior!"

Giacomo straightened and smiled.

"God forbid!" he declared. "I have—other devices."

*T*WO FLOORS BELOW the workroom of Leonardo, Cesare Borgia, now in his customary black velvet, crossed the inlaid floor of the reception hall and extended his arms in a gesture of affection to the French king. To the astonishment of his entourage, Louis started forward at the same time, with the same gesture, and the two men met in the middle of the room and embraced. Cesare kissed the monarch on both cheeks.

"Well," whispered Giovanni Sforza in Latin to the gentleman beside him, "if Louis is annoyed with Cesare, he hides it well."

The king, smiling and animated, put an arm around the duke's shoulders and led him toward the group at the end of the hall. "You know everyone, I'm certain," he said jovially. "Duke Guidobaldo da Montefeltro . . ."

"Whom Cesare drove from his city of Urbino," whispered Giovanni.

"Piero Varano of Camerino . . ."

"Whose father Cesare had strangled."

"Duke Francesco da Gonzaga . . ."

"Whose wife Cesare covets."

"And, of course, Duke Giovanni Sforza of Pesaro."

Giovanni smiled and made an elaborate bow to Cesare. Again, to everyone's surprise, the duke suddenly darted forward, seized Sforza by his arms, and kissed him on both cheeks. "How good to see again, my lord. Is all well with you?"

Guidobaldo stifled a laugh and whispered to Varano, "What a subtle way of inquiring if he is still impotent."

The king gestured to another member of his entourage. "And you are acquainted with His Eminence, Cardinal Georges d'Amboise, of course."

Cesare abandoned Sforza as quickly as he had embraced him, and now he strode across the hall to genuflect and kiss the cardinal's ring. The cardinal, ensnared by the sudden show of affection, blessed the bowed duke. "You are looking well, my son," he said.

Cesare stood erect and smiled charmingly. "And I trust Your Eminence is in equally good health." Then, in a semiwhisper, he added, "The papacy can be an exhausting position."

Francesco da Gonzaga smiled broadly and whispered to Giovanni, "Just what he wanted to hear. The Borgian cardinals will vote for d'Amboise at the next conclave."

"Now," said Louis effusively, "we will dine! Cesare, on my left. Eminence, on my right!"

The three men led the others through the great doors into the banquet as Francesco da Gonzaga and Giovanni Sforza drifted behind the others and Giovanni whispered, "Well, that answers a number of questions. Both the cardinal and the king value the power of the duke and the duke's father more than they value their commitment to Florence."

Francesco nodded. "Now," he said softly, "only God stands between Cesare and all of Italy."

"We should have paid more attention to his motto," said Giovanni. "*Aut Caesar, aut nihil.* Either Caesar—or nothing."

WINDING THEIR WAY THROUGH the Piazza Fontana in the heart of the city, the two burros clipped and clopped over the cobbled streets. Harlequin, seated at the rear of the wagon, began to strum Colombina's old and seldom-used lute. Then he began to sing.

> "The sun is god.
> The moon is god.
> Divine, each brook,
> And sacred, every tree.
> Everyone and everything is god.
> Every blessed thing but me.
> How wond'rous strange.
> The moon can change,
> The stars arrange
> Each person's destiny.
> The moon, the stars
> Are powerful and great,
> But all they could create—
> To godhood, aspirate—
> Was me.
> To these gods, I kneel,
> And yet I feel
> The moon, the stars,
> The sunlight, and the tree
> Will fade away
> While something else
> Survives eternally.
> What a jest if it should be—
> Who'd have guessed that it could be—
> Me?"

Scapino munched an apple in the bed of the wagon and yelled to the troubadour, "That's all very fine, but when do I become a fulcrum?"

*I*N LEONARDO'S WORKROOM in the castello, Giacomo walked to the table, selected a goblet, and brought it over to where the Venetian was sitting. From the pocket of his leather apron, he took a small wad of material and put it in the goblet. Then he struck a flint and ignited it. "Observe," he said as he made a great, dramatic gesture over the goblet.

Suddenly there was a small explosion, and Gentile was swallowed by thick clouds of colored smoke that rolled toward the ceiling and curled back again. He jumped to his feet to try to find his friend in the heavy folds of the smoke. "Giacomo!" he called. "Giacomo!" He began to shuffle forward through the fog when he saw the shadowy outline of the tall assistant before him. "Giacomo, what are you . . . ?" He stopped as the outline grew, altered. Suddenly—from what he took to be Giacomo's body—a huge, twisting head emerged. Through the vapors Gentile saw the head become rigid, solid. It began to form scales that caught the reflected sunlight from the window and flashed and glittered. The great jaws opened to reveal large white, curving fangs and black gums. A forked tongue lashed out toward him, and a bellowing roar echoed through the studio.

Gentile backed away in terror as the dragon grew a body that seemed to fill the room. Massive claws appeared on the thick legs, and the eyes began to glow like white-hot coals. The Venetian nearly choked from the foul stench of the dragon's breath. He called in fright and confusion, "Giacomo! Giacomo!"

"I'm right here!" came the familiar voice, and Gentile saw the heavy clouds suddenly dissolve and sweep away before cool winds that rushed by him. He saw the assistant then, standing by the open windows, arms folded, smiling at him.

Gentile rushed to his old friend. "Giacomo! I'm—I'm astounded! You! A student of the black arts!"

Giacomo put a hand on the Venetian's trembling shoulders and laughed. "It's not magic. It's one of the maestro's tricks that he created to amuse the Moor. I did it all with this." He pointed to a smooth sheet of bronze on the worktable and a smooth cylinder that had a piece of cord emerging from both ends.

"But how . . . ?" Gentile picked up the object.

"The maestro calls it phantasmagoria. He read of it in an ancient book supposedly written by an Egyptian priest or something. If you examine the metal sheet carefully, you will see nothing, but the form of the dragon has been engraved into it. The entire surface has been polished and ground until the image seems to have disappeared. But the metal had been affected somehow, and when light reflects from it, so . . ."

Giacomo adjusted the sheet so the sunlight from the windows reflected from it onto the wall. There was the enormous dragon: scales, claws, fangs, and tongue. "But—it moved!" said Gentile. "It roared."

"No," replied Giacomo, putting the metal down and taking the cylinder from Gentile's hand. "The smoke moved. I ignited a wad of the maestro's powder, which created the smoke. It's effective, but it smells, doesn't it? Of course that adds to the effect. He calls it florabella."

Gentile began to calm down. He shook his head. "But the roar?"

Giacomo took the cylinder in one hand and pulled slowly on the cord. At once there was a great guttural noise, which Gentile recognized as the dragon's sounds. "Leonardo calls it a 'bull-roarer,' " said Giacomo. "It has something to do with the resined cord and the folded membranes inside the cylinder. The duke loves it. He made it bellow like that one evening at dinner when Cardinal Pallavicini was about to sample the soup. The cardinal almost choked to death."

Gentile began to stroke his red beard and study his old friend carefully. "Yes. I see," he said. "You think that you—and some of these devices of the maestro's—might be better protection for my daughter and my art than armed knights."

"Certainly," confirmed Giacomo. "First, who will pay any attention to a peasant man and woman in a cart going east? And secondly, if we *are* attacked, violent men are more frightened by what they can't explain than by a show of force. Why, following Juan Borgia's murder, the superstitious Romans said they saw fantastic lights flowing past the Vatican windows, and the servants reported hearing strange voices. The pope was so frightened he ordered a consistory to consider church reform."

The Venetian slapped a hand on his friend's back. "Giacomo, everyone has misjudged you. You have your own talents and a cunning born of adversity. But—can you get away to take my daughter to Mantua?"

"It's ideal! Leonardo expects me to finish the inventory and oversee the shipment of the devices to Cesena. Mantua is on the way to Cesena, so if we are stopped by inquisitive mercenaries, all I have to do is show them my carte blanche signed by the duke himself. To all appearances, the statues and paintings I have with me are part of Leonardo's collection."

"And if you run into some of Cesare's enemies?"

"That is why we go in disguise," stressed Giacomo. "Be assured. I will see your daughter and your work successfully to Mantua and to the Gonzaga."

Gentile took a leather pouch from inside his blouse and placed it in Giacomo's hand. "Do it! Make this journey safely with my daughter and my art, and this is yours."

"Oh, I couldn't accept anything," protested Giacomo, but he opened the pouch anyway and poured the contents into his open palm. His breath stopped as he found himself staring at five beautiful, polished jewels. "Lord protect us," he marveled, "where did you . . . ?"

"The sultan." Gentile smiled. "He was a generous man. My daughter carries a somewhat larger pouch to present to the Gonzaga for her protection and comfort."

Giacomo's hand began to tremble, and pouring the jewels back into their little nest, he placed the pouch inside his blouse close to his skin, which warmed to the touch of so much wealth and beauty.

"Will the maestro be upset at your—delay?" asked Gentile.

Giacomo beamed. "It will shatter him, I suppose. He relies on me for so many things. But, after all, there's more to life than flying, isn't there?"

He placed a protective arm around the little Venetian's shoulder and walked him from the room. "Now," he said as they proceeded down the corridor, "about these other paintings of naked ladies . . ."

*A*S THE WAGON TURNED into the Piazza Sforza Colombina drew their attention to the clouds of yellow smoke streaming from the upper windows of the castello.

"The duke is in a temper," Harlequin joked.

They laughed together as the antique wagon picked its way through the hundreds of people, carts, wagons, horsemen, clerics, mercenaries, guildsmen, beggars, and children packing the piazza. Soon the vehicle was no more than another speck in the river of humanity that flowed through and around this great city beneath the deep blue sky.

PAVIA

Giacomo and Isabella begin
their journey.
The capitano receives his orders for
combat, and Scapino, Harlequin,
Colombina, Pantalone, and
the two monks are set upon
by mercenaries.

SWITZERLAND Zürich

Bern

THE ALPS

Innsbruck

Salzburg AUSTRIA

St. Wolfgang

Aosta

Biella

POR.

RANCE

Gen

Nice

Zengq

OTTOMAN
EMPIRE

Zara

Piombino Are

Cortona

Ancona

Assisi

Spoleto

Adriatic Sea

CORSICA

TIBER

Aquila

Rome

Pescara

N

APENNINE MTS.

LIRI R.

SARDINIA

Foggia

Naples

Benevento

OFANTO

Cagliari

Brindisi

Tyrrhenian

Sea

Otranto

Cosenza

Palermo

TUNIS

Messina Reggio

SICILY

Mediterranean Sea

Catania

Syracuse

olombina's wagon followed the Ticino River from Milan, a route that took them past the Certosa di Pavia, which Harlequin described as a glorified mausoleum. "This is the final resting place for the more exalted members of the illustrious Visconti family," he told her. "Gian Galeazzo began it, but the construction was halted at his death. The power of his family died with his two sons, and the Milanese territories fell into the hands of a tough professional soldier who had married his granddaughter. The soldier's son was Ludovico the Moor, who, allegedly, murdered his nephew and so established the power of the Sforzas over Milan. It was the Sforzas who had the tomb completed, reasoning that the least they could do for the family they removed from power was to bury them in glory."

"Is there some sort of moral in that?" asked Colombina jokingly.

"Yes, indeed," Harlequin earnestly replied. "A family willing to fight and, when necessary, murder for their honor, deserves to profit from it."

Colombina laughed. "Is that the motto of the Sforzas?"

"No," said Harlequin. "*That* is the motto of the *Italians*."

A LARGE, two-wheeled cart, burdened with an immense load of hay and driven by two hooded monks, creaked and lurched west from Milan on the road to Abbiategrasso and Vigevano in keeping with the ruse devised by Gentile and Giacomo, who had reasoned that the assistant and Isabella, even in this disguise, would attract less attention if they avoided the Via Emilia. This route was a rutted and muddy roadway that had been used and abandoned by the Romans centuries earlier, but was still the principal means of passage from Milan to Bologna. They decided to adopt a plan widely in use among rich merchants and nobles who must travel the roads of Italy: announce loudly and often where you are going and the route you will take, and then take an entirely different one. Consequently the cart would move west to the crossroads at Mortara and then turn east to Pavia.

The air became warmer as the road wound down from the last of the mountains to the plains of Lombardy. The great gray work-horse had obviously not been chosen for speed or beauty, but he pulled the cart and its clerical overseers with no visible effort. Gentile had purchased both the horse and the cart from a wainwright in Milan.

Giacomo had departed the court with the carte blanche signed by the duke. He noted unhappily that the pass was for himself only. So if the couple was asked for their papers, he would have to improvise a reason for his fellow passenger.

Nevertheless he was grateful for the company of the young girl who sat beside him, wrapped, as he, in Franciscan brown, although she had never given him so much as a glance from the time she had been introduced to him by her father, and had not spoken a word from the time she had been elevated to the cart's driving bench.

"I know you must be uncomfortable, signorina," said Giacomo, "but after careful thought, your father and I decided that this would be the most perfect disguise for us."

She said nothing, and the cart lunged and tilted along the country road.

"Once we get to Parma," he continued after a moment, "we can risk traveling on the Via Emilia, and you might be able to rest there awhile in relative safety. Then you could perhaps change into something more womanly and comfortable."

She said nothing.

"I assure you, Signorina Isabella, that there is absolutely nothing to fear. I have devices and secrets that could defend you against any threat." He smiled to give her confidence in him.

She, apparently oblivious to the smile, remained silent, and Giacomo began to question whether the lady could speak Latin. *No,* he reasoned, *she was educated at the court of Urbino, where Latin is the conversational tongue.*

He felt the weight of the bronze sheet that he now carried on a thong under his monk's robe, and he felt certain that the dragon illusion of Maestro Leonardo would do its work. The hay piled upon the cart concealed thirty-three rolled canvases and fourteen separately wrapped statues as well as chests and cases of expensive feminine garments, jewelry, combs, brushes, and additional items that were intended as gifts to the Gonzaga upon reaching Mantua.

"No one will ever question two poor friars with a load of fodder for the monastery livestock," Giacomo continued. "No one will even give us a second glance, signorina." The feminine friar remained silent and unmoving, and he wondered if she had noticed, as had he, the three armed knights on black geldings who had followed them from Milan and then disappeared after an hour or so.

He began to have the uncomfortable feeling that the monk's robes beside him were empty of any human form. He was tempted to touch the leg of the robe to assure himself that there was someone in it, but he reasoned that the action might be taken in a different vein, and preferred not to have discord so early in the journey.

"Is there anything I can do for you, Signorina Isabella?" he asked some time later. "Anything to make the journey less tedious?"

There was no response.

They continued for another hour with not a word or sound or movement from the disguised maiden. When they reached the second fork in the road, Giacomo tried to remember which direction they had decided would be less hazardous—considering their identities—and more comfortable—considering their mode of travel.

"We will take the left fork," he decided aloud. "There should be less traffic along that route, and it is only a few extra kilometers to Abbiategrasso."

He was about to signal the horse to advance when a voice erupted from the cavernous shadows of the monk's hood.

"Imbecile!" it said—in Latin.

"What?" said Giacomo, surprised at the voice, but relieved to find he was not alone on the cart after all.

"No, you great moron!" the voice said, growing stronger and louder with every word. "Isn't it bad enough, you spawn of a jackal, that you forced me to submit to the incomparable degradation of traveling disguised as a man? Now do you propose to prolong the agony, you venomous insect?"

Giacomo's mouth fell open in astonishment. "I—I—"

"If you had the brains of a mosquito, you'd know that the less-traveled road is certainly the one most infested with bandits and brigands, reasoning as we have that they would encounter less opposition along it and thus could lose themselves in the heavily wooded areas on either side."

"Well—"

"Why I let my father convince me to take this journey with an insignificant flea like you, I can't imagine! I can only attribute it to the fact that I am a loving and dutiful daughter, but I want to make it perfectly clear, you pitiful idiot, that I feel I could travel alone, on horseback with skirts and bonnet, and attract less attention than this ridiculous masquerade that you and my father conceived! But then, what can I expect from a peasant whose principal claim to immortality is that he assisted a madman who thinks he can fly, walk on water, raise the dead, and prefers boys to girls? You are possibly just as perverted, although your taste probably runs to knotholes and sheep." She quickly took a breath and continued: "On the other hand, you are fortunate that you made no attempt on *my* virtue, or I'd have skinned you alive, you foul-smelling toad!"

She stopped briefly as the cart suddenly lurched, and Giacomo saw his chance. "All I wanted to say was—"

She overcame him with sheer pitch and volume. "But just to make certain we understand one another before we proceed any further, you pig's arse, I want you to understand that I consider you of even less importance to me than the sweat of the horse pulling this relic of a cart! As far as I can determine, you have none of the characteristics of Man and few of the instincts of the more competent animals! Physically I find you as repugnant as afterbirth, and mentally you are so inferior to me that I find myself astounded that we can communicate in anything resembling language. You have the stability and constancy of the moon and as interesting an expression on what passes for your face. I am reasonably certain that before this journey is completed, I will find myself yoked with the responsibility of protecting *you*, you cringing maggot! And I *can*, too!"

Giacomo took advantage of the lady's second breath to motion the horse forward.

"I think you should know that I have been instructed by some of the best minds in the court of Venice, where I mastered the *trivium* of grammar, rhetoric, and dialectic. And in the court at Urbino I completed the *quadrivium* of music, astronomy, geometry, and arithmetic. I was also privately tutored in fencing. I can speak four languages fluently and curse in ten. I am not afraid of anything that swims, flies, or creeps on its belly, which, I presume, should include you. I can sing, play the lute and the viola da gamba, and tread a merry figure at a ball. There is nothing in the arts of painting, music, or sculpture with which I am not acquainted or which I have not—to some degree—mastered. I am a student of science and can chart a course by the stars if need be. Alchemy is not alien to me, and I possess a philosopher's stone that could—under circumstances I have not fully explored—turn lead into gold, water into fire, and, perhaps, *you* into something remotely resembling a man."

Giacomo grunted.

"So do not imagine for a moment, you parasite, that I will ever need anything like *you* to protect my virtue. Understand that while I possess the unmistakable bearing and appearance of a chaste lady of breeding, I am not totally unfamiliar with the passions of a woman. Not that you should take any encouragement from that, you mole, because—as with all ladies of discretion and experience, I have the highest standards of modesty—which makes this disguise even more repugnant to me. When and if I choose to bestow my favors, it is on men worthy of my intelligence, wit, and breeding and not on changelings created from waste and offal like you!"

"Holy Mother of God," Giacomo muttered to himself.

"And while I am condescending to speak to you, which I will hereafter do infrequently—if at all—I might point out for your education that we have been seated on this jolting, rambling junk heap for more than three hours, and I, for one, being human and feminine, need an occasional pause to perform certain bodily functions which are associated with every animal from the primitive through intelligent mammals, and to which you, apparently, are not vulnerable—which does not altogether surprise me, since . . ."

The cart disappeared over the crest of a hill, but the penetrating and persistent feminine voice echoed and reechoed long after time and distance had swallowed them all.

*C*APITANO FRANCESCO BENEVELLI STOOD rigidly before the table in the great hall of the Castello Visconteo in Pavia, the ancient family estate of the Visconti family and the only palazzo capable of providing a modicum of luxury and comfort for the immaculately attired French commander who sat behind the table studying several maps. The officer was Yves d'Alegre, now attached to the forces of Cesare Borgia. Beside him stood Captain Antoine de Baissey, the bailiff of Dijon, tall and thin and a possessor of magnificent mustaches, who also was on detached duty to Cesare. Beside the capitano stood his second-in-command, Cosimo the Sicilian, whose bearded face bore several scars, some of which were souvenirs of war.

With a jeweled dagger, the French commander marked the passages of three armies upon a large map on the table between himself and the capitano. "The principal needs of the Duke of Valentinois at the present are additional funds and another army to serve under Capitaine Michelotto Corella here in the Romagna." He sat back in the great chair of the Visconti lord and rested the dagger on the map. "Fano has promised twelve hundred recruits and another five hundred have been conscripted at Imola, but we are rapidly exhausting the available young men in that area. That," he concluded, "is where I have need of you."

The capitano beamed. "Anytime and anyplace," he avowed. "My men are ready and anxious for a good fight! Our training has been the best in Italy, and—"

"But of course." The marshal smiled. "*Certainement!* What is needed, however, is to raise an additional force of approximately five hundred from this area." He indicated another spot on the map. "I want you to go to these cities, starting here at Cremona, and recruit young men. I will be doing the same in the Emilia."

The Italian nodded. "Cremona."

"*Exactement!*" the marshal exclaimed. He gestured to the silver platter of breaded meats beside the map. "May I offer you and your aide something to eat, *mon capitaine?* My personal chef prepared these only this morning."

The capitano and Cosimo each took a morsel from the platter and popped them into their mouths. "Thank you, Excellency. They are—ah—delicious," said the capitano.

"My favorites," said the marshal, studying the map once more. "Snails. Bathed in garlic and butter." Both the capitano and his aide stopped chewing at the same time, but the French officer apparently did not notice. "I will give you ten thousand ducats as inducement for the recruits. Give them as much as you need to, but be frugal. Fifty ducats in hand and a promise of spoils works just as well."

The capitano nodded, trying to slip the food under his tongue.

"We have reason to believe the holy father in Rome will soon announce seven or eight new cardinals, each of whom will pay one hundred and twenty thousand ducats for the honor, and that should satisfy our monetary needs."

"I understand, Excellency!" replied the capitano, who then pretended to choke and quickly spat the snail into the palm of his hand.

The marshal sighed. "Naturally, if it were only a matter of military strategy and tactics, it would all be simple. But there are diplomatic questions to be considered. Although Cremona is Milanese, it is close to the borders of both Venice and Mantua, and while they are our allies, there is also some suspicion that they may lodge objections to recruitment so near their own territories."

"Ah!" the capitano said. "If only the diplomats would not interfere with the art of war, eh, Excellency? Things would be so much simpler for gallant warriors like ourselves then, eh?"

The marshal smiled. "Quite right, *mon capitaine.*" He leaned across the table and lowered his voice. "While we have complete trust and confidence in our own troops, some of these Cremona mercenaries you recruit may have hidden loyalties to the doge of Venice and the Gonzaga family. Be very, very careful."

"Deception!" cried the capitano so loudly that he startled Cosimo, who stood beside him, and the hapless aide accidentally swallowed his snail. "What are we coming to, Excellency, when bought troops can themselves be bought?"

"I agree with you." The marshal nodded. He studied the capitano for a moment. "Of course, you have no—difficulties—about facing a possible—insurrection?"

"None at all!" barked the capitano. "Our courage is a matter of record! Perhaps you have heard of our feats of valor in the battles of Campaldino and Caprona!"

The marshal looked puzzled. "I seem to recall a battle of Campaldino that was fought nearly two hundred years ago."

"Same place, different war!" corrected the capitano. "We have so many, I can understand your confusion, Excellency! Suffice to say we defeated a superior force, took the cities single-handedly, and impregnated a battalion of townswomen!"

"I—see," murmured the officer. "Now you understand your mission? Raise an army for me from Cremona and the surrounding territories to the southeast and lead them to Piacenza, where I will rendezvous with you in two weeks."

"Cremona!" said the capitano crisply. "I understand perfectly, Excellency!"

"Bon! Bon!" The French commander rose and headed for the door with his thin aide-de-camp following close behind him. Staff officers gathered the map and other parchments from the table. At the door the marshal turned to face the Italian one more time. "Remember, mon capitaine," he commanded, "Cremona—and then Piacenza!"

"Cremona!" cried the capitano.

The marshal and his aides swept from the great hall, and Cosimo the Sicilian hacked in a useless effort to disgorge the snail. He turned to his commander with tears in his eyes. "Cremona?"

The capitano deposited the escargot that he was still holding in his palm behind a wall hanging. "Are you out of your mind?" he snapped. "Why should we recruit new men when we have enough in our own company to split the ten thousand ducats the marshal is providing?" He clapped a heavy hand on his aide's shoulder. "Besides, I have—another pressing appointment—at Piacenza in three days. You take our men and march east by the end of the week."

"To Piacenza?"

"Toward the junction of the Po. There you will camp for a while and try to stay out of sight. I want the marshal to think we are all busy recruiting. Then, in about two more days—as the marshal commanded—march into Piacenza, where I will join you. I will tell him we enlisted a hundred or so, but the treacherous dogs took all our money and then quickly crossed into Venetian territories."

"I like it." The Sicilian grinned.

They started from the hall. "Why should good Italians die for these damned French aristocrats, eh? Godsblood, they don't even know how to eat properly! Imagine! Snails!"

"A waste of good garlic!"

"Let's find an inn and wash that filth from our lips!"

And they did.

*H*ARLEQUIN, SCAPINO, AND PANTALONE rested in a small park before the ducal palazzo outside Pavia, and Colombina served the three men a suspicious but delectable meal from her magic stewpot.

"Count the horses," said Scapino.

"It's not horse," growled Colombina as she shoveled the meat and vegetables into her own mouth. "If you don't want it, leave it. I'll eat it myself." But the command was ignored by the trio, who attacked the food as if they had been ruthlessly starved for the past two days.

"I have to admit," mumbled Harlequin with his mouth stuffed. "I don't know how you do it, but you do manage to make the most remarkable meals out of very little that I can see. We have hardly any money, but you have been feeding all of us at least two good meals every day since we started this little odyssey."

"It's a gift." Colombina nodded. "But I imagine a fine gentleman like yourself is more accustomed to sweetbreads and artichoke hearts, little cakes stuffed with liver and veal, a soup of pigeons and almond paste. Things like that."

"I like simple food," said Pantalone. "Things created from pasta, tomatoes, and cheese. I remember my mother making superb ravioli and lasagna. And, on feast days, marzipan balls."

"Who did?" asked Scapino.

"My mother," repeated Pantalone.

"I don't remember any woman in Vercelli who could cook that well." Scapino sneered.

"Well, perhaps you should have stopped sleeping with them long enough to take a meal with them!" retorted Pantalone.

"I could do better," Colombina said, "if any of you were a fisherman or knew how to snare quail. What I could do with a red herring! And what sauces I could make if any of you could afford a little wine from the monasteries! As it is, only Pantalone here renews the larder now and again with a rabbit or stolen fruit."

Scapino grumbled and, as usual, wiped his greasy mouth on the sleeve of his blouse. "I recognize the carrots and the beans," he said, "but there are little lumps of something gray in there, that is new to me."

"Truffles," said the proud lady as she handed them small wedges of cheese.

"Truffles?" said Harlequin. "I thought they had to be rooted from the base of trees by a pig. Do you have a pig hidden away somewhere?"

Colombina surveyed the ruins of her meal. "I travel with three," she said.

*I*N FERRARA, Cesare and Lucrezia strolled through the ducal gardens hand in hand, laughing lightly at the news Cesare had brought with him from Milan.

"I swear, I was prepared to grovel—at least a little—and beg his forgiveness," he said, "but damme, the king rushed at me across the antechamber, kissed my cheeks, and called me his 'cousin' and 'my dearest relative.' You should have seen the looks on the faces of my enemies. I thought Montefeltro would pass out, and Gonzaga could only stand and grin like some Barbary ape. Then Louis suggested I choose a horse from his own stables since my poor gray was nearly dead, and he offered me some clothes from his own wardrobe for the banquet."

Lucrezia squeezed her brother's hand. "Tell me about the banquet."

"Why don't we go into the palazzo? You shouldn't be moving around so much. When I arrived two days ago, you were being bled."

"Well, it seems to have done me some good, hasn't it?" She repeated, "Tell me about the banquet."

"Well," said Cesare, "let me see. There was a great deal of seafood: oysters, whale meat, crayfish, salmon, turbot, brill, herring— some salted carp, lobster, mussels, trout, and—oh yes—frogs' legs."

"Frog legs?"

"The French consider them a delicacy. They eat everything. The whale's tongue was roasted and served both in an orange sauce and in a bouillon. Everything floated in garlic, of course. The French think it prevents disease. The salads were bizarre, trimmed with animals made of citron or turnip castles, and stuffed with layers of ham, herrings, anchovies, olives, and caviar."

"Ah," sighed Lucrezia.

"Then we began to eat in earnest."

"Tell me!"

"Venison shaped into lions, pastes of pheasant and peacock . . ."

"Nothing Italian?"

"Eventually. Zabaglione. Frangipane. Tournedos. Minestra and those small, delicate mushrooms you like so much: prugnoli. They dipped them in a light green concoction that they said was Indies sugar." He lowered his voice to a whisper. "It looked like *cantarella*, so I avoided it."

Lucrezia laughed. "It's unlikely the French king would have *cantarella*. I'm told that throughout Italy it is called 'the Borgia poison,' because they think only Father can make it. Did you know they say he suspends a bear killed by arsenic from a hook in the Vatican until a froth appears on the lips—and then he scrapes it off and dries it into *cantarella*."

"In any case I avoided it, and Louis kept lavishing praise and attention on me throughout the evening. He even invited me to join him for his visit to Genoa, but I begged other commitments and rode with him only as far as Asti."

"What do you make of it?"

"The truth," said Cesare. "The king needs Father for some reason of his own, and I can only conclude that he anticipates a war with the Catholic monarchs of Spain over the Neapolitan territories. In which case, the Vatican will be the key to eventual victory."

Lucrezia indicated then that she would like to rest beneath a linden tree in the garden, and her brother coiled at her feet. "Does Louis want you to march on Naples with him?" she asked.

"He assumes I will." The duke shrugged. "But first I want to discuss the possible surrender of Bologna with Ercole d'Este. Father has ordered Giovanni Bentivoglio and his two sons to Rome in fifteen days, and Bologna is vital to the control of the Romagna." He pulled at a tuft of grass. "And there is still the problem of the Savelli letters."

Lucrezia stroked his dark curls. "My poor brother. So many cities yet to conquer, and you're already older than Alexander when he ruled the whole world." She laughed lightly and then bent over to whisper in his ear. "I think you need diversion, my darling. Look to your left, and you'll see the little present I have for you."

Cesare turned his head, and there in the archway leading into the garden stood a young, dark, blue-eyed woman dressed completely in black trimmed with silver. "Sancia," the duke whispered.

"She heard you were here, and she came at once. I remembered how she nursed you back to health in Naples."

Cesare rose slowly from the grass as Sancia walked toward him.

"Bon appétit," called Lucrezia.

*L*ATER, as the creaking wagon approached the Ponte Coperto, Harlequin noticed that the opposite side of the bridge was guarded by a detachment of mercenaries.

"French?" asked Colombina.

"No," replied Harlequin. "That standard is the Este of Modena, but what are they doing this far west?" He thought for a moment. "Well, then again, why not? Cesare Borgia and Ercole d'Este are al-lies. I suppose the duke needs money to support his mercenaries, so they've posted guards along the major roads to confiscate anything of value. If they stop us, let them do whatever they want. We have nothing to hide and even less to steal."

When the mercenaries did confront them, Harlequin and Colombina climbed down and placidly seated themselves under a tree while four of the six men systematically dismantled the wagon. On the opposite side of the roadway, Scapino and Pantalone watched with mild interest.

"These thieves have a talent for this sort of thing, haven't they?" observed Colombina as the sacks and chests came flying out of her wagon and crashed into the roadway.

"Amateurs!" said Harlequin disparagingly. "They do not realize that thieving is an art."

Colombina inquired, "Is it?"

"I mean it," insisted Harlequin. "Hitting some poor traveler on the head and commandeering his purse or confiscating personal property is the last resort of pitiful incompetents who have neither the brains nor the will to imagine a more lucrative, though compli-cated, form of criminal activity. Vandals like these, who use their authority as a club to render us senseless, are an annoyance. A man who sells you the duomo in Florence or walks away with the crown jewels of Naples—now, *that's* a thief!"

"I don't see the difference," said Colombina.

"One is a man of honor with pride in his skill and his profession," proclaimed Harlequin. "The other is a wretch who has no sense of the dignity of his art."

"The victim may find that small comfort," noted Colombina.

"Then the victim should find consolation in the fact that the man who steals will die in the gutter, run through by an intended victim. But a real thief will die on the gallows, drawn and quartered before the eyes of a thousand cheering people—half of whom will weep for him."

Colombina studied him for a moment. "I'm sorry I brought the whole thing up," she said. She turned her attention to the rape of her wagon. "I wish they'd be more careful. I have a good dagger and a lute in there left me by—admirers."

"Don't worry," he said. "They wouldn't know how to use either effectively."

The leader of the mercenaries, a man with a long nose, was itemizing every worthless item that came hurtling from the wagon. "Look carefully!" he bellowed. "Sometimes these rich merchants try to get their wealth out of a city by hiding their gold under the floorboards of their wagons—or by sewing jewels in their rags."

Harlequin rolled over on the grass and laughed softly. "I couldn't get to sleep last night," he complained. "I think it's those jewels sewn in my rags."

"I told you to pry them out of the crowns first," scolded Colombina. Suddenly she became serious and poked Harlequin in the side. "Listen!" she commanded.

Harlequin obediently stood up and listened. From far off, beyond the turn near the trees, he heard what he took to be the screeching of an owl or an eagle. "But birds take time to breathe," he muttered as the sounds continued endlessly and grew louder and more strident. Suddenly, around the turn of the road, a cart appeared with two friars mounted on it. One monk was apparently intoning an endless ritual prayer while the other, who held the reins, waited patiently to respond. It was the silent friar who first spotted the mercenaries on the road ahead and nudged his companion to be quiet.

Long Nose saw the cart creaking toward the bridge and motioned his men to stop them. The cart halted just behind the wagon, and Long Nose and his men surrounded it. "Who are you, and where are you bound?" he demanded.

"Two brothers of blessed Francis," the tall, thin monk said in Italian, "bringing fodder for our animals at the monastery."

"Which monastery is that, friar?"

The question seemed to disconcert the quiet monk, but after a moment he recited softly, "The monastery of Sant'Angelo of the True Holy Cross of Jerusalem, my son. It is—ah—little known— for we are few—and—ah—of humble means."

Long Nose looked at the immense cargo of hay. "You can't be too humble, friar. You have enough fodder there to feed a hundred cows and horses." He gestured to two of his men to search the cart. "Why don't you and your companion step down for a moment, friar, and warm yourselves? My orders are to search every cart and wagon."

The tall thin friar replied enthusiastically, "Why thank you. Thank you indeed." And with that he stepped lightly to the roadbed and crossed to the small fire that had been built to ward off the chill of the early morning. The remaining friar was less nimble and had some difficulty descending. But eventually he joined his tall companion.

As Harlequin watched with intense interest, the mercenaries were now probing the hay with their pikes and swords. "There is something else under here!" called one of the soldiers, and they began to pull away great clumps of hay, which they scattered around the roadway.

It would be difficult for Harlequin later to relate precisely what happened next. All he saw was a great flare of flame to his right, and when he turned to look, both monks were enveloped in huge clouds of thick yellowish smoke, which soon drifted toward the cart and had everyone choking and blinded. From the clouds there came a sound like an ox being strangled.

By this time something huge—and unrecognizable—had formed and floated on the clouds of smoke. Colombina pointed to the towering apparition. "What *is* that?!"

"I have no idea," said Harlequin.

Long Nose and the other mercenaries seemed equally stunned by the sight. "It's some sort of tree, isn't it?" asked Long Nose.

"No," said one of the soldiers, a giant man with a grotesque mole on one cheek. "I think it's a rose. A big, black rose."

Long Nose tilted his head from side to side as he studied the phantom. "Wait!" he exclaimed. "I think it's an animal! A dragon maybe!"

"Yes!" yelled the man with the mole. "That's what it is! It's a dragon!"

Then Long Nose added, "But it's standing on its head!" Harlequin leaned to one side and soon affirmed what the mercenaries had discovered: the image was of a great dragon standing on its head, its clawed feet waving absurdly in the air, and its long, forked tongue licking at the ground.

"Hellfire!" came an oath from the smoke.

"Imbecile!" came another, more feminine cry.

A mercenary lunged through the smoke, pushing along a friar whose hood had fallen back to reveal long, dark hair. The monk suddenly lifted his robe and extended a long and well-shaped leg that sent the soldier flying.

"A brother fulcrum!" screamed Scapino, and he hurled himself at the two other mercenaries who had appeared through the haze to seize the arms of the long-haired monk. But the Mole stepped forward, swung his crossbow, and struck the juggler a blow that sent him sprawling against the wagon.

WHEN HIS VISION CLEARED, Scapino found himself propped against the wagon alongside his companions and the two monks. They were facing the entire squad of mercenaries who threateningly held pikes and crossbows. The clouds of smoke had dissipated in the fresh morning air of autumn. Scapino ran his palm over his head, and when he drew his hand back and examined it, his fingers were smeared with blood. Then he turned and noticed that one of the monks had a beautiful, feminine face. Never had he seen anyone so magnificent, so delicate, so much the lady.

"Well, well, well," said Long Nose as he forced the monk to face him. "Here's a pretty friar indeed. How does one enroll in your monastery, angel?" Then he let out a gasp of air and pain as she snapped a knee into his groin. "Damn!" screamed Long Nose. The Mole hurled the young woman against Pantalone.

"You bastard!" Pantalone snarled.

As the Mole stepped forward to strike Pantalone, who instinctively raised his other hand to protect his head, suddenly Harlequin chanted, *"Non amittuntur sed praemittuntur!"*

He was as stunned as the others to hear the tall monk instantly respond, *"Altissima quaeque flumina minimo sono labi!"*

The deepest rivers flow with the least sound?

The tall monk grinned at him, and Harlequin smiled back. He noticed with pleasure the shock and confusion of Long Nose and the Este mercenaries at this sudden flood of Latin, and he felt he had to move quickly to exploit the advantage. *"Prosperum ac felix scelus virtus vocatur,"* he intoned jocularly to the friar.

"In pace, ut sapiens, aptarit idonea bello," the man replied, laughing with him.

The Mole began to argue in whispers with the obviously bewildered Long Nose when suddenly a group of horseman appeared on the road approaching the bridge. The four armed knights rode like the professionals they were, their chargers glittering with armor and draped with red and yellow brocade. The short, portly horseman they escorted rode a pure white stallion caparisoned in red satin and gold brocade. Behind them came a string of mules loaded with traveling chests with trappings of striped yellow satin and bearing the crest of a bull.

"Make way!" commanded the leader. "Make way for the physician Gaspare Torrella, servant to the Duke of Valentinois! Make way!"

There was momentary bedlam as the Este mercenaries tried to pull Colombina's wagon and the cart far enough to one side to allow the entourage to pass. During the process, Harlequin came to the edge of the roadway, and Colombina watched as one of the mounted knights started to talk to him. Harlequin handed the knight a parchment, and after a moment the knight motioned Long Nose to join their conversation. The knight passed the parchment to Long Nose, and after more whispered conversation, the physician and his entourage continued down the road, and the mercenary captain and Harlequin returned to the others.

"All right!" Long Nose growled. "Throw this refuse back in the wagon!" Soon the mercenaries were hurling the sacks, chests, pans, and bolts of material into the rear of their wagon with as much enthusiasm and careful attention to detail as they had shown in removing them.

Harlequin returned to Colombina's side. "You spoke to someone in that party," she said.

"He was announced as the personal physician to Cesare Borgia," said Harlequin softly. "I merely asked one of the party if it was true that he had a cure for syphilis."

Colombina gave him a searching look. "Oh? And what did he say?"

"He said yes." Harlequin smiled.

Long Nose and the Mole huddled together with the mercenaries, and Harlequin caught only a few words of their heated conversation, but it was enough to indicate to him that the Mole was questioning the whole procedure. Finally the Mole grabbed the parchment from Long Nose and crossed to Harlequin.

"Where did you get this?" he snapped.

"That should be obvious."

The Mole gestured to the two "monks." "And these two! Are they with you?"

"Yes," said Harlequin quietly.

"Then why didn't you arrive together?"

"They got confused and took the wrong road."

The Mole snorted and slapped the parchment against Harlequin's chest. "Why the hell didn't you show us this at once?"

"You didn't start striking people until the cart arrived."

"Then why didn't you show it to us directly instead of taking it to the knight?"

"It's in Latin. I wasn't sure you could read Latin, so I thought the knight might assure you of the contents."

The Mole snorted again and growled, "Get the hell out of here! All of you!"

The cowled lady lunged forward. "Indeed?" she shrieked. "Well, I'm not through with you, you pompous, arrogant son of a—"

Harlequin clapped a hand over her mouth and glared at Long Nose. "We will continue our—mission. Thank you." He gestured to Colombine, who seized the female monk and almost hurled her into the rear of the wagon. Pantalone assisted Scapino to mount the bed of the wagon beside her.

Within minutes the wagon and the cart proceeded across the bridge into Pavia with the mercenaries glaring on either side as they passed. Pantalone and Colombina urged their burros to maximum speed, and Harlequin and the tall monk drove the cart.

The cowled lady was out of his sight in the back of the wagon, and the other monk's attentions were centered, at least momentarily, on attending Scapino's head wound. But as the two vehicles rattled down the roadway, even distance could not prevent Long Nose and his mercenaries from hearing the lady's high-pitched, feminine shriek of farewell.

"Castrate the villains!"

*P*AVIA WAS A BUSTLING CITY, full of construction and demolition simultaneously. The wagon and the cart had to pick their way through the masses of seminarians and young men in elaborate dress near the Collegio Castiglione. It took nearly a quarter of an hour for the small caravan to traverse the square dominated by a great statue of Pius V and fronted by the new facade of S. Francesco da Paolo and the Collegio Cairoli, the most prominent seminary.

"Just what the country needs," grumbled Harlequin, "an army of new priests." As customary, the men conversed in Latin.

"What was that parchment that saved us?" asked Giacomo.

"A carte blanche signed by the Roman pontiff himself. It specifies that the bearer is not to be prevented from passage anywhere in Italy—under pain of excommunication."

"My God!" exclaimed Giacomo. "Where did you get it?"

"I bought it from a monk in Geneva for two florins." Harlequin laughed. "Have you heard of Archbishop Flores of Cosenza?" Giacomo shook his head. "Well," said Harlequin, "he was the pope's private secretary, but he also ran a private enterprise. He sold forged papal bulls. Thousands of them. Dispensations of marriages. Legalizations of bastard children. Cartes blanches. I bought one of the better ones."

"It is a forgery?"

"Of course. You don't think the pope would grant someone like me a pass through every city in Italy? That's why I didn't show it at once. When I saw the knights coming, I thought I better risk it."

Giacomo gave a light laugh. "What happened to Flores?"

"The pope found out, had him imprisoned, and let him die there of starvation."

Suddenly one of the clerics, garbed, unlike the others, in a white mantle with a huge red cross on both the front and back, separated from the seminarians and approached the cart.

"God be with you, sirs," the cleric addressed them in Latin. "Would you be going to Mantua, friends?"

"No," said Harlequin softly. "To Piacenza, then south and east."

"Ah," replied the cleric. "That is unfortunate. There are reports of a miracle in Mantua. They are rebuilding the Cathedral of Santo Pietro, and they uncovered a marble sarcophagus. No one knows who is buried inside, but letters are said to have been mysteriously burned into the hard substance before the eyes of many parishioners."

"What do the letters say?"

"No one can read them." The cleric shrugged. "That's the mystery, but there is a scholar from the Este family trying to decipher them. Well"—he sighed—"I was hoping you were en route to Mantua and would be willing to take me with you so I could see for myself."

"I'm sorry," Harlequin reiterated, "we are going to Piacenza."

"Ah," repeated the cleric. "Then go with God, my sons." He blessed the two men and disappeared into the flood of seminarians now flowing into the collegio.

"Who was he?" asked Giacomo.

"One of the *piagnoni*, the weepers. Former followers of Savonarola. Four years ago they were the most powerful men in Tuscany. Now they seethe in quiet conclaves and plot revenge."

When they turned into the Piazza della Vittoria, a market square, Colombina stopped the cart and took the last of Scapino's coins to make some purchases.

"My God!" exclaimed Giacomo suddenly. "Hide me!"

"From God?" asked Harlequin.

Giacomo was trying desperately to climb into the back of the cart. "From that man over there. See him? The tall bearded man surrounded by the masons and carpenters?"

Harlequin looked and saw the man in question, who was obviously overseeing the reconstruction of the cathedral. "Who is it?" he asked. "A duke?"

"Worse," mumbled Giacomo. "That—is Leonardo da Vinci!"

*A*T THAT PRECISE MOMENT the great master looked up from the designs for the cathedral, and briefly his eyes met those of Giacomo, who quickly hunched his shoulders and threw the hood of the monk's robe over his head. Openmouthed, the artist watched as Harlequin urged the cart forward and past the reconstruction site.

"No," Leonardo mumbled. "No, no, no. It was just a bad memory."

And he returned to his labors.

PIACENZA

*The capitano is taken in combat
and is sentenced to die.
Giacomo gets a new name,
and the two monks join the company.
The sermon to the piagnoni.
Pantalone eavesdrops.*

SWITZERLAND Zürich AUSTRIA

Bern Innsbruck Salzburg St. Wolfgang

THE ALPS Aosta

Biella

POR. Zengg

FRANCE Gen. OTTOMAN
EMPIRE
Nice Zara

CORSICA Piombino Are... Adriatic Sea
Cortona Ancona
Assisi
Spoleto
N Aquila
TIBER Rome Pescara
SARDINIA APENNINE MTS.
LIRI Foggia
Cagliari Naples
Benevento
OFANTO
Brind

Tyrrhenian Otranto
Sea

MILES
0 10 20 40 60 80 100 Cosenza
KILOMETERS
0 20 40 80 120 160

Palermo
TUNIS Messina Reggio
SICILY Mediterranean Sea
Catania

Syracuse

Claudia Carlson © 1993

Capitano Francesco Benevelli elevated himself on one elbow to better survey the soft, fragrant terrain of curves and valleys beside him in the bed. He bathed in the warmth of the conviction that this woman, this Annamarie, was the one true love of his life—even though she was now married to Filippo Masaccio—whose only claim to distinction was his recent ascendency to the post of grand master of the clothmakers' guild.

Annamarie and the capitano had been sweethearts and companions in younger, sunnier times when they had loved in the fields and, once, on horseback; and now, on his frequent visits to Piacenza, they were lovers again.

What elevated Annamarie above the other women he had bedded on occasion was the incontrovertible fact that she was faithful to only him—and, infrequently, to her husband. Capitano remembered that his father had argued that the quality most universally admired in men was courage, and in women, fidelity. He reflected on this now: that if only he had not chosen the military life to display his courage, he might be the husband every night in her great, comfortable, smothering, canopied bed in the house of Masaccio on the Via Belcredi.

It was true, of course, that Annamarie had added spare centimeters of luminous flesh to her basic frame over the years, but Capitano found them even more of an attraction. It was equally true that her once midnight hair had an occasional silver invader hidden among its strands. But now he, too, had a few silver hairs—which, he acknowledged, was not quite the same thing, because, he believed, a silver crown gives a man the appearance of a distinguished monarch, while it only makes a woman look like an extinguished dowager.

The capitano was snapped from this deep philosophical reverie by the sound of—what?—something beyond the bedroom door. "I think I heard something," he whispered into the delicate ear of his lady.

"Nonsense," she whispered back as she nibbled his ear. "I told you Filippo is in Parma arranging for a new guild wagon, and our servant girl, Marisa, is asleep." Her serpentine tongue licked at the dark hair of his chest. "Furthermore Marisa does not so much sleep as die and resurrect with the dawn's first light." The roving tongue moved lower. "Now," she purred, "what were you saying about the campaign in the Romagna?"

He smiled and pushed her back against the pillows. He gently lowered the sheet to reveal her breasts with the nipples that always reminded him of golden florins.

"It is simple, my love," he began, and brushed his lips against her right breast. "This is Milan." He flicked at one coin. "And this is Cesare Borgia, replacing a Sforza married to an Este and—"

His lessons were interrupted as the bedroom door slowly swung open to the discordant accompaniment of shrieking hinges. There, framed in the doorway and holding a lantern high above her head, was a young, wide-eyed girl in a long sleeping gown. "Signora?" she whispered.

The capitano sprang from the bed, pulled a sheet up over his head like a hooded toga, and began, "I see, Signora. And you say the pain is—where?"

But the deception was lost on the servant wench, who wheeled quickly and hurled herself down the stairs, proclaiming, "Rape!" with every step. Instantly the capitano hustled himself into the scattered portions of his uniform. "Dies and is resurrected, eh?" he complained as he stuffed one foot in the wrong boot.

Annamarie sat up unhappily and watched her lover attempt to reassemble himself. "I swear," she muttered through clenched teeth, "that girl has slept through two fires, a robbery, a riot outside our very windows, and a cannon duel. Tonight she awakens to the din of a pillow fluffed against a bed!"

Her lover was barely clothed and had begun to buckle on his sword. "Too bad," he murmured. "You'd have adored the assault on Naples." He headed for the door precisely as the aide of the French marshal appeared in the opening and the officer's naked blade was pressed insistently against the capitano's throat.

"Well, *mon capitaine!*" He grinned. "And how are they going, the enlistments in Cremona?"

COLOMBINA'S WAGON and Giacomo's cart rested in a nest of birch trees and bushes where the Tichino joins the Po River west of Piacenza. The burro they had named Death and the great workhorse grazed together on the cool grass. The five human travelers were scattered about the encampment, nibbling on wedges of cheese and smoked meat. Isabella, as usual, was giving everyone the benefit of her oratory in excellent, if incomprehensible, Latin.

"I said it a million times!" She wheeled on Giacomo, who slowly chewed a portion of the meat and wished it was Isabella's heart. "Didn't I say it? Didn't I?" She turned back to the group, who watched the lady in awe as they ate. "I said, 'Do not take that road! That road,' I said, 'will be the very one that the mercenaries will use.' I said that! I said it a hundred times!"

Scapino, cupping a wet cloth to his head, interrupted. "I seem to be bleeding again," he said in Italian.

Isabella raged on. "My instructors in strategy and tactics were the best condottieri in Urbino. I have trained my mind to think like an opponent and at least a month in advance—which is why I am excellent at chess and undefeated among the members of the doge's court."

"It's only a small stream of blood," said Scapino. "I mean, it's not *gushing* or anything."

But Isabella was not to be distracted.

"A mere glance at a map would have shown that the key points for a mercenary army would be the bridgeheads and those roads which are, at least, reasonably paved with great expanses of open land on each side! But no! My idiot guardian simply ignored me and rode blithely into their checkpoint!"

"I mean," mumbled Scapino, "I can probably live on for—oh—two or three minutes."

This quiet statement brought Giacomo to his feet, and he crossed to the bleeding juggler and began to examine the wound.

"It was idiocy!" shrieked Isabella after him. "Are you completely unacquainted with the battle of Crécy?" She began to scratch a diagram in the earth. "Did no one ever tell you how the Count of Alençon and the Duke of Lorraine were astride the hill by the old

Roman road, and Northampton and the forces of the Prince of Wales were drawn across the Valley of the Clerks controlling the road to Abbeville and the Bois de la Grande?"

"On the other hand," Scapino grumbled, "I could expire any minute now."

Giacomo opened a small purse attached to his belt and extracted a leaf, which he crushed between his hands.

"Have you never read," railed Isabella as she graphically illustrated her point, "how the English archers were positioned behind and between the men-at-arms while the Genoese crossbowmen were spread in an arc before the French infantry?"

Suddenly Scapino was on his feet and glaring into the lady's face. "I am sorry to interrupt your ravings in the language of the Church with the fact of my dying," he said coldly, "but I think it would be better if you temporarily closed that mouth of yours!"

The lady was stunned. So much so that she replied in the vulgar tongue. "Wh-what?"

Scapino snapped, "Not another word! You make my head ache!" Then he lowered his voice and said, "You are the most beautiful woman I have ever seen in my life. Your—your wonderful face glows with the warmth of the sun, and your eyes could drive a man mad with desire for you, but when you open that big flapping mouth of yours, your nose grows warts, great gaps appear between your teeth, and your breath would suffocate an ox!"

And with that declaration of his love, Scapino collapsed back on the box. Giacomo dipped the crushed leaf in a bowl of water and applied it to the wound.

Isabella abruptly sat down on a keg, speechless and wide-eyed, and that silenced the others. It was Colombina who smiled and crossed to hand Isabella a plate of the meat and cheese. "Eat," she said in Italian. "It will keep your mouth busy."

Harlequin took advantage of the conversational lull to survey his extended and extensive family "Well, it would seem that we have been joined—at least for the moment—by a vocal young lady and what appears to be a lecherous cleric."

"I am not a lecherous anything," grumbled Giacomo in Italian as he worked over Scapino's lacerated head. "And I am most certainly not a cleric." Isabella penetrated Giacomo with an icicle glance.

"Are you a monk?" asked Harlequin.

"No," he replied.

"Then why do you travel in a monk's robe?"

"Protection."

"From God?" asked Scapino.

"From thieves and brigands," explained Giacomo. "You may have noticed that I travel with a young lady."

"You certainly do." Scapino grinned. He looked at Isabella, who was ravenously attacking the smoked meat with the same dedication she had earlier given to oratory. Scapino noticed both her appetite and the fact that the monk's robe left her trim ankles exposed.

"I noticed," replied Harlequin, "that you travel with a woman who is reputedly a lady, but she speaks as no lady I have ever encountered before—in any language."

"Yes," agreed Giacomo. "She is—unique." He contemplated his charge for a moment and then continued the conversation with Harlequin in Latin. "Well, her father felt it was necessary for her to travel incognito to Mantua."

"Mantua?" asked Harlequin. "Why Mantua?"

"The Gonzaga family would protect her."

"Ah." Harlequin nodded.

"And I thought it would afford her better protection if we traveled together as monks."

Harlequin shook his head. "You would have afforded her better protection if you traveled as plague victims—or armed knights." He crossed to Isabella and asked in Latin, "Have you a name, signorina?"

"Donna Isabella Zappachio," she spat.

"Her father felt Milan and Venice were not safe," said Giacomo.

"For her enemies, you mean," said Harlequin with a wink at the tall man.

"You have a point." Giacomo sighed.

"And what is your name?"

Giacomo stopped then and wiped his hands on the wet cloth.

"Since there is an element of danger," he said softly. "I do not choose to give you my name."

"Who wants it?" Harlequin shrugged. "I have a perfectly good name of my own." He glanced at Colombina. "But I respect anonymity." He examined Scapino's wound and switched the conversation to Italian. "This is very good work. Where did you learn this art, pray?"

Giacomo applied another leaf. "I—ah—served a madman. And the—experiments—of this gentleman occasionally resulted in my being—wounded. In addition, he had some knowledge of anatomy, which was not wasted on me; so I learned to—doctor—myself a little."

He examined Scapino's poultice once more. "Well, we must call you something, and since you apparently have some skills as healer, you shall be our good doctor, our dottore."

Giacomo threw the bloodied water into the bushes. "I will answer to anything." He looked at Harlequin and grinned. "Save a call to arms."

Colombina whispered something to Isabella, who rose abruptly. "I think this young lady is weary and could use a little rest to get her breath back. I'll fix her a place in the wagon."

Harlequin nodded and turned again to Giacomo. "How is the wound?"

Giacomo sighed and led Harlequin aside. "There are some things I do not understand. This wound is one of them. It is hardly more than a laceration of the skin. I would think that a blow with the butt of a crossbow could crack the skull, but—well—the blow was precisely administered."

"What does that mean?"

"The mercenary who struck him didn't want to really hurt him."

"What do you make of that?"

Giacomo shrugged. "A compassionate mercenary?" He lowered his voice again. "And then there is the matter of the horses."

"Horses? What horses?"

"When the girl and I rode out from—from where we came from, I thought we were followed by three men on black gelding horses. I think I saw one picketed with the horses of the mercenaries at the bridge."

"So? There must be a thousand black geldings in northern Italy. What do you make of that?"

Giacomo shrugged again. "A compassionate mercenary with a black gelding?"

Harlequin commanded, "Tell us how you created that strange illusion at the bridge."

Giacomo smiled. "A device of the madman I mentioned earlier. The principle is reflection of shadows on smoke." He was suddenly embarrassed. "But I—ah—projected it upside down, and the—ah—the bull-roarer fell into the fire."

Harlequin lowered his voice. "And this—madman. Could it have been that same Leonardo da Vinci you wanted to avoid in Pavia?"

Giacomo studied the man in the colorful cloak. "Italy is full of madmen," he said.

"All right. We won't pursue the matter. What was behind those bizarre Latin expressions of yours at the checkpoint?"

"When I heard you start to speak Latin, I thought I knew what you were trying to do, so I wanted to say something—that sounded strange but important. The first thing that came to mind was a passage from Seneca and another from Horace that I had to memorize for Maestro Verrocchio—to be carved on monuments. Patrons prefer Latin inscriptions on their portraits and statues." He murmured, *"Ars longa, vita brevis!"*

"I agree." Harlequin smiled. "Art *is* long, and life *is* brief. Well, it confused them and bought us some time—which is what I hoped for." He searched through a now empty sack for any remaining apples.

"I used the last of the money from Scapino's purses to buy supplies in Pavia," said Colombina, coming down from the cart. "Has anyone here anything of value that we might use to keep us alive?" She turned toward the cart. "What have you in here, dottore?"

Giacomo instinctively stepped forward to stop her. Before a word was said, however, Scapino stood unsteadily and stepped in front of

Giacomo. "Careful, good doctor," he said softly. "I may be wounded, but I am halfway to becoming a fulcrum."

"Don't be afraid, Dottore," said Harlequin softly. "We are not thieves or brigands. No one is going to violate your trust."

Giacomo studied Harlequin's face, and then, finally, he nodded. Colombina took advantage of the moment to push aside the hay in the cart. "Let's see what our friends have here." She found and opened one of the two *cassoni*, elaborate wooden chests bearing a quartered motif in yellow and red. "Well! Some—gowns—and other feminine ornaments. Beautiful, but we can't eat gowns!" And she began to rummage through the other chests and cases.

Harlequin crossed to the wagon and withdrew two rolled canvases. He smiled at Giacomo as he untied the leather thongs around one of them. He spread the fabric between his hands and gasped in wonder.

What he saw was the painting of an assembly of lovely women and bearded men with the legs of goats. They were dancing and coupling around a verdant tree set against a Venetian landscape. Harlequin gave a low, drawn-out whistle. "Sweet Mary and Joseph," he whispered, "it's magnificent."

Giacomo, relieved that his new acquaintances posed no threat and seeing no further need for secrecy, came behind Harlequin and looked over his shoulder. "The man who created that called it *A Company of Wayward Saints*."

"Are they all like this?" asked Harlequin as he unrolled the second canvas. Giacomo nodded. This was a painting of a reclining woman on a plush divan. She held a small feathery fan in one hand and the other rested lightly on her bare stomach. "He called that one *Houri*," said Giacomo. "I'm not being indecent. That's what they call dancing girls in Constantinople."

Harlequin studied the portrait for some time. "Look how the skin glows with warmth! Look at the texture of the skin! I've never seen anything so beautiful in my life."

"Of course you noticed she's—ah—she's—naked," whispered Giacomo.

Harlequin grinned. "Only because she has no clothes on." He

rolled and tied the canvas as Giacomo nodded, without understanding, at the logic of the statement.

"They are the work of my father." The words came from Isabella, who reappeared now on the steps at the rear of the wagon, now speaking in Italian. "But he felt they might be damaging to his reputation. So I am taking them to our friends the Gonzaga in Mantua."

She smiled then and descended to the ground. "I personally feel it is absurd for us to continue our travels disguised as monks." She looked momentarily at Scapino. "If you have no objections, I think it might be safer to travel with you. Would you, by any chance, be going to Mantua?"

Harlequin approached the young woman. "I'm afraid we have no—mutual destination, signora. Actually we are not *really* together. I mean, I, for one, am only traveling south with—ah—these people—until I—choose to leave. In the process, I have agreed to teach this robust creature to read and—dance." He gestured to Colombina.

"He's teaching me to be a fulcrum!" added Scapino. Isabella's confusion was echoed in the face of Giacomo, who suddenly collapsed wearily on the grass.

"However," said Harlequin, looking at the others, "I quite agree that you should not continue the journey disguised as monks. Indeed, I think you would look less suspicious and be more comfortable in something more—feminine and, ah, traditional." He crossed to Colombina. "Would you have any objection to a—temporary diversion—to Mantua?"

Colombina shrugged. "One city is much like another. But," she pointed out, "we need money to feed us along the way."

"If you escort me to Mantua," Isabella said as she produced a small leather pouch, "I will share this with you." She opened the pouch and poured the contents into her palm. The gems sparkled in the afternoon sun.

"Mother in heaven, who did you rob?" muttered Scapino.

"Whom," corrected Isabella.

"Where did you get them?" scowled the juggler.

"My father received them as gifts from the sultan in Constantinople."

Harlequin frowned. "I never knew the Turks to be so generous."

"He painted portraits of the sultan's family."

This satisfied Harlequin. "Then, signora, I think you have employed some companions." He crossed to where Giacomo reclined on the grass and whispered in Latin, "As for you, dear dottore, there are two ways to disappear. One is to become exactly like everyone else."

He looked around at the assembly. "Which would be nothing short of a miracle for this lot: a thief who poses as a juggler and who dreams of becoming a fulcrum; an apprentice thief who doesn't acknowledge his own name and who thinks with his masculine member; a lady with the breeding and education of nobility and an unbridled mouth; and a mysterious healer who travels with beautiful art and sees nothing but the nakedness."

Giacomo stirred, amused.

Harlequin continued to whisper to him. "Or! One could disappear like *me*. Dress so outrageously and so *unlike* everyone that people cannot help but notice the wardrobe and fail to observe the person in it."

Giacomo sat upright. "Are you hiding from someone, too?"

"Every man has a reason to hide *something*." Harlequin smiled as he replaced the canvases in the cart. He replaced the hay over the items and paused momentarily to examine a crest on Isabella's traveling case. Then he covered everything with the fodder. "But sometimes your enemies are strong and legion, and their power is so far-reaching that—there may no longer be a place to hide."

"What do you do then?" asked Giacomo.

"Then, dear dottore," Harlequin replied, "I avoid looking up." He placed a hand on Giacomo's shoulder. "You're an unusual man, friend. You deal in illusions, speak Latin plagiarized from monuments, and heal physical wounds and ignore the spiritual ones." He laughed and walked away, throwing the words back over his shoulder. "If you're not careful, you'll be the next pope."

I find myself allied with an assembly of lunatics. Giacomo smiled and lay back in the cool grass. *Ah, well, at least they haven't thrown me from a window—yet.*

And he was soon asleep.

Harlequin turned to Colombina. "Where is Pantalone?" he asked in Italian.

"I told you. We're at the end of our supplies," she said, "so I sent Pantalone into Piacenza to get what he can. In the meantime we have to wait for his return, because he is riding Destruction, our other burro."

Harlequin sighed. "Do you realize I could have leisurely walked from Aosta to Piacenza in one third the time it has taken us to get this far? What with breakdowns of that antique cart, dying horses, and having to lose a day or two while we searched for supplies, we have been together for nearly two months!"

Colombina smiled. "That's all right," she said. "Don't thank me."

*I*N THE SMALL CHURCH of Santo Savino, the *piagnoni* stood before the huge wooden crucifix before the high altar and intoned *Missus a Deo*. They had come to hear their leader speak on the life and work of the Dominican they considered "sent from God," Girolamo Savonarola.

"What I tell you now is not my words," cried the tall, thin priest in the pulpit. "And Fra Girolamo said they were not his words, but God's! He said he had seen God's almighty hand clutching a dagger aimed at the wicked and vain heart of Florence! He cried out against those who dwell in palaces and the courts of the mighty and against those who shelter ribalds and malefactors! He cried out against those who have placed a love of oratory and poetry above the love of God, who alone is worthy of our love! In the palaces of these great prelates and lords—even to the chambers of the Vatican itself—they can be seen, these proud men clutching books on the humanities, attempting to guide themselves by the light of Virgil, of

Horace, of Cicero. Fra Girolamo warned us! He told us, there is only one book to which man must look for guidance! To the sacred book! To the holy book! To the words of God Himself!"

The leader swayed a little in the pulpit as if his tall frame were racked with the intensity of his own emotion, and continued:

"He warned the people! He said they must turn to Christ! On the walls of every church in Rome are great works of lasting beauty! Of truth! Because they represent for us the beauty of God and His glory. Their subjects are holy and their works sacred. By their fruits ye shall know them! By their fruits! But there are other pictures as well! Images of gods! Of pagan gods! Portraits of the women of the streets! He warned them! 'Painters, you do ill!' he cried. 'You bring vanity into the house of the Lord! You vest the Blessed Virgin as though she were a common woman!' This was the guidance Fra Girolamo, the blessed one, left us. With what words, what can I say to remind you to keep firm his convictions? How can I describe the great evils committed by these portrayers of wickedness? What can I say?"

The question echoed through the church.

What can I say?

"WHAT CAN I SAY?"

In the small Sala del Sibille in the Borgia apartments in the Vatican, the Pontiff of Rome, Rodrigo Borgia, Alexander VI, looked at the ceiling frescoes depicting the ancient pagan gods Osiris and his sister-wife, Isis, and then turned to face his secretary-priest, Francesco Troches.

"Why should Your Holiness say anything more than you have? As the Pontiff of Rome Your Holiness would naturally be solicitous about peace in Bologna. What is more natural than to request that Giovanni Bentivoglio and his two sons come to Rome in fifteen days and discuss the matter?"

Rodrigo looked down into the gardens and listened to the musical pattern of the fountains below the tower. "It is the fifteen days.

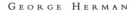

It sounds like an ultimatum, doesn't it? That's what has alarmed Louis of France and the Bolognese!"

The secretary shrugged and approached the pope. "Why is the time so important? Fifteen days. Twenty. What does it matter? It is simply a question of assuring peace in the Emilia. There is no threat implied. No accusation made."

The pontiff wheeled and slammed the parchment he had been carrying on the desk. "Giovanni Bentivoglio is no fool. My agents report that he has taken the matter to the people. He tells the Bolognese that I have ordered him and his sons to Rome. He warns them that if they come, I'll slap them all into prison; and if they don't, I'll order Cesare to take the city—which is exactly what I planned to do. But Cesare is still dawdling in Ferrara with his sister and Sancia of Aragon, and I have reports that his condottieri will refuse to attack the city, because they signed the treaty with the Bentivoglio and it would violate their honor! Their honor!"

He suddenly snatched up the parchment and darted from the room, and Troches had to run to keep up with him. The pontiff just as suddenly paused in the middle of the adjoining room, where Pinturicchio had painted Lucrezia as St. Catherine of Alexandria and Cesare as the Emperor Maximinus. The pope looked at the figures who stood before an arch bearing the insignia of the Borgian bull and the legend *pacis cultori*. "To the peace bringer."

"The condottieri would not rebel against the duke," Troches panted as he raced into the room. "They are not that foolish."

"And what of this inquiry from the French king?" continued Rodrigo, waving the parchment. "He reminds me that he has promised the Bentivoglio that Bologna will be safe from Cesare, and the terms of the treaty will be honored. He inquires now why I have sent the duke an ultimatum! He uses the word! Ultimatum!"

Troches opened his mouth to speak, but the pope roared, "And what shall I tell him? What can I say?!"

"WHAT CAN I SAY?" pleaded the half-naked capitano before the small table in the anteroom above the marble arcade of the Palazzo Comunale.

The French commander, Yves d'Alegre, did not smile as he faced him. "You can tell me, *mon capitaine*," he hissed, "how you raised a mighty army so quickly."

The capitano snapped his heels together in approved military style and attempted to salute—which was somewhat difficult with his hands bound together in front of him. "I have, Excellency! Two hundred skilled and fearless men, and all I need now is an additional five hundred ducats! I personally came to Piacenza at once to inform you of my achievement!"

"*Eh bien.*" The marshal nodded. "And why did you expect to find me in the bed of Madame Masaccio? I hardly know the lady."

The Italian relaxed a little, stood on one foot, and replied, "Well, Excellency, that was only a little diversion, you understand?" He winked at the commander. "An interlude. After all, we are both soldiers, yes? We military men, we understand these things."

"*I* am a military man!" screamed d'Alegre. "*You, capitaine*, are a cowardly dog!" He rose quickly and slammed his baton hard against the table. "So, you enlisted two hundred Cremonese?" He began to pace behind the table. "Then you are something of a magician who can appear in two places simultaneously! The lady's servant says you have not stirred from Madame Masaccio's house in four days!"

"The servant wench said that? What an incorrigible liar! Pay no attention to her testament, Excellency. The wench is obviously a sworn enemy to all military men. Probably an unfortunate love affair or—"

The French officer slammed the table with his baton once again. "You have not enlisted an army, you lying scoundrel! Not in Cremona! Not in Parma! Not anywhere!"

The capitano seemed genuinely surprised. "A moment, Your Grace! Are you . . . ? Could you possibly be doubting my word?"

The marshal gave a small, involuntary cry of frustration as though he were strangling on his rage. "Take this man out and hang him!" he roared.

The capitano resisted the efforts of the Frenchman's mustachioed aide to turn him around. "Hang me? But why?"

"Because," the commander sputtered, "I haven't the time to have you drawn and quartered!"

The Italian broke from the aide and leaned across the table. "But what have I done that is so terrible, Excellency? I kept my own men fresh and alive so they could march with you against the Neapolitans for the glory of France! What is so bad about that?"

"What men?" the marshal roared as he again beat the table with his baton. "Where is your company? We've seen no sign of this mythical army you raised among the young men of Cremona! And where is the ten thousand ducats I gave you for enlistments? We only caught *you*, because Captain de Baissey here was in Piacenza to pay a—social call—on Madame Masaccio when her servant ran out screaming of rape!"

The capitano stammered, paling, "A—social call? On Signora Masaccio?!"

"And what I want to know is—"

"A social call, you say? A matter of business perhaps? Surely you are not implying something—romantic?"

"Forget Madame Masaccio!" bellowed d'Alegre. "The rape was—"

"Ah! I see, Excellency! I assure you it was not a rape at all! It was—a misunderstanding! Signora Masaccio is a veritable angel and a woman of great fidelity!" The Italian struggled to ignore the small laugh that emanated from the aide. "As an officer and a gentleman," the capitano declared, "I will, of course, accept full responsibility for the affair!"

"I do not wish to discuss Madame Masaccio! Where are your men?"

The capitano straightened and took a breath before he replied calmly, "They, ah, they should be encamped at the fork of the river."

D'Alegre struck the desk again in his fury. "They are not! And where is the money I gave you to enlist an army for me at Cremona?"

"Well, not to diminish your judgment, sir, but, begging Your Excellency's pardon, the men of Cremona are notoriously stupid and really not adaptable to the style of combat to which my own men are accustomed: hand-to-hand, sword to sword, tooth and claw . . ."

The marshal fell into his chair in amazement. *"Mon Dieu!"* He sighed. "This man could talk the devil into receiving Communion!" Then he roared again, "Hang him at once!"

Once again the Italian resisted all efforts of the younger officer to turn him away from the table. "Excellency, you can't hang me in good conscience!"

"Then, damn it," the French commander snarled, "I will hang you in *bad* conscience! But hang you I will!"

The capitano snapped to attention. "I must remind Your Excellency that I am a soldier like you!"

"God forbid," muttered d'Alegre.

"I have devoted my life to the military!" the capitano exclaimed. "As did my father and his father before him—back ten generations! To hang me would disgrace and insult my entire family!"

The commander ran a hand over his forehead. "But it will do *me* a world of good," he said. "You should have thought of the disgrace to your family before you ignored my commands to raise an army at Cremona!"

The capitano remained at rigid attention. "I did not ignore my assignment at Cremona, Excellency. I merely—revised the general strategy."

D'Alegre rose furiously and struck the table still another sharp blow with his baton. *"I dictate the strategy!"* he shouted.

The Italian looked at his commander in surprise and pain. "Well," he said quietly, "if I knew you were so sensitive about your authority . . ."

The French officer seemed to lose his balance. He staggered back to his chair and sank into it, his arms by his side. "Hang him," he moaned. "Please, somebody, hang him!"

"At least grant me the right to die like a soldier—with a sword in my hand. And in my uniform."

D'Alegre loosened the collar of his own tunic and appeared to be dying of suffocation. "I'd sooner give a cannon to a Barbary ape," he hissed. "You came naked into the world. It is only just that you depart the same way."

"Then," retorted the capitano, "let me die in the tradition of the military—at the hands of a brother officer—quickly and efficiently!"

"You have no right to ask for privileges!" the marshal bellowed. "None!" He rose furiously to his feet and struck the table again—which promptly split in two and collapsed. D'Alegre stared at the shattered table as though it were his only son. "Take him out of here." He began to sob to the smirking aide. "Take him into the woods and cut his throat! Shut him up! See to it personally! Is that clear?"

The mustachioed aide saluted smartly. "Yes, Excellency!" he barked, and then, grabbing the short length of leather that dangled from the capitano's bound hands, he dragged the officer behind him from the room.

D'Alegre evaporated into his chair again. "Saddle my horse," he groaned to another aide, who saluted, wheeled, and left the room.

The marshal laid his head against the back of the chair and looked at the ceiling.

"If I'm lucky"—he sighed—"I may die today."

WITH THE ENTHUSIASM of authority and the dedication of a sadist, the aide dragging the capitano would pause now and again to deliver a sharp kick or a stab with his drawn sword when his prisoner staggered and fell.

The Italian, on the other hand, was unmistakably agitated and muttered incomprehensively to himself as he was roughly tugged into a patch of woods bordering the villa. At the very edge of the trees, the leather binding his hands was given a yank that plunged him headlong into the dirt and rocks.

"Get up, you bastard!" the aide commanded, and gave the fallen soldier another kick.

"Certainly, Excellency," the capitano murmured as he rose awkwardly to his feet. "I—I apologize for my clumsiness."

"I am not as tolerant of insolence as the marshal," the aide snarled, and struck the capitano with the hilt of his sword, opening a gash on his right cheek.

"I'm—sorry," mumbled the capitano.

The aide then abandoned the leather thong and gave the capitano a violent push into the woods. They proceeded that way for a short distance: the Italian in front and the young Frenchman prodding him impatiently from behind with the point of his sword. "Faster!" This time the older man tripped and fell on one knee, and the aide moved around him quickly and slipped one hand under his arm to raise him. "Up! Up!" he growled.

It is doubtful that his captor ever saw the sharp rock, concealed between the bound hands of the capitano, that caught him in the throat and hurled him back against a tree. It is quite certain he did not see the second blow from the rock, which came swinging down from above him and shattered bone, flesh, and cartilage between his eyes.

The Italian managed to get to his feet. He quickly knelt and removed the aide's knife from its sheath. Then, with the blade sandwiched between his teeth, he sawed the leather thong until his hands were freed.

He paused then to look down at his bleeding victim. "Poor fool," the capitano said quietly, "you would not have survived a day in Milan." He knelt again and slipped the aide's knife into his waistband, and removed the man's belt and scabbard, attempting to tie it around his own ample waist. Seeing that this attempt would simply never succeed, he threw the belt and scabbard into the woods and knelt again over the body to remove the Frenchman's tunic, which he placed around his own naked shoulders. Then he pried the sword from the dead aide's hand. "That," he taunted to the deaf ears, "is for daring to malign the reputation of my faithful Annamarie!" He stood, slipped the sword through his own belt, and surveyed the terrain. "A horse, a horse," he murmured as he set out for the stables.

At that very moment a young lieutenant was leading the duke's great chestnut stallion to the inner courtyard. Capitano moved from the shadows of the villa walls, more shadow than substance himself, and the knife flashed in the light of the setting sun.

The lieutenant tumbled to the earth, his fallen hose around his knees, and in a moment the capitano was mounted upon the stallion and galloping south. As he raced along the road he heard the rumble of thunder in the distance.

"No, lord," he assured. "I'm only borrowing it."

*T*HE BURRO NAMED DESTRUCTION waited patiently, tied to the large iron ring on the wall of the tavern where the Via Bartolomeo meets the Via Campagna in Piacenza; and inside, Pantalone waited less patiently for the serving wench to bring him the wine and cheese he had ordered. He crouched behind a small table in a shadowed corner, trying to look older than his years and more worldly than his experience. He placed the small, joined sacks containing the necessities Colombina had requested on the table before him and relaxed, his back against the wall, with a sense of satisfaction in having completed his assignment, now contemplating a little stolen time for himself. The merchant in the Piazza dei Tribunali had agreed, for a specified sum, to have the fresh vegetables ready when Colombina and the others arrived tomorrow.

In the meantime Pantalone luxuriated in the knowledge that his purse still contained a few odd coins, and that he was warm, invisible, and relatively carefree. The persistent smoke from the great fireplace to his left had begun to make his eyes burn, so he closed them for a moment. This sharpened his hearing remarkably. He was always surprised at the degree of change. As he sat there he could hear and clearly distinguish between the crackle and hiss of the roast turning on the spit, the dull clunk of the pewter mugs and decanters against the wooden tables, and the babble of several conversations.

He played his game of isolating one conversation from all the others. It was one of his favorite amusements to sit in such places as this tavern or in the piazzas and to try to identify the travelers, merchants, mercenaries, and guildsmen from their voices: the rhythms, the accents, the nature of their conversations. He heard now, quite distinctly, the dark, raspy tones of an older male to his left.

"I don't quite understand, Lieutenant Angelo. A dragon, you say? And standing on his head?"

Pantalone's eyes snapped open. The speaker was a black-robed priest seated with a giant mercenary only a table removed from his own. The reflection of the flames in the fireplace bathed the priest's narrow, black-browed face with diabolical, flickering shadows. He wore a small, trimmed goatee and mustache. He looked well fed, but there was still a rodentlike hunger about him, and he wore his Bible-black hair long and thick. The giant mercenary had his back to Pantalone.

"Not a dragon," the mercenary growled, "but—well—the appearance of a dragon."

Pantalone winced. That voice. Where had he heard that voice before? In an instant he knew: the Mole. The second-in-command to Long Nose. The mercenary who had struck Scapino. The mercenary who had argued with his condottiere about the parchment.

"Well," whispered the dark priest, "the parchment interests me. It bore the Borgia crest?"

"Yes. But I'm certain it was a forgery. I've seen four or five like it in the past year." He took a drink from his cup and continued. "There were six people in both parties. Two were dressed as monks. And one of these clerics turned out to be a woman. That stupid commander insisted they must be agents of the pope, because of the carte blanche, so we had to grant them free passage.

But I tell you, there was something about them. They had—a certain *look*. You understand?"

The ferret-faced cleric leaned across the table. "The leader of this company of rabble," he said in that low, raspy voice, which was menacing in itself and which frightened Pantalone just to hear it. "Describe him again."

The Mole spoke slowly. "A tall man in a wide-brimmed hat like a bird's beak. Dressed in rags and shreds of many colors."

"These rags," hissed the priest, "were there designs on them?"

"Designs?"

"Were they plain? Just shreds of cloth in solid colors or were some of them—did some of them have heraldic symbols on them? Or stripes perhaps?"

"I don't remember, Father Sebastiano. Is it important?"

"It could be, Lieutenant," rasped Sebastiano. "Do you remember the stories of defeated Swiss mercenaries who retreated from the battlefield tearing their flags and standards into strips? Did you never hear how they sewed these strips over their tunics as a vow to revenge their defeat?"

The Mole shook his head.

The dark priest continued. "Those many-colored rags often cover scaled armor after the style known as brigandine." He leaned closer, his voice more hushed than ever, and Pantalone felt himself leaning in the direction of the priest's table. "Such men are professionals. Dangerous men. Skilled in arms." He sat back then and took a swallow from his mug. "Very interesting. You say you thought you recognized one of them?"

The mercenary nodded. "The tall one dressed as a monk. I had to think about it for a long time, but I remembered only yesterday where I had seen him before."

"Where?"

"He was at the court of Duke Sforza. I remember him, because we almost collided when I accompanied the Duke d'Orléans to the Milanese court three years ago. He was wearing huge flat shoes and carrying a pole in either hand, and he kept falling down, and—I'll never forget this—he jumped into the garden pool and nearly drowned."

The priest frowned. And he sat silently for some time, taking deep drafts from his mug. "A servant to Duke Sforza traveling with agents of the Borgian pope and a Swiss mercenary? Confusing." He placed a hand on the mercenary's shoulders. "What else did you observe of this band of travelers at the bridgehead?"

"Nothing more," he replied. "Except—the man in the patched cloak and the tall monk both spoke Latin."

"Indeed? What did they say?"

The Mole shrugged. "Nonsense! Platitudes! But it sounded serious at first, and then the monk said something that made the other man laugh."

"What, specifically, did they say?"

"The man in rags said something about someone or something being 'Not dead but gone before.' And then the monk mentioned something about deep rivers flowing silently, and the first man said something about successful crime being virtue, and they both laughed, and then the monk said something like 'in peace, a wise man prepares for war.' "

Sebastiano paled. "My God," he whispered, "they are talking about Cesare Borgia!"

"How did you deduce that?"

"The use of the word 'virtue' connected with crime! That's the way Machiavelli wrote the Venetian court about Cesare! A man of *virtù*, he said! The one who is not dead, but gone before, that could be Savonarola. Or Juan Borgia. And then that warning about preparing for war in the midst of peace, that's certainly about Cesare's plans to take Bologna!"

"I say it's nonsense. One of those statements is from Seneca. I remember my tutor making me memorize it. And one of the others is a quote from Horace."

The dark priest drank again and smiled, exposing a missing tooth. "That, Lieutenant Angelo, is why they spoke that way. They wanted you to *think* they were merely quoting random phrases from the Romans. Actually they were passing information to one another!"

"Why would they go to all this trickery?" the mercenary insisted.

"Think!" snarled the priest. "Did the cart and the wagon arrive together?"

"No, the wagon arrived first."

"But they left *together*!"

"Yes."

The priest finished his drink. "I will inform the cardinal at once."

The mercenary put a hand on the priest's sleeve. "But wait! What of the letters? What news from Modena?"

"Little," Sebastiano responded. "All we know is that the letters are heading south. The last report said they were in the possession of a priest, but that is not very helpful. Cardinal Ferrari says the pope is very agitated. He feels the letters will destroy the delicate alliance between France and Rome."

The lieutenant protested, "We had detachments at every approach to the city. If the letters passed through Pavia, we would have found them."

"Well," snapped the priest. "They have entered Italy, we know that much, and our latest reports say they are in this vicinity."

The Mole shook his head. "I don't believe it," he murmured.

"The cardinal has complete faith in his agents," declared Sebastiano.

The mercenary growled something inaudible, and the priest rose to his feet. "Cardinal Ferrari must hear of this." He paused, leaned over the table, and whispered to Lieutenant Angelo. He straightened up as the soldier finished his cup and also rose to his feet. "Come walk with me a little."

Pantalone could hear no more, and he had neither the time nor the inclination to follow them. It was enough that he had heard what he heard, and that he didn't understand more than a third of it.

Harlequin—a Swiss mercenary? *Well, why not?* he said softly to himself.

The serving wench appeared then with his wine and cheese, and he noted with some pleasure that she smiled at him and bent over his table a little lower than necessary to reveal two of her better assets. He, in turn, had flung his payment to her with the air of a man accustomed to throwing wealth about. He was disappointed when, instead of swooning at the sight of his reckless disregard for money, she concentrated instead on examining each coin in quick succession to affirm their value.

Satisfied that they were genuine, she cooled, turned indifferently from him, and went back to the tavern keeper, swaying as she walked to avoid the tables and the groping hands of the customers.

Pantalone sat for a while silently chewing the hard cheese and sipping the wine, which was of uncertain quality and parentage, and surveyed the room.

There was another, older mercenary sitting alone on a small stool before the fire, and Pantalone bristled to see the soldier's hand travel up the leg of the serving wench as she delivered his wine. He was even more annoyed when the mercenary suddenly grabbed the girl by the waist, pulled her down on his lap, and kissed her to the cheers and laughter of the other customers. The sight of older, audacious men having their way with women always irritated Pantalone. He was reminded of the rapacious older boys of his village.

Deep in his soul a little voice seemed to say, *If you're not getting it, Pantalone, no other man should!*

But Pantalone became even more furious when the girl pulled herself loose, rose with a laugh, and wiggled her way across the crowded room. *Bitch,* he snarled to himself.

But it was the aged mercenary on whom he decided to release his smoldering rage. He watched carefully as the old veteran played a game of stabbing his dagger between his spread fingers so rapidly that it made the blade blur.

Godblood, he said to himself. *That's not so hard. I could do that.*

He stood up, slung the joined sacks across one shoulder, and walked slowly to where the mercenary was tilting back on the small stool. Suddenly Pantalone swung his foot against the back leg of the stool and sent the man—armor and empty mug—crashing to the floor. The noise attracted everyone in the tavern, who looked with a mixture of horror and fascination at the boy and the soldier. There was a momentary hush, broken only by a brief, worried word of alarm. Pantalone noted with satisfaction that the serving wench also watched and appeared concerned. But for whom?

The boy then reached down, grabbed the startled mercenary by the throat, an action that sent the soldier's helmet flying, and pulled him to his knees. "Damme." Pantalone sneered in his best imitation of an older, dangerous inhabitant of southern Italy, where, he knew, the more lawless of his countrymen reigned. "You French toadies think you can just put your stools wherever it pleases you!"

He snarled in what he considered to be a menacing tone, but the old soldier, having recovered his wits and his footing, gave the boy one quick shove that sent him hurtling back into another table. *Damn,* thought Pantalone. *He's not so old after all!*

"You have no sword, boy," the mercenary growled in that unmistakable accent that Pantalone had been attempting to imitate. "May I provide you with the blade to mine?"

With that, one gloved hand flew to the hilt of his sword, and he drew the weapon quickly and cleanly. Pantalone saw the flames dance and color the blade with the appearance of someone's blood. He backed toward the fire in an attempt to circle his opponent and open a path to the door, when suddenly the soldier lunged forward. The boy, remembering a portion of Harlequin's instructions to Scapino on how to be a fulcrum, sidestepped with that natural agility that, by the grace of God, did not desert him now.

The mercenary, expecting resistance to his blade, went headfirst into the fire, where his thick and heavily oiled hair instantly burst into flame. His screams awoke everyone in the room, and they started forward as one to assist the poor human torch. Pantalone took advantage of the confusion to dash out the door, untie Destruction, throw the sacks over his back, and prod the poor beast into some semblance of a rapid trot.

"*Arri!*" He urged the animal forward up the steep street and as far from the tavern as he could get. He headed west and was relieved not to hear sounds of pursuit. Indeed, he was concentrating on making as much speed as possible, so he never heard the rapid tattoo and the clank of armor in front of him until it was nearly too late.

From around a corner of the street plunged a great war-horse covered deeply in shining plate and mounted by a half-dressed madman waving a naked sword. Pantalone managed to jerk Destruction to one side, but the blade of the warrior nicked his arm in the passing as the wild horseman screamed at him, "Clear the way, you pig's behind!"

As the capitano disappeared into the shadows of the street, Pantalone thought to himself, *Godsblood, I hate the military!*

THE CAPITANO ROSE from the grass and rubbed his hand down the smooth flanks of the war-horse. That reminded him of his beloved Annamarie, and *that* reminded him of the insinuation that the woman had other lovers. *No,* he told himself. *Impossible.*

He had stripped the animal of the armor and allowed him to graze and drink. Now he looked at the immensity of the stallion with open admiration. "You're no ordinary horse, are you? You're Mantua-bred! And with that armor removed, I'll bet you can run like the wind, can't you? I'll bet you can. In fact, that's what I'll call you! Zephyr!" He backed away to let the horse finish grazing. He was reminded then of his own hunger, but he reasoned that it might be safe to stop in Parma and barter for something since there had been no indication that he was being pursued. *Now,* he thought, *if I only had something to barter.*

He had been dragged from the bedroom of Annamarie with few items of clothing, retaining only his pants, boots, and hose when they brought him before the duke. He also wore the belt of his own uniform, but they had removed the sword and scabbard and dagger from it. This he had replaced with the naked sword and dagger taken from the dead aide.

"Even if I wanted to kill game," he murmured to himself, "I have nothing to use." He thought then of taking the time to make a trap, or to attempt to find Cosimo and his own company of mercenaries, but from what he could glean from the marshal's tirade, the soldiers had divided the enlistment money and dispersed. *Which*—he shrugged—*is exactly what I would have done in their place.* Still, time was his enemy, and he reasoned that it would be best to keep running.

There was a mysterious packet wrapped in a waterproof membrane from some large animal and tied tightly with leather thongs. It had been secured to the horn of the saddle, and until now he had overlooked it. Now he considered that it might be something of value he could trade for food. He had to cut the thongs to open it. When he unbound the contents, he was surprised to find two long objects with which he was not unfamiliar. He smiled then and blew a kiss to the west.

"Bless you, Excellency!"

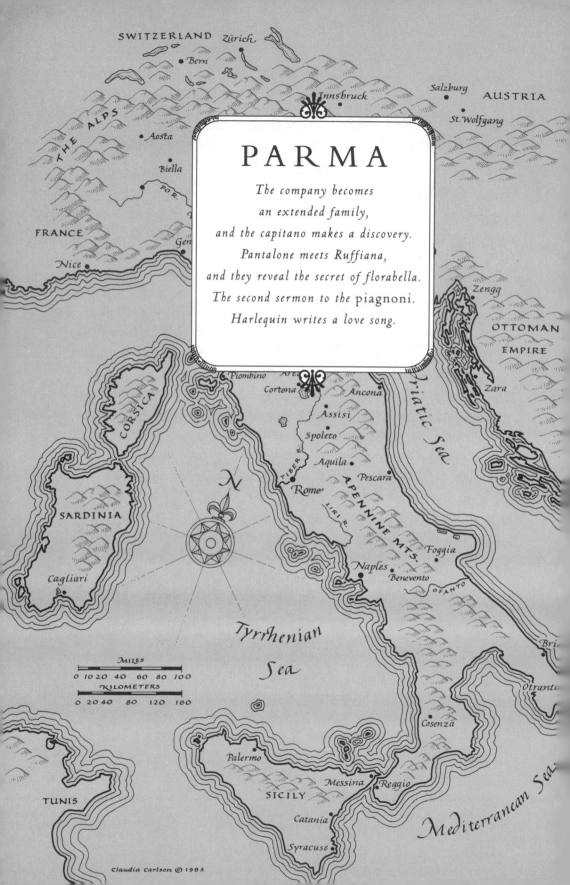

PARMA

The company becomes
an extended family,
and the capitano makes a discovery.
Pantalone meets Ruffiana,
and they reveal the secret of florabella.
The second sermon to the piagnoni.
Harlequin writes a love song.

The cart and the wagon inched their way along the main roadway leading northeast out of Piacenza. The route picked by Harlequin for the safe delivery of Isabella and Giacomo to Mantua ran along the main stream of transients through Cremona, and then directly east. Pantalone's story of what had occurred at the tavern in Piacenza seemed to give Harlequin a moment of indecision, but then he told them that he felt their best chances might be to continue on the paved roadway rather than cut cross-country.

"Should the Cardinal of Modena send the Este mercenaries after us," Harlequin told them, "there would be more chance of encountering them to the south in his own see. Whereas if we continue northeast, we should arrive within the areas controlled by the Gonzaga of Mantua within a day or two." Then he added, "Of course, the forged carte blanche has outlived its usefulness. From this point on we will have to rely on our wits and the grace of a benevolent God."

He then offered Scapino, Pantalone, and Colombina the opportunity to divide from Isabella, Giacomo, and himself. "You are in no danger at this point," he said. "The condottieri of the Savoy would never look this far south and east for two cutpurses, and Colombina has offended no one—with the possible exception of Terpischore, the muse of dance."

Colombina snorted. "You'd starve without me."

And Scapino added, "You agreed to teach me how to be a fulcrum. If you think I've completed the study, why did I get my head broken in Pavia?"

Whereupon Harlequin sighed and murmured, "Well, I knew you'd insist on coming along, but it was worth a try."

*T*HE AUTUMN WAS MILD in northern Italy that year. Fall lingered lovingly over the fields and pastures and foothills of the Apennines, and there was, as yet, no sign of the winter rains or the cold *tramontana*—the bora winds that sweep into Italy from Central

Europe. The oaks, the junipers, the pine and laurel, the broom trees—everything remained green into late October. The darting silver tongues of the olive trees gossiped of the passing of the strange ensemble from Piacenza toward Cremona, and falcons and kites screamed defiantly overhead as they searched out their prey, hapless field mice.

It was good hunting weather.

As the small caravan wormed its way toward Cremona, the capitano, resplendent in armored mail and a black robe cinched at the waist by a gold chain, raced southeast on the back of Zephyr, whose armor he had traded for his own at the Abbazia di Chiaravalle della Colomba in Alseno.

The abbey, which was founded by St. Bernard of Clairvaux nearly two hundred years earlier, had been plundered and sacked innumerable times by one army or another and, as a result, had amassed an impressive collection of discarded armor and weaponry. Knowing that monasteries and abbeys always afforded transients a free meal if so requested, the capitano had sought refuge there for a day or two, traded the horse's armor, and bade the monks farewell as he proceeded down the south road to Fidenza.

In Fidenza he took the opportunity to tap into that invisible network that exists for professional soldiers. From an old companion-in-arms who had retired to the softer life of the small town, he learned that his mercenary company had performed exactly as he had reasoned they would. When Cosimo returned with the enlistment monies, the ducats were divided equally among them, and then they had scattered in a hundred different directions. Capitano knew that their easily acquired wealth would be lavished on fine food and drink and a woman or two before the veteran soldiers would find themselves once again in need of financial assistance and immediately enlist in another army.

But from the monks of the abbey—where information was often exchanged for a meal, providing the Vatican with a spy system second to none—the capitano had learned that Cosimo had apparently reported the deserters to the marshal, whining that they had robbed him of his own savings and had departed in the dead of night. Whereupon the marshal had bestowed a small recompense on the Sicilian and given him a special assignment: to find and kill the capitano.

The capitano thought of that now as he raced the great warhorse toward Parma. *If I can reach Reggio,* he told himself, *I have a chance.*

O CCASIONALLY THE CART and the wagon passed ancient, eroded tombs that marked the kilometers along this road to Cremona, which had been built of lava rock by the Romans. Herds of sheep and goats were everywhere and congregated on the roadways to baa their litanies.

Despite the passage of the forces of death during the previous invasion by the French, life now filled the fertile countryside. Occasionally they would come across a discarded bill—that curious pike that combined an ax blade, a sword blade, and two pointed prongs at right angles to one another, all mounted on a long pole. One day they counted five discarded bows, and Harlequin said these weapons were probably abandoned by the French peasant conscripts in their rapid retreat from Naples two years earlier.

"The French king," he told Colombina, "thought it might be nice to have a standing army, so he ordered the entire male population to be trained in the use of the crossbow. The nobility quickly pointed out that an armed peasantry could result in insurrection and revolution, so he rescinded the order but, still needing an army, decreed that every fiftieth household should provide one ablebodied man trained in weapons of war. Once a year they would meet, swear their loyalty, and play war games." He laughed at the memory. "But when it came to actual combat, they proved worthless, and those abandoned bows are a testimony to their inefficiency. We called them chicken killers."

"We?" asked Colombina.

Harlequin smiled but said nothing further. Later, however, as the small caravan moved slowly east, he would from time to time describe battles fought by night with small flashes of light and sounds like muffled drums. He described in detail the sounds of the big, new cast-iron artillery mounted on two-wheeled carts that he called ribauldequins; and this, in turn, led Pantalone and some of the others to believe the ragged vagabond was indeed a former mercenary.

The progress of the company was slow and frequently impeded. Harlequin had failed to consider that the journey would also include frequent breakdowns of either the cart or the wagon or, occasionally, both; and he failed to consider a week's delay when they attempted to cross the Po at a point that Isabella had sworn was an ancient fording place.

Nor had he anticipated Scapino's remarkable plunge into the raging waters in an attempt to rescue one of Isabella's traveling boxes, and the juggler's subsequent fever and chills that kept him—and the company—immobile.

But as a result of these unforeseen adventures, autumn had worn on by the time they neared the outskirts of the city.

Pantalone's story of what he had overheard in Piacenza had affected the company in different ways. Harlequin had been most interested in the dark priest, Sebastiano. Three times he made Pantalone repeat the description of the ferret-faced cleric and how he'd interpreted their nonsense Latin. Then he had walked apart from the others to sit alone for more than an hour.

Giacomo, alias Dottore, became alarmed that Sebastiano had expressed such a strong interest in Isabella. Despite his past incompetent attempts to protect her—which he could attribute to his inexperience in matters of intrigue and adventure—Dottore had taken his commission from Gentile Zappachio seriously, and despite the girl's attitude of superiority toward him, he liked her. And he had never underestimated the possible danger imposed on them by the nature of Gentile's art.

One night he regaled the group with the stories told in the Milanese court of the great "bonfire of the vanities" supervised by Savonarola in Florence a year before, of the eyewitness account of Cardinal Sforza to Duke Lodovico, and of the internal warfare that erupted—and still existed—between the religious orders of the Church.

Indeed, he did not wear the monk's robes anymore, because Harlequin had felt that a complete detachment from all things religious was additional protection in these times. The ragged vagabond pointed out that "a communion of saints" was merely a theological phrase to the Dominicans, who were espousing the cause of their Sister Colomba for sainthood because of her religious ecstasies, while warring with the Franciscans, who were advocating the cause of *their* Sister Lucia de Narni, who, they swore, was inflicted with the stigmata. "Even the Cluniacs are differing with the Cistercians," said Harlequin, "although both are segments of the Benedictine rule."

In addition, he pointed out that they were encountering more and more of the mysterious and mystic "black monks," who were reportedly from England. These men slowly trod the Italian roadways in pairs or groups of four, seemingly without cause or destination, and on occasion they would cross the path of one or more of the "solitaries" who measured their lives and devotion by the austerities they suffered and who were themselves on their way to bleak caves tucked into the Apennines. Consequently it was agreed that it was far safer to be associated with no clerical order of any kind.

In his spare time Dottore had returned to sketching and painting, always searching for that elusive "secret" that Verrocchio had passed on to da Vinci and not to him. He was temporarily convinced that the secret had to do with the brushes used, and that was why the burro nicknamed Death now had a bobbed tail.

Scapino was equally upset that Isabella seemed to be in potential danger, since an unusual relationship had blossomed between the juggler and the painter's daughter. It was unusual because, as far as the others could see, Scapino made no visible overtures, was not known to speak romantic phrases to her, and indeed once, when she began one of her marathon monologues over the evening fire, he told her quite sharply and clearly to stop.

And stop she did.

He never assisted her in climbing up or down from the wagon or the cart, nor did he serve her an unequal portion of their food. He did not serve her at all, and was known to talk right over her when he felt that the topic of her conversation was of no interest to him or she began to speak Latin. As a consequence, she rarely indulged in that aristocratic tongue anymore.

But Scapino was protective of her, and she, in turn, felt safe and comfortable when she was with him.

As a consequence of their relationship, he had intensified his study with Harlequin and had become quite an adept acrobat, spending long hours at juggling practice even as they rode through the countryside. He had, in general, sharpened all his skills and disciplined his body.

Isabella, on the other hand, was delighted that for the first time she never had to play the lady for anyone. Indeed, she did not have to play any role for anyone. What she was—what she revealed to them all, and especially to Scapino—was what she was, and he accepted and appreciated her honesty. At the same time they were all confused as to her education. The arts taught young women in the courts of the dukes and marquises did not normally include fencing, military tactics, or romantic literature. Indeed, they puzzled how and why a daughter of a Venetian artist was welcomed into the courts of Venice and Urbino in the first place, but Isabella had described—at interminable length—the depth of compassion and support shown her family because of Gentile's skill at portraiture.

Like Dottore, she no longer wore the monk's robes. Now Isabella sported a scoop-necked, long-sleeved blouse—much too large for her—and a full skirt with red petticoats, all supplied by Colombina. She secretly hungered for the feel of her own silks again, but Harlequin had stressed that they must not draw attention to themselves, that nothing would attract more curiosity than a fine lady traveling with a herd of vagabonds. Even in peasant clothes she looked well-bred, and so they provided her with a heavy, black shawl that she used to cover her hair and shadow her face when they passed through the cities.

Oddly, when Pantalone related the interest shown in her by Sebastiano and Lieutenant Angelo, Isabella was surprised to find that she was not afraid but exhilarated.

On hearing about that conversation at the inn, however, Harlequin, puzzled, had reexamined her traveling case. The chest was decorated with a quartered *impresa* in black, red, and yellow with gold leaf applied in some areas. The top left quarter depicted an elaborate censer wound with four gold suspension chains. The motif on the top right was basically five wavy red flames against a golden background. The bottom left design was a series of five gold *papellone* laid upon five red shingles, which, in turn, mounted five black panels. The final lower right quarter was a large letter *A*, black with white dots, tilted on one leg and laid against a golden sky. Around the border of the *impresa* was a series of florid monograms that seemed to depict two letters intertwined, but the inscription was so ornate that it was nearly impossible to discern what the letters were.

If her case bore a coat of arms, it represented a combination of several houses. Isabella, when questioned, said she had been told the *cassone* had been her mother's. She could not explain how the wife of a Venetian painter had merited an *impresa* of any sort.

Pantalone and Colombina were alternately afraid and delighted by the new turn of their odyssey. The boy felt that everything promised a greater sense of adventure and excitement than his more routine experiences as a purse cutter. He was of the opinion that if he had to go, he would like to have such pleasant company with him at the time. The threat by the old mercenary in Piacenza had reawakened his desire to master the devices and the tricks of Dottore and the fighting skill of Harlequin, as well as the sleight of hand of his father, Scapino, but this was tempered of course by the young man's personal code:

I can do that!

Although, in a spirit of precise honesty, most of his time was taken up in daydreaming of that elusive, timeless sexual adventure with a genuine, professional woman of the night—like those incredible (and impossible) encounters narrated with great relish and exquisite detail by the older boys of Vercelli.

Colombina, for the first time, belonged to someone and something outside her own narrow world. She reveled in her role of mother to them all. It was she who reassured and comforted and fed and encouraged them. Furthermore Harlequin had kept his promise, and every evening he took her apart from the others and taught her the formation of letters and words and phrases. On occasion he resurrected the things she had forgotten about balance and fluid motion and body discipline. But above all he showed her that she had forgotten the pleasure and the personal necessity of dancing—that secret that every dancer understands and reveals in the art. He made her see that she danced badly because she had no reason to dance—other than to earn money—which, he argued, would never produce a truly great dancer. He said repeatedly, and she struggled to understand, that art is truth made visible, and while a lie can please for a moment, the effect would not be lasting. Certainly not for eternity, which, he told her, was the minimum testing period for great art.

Now, in the lazy afternoons, Isabella assumed the role of instructor to Colombina for reading and writing while Harlequin remained an advocate of the arts.

Harlequin was the unmistakable leader of the group. Apart from Isabella, he was obviously the best educated, and his knowledge went beyond that acquired through the universities of Bologna or Padua or Pavia. He quoted statements by Strazzi of Florence and Giustiniani of Venice concerning a "new consciousness," a new way of interpreting experience. The others did not always understand these things, but they noted the intensity and conviction with which he spoke.

He could, indeed, speak Greek as well as church Latin, and from his ability with the vulgar tongue, they reasoned that he could probably speak other languages as well. He possessed some knowledge of the things they had often wondered about: where the stars go in daylight, the shape and history of the earth, the origin and

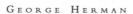

habits of a variety of birds and other, more legendary animals; and he frequently had friendly arguments with Isabella on topics the others could not comprehend.

He was also the most widely experienced. It was not so much that he always knew what to do, but that he always did *something* when some action was necessary. When he was right, they all prospered, and when he was wrong, he suffered with them. When he felt it was a matter of some dispute, they "went to the hands" and the majority ruled. "We are all working to avoid encountering Italy's numerous autocrats and tyrants," he counseled. "Let's not substitute one tyranny for another."

He was a magnificent storyteller and would spin epics by firelight in the evenings about ancient wars and peoples, about the loves of Paris and the heroism of Hector.

He could sing and play the lute, and knew, apparently, hundreds of songs—many of them surprisingly ribald and suggestive, but bright and merry and great fun.

But if they respected Harlequin for his knowledge and experience, they grew even closer to him for his sheer sense of absurdity. They each, in their individual spheres, had encountered "scholars," especially the principal products of the universities—the *notaria*—whose higher education prepared them only for medicine and the law; and the universal opinion was that such people were dull, uninteresting individuals who could pontificate for hours on the probable number of angels that could stand on the head of a pin or the proper preparation for a legally binding contract or why bleeding was the proper response to most ills. And they had all noticed, like the peasants and thieves and laborers of the "lower classes," that these same well-educated gentlefolk could be easily bilked in a bartering engagment, cuckolded by the score, and could not roast a pullet without burning it.

Harlequin never said anything important that was not also linked with something trivial or absurd. It was as though he stood apart from himself, watching himself move and hearing himself speak, and judging the entire procedure as pointless and ridiculous. When asked, he would launch into a long and detailed explanation of something and then, realizing he was lecturing, would turn it all into a jest. His most biting gibes were aimed at himself, and he had the wonderful gift of being able verbally to chastise someone with a laugh, so that the victim was never really certain if he had been taken to task or simply shared an amusing experience.

Harlequin laughed more than anyone else in the company and constantly delighted Pantalone with his observations on human behavior. The boy had laughed to tears when a procession of the family of a rich merchant, full of pomp and pretentiousness, passed by them, and Harlequin attributed the pained and aloof expression on the face of the fat marketeer to the fact that he had just defecated in his tights.

And Harlequin's bizarre and irrevent humor had become infectious. The entire company, after a while, became equally adroit at spotting the fear beneath the bravado, the foolishness in the wise, and the absurdity in nearly all of man's behavior. Despite the danger and the threats constantly around them, they were a bright and merry band of rabble who took their collective triumphs and small tragedies in stride, and who grew, individually, for this brief time, in the same direction.

They had become a small, unique society of scholars: Scapino and Pantalone studied to sharpen their skills; Colombina quaffed knowledge from Isabella and Harlequin; and Dottore, possessing a wide range of talents and information, taught everyone.

Like all societies, however, they shared an indefinable mistrust of each other, occasionally voiced in objections to Isabella possessing "the arrogance of her class" or to Harlequin "assuming leadership" or Pantalone "sneaking looks at Isabella when she's bathing." Like all societies, they begrudingly accepted responsibility for cleaning or grooming the animals or fixing a wheel or an axle or drawing water, but occasionally they also expressed—with only a minimum of embarrassment—a genuine affection for each other. Like a true family, they were full of differences that made no difference and were at odds on every insignificant matter except the fact that in times of conflict, they had to act and respond as one.

They were, like so many in those turbulent times, enlarging their horizons rapidly, because two of the doors to personal freedom were now open to them: an equal dispensation of knowledge, and the time and patience to develop individual skills. Only two remaining elements were still lost to them: a worldly and practical wisdom as to how to use their knowledge and their skills most effectively. And the universal truth that made it all relevant to living.

When the axle on Colombina's wagon broke for the fifth time just three hours west of Cremona, as they were approaching the fork where their gutted dirt road joined the Via Emilia, there was no great dismay over it. The matter was soon settled and the wagon abandoned. The contents that were vital to them were transferred to the cart, where they substituted for the hay camouflaging the paintings and Isabella's personal wardrobe.

Death and Destruction were harnessed to the cart, which now proceeded slowly down the ancient Roman road. There was some disagreement at first over who should walk and who should ride. Colombina had advanced the romantic notion that the women, being women, should ride, and the men, being men, should walk. Scapino voiced the opinion that this was nonsense, since they each had two legs, and that they should all take turns riding.

He won his case, because Harlequin and Pantalone, though instinctively romantic, were equally averse to treading any great distances over a worn and cobbled roadway.

ZEPHYR THE WARHORSE galloped down the Via Trento in Parma, scattering merchants and workers, farm wives and students in all directions. Just outside the shop of Gasparo the Wainwright, Filippo Masaccio, the reed-thin grand master of the clothmakers' guild, shook an angry fist in the capitano's direction, and then turned his attention to the aging wagon maker.

"When, then, *will* it be completed, you avaricious antique? You have made four trips to Piacenza to review the plans with me, and I have had to make six journeys here to Parma to oversee the construction!"

The wainwright countered, "When will you have the rest of the money, you miserable miser?"

Filippo placed a bony hand on the old man's shoulder. "I just met with a representative of the Monte dei Paschi of Siena. The bank has agreed to advance me the money against this winter's profits of the clothmakers' guild, at seven percent." He prodded the carpenter with a stilettolike finger. "I wouldn't have had to resort to a loan, you decrepit woodworm, if you hadn't raised the price for the third time!"

Gasparo shrugged. "Is the price of your cloth the same as it was six months ago, you tightfisted toad?"

"You know perfectly well the price of my cloth has had to rise if I am to make a profit. Can I ignore the newly imposed city-gate tolls? The new duties on salt and milling and wine? And the increased taxes on meat and fish, fats, oils, iron, and white bread? Hasn't the trouble with Constantinople affected the silk trade, yes or no? Haven't the Venetian merchants raised their prices as well? And do you think that the legislation in Florence denouncing guilds as contrary to Christian charity and the brotherhood of man hasn't affected my business, eh?"

The wainwright disagreed. "The reason your price rises is due to the appetite of your beautiful and gracious wife, Annamarie, for *gentilezze*—expensive baubles. Not that I blame her, the poor thing, since nothing but your prices can still rise, I warrant."

Filippo growled, "My wife's taste for jewels has nothing to do with your prices, you greedy nail pounder." He lowered his voice. "I have to consider the possibility that more of the *popolo* will begin to form their own guilds and drive me to the wall, don't I? We agreed on a revised price for the wagon on your last visit to Piacenza, and now you tell me it will cost nearly half as much again! If I wasn't concerned about my prolonged absence from that beautiful wife of mine, I wouldn't even be discussing the matter with you. There are other wainwrights in Italy."

"None that can make such a wagon! And this is not an ordinary wagon," Gasparo argued. "Come look at it, you impotent mummy!

It is not even an ordinary guild wagon. It is lighter. A single horse can pull it. Yet it is stronger than the trees we made it from!"

They walked out of the shop into the piazza. There against the side of the building was a strange-looking vehicle. It was certainly wider than the average wagon, and taller. It looked as though one large wagon had been placed directly on another. From the four corners of the basic wooden bed rose four heavy supporting columns, which supported a wooden floor. On top of this floor two additional supports had been mounted on the left side of the wagon and a cross beam anchored between them. Heavy green curtains had been mounted around the bottom area and were suspended from the "roof" by strong metal rings.

"You haven't completed the upper floor!" Filippo protested. "It needs two more supporting pillars and a roof over all!"

"I know, I know." Gasparo nodded. "What do you think, you sheep's barber? That I've never witnessed the *sacra rappresentazione* on the feast days?"

"And there should be curtains completely around the second level, you creaking monstrosity! I sent you two complete sets of drapes, did I not? Where are the others?"

"What do you think, you stupid bastard, that I wiped my ass with them? Do you imagine I ate them? Do I look like some sort of a moth to you?" He poked the clothmaker's belly. "Do you think my wife and six daughters have converted them into ball gowns? The curtains for the top area are stored there—in the bottom well—until we've finished the construction. What do you think we could hang them on, you eater of cow dung? Our pricks?"

"And what about the roof?" Filippo nagged. "Our costumes are made of delicate fabrics and must be protected against the sun and the rain. You may remember that I told you that earlier, you senile old ass."

"I tell you I've seen guild wagons before, damn your eyes to hell! Look! Look! Look!" Gasparo half dragged the cloth merchant into his shop again. "See?" He pointed. "My assistants and apprentices already finished the supporting corner poles and the cross beams!

We have only to mount them and hang your cheap curtains, you cheater of widows and orphans!"

"And why is my new, unfinished guild wagon left outside to brave the elements, you raper of pig bladders?"

"Because I intend to harness a horse to it within the hour," the old wagon maker wheezed, "to test it for weight and stability. If that's all right with Your Exalted Majesty, father of farts!"

"Just as long as my unfinished wagon is completed by tomorrow, you dottering old carrier of disease."

"Your unpaid-for wagon will be ready when you have the rest of the money, you breeder of maggots!"

Filippo slipped his arm over the old man's shoulders and drew him to one side. "If you are testing the weight," he whispered, "remember the wine I will be carrying back to Piacenza."

Gasparo laughed softly and led the clothmaker back to the wagon outside. He drew back the curtains to reveal four hogsheads of wine resting in the bed. "It was delivered this morning"—he chuckled—"and I had it loaded at once. I trust you don't intend to carry wine with you when you perform religious plays on All Saints?"

"That, you old fart, is not merely wine," confided Filippo. "That is ambrosia, an incredible vintage, and our guild is accepting it from the vintners' guild in payment for curtains and costumes for their presentation on All Saints. So we sidestep the taxes, you understand? My guildsmen will toast the feast day with a veritable elixir. Aren't you jealous, you stinking bag of rotting guts?"

"Why should I be jealous of a guild of drunken weavers whose fabrics dissolve in the rain?" growled the wainwright as he ambled back into his shop with his old friend.

"And the wagon must—absolutely must—be finished tomorrow, you spawn of dung beetles. I will bring you the rest of your exorbitant fee, and the wagon must be ready to go with me to Piacenza. My poor wife has been without me for a week."

"Fortunate woman," said Gasparo. "At least she has been given the brief opportunity to sample the stamina and equipment of the neighboring males."

Filippo laughed, patting the old wagon maker lightly on his bent

back. "I never worry about Annamarie. She is a model of fidelity."
They walked together. "Come see us perform in Modena on All
Saints' Day," he said. "We have been assigned *Abraham and Isaac* this
year, and I may even save you some of the wine, you pitiful, dying
lecher." Both friends heartily waved good-bye to each other as
Filippo left the shop, rounded the corner, and disappeared from
sight.

"Godsblood"—Gasparo laughed until his eyes ran—"how I hate
that bastard." Then he remembered the many extreme personal
kindnesses shown him by Signora Masaccio during his last visit
to Piacenza. *Oh well,* he thought. *I'll just arrange for one more
trip to Piacenza to discuss modifications and then add forty florins to his
bill.*

*T*HE FOCAL POINT of Cremona is the Piazza del Comune
dominated by the Torazzo, a towering facade that is easily visible for
miles. Here in the shadow of the western facade of the cathedral,
where the months are depicted with figurines after Antelami, the
cart paused long enough for Colombina to make some small purchases and for Harlequin to eavesdrop on the local merchants.

What he heard and reported to the others was not encouraging.
"The Este family," he announced, "has cut the only western approach to Mantua just east of the crossroads near the Oglio River.
According to what I overheard, they are searching for a wagon and
a cart that slipped past the sentries at Pavia, and in light of Pantalone's observations in the tavern at Piacenza, it is clear that the mercenary's report to Father Sebastiano had alarmed the Cardinal of
Modena and the Estes about us.

"So," Harlequin concluded, "I propose we play a little game with
our pursuers by heading south to Parma. By running parallel with
the Po and cutting cross-country to Busseto, Soragna, and
Fontanellato, we can avoid any Este mercenary patrols on the main
roads. It will mean still another delay, and I realize that each step
takes us closer to the duchy of Modena instead of Mantua, but no

one will expect us to approach Mantua—which they seem to know is our destination—from the south. They also do not expect to find us reduced to only one vehicle—which may or may not be an asset. In any case, I think it is the best plan."

Dottore concurred. "It is the *only* plan."

So it was unanimously agreed by "going to the hands" that the party would turn south and go cross-country to Parma and then north into Mantua.

"Which," Isabella observed to Colombina, "is like the fly telling the spider, 'I know it's your web, but I'm just passing through. Ignore me.'"

UNKNOWN TO THE COMPANY, there was a moment of danger outside Fontanellato. Just as the cart had reached the main road into Parma, they came upon a carriage that had thrown a wheel at the crossroads, and the fugitives had to work their way around the vehicle, which blocked the thoroughfare. From the curtained window of that carriage, Leonardo da Vinci, hastening to join his master, Cesare Borgia, at Cresena, imagined he saw his old assistant, Giacomo Martinelli, walking and laughing with two peasant women as three men attempted to cajole, pull, and push a team of obstinate burros around his broken vehicle.

No, he told himself. *I've just been working too hard.*

OUTSIDE PARMA, Harlequin pointed out that the jewels owned by Isabella and Dottore were useless for barter, because they would certainly arouse suspicion as to how the ragged travelers came by such valuable gems. Their need for food was therefore limited to a judicious use of Dottore's remaining funds in the marketplace.

"This austerity will be temporary at best," Harlequin proposed "because I think a large purchase—such as a wagon—might be paid for with a jewel. What we need is to find one of the *marranos* in Parma who asks no questions and knows a bargain when he sees one."

The *marranos,* he had enlightened them, were "secret Jews." When the Spanish king had demanded some years earlier that all Jews either convert to Christianity or be deported, scores had migrated to Italy for protection. To the horror of the devout Catholic rulers, the Borgian pope had instead sheltered them, allowing them to erect colonies of tents along the Appian Way.

Some, however, to be absolutely safe, practiced their faith in secret, and dressed and worked among the Christians. They had also become money changers, and that of course was the main reason Pope Alexander had befriended them.

As the ragged travelers neared Parma, Pantalone had the pleasure and the responsibility of entering the city ahead of the others on the workhorse that had been named Salvation. He was given Dottore's last *zecchino* to purchase the supplies they urgently needed, because—as Harlequin also pointed out—the boy possessed a youthful curiosity that had resulted in his hearing and observing everything.

Unhappily Pantalone also possessed a young and facile body that was composed of eighty percent water and twenty percent hormones.

From his arrival at the doorway of adolescence, his sexual appetites were persistent and almost never satisfied, and his initial dalliances simply routine for a boy of his age and ability. He had made love to gamesome young farm girls and to the fat and fatuous village whore, who—like the customary idiot—seemed to be assigned one per region. Sometimes there was an occasional, neglected wife, but these were uninspired encounters that left the young man thinking at times that sex wasn't the supreme pleasure that the older village boys had declared it to be. He enjoyed it, of course, and he never ran from an opportunity when circumstances—and his equipment—might arise, but this was due partly to his appetite and partly to his sincere religious conviction that to refuse sex when offered was a grievous offense against all the gods of nature and the universe.

But at the heart of it, he also felt that he was missing something, something unique, something secret that was known only to those who made love a genuine art form. Not the unfortunate village woman who needed subsistence and diminished the act to one of submission so complete that compost heaps would have offered greater warmth and motion. He desired someone young and exciting, bosomy, and strong. Someone who brought to the act the same degree of imaginative dedication that he did.

The only other requirement of this ideal bedmate was that he, Pantalone, had to be her only lover, but that was a minor concern, because he was convinced that once they had mated, his talents and skill would keep his partner faithful and devoted through the rest of her life.

It must be noted, too, that for the many weeks it had taken the company to reach Parma, he had made love only two or three times. He couldn't count the episode Scapino had interrupted in Aosta. There was one time with the giggling young farm girl in the bushes at Biella, whom he had left asleep and satisfied and from whom he liberated her two grazing burros, Death and Destruction. Then once with a tavern wench in Milan when he had temporarily separated from the others.

No, he remembered now. *It was twice with the tavern wench.* But that was beside the point.

He had resorted to a more solitary solution in the late dark when the others in the company were asleep, but he found it less than satisfying. No one ever had the opportunity to point out to the boy that he made love to himself as he did to women: as though the fortress was under siege and he had only a few minutes to make his attack and retreat before the reinforcements arrived.

So, when an exciting, wild-haired, radiant-eyed young whore suddenly appeared at his elbow in the marketplace on the Via Bottego in Parma, it was not merely a chance encounter. It was manifest destiny.

He was examining some shanks of meat, decorated with flies, at a farmer's stall when she appeared, red-haired and tawny, in a dirty gray blouse that revealed as much of her round, firm breasts as she wanted revealed. She was older than he by perhaps five or six years, but one look at the nut-brown firm legs and trim ankles below her scarlet skirt and petticoat, and Pantalone felt the barrier of age disintegrate. She brushed invitingly against him and pretended not to notice, but he felt the hard nipples and the heat of her through the flimsy blouse.

"Don't buy the meat," she breathed in his ear.

"What?"

"It's dog," she whispered, "and diseased at that. One bite, and you'll die with a bellyful of little, fiery worms." She tapped his belly then, and the long fingers casually stroked him so briefly, so well, and with such controlled skill that he felt himself harden. He also began to tremble. "Oh, poor boy, you have a chill," she said, smiling at him. Then softly, "I have a remedy for that."

"I—knew you would." Pantalone smiled back at her. Then, in a completely reflex action, he heard himself blurt out the words, "How much?"

The sudden and direct presentation of the question delighted her, and she laughed. *Her laughter,* thought Pantalone, *is miniature cathedral bells.*

"Oh, I'm very expensive," she lied as she lightly brushed her magic hands down his chest and directly to his crotch with such a studied and experienced gesture that an onlooker, less than an arm's width away, would have noticed nothing.

Pantalone, however, noticed something. "How—how much?" he repeated, feeling as though someone had removed all the air from the piazza.

"Wait," cooed the girl. "What's your name?"

"Pantalone," gasped the boy. "How *much?*"

"My name's Ruffiana." She stroked him again. "And I am really more in the market for a wealthy guildsman or a condottiere."

"I have a *sequin!*" he offered, and held the golden coin in the air for her to see.

Her bright yes flashed in astonishment, and she quickly grabbed for the coin. Pantalone, however, waved his hand, and the gold instantly disappeared. It was a trick taught him by Harlequin. He was delighted that it worked.

"Sweet Lamb of God," said the girl in a hushed voice as she blessed herself quickly with the sign of the cross. "Are you—a demon?" And she stepped back from him.

He felt he was losing her and instinctively made a move toward her, but she backed away as rapidly as he advanced. "Stay where you are!" she said, and held up a small wooden cross that she wore on a thong around her neck. "I'm not afraid of you!"

"It was only a trick!" wailed Pantalone. "I know lots of them. I can make birds appear from an empty chalice and change the color of silk by passing it through my fingers. I can make water flow uphill!"

She studied his face then and let the cross fall back against her dark skin. "Well," she said slowly, "I know a few tricks myself." She circled him. "The *sequin*. Was that real?"

"Oh yes!" He made the coin reappear at the tips of his fingers and, on an impulse, tucked it between her breasts. "You see?" He beamed at her.

"It feels real enough." She smiled back at him. Suddenly her hand shot out and quickly brushed against his crotch again. He fought not to bend over in the exquisite agony of her touch. "And so does *this*," she teased. "I guess you're not a demon after all." Then she took a step away from him, smiling at him over her bare shoulder. "A *sequin* is a great deal of money. What do you expect me to do for it?"

Reassured, he moved forward and swept her along the piazza with an arm about her waist. "Let us consider that problem together."

On THE SOUTH ROAD approaching Parma, the cart and its ragged escort moved slowly and deliberately in the bright afternoon. Scapino and Isabella drove Death and Destruction from the seat of the cart, and Colombina and Dottore walked on either side. Harlequin preceded the burros like a mad pied piper, strumming the lute and singing to the rhythm of their hooves against the cobblestones.

And naturally, on such an afternoon, he sang of love.

> "The cloud and the sea are lovers,
> And anyone can see the reason why.
> The sky doesn't want to cling to the cloud.
> The cloud doesn't hang on the sky.
> They are lovers. They are two.
> But the white cloud is only vapor,
> Till it rests on the breast of the blue.
> The cloud remains a cloud.
> The sky is still the sky.
> They are lovers,
> And don't know why.
> The tree and the bird are lovers,
> As all who see must agree.
> The tree doesn't try to fly like the bird.
> The bird doesn't stay with the tree.
> They are lovers. Never one.
> For the bird brings song to the linden,
> And the tree protects from the sun.
> Still the tree must stand and grow.
> The bird must soar and sing.
> They are lovers—
> For an hour—
> Every spring.
> You and I are forever lovers,
> And our love is forever true.
> You and I.
> Me and you."

He strummed a single chord, which hung on the air and vibrated for an eternity. Then he sang the final word.

"Two."

"That's a pretty tune," muttered Scapino.

"It's doggerel." Isabella sniffed.

"I don't care who wrote it," Scapino snapped at her. "I like it."

They rode on in silence with Isabella's hand resting on his knee.

*H*UDDLED TOGETHER in the small pharmacy in the church of Santa Giovanni Evangelista, a group of white-robed clerics listened with fascination to the speaker. Tall, mesmerizing, the leader of the *piagnoni* repeated the teachings of their "martyred" leader, Savonarola.

"Fra Girolamo pointed out that these excesses of vanity lead to worship of the body and away from the worship of God. The temptations of the lip and the scented hair are strong, but remember, he told them, all living creatures die. The warm lip and the soft mouth become the nesting places of worms and maggots. The vile things below the earth will feast upon the ivory flesh and the fluid eye! When tempted, think on this! The body will become food for worms, but the soul will go on, turning and twisting in eternal flame, seared and burning without end, subject to the screams and cries of the damned without hope, hour upon hour, day upon day, eternally!"

There was a murmur through the massed congregation. The orator's voice became stronger and filled the small room with its pungent herbs and spices, dried animal tissue, and exotic scrapings the monks considered medicinal.

"Repent your vanities, he told them! Destroy those who seek to destroy your own immortal souls with their wicked representations of common women and pagan gods! Destroy them before almighty God in His wrath and justice lets fall the sword upon this city of licentiousness! Do not let Florence become like Sodom, like Gomorrah! Do not let our courts become like those of Herod! Destroy these evils! Destroy those who would lead you into sin and damnation! Destroy!"

As the murmur rose up from the white-robed assembly, the dark priest—who was also the tall cleric who had encountered Harlequin and Dottore in Pavia—turned to those around him. "For these truths he was tried, condemned, and hanged. Then his body was burned, and the ashes thrown in the river so he could not be justly venerated." The priest drew a small vial from under his robe. "But there was a substitution. I have the ashes of the saintly prophet, and I will leave this vial here for you, to remind you to be true to his principles, and to beware of the eyes of the infamous Borgia—which are everywhere."

The assembly gathered around the priest to examine the vial, and unnoticed, one monk, hooded and invisible within its dark folds, slipped out the small doorway into the Piazzale Santo Giovanni.

*I*T WAS MORE THAN PANTALONE had expected and much more than Ruffiana had bargained for. They had made love, at first, against a damp, shadowy wall near the Viale Bottego, and then under the bushes in the communal gardens, and finally under the north bridge over the Parma. They had made love standing up, lying down, bent over, and on their knees like the animals. They had experimented from the front, from the back, upside down, and on the bias. It was, for Pantalone, the culmination of every exaggerated story told by the older boys in his village and created by his own vivid imagination.

And Ruffiana, who thought she might earn a *sequin* with a minimum of effort, soon realized, panting and wet with perspiration, that she had never encountered anyone quite like this young boy with the smell of mating about him. She concluded that his previous experience must have been limited to wild boars and undomesticated farm animals.

After finally conceding that he had received his money's worth, he paused for breath. Ruffiana felt as though she had been taken by the entire French cavalry—including their horses.

Pantalone, of course, looked upon every sexual encounter as a test of his manhood and his prowess. He constantly measured his abilities against the imagined feats of stronger boys and the gibes of cruel, older girls. As a consequence, he always concluded these acts with a ballad of a single tune: "How was I?"

Ruffiana leaned against the wall of the duomo and sighed. "Wonderful."

He beamed. "Was I really?"

"Amazing," she replied. "If it weren't for the fact that I can neither stand, sit, nor squat, I wouldn't have believed it happened."

"I have a big reputation with women," Pantalone confided, repeating the canticle of the older boys in his village.

"And elephants, too, I imagine," she mumbled through clenched teeth.

"What?"

She looked at his curly, handsome head and forgave him the vitality and impatience of his youth. "Small talk." She smiled. "*Grazie* for the *sequin.*"

He sat on the steps of the duomo. "Oh yes," he murmured, "about that *sequin.* It—ah—it was supposed to buy food."

Ruffiana nodded, familiar with this turn of the conversation. "It will," she cooed, patting his cheek. "*I* eat."

Pantalone slowly realized the full extent of his problems as the real world collided with his fantasies. "Look, if I—ah—if I don't come back with food for the others, Harlequin and Scapino will kill me."

"Others?"

"At the wagon."

She turned slowly to face him then, intently. "You—have a wagon?" she asked.

He nodded. "And two burros and a horse."

Suddenly words poured from her. "Can you take me with you? Please? I have to get out of this city as soon as I can, and I have no way of doing it."

"Why do you have to get out of the city?"

"Well," she began to explain, "there's this condottiere—a very important man—very rich and powerful. He's a little upset, you see,

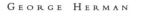

because I gave him what he wanted, you understand me? But he, ah, he also got a little—something—or some *things* he, ah, he *didn't* want, you understand?"

It took Pantalone a little while to comprehend what she was telling him, and then the full horror of the confession—with all its ramifications—broke over him. "Oh wonderful!" he wailed.

"It's not the pox," she reassured, and pulled him next to her. "And it's all right now. Even if one or two survived, your incredible performance would have crushed the little bastards."

He inched away from her just in case, and he began to imagine that some minute dragons were devouring his crotch even as he sat there. He had to concentrate very hard on what she was telling him.

"So I have to get out of the city, because he has his soldiers looking for me. If he catches me, he'll kill me. He's insane, a wild lunatic." She grabbed his arm. "Can't I go with you and your friends? I'd be safe with others around me, and I have no other way of escaping and—"

"I don't know," moaned Pantalone as he scratched his belly.

"Look." She smiled and pulled him closer. "Perhaps I didn't make myself clear. About you, I mean. You were amazing! Astounding! I can't get enough of you!" He tried to back a little, but her hand shot to his crotch again, and he felt the old compulsion return. "Normally," she rattled on. "I don't care much for young, handsome boys like you, because they seem so—shallow and inexperienced. But you are a magnificent lover! And smart!" Her volume increased. "I like to share things with a man—besides my body, I mean. Like—like music. And—talking. Godsblood, you don't know how I ache sometimes for some intelligent man to talk to, you understand? You *must* take me with you!"

Pantalone felt his mouth turn to dust, as her hand explored between his legs again. He wished with all his heart that she would stop stroking and scratch instead. "I—ah—I don't know," he croaked.

She held him even tighter. "Listen," she cooed as she rubbed her breasts against his arm and increased the pressure of her fingers.

"You're a man who needs it often, aren't you? I can tell, you understand? I mean, if we were together . . ."

Pantalone stiffened at the thought of it. "Every night?" he whispered.

She sighed, slowly nodded, and murmured, "Every—night."

"And sometimes during the day, too?" Pantalone continued.

"What?"

"I mean—if we're sent to bring back water together, or resting near the bushes at midday maybe, or together in the back of the wagon?"

"Yes, yes," she moaned wearily. "Any time you say."

"Oh, I forgot!" he blurted, suddenly sitting upright on the steps. "We don't have the wagon anymore. All we have now is the cart for the six of us, and the two burros, and Salvation."

"Salvation?"

"The horse."

Ruffiana withdrew her hand from between his legs and leaned back against the steps, deep in thought. "Six, you say? Any women?"

"Two," said Pantalone, "but they won't be a challenge to you."

"Which leaves four men," she reflected.

"They won't be a challenge to *me*," he boasted.

"And one cart."

Pantalone nodded. "And no food—because you have our *sequin*."

"*My sequin*," she snapped. "I earned it!" She rose to her feet and began to pace. "Six people. Two burros. One horse. No food." She paused a moment and then pulled Pantalone beside her. "Come with me," she demanded. "I think I have the answer to your problems. But first you have to promise to take me with you if I do this for you. Is that a promise?"

"Do what for me?" asked Pantalone hopefully.

She whispered her plan to him as they walked arm in arm toward the piazza. His face broke into a wide, bright smile. "It's a promise!" he roared, and as they turned the corner of the street he violently scratched his backside.

*A*t that moment the tall, thin Dominican stood just outside the pharmacy in the Piazzale S. Giovanni, with five or six of his *piagnoni*.

"Fra Girolamo foresaw it, and I sense it as well. The very foundations of Italy will be shaken in war and disease! The first shall be last! Unhappy Italy! There shall be war upon war, abomination upon abomination! The law of the priesthood shall perish, and priests shall be denied their place! Princes shall be forced into haircloth, and the people shall be crushed by tribulation!"

And in Imola, Cesare Borgia prepared his officers for war.

*T*he youth appeared at the shop of Gasparo shortly after the departure of Filippo, much to the annoyance of the old wainwright. For one thing, these constant interruptions kept him from his work, and second, the boy did not have the look of money.

Still, his opening words were promising.

"Is this the shop of Gasparo the genius?" he heralded.

The old man shuffled to the front of the building toward the boy. "It is my shop, yes," he responded.

"My master has need of a—device," the youth began. He waved his hand through the air, and a gold *sequin* flashed in the light of the torches.

Gasparo was impressed, but cunning businessman that he was, he expressed nothing. "I am apprentice to a great magician and sorcerer," the boy continued, "and he requires a device to be made of wood in which he shall turn a woman into an ape."

"Why would he do that?" asked the wainwright.

"Or an ape into a lady." Pantalone shrugged.

Gasparo studied the boy: he was dressed poorly enough to be an apprentice, but on the other hand, clothed better than Gasparo's own apprentices, so it was possible that he *was* the assistant to a great and powerful man.

"It will cost fifty florins extra!" the old man declared.

Pantalone was surprised at the suddenness of the decision. "How can you determine the price when you haven't been given the specifications of the device?"

"Whatever it is," replied Gasparo, "it will not be ordinary, and everything extraordinary costs fifty florins extra."

The boy nodded at the logic of the system. "Well," he said softly to the old man, "my master insists that the device be made of florabella wood."

Gasparo looked warily at the youth. "Of what?"

"Florabella," Pantalone said slowly and distinctly.

"What the devil is florabella wood?"

"You know," whispered the boy, "wood that will not burn."

But Pantalone hadn't figured on the wainwright's declining ability to hear whispers. "What?" screeched Gasparo. "Speak up, boy!"

"Wood that will not burn!" shouted Pantalone. Every head in the shop turned to face him.

Gasparo was appropriately impressed and his eyes widened. "Wood that will not burn? I—I never heard of such a thing!"

"Ah, that will make the arrangements a little more complicated. My master can provide the florabella, of course, and you can treat the wood, but the cost will have to be adjusted to—"

Gasparo seized the boy by his ragged collar. "You have a substance that can prevent wood from burning?"

Pantalone nodded as he struggled to release himself. "Of course!"

Gasparo let go of him. "Wood that will not burn. I don't believe it."

Pantalone fidgeted as though these minor details were annoying. "My master learned the secret in the East, where houses are only wood and paper, and they never burn. The secret is a powder called florabella, which is used to treat the wood."

Gasparo exchanged looks with his workmen, who were now attending the exchange with undisguised interest. His eyes glistened greedily in the light of the oil lamps. "Wood that does not burn." He mused. "Such a secret would make me rich!" The others began to murmur among themselves at the thought of it. "If you share this secret with me," he told the boy excitedly, "I will build your master's device for nothing!" He stopped then, realizing that perhaps he had gone too far too fast. "How do I know it will work?" asked the old wainwright carefully.

"Wellll," said the youth, "I am reasonably certain my master wouldn't expect a man of your reputation and ability to accept the arrangement on faith." The pause was deliberate and effective. "I am prepared to give you a demonstration."

"Bravo, young man! Good!" chortled Gasparo. "I assure you, young worthy, that if what you say is true, I will keep the secret to my own shop and build any future device of your master for absolutely nothing." There was another brief period of silence. "Or—at cost."

"Now," ordered the boy, stepping into the center of the shop, "I will need a pile of shavings and strips of old wood." Gasparo nodded to his workmen, and soon a small mountain of sawdust and splinters arose in the middle of the low-ceilinged room.

"Shouldn't we be doing this in the piazza?" asked Gasparo warily.

"Where everyone can see and realize what a secret you have been given?" said Pantalone. "It would be the topic of conversation throughout the city in an hour's time!"

Gasparo quickly agreed. "Of course."

"And now," the boy continued the demonstration, "Florabella!" He took a small pouch from his blouse and spilled some of the contents into the palm of his hand. "Observe," he intoned in his most mysterious voice as he replaced the pouch and then poured the substance from hand to hand. The carpenters and the apprentices moved in closer to get a better view of the proceedings. This provided Pantalone time to glance quickly through the open door of the shop. He smiled as the unfinished guild wagon rolled silently and slowly past, Ruffiana in the driver's seat.

"It looks like common sand," muttered one of the workers.

"Nothing magic about that," said an apprentice. "Everyone knows sand won't burn."

"Too fine to be common sand," noted another.

"Get on with it!" growled Gasparo, realizing that his entire shop had ceased work to attend the miracle.

Pantalone picked up two or three pieces of the wood and rubbed each with the powder. When he finished, he sprinkled the remainder of Dottore's "magic dust" on the shavings. "I am ready!" he declared. "A flame, please!"

One of the workers handed a small oil lamp to Gasparo. "You are certain of this?"

"On the soul of my wife and children," the youth intoned, "this wood will no longer burn!" Gasparo nodded, and one of the workmen lit a taper from the lamp and handed it to Pantalone, who bent and applied the flame to the wooden mountain. In an instant thick, yellowish smoke billowed up, curled back from the low ceiling, and completely engulfed the shop. The workmen and apprentices began to cough and flail wildly at the heavy, suffocating cloud, colliding with one another in the process and cursing with every movement. They thought they heard the voice of the boy, fading slowly away: "Of course, I didn't say it wouldn't *smoke!*"

In his confusion, Gasparo dropped the lamp, which promptly shattered. In an instant flames ignited the shavings and sawdust on the floor and began to lick up the beams and supports of the shop. Some of the workmen who had stumbled out into the cool air of the piazza began to shout "Fire!" through the streets, and an apprentice started a clamorous clanging of a bell. Townspeople poured forth to assist the wainwrights. Pails of water from the communal well passed from hand to hand, but it wasn't long before Gasparo sat on the edge of the fountain and surveyed his ruined shop. It was then that he first discovered that the guild wagon was gone.

"I knew it!" he screamed. "It was that bastard Filippo! He couldn't raise the rest of the money to meet my price, so he stole the wagon!" The old man stumbled to his feet and waved an angry hand toward the sky, now alive with glowing embers and the glimmering evening star. "May the moths devour your cloth, you treacherous eater of dung!"

*H*ARLEQUIN NOTICED the column of smoke rising from the heart of the city sometime before he saw the strange vehicle moving toward him. It took a while, in the gathering dust, to recognize Pantalone and a red-haired wench driving Salvation as though the devil were licking at their heels.

"Surprise!" caroled the youth, "we have a new wagon!"

Colombina looked with amazement at the strange conveyance. "What is it?" she asked.

"I haven't time to give you all the details now," answered Pantalone. "Let's just say that I have the supplies you wanted, this new wagon, and we still have the *sequin*, thanks to this young—lady."

The "young lady" in the meantime had proceeded to climb down from the wagon behind him, revealing a fine expanse of tanned thigh.

"She's known as Ruffiana, and she isn't certain of her last name." He gestured quickly to the others. "This is Signori Harlequin, Dottore, Scapino, and Signorina Isabella and Signora Colombina." He wheeled back to face Harlequin. "Ruffiana's going with us," declared the boy, and then added for Harlequin's benefit, "Isn't she?"

There was a pause in which Isabella and Colombina inspected the wagon, and Dottore and Scapino visibly inspected Ruffiana. Finally Harlequin shrugged, turned to the company, and said quietly, "From the looks of things, I think we better cut through the woodlands and bypass Parma." He glared at Pantalone.

"The city seems burned up over something," he said sharply.

MODENA

The miracle of Santa Lucia and the
story of St. George and the dragon.
Capitano meets with Alviano as a
trap is prepared for Cesare Borgia.
The company encounters a hostile
audience with a different concept of
entertainment and nearly fails
to survive for an encore.
The capitano enters.

SWITZERLAND   Zürich

Bern

THE ALPS

Innsbruck

Salzburg   AUSTRIA

St. Wolfgang

Aosta

Biella

FRANCE

POR.

Gen

Nice

CORSICA

Piombino   Are

Cortona

Zengg

OTTOMAN

EMPIRE

Zara

driatic Sea

Ancona

Assisi

Spoleto

Aquila

TIBER R.

Rome

Pescara

APENNINE MTS.

LIRI R.

N

SARDINIA

Cagliari

Foggia

Naples
Benevento

OFANTO

Bri

Tyrrhenian

Sea

MILES
0 10 20 40 60 80 100
KILOMETERS
0 20 40   80   120 160

Otranto

Cosenza

Palermo

Messina   Reggio

SICILY

Catania

Syracuse

Mediterranean Sea

Claudia Carlson © 1993

The great guild wagon and the small two-wheeled cart rattled back onto the Via Emilia northeast of Parma, not far from the border that marked the limits of the duchy of Milan and the beginning of the authority of the Gonzaga family, who ruled the north from Mantua. But after two hours and a quick conference of all the company, the caravan camped, hidden in the thick underbrush along the banks of a Po tributary, while Harlequin and Pantalone took the burros and headed into the mountains to Santa Lucia, a tiny, isolated village older than time. Its largest piazza was treeless and worn in this late October. Harlequin and Pantalone tied Death and Destruction to a road marker not far from the village church and began to walk.

YOUNG FRA GIOVANNI SAT ALONE and unhappy in the curtained, airless, dark closet that served as a confessional for the faithful of the little parish. The bleak receptacle also served as an instrument of his own personal penance. Of all his duties, hearing confessions was the one that repelled him most. His commission, pronounced at his ordination, that "whose sins you shall forgive, they are forgiven them; whose sins you shall retain, they are retained," frightened him with the immensity of that spiritual responsibility.

He was a young man who wished to serve God not judge his brothers, and as a consequence he soon had the reputation of being an "easy" confessor. Great malefactors from as far as Reggio or Modena trekked to Santa Lucia to confess to this gentle youth, whose penances seemed limited, at the most, to "a decade of the Rosary for the poor souls in purgatory." Prior to the great Feast of the Resurrection when everyone was compelled to receive the Eucharist, the farm girls would wait patiently outside Fra Giovanni's confessional to confess their dalliances with the lusty country boys rather than receive a quicker—but more severe—judgment at the portable confessional erected for the visiting priest.

For this youth, who measured his life in six of the seven sacraments, there was only one remaining, and the depressing thought of Extreme Unction, coupled with the recent ill luck in his small parish, made him meditate on pilgrimage, perhaps to the shrine of Santo Gregorio in Modena, where he had been born, baptized, confirmed, made his first confession, received his first communion, and was invested in holy orders.

As with most others, money was at the root of all his problems, of course.

The generosity and love of the young priest was known to everyone in the village, and as a consequence he not only supported the poor and the hungry, but every glib liar and lazy lout for kilometers in every direction, which left little for his own subsistence.

He knew his sermons failed to inspire or move, but they were so blessedly short that his faithful stayed awake out of loyalty and devotion to their pastor. He spoke from the heart always, with personal conviction, but his themes were not the popular ones. He did not announce the end of the world for next Thursday, for example, although his superiors had taught him in the seminary that a good "doom and gloom" prediction would always bring in a little something extra if you frightened the guilty enough. He wished sometimes for a gift of inflaming oratory that would somehow milk a few extra coins from those few miserly parishioners who had wealth to share but did not.

But instead the gentle priest preached of infinite love and compassion, of a Father who would provide not everything wanted but all that was needed to do what He expected of you. Fra Giovanni meant it to be consoling, but it was not a popular theme with the majority of his congregation, who found themselves yoked to poverty by a system founded by, and dedicated to the welfare of, the landowners and the nobility.

He was reflecting on this when he heard a movement in the confessional booth to his right. He sighed, drew back the small curtain over the grillwork opening, and gave the initial blessing. He waited, then, for the recitation of sins; but nothing was heard from the opposite side of the window.

"Is anyone there?" whispered the young priest.

For a long time there was no reply. "Fra Giovanni," came a voice at last: low, soft, slow, and melodic. "Fra Giovanni," it repeated, "you must go to Parma." This startled the cleric, and he twisted his head to try to peer into the dark interior beyond the grillwork, but he saw nothing.

"You must go to Parma," the voice repeated, "in pilgrimage to the duomo of Santo Giovanni, your namesake."

"Who—are—you?" whispered the thoroughly frightened young priest.

"Search your heart, and you shall know me," answered the voice.

Now Fra Giovanni became terrified. His heart pounded. The reply was precisely the type of vague, oblique response he had been taught to expect from supernatural visitors. And, to strengthen that premise, the voice spoke in Latin.

He again tried to see into the booth, and again he was certain there was no one there.

"But—why Parma?" he managed to ask.

"You must go and console one of my beloved, Gasparo the Wainwright, with whom I am well pleased." There was a brief pause. "Somewhat."

"Gasparo the Wainwright?"

"In the confessional, my son, you will find a jewel of great value wrapped in yellow cloth and placed upon a *zecchino*. The *zecchino* is for you, my faithful servant, for I am aware of your needs."

"A jewel?"

"A jewel of great worth, which you must give to Gasparo the Wainwright that he might use it to rebuild his shop."

"His shop?"

The words were coming too fast for the little priest to understand fully, and he felt the perspiration sprinkle his forehead and run in small streams down his body.

"Tell him his prayers are answered. Now I must go. Cherish God, protect the widow and orphan, believe in love, and you better get started at once," the voice advised.

Fra Giovanni assented—he would go to Parma. "But where will

I find this Gasparo?" he asked. He waited for a reply, but there was only a hushed, whispered rustling, and then nothing.

After a while the young cleric stepped from his confessional and surveyed the interior of his little church. It was empty save for a shawled, black-garbed woman kneeling before the burning candles of the shrine to the Blessed Mother. He recognized her both from her appearance and her loud intoning of the Rosary. He turned then and apprehensively pulled back the curtains of the booth. On the small wooden ledge beneath the grillwork opening was a yellow packet. When he lifted the little bundle, he saw the gold *zecchino* beneath it. He was so busy examining the jewel, its wrappings, and the coin that he failed to notice the small hole in the outer wall of the booth to the immediate left of the window.

Had he noticed it, and had he placed his eye to it, he would have seen two odd figures disappear around the corner into the piazza: the tall man in the bizarre cloak of rags and patches and the strange hat with the bird's beak, and the ragged youth with no distinguishing characteristics.

*P*ANTALONE STRUGGLED to keep up with Harlequin's long strides. He reflected on what he had seen Harlequin do: the boring of the small hole in the wall of the church with his dagger, the insertion of the tube of rolled parchment, the trick of twisting the outer end so it formed a funnel or cone on the inside of the booth by the confessional window. With this, he knew, Harlequin became the voice of the supernatural.

He, in the meantime, had entered the booth and placed the jewel and the coin where he had been instructed to, and then he had remained outside the booth, preventing anyone from entering until he heard Harlequin's code words: "Cherish God." Then he had left the church in time to see Harlequin reroll the parchment back into a tube and remove it.

"Now, why did we go through all that?" asked the boy.

"Because we are responsible for our actions. You may have intended to make smoke to distract from the theft of the guild wagon. But the result was a fire that destroyed a man's livelihood. You are responsible; and all of us, being one with you, are also responsible." Harlequin moved faster up the narrow passageway. "Restitution had to be made."

"Why?" complained Pantalone. "Priests sell indulgences. Cardinals sell dispensations. The pope sells cardinals' hats. Fathers sell their daughters. Wives sell their favors. Merchants sell rotted goods and unneeded services. Mercenaries sell their blood and their skill, but beneath it all, they are all cheating someone. Everyone lies and deceives and makes promises they do not intend to keep and steal what they can from anyone who is stupid enough to be taken by them. Why should we be different?"

"Are you like all the other boys your age?"

"No!" Pantalone snapped. "I'm faster! And a lot smarter!"

"That's why we pay for what we use. We're different. We're odd. We're bizarre and ridiculous and absurd." He smiled warmly at the boy. "But remember, without something good, nothing would be evil. We keep the universe in balance."

They strode quickly through the piazza in silence.

"Will the priest go to Parma?"

"Yes."

"Can he be trusted to deliver the jewel to Gasparo?"

"Yes."

"How can you be sure?"

Harlequin stopped suddenly and turned to him. "Listen, boy! If you have to trust someone in life, you could do far worse than trust a poor priest—or a poor physician—or a poor teacher. Their poverty is a testament to their dedication and belief in the nobler principles of their professions. Professions, I might add, that easily and naturally lead down the paths to greed, arrogance, and hypocrisy."

"But how can you be certain that the jewel won't tempt him?"

"Of course it will tempt him, child! He's not God!"

Pantalone smiled smugly at the tall, bizarre figure. "I don't believe in God anymore," he said.

Harlequin snorted. "Don't be impertinent, boy. Who cares if *you* believe in God? The basic question is: Does God continue to believe in *you?*" He turned then and continued up the narrow walkway.

Pantalone raced after him, and when they reached the burros, he said, "I didn't understand what you said back there."

Harlequin stopped and grinned at him. "Then do what I do." He climbed aboard Destruction, hidden amid the shadows of a neighboring house. "When I start talking that way, I stop listening to myself."

The boy frowned as he tried to decipher what Harlequin had just told him, and then he mounted Death and soon was out of sight down the shadowed street.

*T*HIS IS THE STORY behind the "miracle of Santa Lucia"— repeated throughout the villages and towns of the Modena for more then two decades. A morality play wherein a divinity of love, through the services of a poor priest, rebuilt the shop of Gasparo the Wainwright of Parma, whom, for some inexplicable reason, God loved.

Filippo Masaccio, of course, never believed a word of it and said as much to his parish priest. "It's ridiculous that that old miser and thief should be so loved by our Creator," he argued. "It's widely known that he is selfish and arrogant and treacherous."

"Yes." The priest sighed—as if the sigh explained it all.

Annamarie Masaccio, of course, doubted the whole thing, but felt sorry for the poor wainwright and found an opportunity some weeks later to console him.

*H*ARLEQUIN AND PANTALONE DROVE the guild wagon where Colombina, Isabella, and Dottore sat among Filippo's hogsheads of wine and supplies in a division that had been established since the arrival of Ruffiana, who rode with Scapino in the cart behind them. Isabella and Colombina were always apart from the new woman in the assembly; and Ruffiana, on her own, made no attempt to bridge the gap between them, which widened every minute.

She had proved an instant favorite with the men—which might explain some of the animosity of the women. Dottore became a second father to her since she confided to him that she had lost the original model in her infancy due to her mother's confusion with foreign faces and the natural wanderlust of the military. Scapino liked her at once, and they understood each other instantly. Their easy banter and joking discourse only served to heighten Isabella's opposition, of course; but for Ruffiana, it meant the acquisition of a special friend who shared with her a communion of experience, for if Pantalone suffered an appetite for women, Ruffiana had a ravenous appetite for everything.

Harlequin had become an additional protector—which Colombina, like Isabella, attributed to natural lust. But the fact was, from the time she joined them, Ruffiana had been her own woman.

Nevertheless what had become a tight little society began to unravel upon the prostitute's arrival. And as with marriages, it was a series of small differences that provoked the animosity of Colombina and Isabella. Ruffiana took too long to get dressed in the mornings. Ruffiana used Colombina's comb without permission. Ruffiana was caught looking at Isabella's hidden wardrobe.

So Ruffiana decided that she would leave the assembly without telling anyone as soon as the opportunity presented itself. Any city, town, or village, she reasoned, could permit her some degree of anonymity and provide her with employment. What was most important, she was out of the jurisdiction of the Milanese condottieri and could find, as a last resort, enough potential clients that she would not starve.

*I*N REGGIO, at a tavern off the Via Farini, Capitano turned to the innkeeper and murmured a name. The ancient, fat, and bald innkeeper studied the mail-suited condottiere and then gestured him to a dark corner of the room.

"You are Captain . . . Captain . . . ?"

"Francesco Benevelli! Yes!"

"I was told to ask you the name of the only woman you ever truly loved."

"Annamarie."

"Yes," confirmed the innkeeper. "That was it! Fine! Ah—here is the message. He said—that I should tell you—that he is pleased— that you wish to become a—a—"

"A matador!"

"No, it was more like a—I forget. What's a matador?"

Capitano became annoyed with the man's hesitations. "A bullfighter! Continue!"

"That's right," the man persevered. "That's what he said it was. A bullfighter. Why do you want to fight bulls?"

"Because I hate horny creatures!" exploded the capitano. "Tell me the rest of the message before I gore *you!*"

The innkeeper paled. "Oh! Well! He said—he said—to become a—what you said, you must go at once to—to—" He scratched his head. "Someplace that begins with an *M.*"

The capitano groaned. "An *M*? An *M*! Modena? Milan? Messina?"

"It had something to with sorcery."

"Sorcery? You mean sorcery as in magic?"

"That's it," cried the enlightened old man. *"Magione!"* He then lapsed again into confusion. "I *think* he said Magione. Do you know someplace called Magione?"

Capitano was exasperated. "It is a stronghold above Lake Trasimeno, about ten kilometers west of Perugia. It belongs to Cardinal Orsini! So?"

"Above Perugia? I've never been to Perugia. I've never even been as far as Bologna."

"If you don't hurry and tell me the rest of the message, I'll kick you *beyond* Bologna. Why must I go to Magione?"

"What?" The old man faltered.

"*Why* must I go to Magione?"

"Oh! He said—he said"—the innkeeper scratched his head—"something about the bull turning on the house, whatever that means. And he says you should contact a—now let me think—a Bartolomeo—something or other—from Venice."

"Bartolomeo? Bartolomeo Alviano?"

"That's the one. He said this Bartolomeo could use you."

The soldier smiled, relieved, and turned to leave the tavern.

"Wait!" shrieked the old man. "He also said you would give me a florin for giving you the message."

The capitano posed momentarily by the door.

"He lied," he said.

*A*WAKENING AT THEIR ENCAMPMENT outside Sabbioneta, the company realized that Ruffiana was no longer with them.

"Just as well." Isabella sniffed.

Harlequin led her aside and said softly, "You are the sole reason this company is going to Mantua. The rest of us have no reason to risk our necks for you, but we decided we would. Do you know why?"

"My jewels will feed you," she said.

His eyes narrowed. "Your jewels? Madonna, I have lived without your jewels for some thirty-odd years, and I could go on living without them for the rest of my unnatural life. If you believe that I agreed to escort you to Mantua for money, then you better go on alone." He wheeled then and started away from her.

"Wait!" Isabella called after him.

He turned slowly to face her. "What?"

She seemed about to weep, but her voice was strong and proud. "You—you agreed to escort me because because "

"Why?" snapped Harlequin.

"Because—I needed you."

Harlequin smiled and slowly came back to her. "That's right. And although Ruffiana has only been with us for three days, in that time you and Colombina have given the poor child no opportunity to show you how much she needed you!"

"Me?"

"You!" he repeated. "And Colombina! And me and Scapino and Dottore and Pantalone! We were something she never had before: a family! And it takes time and patience and love to mold a family from a handful of alien personalities! She needed you, and you turned away! Now the only remaining question is: Why should *I* stay with you?"

She did begin to weep then, and after a moment or two of hushed conversation, they walked together to face the others.

*R*UFFIANA FOUND HERSELF backed against a bare, damp wall in a dark and isolated room of the worn and weary tavern in Gualtieri. On the table—which she had managed to keep between herself and the three mercenaries—were the remnants of their little game for the afternoon: a purse stuffed with florins and ducats that spilled out over the table, eight empty tankards of honey and wine, and the remains of a roast pig and dumplings. She stood quietly, watching them carefully, and mentally computed the odds of escaping through the one door on the opposite side of the room.

At first there had been only herself and the young, chestnut-haired mercenary who gave his name as Matteo. Their arrangement was understood and agreeable to both, but after she had agreed to go with him to this dingy, sequestered back room, they were soon joined by a scar-faced soldier and a Sicilian condottiere with huge hands.

The introduction of these others—and especially the Sicilian, who described to Ruffiana and his companions what he liked to do to women with his ivory-handled dagger that he called "my pretty, pointed tooth"—made the proposition lose some of its attraction.

The soldiers had spent some time at first in small talk about the war and the hundred ducats the Sicilian would receive for finding and killing a man they called Captain Benevelli. From the conversation, Ruffiana judged that Cosimo, which was the Sicilian's Christian name, was seeking his former commander with instructions to kill the officer on sight—to spare the French time-consuming court-martial proceedings.

Ultimately the conversation turned to women. "By tradition," Cosimo insisted, "all Sicilian women are virtuous ladies, and no Sicilian man would ever take liberties with one, because that would dishonor her, you see?" The others nodded, and the Sicilian elucidated, "Of course, rape is all right, because if you rape a Sicilian girl, she is still technically considered a virgin, and one can marry her later without shame."

They had gone on then to the specific subject of rape, and from there the activity had shifted to rough pawing and grasping and the occasional slobbering kiss, and finally Ruffiana had maneuvered herself to her present strategic position. Though the soldiers were now stripping themselves of weapons and armor that might interfere with their sport, she noted, with some dismay, that the Sicilian retained his "pretty, pointed tooth." She knew instinctively that once they attacked her, there would be little she could do about it; and the last thing she could expect was a knight in shining armor to ride to her rescue on a great white charger and sweep her away from danger.

Which proved a realistic judgment, because her salvation suddenly appeared in the doorway blanketed within a great brown hooded monk's robe, emitting a distinctly familiar voice.

"Signorina Bacchae!" the monk scolded. "You naughty, naughty girl!" He elbowed his way into the room. "How many times do we have to warn you not to play these little games anymore?" He pushed his way past the burly Sicilian and the scar-faced mercenary and came around the table to her. "My apologies, gentlemen," he said, "but we can thank the good Jesus that I have been in time to save you!"

Cosimo frowned as the monk put an arm around Ruffiana and started to guide her around the table and out of the room. "Save us?" the Sicilian objected, placing himself between the couple and the door. "Save us from what?"

"Ah!" shrieked the monk, which made everyone instinctively back away. "It's too terrible to name! Much too awful! Suffice to say that you will know it when it inflicts you: the fires in the belly, the succession of red-hot pokers up the arse, the agonizing pain through every toenail, and in the last stages, the eyeballs go simply—*plop!* In your hand!"

"God in heaven," mumbled the Sicilian. "What do you call that?"

The cleric hesitated. "Surely you've heard of—the Black Death?"

"Your eyes don't fall out from the Black Death," said Matteo, the chestnut-haired mercenary.

"I didn't say they did!" haughtily replied the monk, as though he were addressing an assembly of rebellious schoolchildren. "I simply asked if you knew the name, didn't I?! *This* disease—the one this poor, unfortunate wench carries—is called—the Green Misery, and it makes the Black Death look like a mild annoyance."

"The Green Misery?"

"Because of the tongue, you see. I mean the way it swells and elongates and grows up into the nose and suffocates the unfortunate victim. That happens, of course, after the subject's skin turns bright green with ugly, red, oozing sores of putrid-smelling pus and—" He started again to guide Ruffiana toward the doorway, but Matteo stepped in front of them.

"She isn't green!" argued Matteo.

"And there's nothing wrong with her tongue." The Sicilian leered.

"We'll show you," snarled Scar Face as he reached for Ruffiana.

"No, no, no," insisted the the monk, becoming even more irritated and pulling the girl behind him. "Now pay attention! She will continue to look the way she does until the later stages of the disease. One day—soon—her eyes will simply—*poof!* Right on the floor! That is the way this disease works with the carriers. But I warn you, right this instant her very breath is fatal! Absolutely! She broke away from her attendants two days past, and now we have seventeen men dead from Mantua to Modena! And it's only Tuesday!"

But Matteo argued, "How can *you* touch her then and not get the disease?"

The logic of that statement was not wasted on the Sicilian, who moved menacingly behind the monk and the girl, and Ruffiana considered the possibilities of making a dash past the other two theatening them. But then the cleric suddenly reached up and threw back his hood.

It was Scapino, of course, or at least something that remotely resembled Scapino. But his skin was bright green with running sores scattered over it; and worse, where his left eye should have been was a gray, gelatinous mass of liquid and membrane that dangled and oozed down to the cheek.

The chestnut-haired mercenary stood paralyzed, and then he gagged and turned away to face the back wall.

Scapino and Ruffiana moved quickly past the scar-faced mercenary and the Sicilian, who stood as if they were cast in bronze, and they worked their way through the main room, where the other patrons were similarly affected at the brief sight of the oozing sores and green flesh. No one attempted to stop them. Indeed, a path opened wider than that of the Red Sea for Moses.

As they stepped into the street Matteo could still be heard depositing his midday meal on the backroom table. Scapino replaced his hood, wiped the crushed grapes from his left eyelid, and motioned for Ruffiana to mount Death. He climbed aboard Destruction, and the two burros were urged quickly up the narrow street.

"We went to the hands as to whether or not you should be brought back," explained Scapino, still picking the fruit from his face. "You lost unanimously, so here I am."

Ruffiana looked at him. "Unanimously?"

"That's a Harlequin word meaning 'everybody.'"

"I can't go back," she said softly.

"You must."

"No. Your—friends—they don't really want me."

Scapino grinned. "I told you the hands were unanimous. Oh, Colombina and Isabella were jealous, because they weren't sure which of the men you wanted. It never occurred to them that you have better sense and wouldn't want any of us. But—after being enlightened by Harlequin—even *they* want you back." He kicked the burro into a somewhat faster pace. "You *must* come back with us."

She smiled despite her feelings. "Why?"

"Because with us, you won't be raped without your permission. Besides, Harlequin says running away becomes a habit that solves nothing."

She made a face at him. "Oh, don't tell me that! You and your friends—you're all running away from something!"

"Well, yes and no," he said as he urged Destruction on. "Harlequin sees it differently. He says perhaps we're being drawn *toward* something."

"What?"

"I don't know," he admitted.

"It will probably be your mutual destruction," she grumbled.

"Maybe so." He smiled at her. "But we feel you should be a part of it. After all, how many times in your life are you given the chance to die slowly—but with dignity?"

She laughed then, and he winked with his still-gelatinous eye and began to whistle a bright and airy *saltarello* as they rode out of the city.

WHILE SCAPINO WAS RESCUING RUFFIANA, Harlequin moved the company still farther south and east. Like some malevolent magnet in the duchy of Modena, they were being drawn closer and closer to the see of Cardinal Ferrari.

They went southeast into Correggio and then directly east to Carpi into Modena from the south. "We will not stay long," he estimated, "just long enough to convert a jewel into currency and get supplies. For this we need a banker, and that means a city, and Modena is the closest."

Outside Modena, Harlequin proposed that he, Pantalone, and Dottore should enter via the cart drawn by Salvation, obtain their money, and make all the necessary purchases at a variety of stalls. The women and Scapino were to remain with the wagon outside the city. He explained that the clothmakers' guild might be searching for the stolen wagon, and that three individuals making moderate purchases would arouse less curiosity than one individual buying enough to feed a small army. Furthermore three sets of cars and eyes could learn much more of value.

IN THE FORTRESS of Magione, the capitano waited in the cold and empty corridor outside the anteroom and paced the floor. After a moment he was joined by a shorter, stocky gentleman in breastplate and mail bearing the *impresa* of the lion of Venice.

"Captain Benevelli?"

"Yes, Excellency."

The Venetian condottiere motioned the capitano to sit on the stone facing before the bay window. "This will have to be brief, but you are recommended by a man I trust and respect. He informs me that you are—in some difficulty with Cesare Borgia's French allies. Is that correct?"

"Yes, Excellency."

The condottiere looked around quickly and lowered his voice. "Then you may have come at a propitious time. In that room are several of the condottieri of Cesare Borgia including Vitellozzo Vitelli and the Baglioni brothers, Gentile and Giampaolo. They are meeting with Cardinal Orsini, Pandolfo Petrucci of Siena, Hermes Bentivoglio of Bologna, and Oliveretto of Fermo, and they are talking of preparing a trap to capture and kill Cesare Borgia. Do you understand?" The capitano nodded. "I am here to represent Venice, but the doge is not committed to any attack on the Borgias—yet. If I like what I see and hear, I will send you to Venice immediately, and I will join the conspiracy."

The capitano felt his mouth dry, and he was about to speak when Bartolomeo rose, gestured him to wait, and then went through the great doors into the anteroom.

*I*N THE ANTEROOM of the Palazzo Vescovile in the fortified city of Imola, Cesare Borgia tapped a point on the great wall map with his jeweled dagger and said, "The villagers of Santo Leo have rebelled and taken the fortress."

Michelotto Corella and Ramiro de Lorca studied the map as they sipped wine from the silver chalices. "Any others, sire?" asked Michelotto quietly.

"Six," replied the duke, "and the citizens of Urbino have rebelled and called for a return of that idiot Guidobaldo! The governor I appointed barely escaped with his life." He turned then and the condottieri were surprised to see him smile. "And fifteen mules packed with the city's treasury."

Ramiro laughed lightly and said, "That will be welcome news for our mercenaries, sire."

"What I need now," said Cesare, "is for you, Michelotto, to regroup here at the Rimini with reinforcements from your ranks, Ramiro. Then I want you, Michelotto, to join with Ugo da Moncado along here, from Pergola to Fossombrone, and put down the insurrections."

The giant condottiere nodded. "Restrictions?" he asked softly.

The duke's smile returned. "These rebels are ignorant and misguided, Michelotto. Teach them for me."

Michelotto nodded and started toward the door, but Ramiro turned and said, "There is a rumor of a rebellion among your own condottieri, my lord duke. I wish to assure you that I am not in their number."

Cesare sipped from his goblet. "I know," he said. "I know—everything."

*T*HE THREE TRAVELERS STOPPED first at the small establishment of Aaron the Jew on the Loggia della Mercanzia, who converted the small emerald into ducats that Harlequin divided equally with Dottore and Pantalone.

Pantalone, the perpetual dissident, protested at the amount charged by the money changer, grumbling, "I don't like doing business with Jews. I don't like people who deal in money."

Harlequin shook his head. "That doesn't prevent you from dealing with whores and merchants, does it?" He then patiently pointed out that the Jews were in the occupation of changing and loaning money "because Christian authorities forbid the Hebrews to engage in any other business. Christians were forbidden to deal in money changing by order of the holy father unless," he added, "your name is Bardi or Peruzzi. Even then you are not expected to charge interest—which is why so few of the wealthy and powerful lords of Italy have actually gone into banking.

"It's true," he said, "that the Jewish *banchi di pegni* charge as high as forty percent a year, but the number of banks available to us are limited. Thirty-three *banchi grossi* collapsed in Florence when the Medici were driven out, and although the city-states like Siena operate banks and make loans at only seven percent, that usually only applies to merchant loans. I understand that the Franciscans have started their own bank known as *monti di pieta* and charge only five percent interest, but that's in Perugia."

Then, carried away by his topic, he instructed the youth on the basic facts of economics. "Merchants frequently have all their wealth tied up in trade goods being taken on long and distant voyages. In that interval, the merchants must have enough money to maintain their businesses, and the Jewish money lenders agreed to advance such monies against the probable success of the trading missions. But many of these ventures have failed with great losses— which is why the Jews charge such high interest on risky arrangements. Besides," said Harlequin, "the Jewish money changers keep their promises and hold their tongues. You would be a wiser boy if you cultivated those arts yourself."

Ah, thought Pantalone, *chapter fourteen, verse twelve, from the third epistle of Harlequin to the Underlings.*

And it's only Tuesday.

O N THE PIAZZA GRANDE, Dottore made his required purchases and drifted toward the Street of the Clothmakers. He surveyed the rows of stalls laden with bolts of material: wool and lace from the West, and silks and satins from the East. His artistic eye examined the effect of the sun on the texture of the materials, and he reflected once again on the Verrocchio secret. "It must be the light," he grumbled.

"Gasparo the Wainwright of Parma," he heard the elderly guildsman tell his journeyman, "accepted the commission, you understand? But then, when a fire destroyed his shop and the unfinished guild wagon, he swore that brother Filippo of Piacenza had stolen it! So the scoundrel tried to get a judgment from the duke against brother Filippo to offset his losses, the greedy carpenter!"

"The world is full of thieves." The journeyman sighed.

"But brother Filippo knew that Gasparo was trying to cheat him, and despite the pleadings of his beautiful and saintly wife for compassion, he warned the brotherhood against any further dealings with the rascal!"

"Rascals and thieves," the journeyman moaned, and shook his head sadly.

"Fortunately Mario the Wainwright of Mantua had already constructed another guild wagon for the guild of masons which was not paid for, so he sold it to brother Filippo and our brothers will use it to play *Abraham and Isaac* here on the Feast of All Saints to-morrow." Suddenly a young boy pushed past Dottore, grabbed a silk scarf from the stall of the clothmaker, and was gone up the narrow passageway before the guildsman could stop him. "A curse on you!" the elder shouted after him. Then he sighed and stepped back behind his display stall. "Modena was once such a lovely city," said the guildsman. "Now look at it! As bad as Parma or Milan! You aren't safe in the streets!"

The journeyman nodded. "And have you heard about the renegade band of mercenaries roaming around in the north? Their patrons ran short of funds to pay them, so the devils have been wandering around, murdering and plundering the duchy as they work their way west to Genoa and a possible sea route home to Venice."

"Murderers and plunderers?" The guildsman shuddered. "Where are they from? Are they Swiss? Flemish? French?"

"No one knows. Some say they do not use heavy armor, so they move quickly. I was told they raided a farm not a day's journey from Reggio. Killed the old farmer, stole his crops, slaughtered his sheep, and raped his wife and daughter! Shameful! Shameful! But the Duke d'Este has his mercenaries patrolling every road to the north, so they won't be able to come to Modena."

Then the cloth merchants noticed Dottore still fingering the same piece of material, and the old guildsman examined him from head to toe with an experienced eye. After a moment he and the journeyman both began to walk slowly around the stall and toward Dottore, who, wisely judging it was time to move on, bobbed with a modicum of respect and then bounded down the street.

*B*ARTOLOMEO ALVIANO EMERGED quickly from the anteroom in Magione, flushed and anxious, and crossed to the capitano, still waiting in the cold corridor. "This will prove disastrous," he whispered to the capitano as he half propelled him by one arm toward the staircase. "Listen to me, and listen carefully.

These men are fools. They laid out their plans completely, and it was obvious even to me that more than half of them are petrified of Cesare Borgia. Within an hour, mark me, Cesare will know every word spoken in there." He wheeled suddenly and pressed Capitano against the wall. "I cannot trust this information to anyone. I must leave for Venice myself, this very minute. All I can offer you, my friend, is possible employment upon my return, but as of now, I have no mercenaries, and if I did, I would not commit them to this doomed enterprise."

The capitano stammered, "But—what shall I . . . ?"

"Take this," said Alviano, pressing a purse in the capitano's hand.

"But . . . !"

"Ride as far from here as you can. Stay off the main roads. Depending on what my instructions are in Venice, I may return, and if so, I will look for you—oh—in Bologna. That is still Bentivoglio territory."

The capitano nodded and was about to speak again, but the Venetian was already down the stairs, two at a time, at full gallop, and was gone.

NEAR THE PORTO SAN AUGUSTINO, by the great duomo in Modena, Pantalone and Harlequin watched a score of white-robed friars scurrying in and out of the houses bordering the piazza, their arms filled with clothing and furnishings. The clerics carried statues and paintings, great chairs, and ornate decorations torn from the walls, and they hurled them onto a blazing bonfire. The townspeople, for the most part, watched silently as the robed figures went about their labors to the slow, steady, monotonous beating of a drum.

"What's it all about?" whispered Pantalone. "What's happening?"

"A last gasp of the *piagnoni*, Savonarola's diminishing followers. They're burning—things," said Harlequin quietly.

"I can see that," hissed Pantalone. "What are they chanting?"

"Vanities."

They watched silently for a while. Now and again some townsman would try to retrieve one object or another only to have it pulled back by the white-robed monks.

"Look at all those beautiful things they're throwing into the flames. Now they're bringing out tapestries," whispered Pantalone as four of the white robes entered the piazza from a house with a huge, rolled hanging on their shoulders.

"Yes," said Harlequin quietly.

"Why?"

"Because Christ or the saints are not depicted in the tapestries. Because angels are not inscribed on the furniture. Because they are beautiful and give pleasure—but they do not inspire to religious ecstasy."

They watched again silently, and Pantalone then asked, "How can he get people to do this? What power does this Savonarola have over them?"

Harlequin dryly responded, "He said God talked to him."

Pantalone turned to stare at him. "What?"

Harlequin did not look at him. He kept his attention focused on the scene as if he never wanted to forget it, but he replied, "He said God talked to him. That he saw the hand of God in the clouds above Florence, clutching a flaming sword, and a voice told him that God would permit the French to destroy the city, to destroy all of Italy, unless the people repented and destroyed their things of vanity, their items of pleasure. When the French did not fulfill his prophecies, he argued that they, too, were wicked in the eyes of God. The people themselves must turn from their lives of sin and corruption."

Pantalone's brow became furrowed. "Is it true?"

"Who knows?" Harlequin sighed and shrugged. He faced the young man. "Is it true there was a great flood, and someone built a boat and brought two of every species aboard?" He turned his attention back to the fire and the chanting, robed figures.

"But—did God speak to him?" Pantalone persisted.

"How should I know?" Harlequin snapped. "Who am I, the pope? I'm told God speaks only to popes, and the pope is a decadent with an army of children and mistresses. If God chooses to speak to a debaucher, why not a fanatic like Savonarola?"

"Well, no god ever spoke to me," Pantalone reminded Harlequin. "Did God ever speak to you?"

"Once. He said, 'Stop asking so many questions,' and that put an end to our conversations." Then Harlequin's voice lowered. "I heard of a monk once, who not only talked to God, but to all living creatures as well. Birds. Dogs. Lambs. Everything. He walked barefoot around the countryside, and wild and beautiful things would come to him. Birds would roost on his shoulders."

"That could be a problem," observed the practical Pantalone.

"They apparently behaved themselves around him."

They did not notice, at first, the tall, thin, white-robed priest who insinuated himself beside Harlequin. "Isn't it wonderful, my son? Isn't it beautiful? It is the end of social injustice and the tyranny of the wealthy."

Harlequin nodded. "Well, I'd like to see *that*," he murmured.

"Fra Girolamo made many converts among the wealthy," said the priest. "These people have willingly consented to put an end to their vanities."

"Their vanities?" asked Pantalone.

"Shameful, ornamental gowns and robes, great mirrors in gilded frames, paintings, *gentilezze* such as cameos and scent boxes!"

"And you say the rich have fed these pyres of their own will?" asked Harlequin.

"Oh yes! Isn't it wonderful! And on the eve of All Saint's Day! It's marvelous!"

"Marvelous," echoed Harlequin, and he felt a cold wind touch his spine. "And what does the pope say of all this, Father?"

"The pope? The pope is corrupt!" the man asserted. "It was the pope who had Fra Savonarola executed, because he preached against the Borgia's excesses and his obscenities and called upon him to repent and reform his practices! In response the Antichrist in the Vatican first excommunicated Fra Girolamo, and then sent Mariano de Genazzano to Florence to denounce the Blessed One as a great drunken Jew."

"A Jew?" cried Pantalone.

"And a son of perdition," declared the priest. "But Fra Girolamo replied that *he* was not the one who kept concubines or young boys for pleasure, that he merely preached the faith of Christ."

"Yes." Harlequin nodded. "Well—thank you, Father." Then, suddenly, he pressed a ducat into the man's palm. "To assist you in such good work, Father."

"God bless you, my son! God bless you!" the priest replied. "In gratitude, may I present you with this small card on which the prayer of St. Dominic is copied?" He took Harlequin's hand and placed the card in it. Then he turned and quickly became part of the white-robed, chanting sea.

"Isn't that the same priest who stopped us in Pavia and wanted transport to Mantua?" asked the boy.

Harlequin shrugged. "All priests look alike to me."

"We better get back," said Pantalone, "before the incendiaries find *our* vanities." Harlequin nodded, and glanced quickly at the small card. Then, inexplicably and quietly, he tore it into pieces and spread the fragments along the roadway. They were joined by Dottore, who had completed his shopping at the marketplace.

In the shadowed facade of the Cathedral of S. Geminiano, the giant mercenary with the mole on his cheek and the black-robed, ferret-faced Father Sebastiano watched the trio make their way toward a narrow street where the cart awaited.

"Follow Manciano," Sebastiano said. "I'll inform the cardinal."

*B*Y THE TIME HARLEQUIN, Dottore, and Pantalone returned to the encampment, Scapino had reappeared with Ruffiana. He had washed away all the dye that had produced his green face, and all signs of the red sores that had been made with cherry juice. Isabella and Colombina were embarrassingly polite to the young girl but still obviously annoyed, especially since Scapino had run off with the burros, leaving the two women with a potential problem had flight been necessary.

Harlequin seemed pleased that the venture into Modena had gone without difficulty, and when Dottore reported that the clothmakers' guild assumed the guild wagon was destroyed in the fire and were no longer looking for it, the company decided their collective future looked somewhat brighter.

So they decided to celebrate a little. "This is the eve of All Saints' Day," cried Harlequin. "A day sacred to the memory of the dead! And since we may all be numbered in that congregation before we ever reach Mantua, let us enjoy what we can while we can!"

They lit the torches and brightened the encampment around the communal fire. They bunged two of the hogsheads of wine they had uncovered in the well of the wagon, and laid out cheese and smoked meats. They ate and drank to their individual satisfaction, and they sang songs of love and heroic deeds.

Later in the evening the three ladies appeared in Isabella's personal stock of beautiful, rich gowns from Venice and jovially dabbed on her flowery perfumes. Colombina was too large for Isabella's clothing, of course, so she had been more or less stuffed into certain portions of her outfit and overflowed others. The overpowering scents, everyone decided, were a nice change from the usual smells and would keep the insects busy.

The songs became more ribald, focusing on stories of wealthy, fickle ladies who came to bad ends by their unbridled affection for wicked men and describing in detail their fall from virtue.

Dottore, like most of the others, had gotten quite drunk, but Harlequin was as straight and sober as an oak tree. It was well into the night when he studied the unfinished guild wagon and suggested that they modify the vehicle so it would look less like an unfinished guild wagon.

"As it is at present," said Harlequin, "it reflects the stern, sober personality of the clothmakers' guild. I think it should be more—rustic, less—perfect. Besides," he added, "then we could take it into the cities without attracting attention from townspeople expecting us to perform on it."

"But it is a stage!" argued the staggering Dottore. "It is consecrated to the *sacre rappresentazioni!*"

"Make mine spaghetti!" yelled Pantalone. "*Sacre* gives me gas." He made an obscene noise and aimed his buttocks across the fire at Colombina, who shrieked with drunken laughter.

"It would be sacrilege," insisted Dottore, "to alter one board of this holy vehicle until it has been baptized with at least one religious, moral epic!"

"I agree!" cried Pantalone.

"Especially since this is the Feast of Fools, the eve of All Saints' Day!" expanded Dottore. "Tomorrow the clothmakers' guild will perform in Modena. It is only fitting that we perform—something—on their stage tonight!"

They went to the hands, and the idea was quickly adopted. The selection process began with Colombina proposing they perform the Nativity.

"Wonderful," said Harlequin, "and you can play the Virgin and give birth to a pound of dead horse meat."

"Make mine spaghetti!" Pantalone yelled again. "Horse meat gives me gas!"

"The Annunciation!" shouted Dottore.

But that topic was quickly eliminated when the angelic Scapino shortened the play by turning to the virginal Isabella and intoning, "Guess what! You're pregnant!"

"I have it!" called Colombina. "The story about the—the man on a horse!" She wheeled on Harlequin. "You remember! That stained-glass window in Aosta!"

"St. George and the dragon?"

"That's it!" she said. "St. George and the flagon!" Then, realizing and delighted with her error, she dissolved into laughter.

So they decided then on *St. George and the Dragon*, because there were no traditional lines that had to be remembered, and it would provide Pantalone with the opportunity to act out one of his fantasies by playing an animal.

Scapino volunteered Ruffiana for the role of the fair young

maiden imprisoned in the tower, but Ruffiana argued that she was unfamiliar with the tale. "What *is* a dragon?" she asked.

Harlequin informed her, "A dragon is a terrifying creature with scaly skin and stinking breath who seeks out young women and eats them."

"Oh," squealed Ruffiana. "Him!"

She declined nevertheless, saying Isabella was more of a lady and would use the proper words.

"That's what I'm afraid of," said Scapino, disappointedly.

But Isabella agreed and was assigned the role of the ingenue.

Scapino was chosen as St. George, because he treated them to a wonderful audition of a horseman who kept swaying and falling off, trying to climb back on, and riding under a horse.

Finally Harlequin stepped to the front of the wagon, gestured to the upper floor, which served as the stage and which was now aglow with torchlight, and announced, *"The Saga of St. George!"* Scapino instantly fell off his imaginary horse.

"And the Dragon!" continued Harlequin. Pantalone danced out with a torch between his teeth and nearly set fire to his blouse.

Colombina and Ruffiana were already laughing.

"In the fifty-foot tower in the dark woods," Harlequin began, setting the stage, "is the beautiful Princess Alabastard."

"That's Alabaster," prompted Dottore.

"She never knew her father." Harlequin winked. On the stage, Scapino lifted Isabella to the top of one of the now empty hogsheads, which represented her prison. "She is held prisoner," narrated Harlequin, "by the wicked and ferocious dragon Puffball!"

"Puffball?" objected Pantalone.

"I'm tired, and my imagination is limited!" apologized Harlequin. "Back in your cave, Puffball!"

Pantalone quickly hid behind Isabella's skirts and the hogshead. He took advantage of this position to run his hand up Isabella's leg, and she shrieked, developing a subplot that had to run its course before Harlequin could resume the story.

"The fair princess is threatened with a fate worse than death," the orator maintained.

"What's worse than death?" asked Ruffiana.

"Life, dear." Colombina smiled and patted her knee.

"Enter, the beautiful, heroic St. George!" heralded the Vagabond, and Dottore, Ruffiana, and Colombina cheered lustily.

Scapino had placed a pail on his head and attempted to juggle a long pole as he mimed galloping across the stage, circling, galloping back, falling off his horse, and nearly impaling himself on his own lance. In the process he had dropped the pail and somehow got his foot stuck in it, and thus for a period he limped around in small circles. Finally he reassembled himself on the very edge of the platform and pretended to be in danger of falling off.

Colombina was rolling on the ground in Isabella's Venetian gown, roaring with laughter.

"On approaching the tower," Harlequin went on, "St. George sees the beautiful maiden, who calls out to him." He turned to face his actors, but everyone was busily examining their nails, picking their noses, and scratching their behinds. "The maiden speaks!" demanded Harlequin, and Pantalone ran his hand up Isabella's leg again.

"That's *you!*"

Clearing her throat, Isabella began a singsong recitation. "Oh, Sir Knight! Sweet Knight! Strong Knight! Good Knight!"

"Good night," said Scapino, and he pretended to leave the stage.

"Damme," exclaimed Ruffiana, "that was a short play!"

"Oh, beautiful Sir Knight," chanted Isabella, "pray rescue me from yon fierce dragon!"

"What should I do first," Scapino asked, "rescue you or pray?"

"Rescue me"—Isabella smiled—"and then *I'll* pray."

"What do *I* get if I rescue you? Will you answer *my* prayers?" asked Scapino lasciviously.

Isabella began to laugh, but regained her composure and fitted a stern, virtuous, vacant expression on her face. "Oh, Sir Knight, heaven will reward your kindness and shower you with blessings."

"I do a good deed, and I get rained on?"

"I mean, the gods will smile upon you and bless your every enterprise."

"Who needs it? I have a rich father," replied Scapino as his "horse" began to prance about in circles. "What can you offer for my immediate future?"

Isabella fell into the irreverence of the moment. She stuck out one hip, cupped a hand over her breasts and another over her belly, and cooed, "How about a kiss?"

Scapino choked, but he managed to mutter, "Best offer I've had since Sister Superior finished the wassail last Michelmas. I accept!" He then proceeded to gallop in a small circle around the stage, roaring, "Dragon! Come out and get your just deeeserts!"

"A little pastry maybe," said Pantalone as he stuck his head out from behind Isabella's skirts, "and not so many eggs in the cream this time!"

"Silence!" roared Scapino over the laughter from the quartet watching him. "I am here to slay you, dragon, and rescue the fair damsel!"

"You can make a living at this?" asked Pantalone.

"I have been promised," said Scapino, "a kiss from her dainty lips!"

"From her dainty lips!" bellowed the dragon in an outraged tone. "The lady screams every time I even run a hand up her leg!" He demonstrated the process on Isabella once more, and she obligingly shrieked and hit him on top of the head. "I ask you, fair damsel," he squealed, "is this fair, damsel?" And he spent a few minutes performing a staggering, weaving, delirious walk around the stage.

It was up to Scapino to bring them back to the plot. "Prepare yourself, dragon!" he roared. "I am about to attack and destroy you!"

Pantalone then spent the next few minutes pretending to be a coward. He attempted to hide himself under Isabella's skirts, under the floorboards of the stage, behind a thin torch, and finally he came down to Scapino with both hands held, palms out, before him. "Can't we talk about this? Whatever happened to diplomacy? Is this good politics? Is that all there is? Just 'Prepare yourself, dragon! I am going to attack and destroy you?' Is this the old Italian way of doing things?"

"Yes, it is," curtly acknowledged Scapino as he made his imaginary steed rise on his hind legs and paw the air. "Prepare!"

"A moment!" pleaded Pantalone. "One moment, please! I am bound by the laws of this country to inform you of my reputation. My breath is deadly."

"I know, I know," groaned Scapino, pretending to gag.

"And I am the recognized champion and laurel-wreath holder in freestyle fang-and-claw combat!"

"I have a twelve-foot lance."

"A pointed argument." At that the knight started forward again, but the dragon raised his hands to stop him. "Look," Pantalone whined, "this wench means so much to you?"

Scapino shrugged. "It's one way to pass a dull afternoon."

Colombina's laughter turned to a hoarse, choking cough, and the performance stopped briefly to allow Dottore and Harlequin enough time to pound the poor woman into a semblance of sobriety.

"Let's trade a little," said Pantalone. "What have you in your saddlebags?"

"A sausage," said Scapino.

"Wurst?" said Pantalone.

"I've seen better."

Harlequin emitted a loud, mocking moan at the pun, and Scapino thumbed his nose at him as Pantalone wiggled his buttocks at the audience.

"All right," said Pantalone, "I propose a trade. I'll trade you a little romp in the meadow with the wench in exchange for half of your sausage."

"Which half?"

"Which half would you prefer for a little romp in the meadow?" asked Pantalone, puzzled.

"I meant which half of the sausage?"

"The half you haven't gnawed on." Pantalone smiled. "And in return I'll give you the half of the wench that *I* haven't gnawed on."

"I don't know," murmured Scapino. "Is she a virgin?"

Pantalone feigned shock and surprise. He staggered around the stage in mock dismay. "Is she a virgin?" he shrieked. "Is she a virgin! Does the moon light? Does a horse fly? Of course, she's not a virgin! Is your sausage a virgin? I doubt it very much! One can only imagine what's been jammed into that sausage skin!"

"All right," agreed Scapino, "it's a deal!" He pretended to throw something to Pantalone. "Your sausage!"

Pantalone raced to Isabella and swept her from the hogshead into his arms. He then ran back to Scapino and draped the girl over his shoulder, slapping her on the behind. "Your wench!" he boomed.

Dottore, Ruffiana, and Colombina were in tears from laughing. Until that moment Harlequin had been carefully watching the show and its "audience," but now he left the front of the stage and was slowly circling the fire and peering into the woods around them.

Scapino was the first to notice him. He set Isabella down and asked quietly, "What is it?"

"Put out the torches," Harlequin whispered. Instantly the troupe began to smother the torches in the pails of water that stood near the cart for the burros and the horse.

"Shall we put out the fire?" asked Pantalone, coming beside Harlequin.

"Not yet," said the Vagabond as his eyes scanned trees for something. "Get the women inside the wagon."

The boy nodded and began to herd the women behind the curtains of the guild wagon. Harlequin walked forward and slipped a sword from its scabbard in the cart. Then he disappeared into the trees.

*A*FTER A WHILE Harlequin's many-colored cloak was only another shadow among the others in the dark wood. The moon had gone behind a cloud, and he picked his way carefully, with the silent tread of a hunter or a hunter's prey, pausing with every other step to listen. He heard nothing, and that troubled him.

Where were the night creatures? Why was the owl suddenly silent? What was out there, barely rustling the leaves and the bushes as it passed?

Then, as the moon broke out from behind the masking clouds, he saw five armed men in tattered remnants of uniforms with pikes and swords, moving quietly, spread out, approaching the camp. He decided to give an alarm, and at the same time to divert the attention of the mercenaries from his company. *Perhaps, if the intruders have not yet seen the camp, I might lead them away.*

He gave a wild yell and began to run through the brush and the trees away from the encampment. He was pleased to hear a series of cries behind him and the crackle and crash of pursuit. He dodged and swerved between the narrow spaces between the trees and took great leaps over the fallen trees and the high bushes, spreading his long legs in a smooth, effortless motion.

The arrow that struck him from behind knocked the wind from him, and he tumbled down an embankment into a small pond, facedown in the green slime and the mud.

ONCE THE WOMEN WERE HIDDEN behind the curtains of the guild wagon, Scapino patrolled by the fire, poised on the balls of his feet as Harlequin had taught him, to await the attack. He held a sword in one hand and a dagger in the other, and he quickly ran down a mental listing of his lessons with Harlequin.

You cannot take the time to think. If you say to yourself: here he comes, you are a dead man. It must be all reflex. You must see and instantly respond!

He struggled to remember his instructor's words about being a fulcrum.

A man's weight can be used against him. If all his power, his force, his movement is directed to one specific area, and if you are not there when he strikes, the slightest force applied to him at right angles will send him flying, and he'll land hard. And he remembered: *a man's arm is hinged to operate in only one direction. Using your forearm as a fulcrum, and applying pressure at the elbow, you can direct the man's arm anywhere you desire. And where his arm goes, his body must follow!*

He remembered all this quickly, without thinking of it, and he felt himself ready when the first ragged and dirty mercenary emerged from the wood. At the same time the desperate man saw Scapino and leveled his pike at him. Noting the juggler's weapons, the invader approached very slowly, making a small circle with the point of his pike, and then, suddenly, he lunged. The handguard of Scapino's dagger forced the point of the pike down with little effort, and the fulcrum wheeled and slashed a deep furrow across the renegade's shoulders as the intruder screamed in shock and agony.

Suddenly there was the sharp stab of pain to the back of Scapino's head, and he suddenly remembered Harlequin's most-repeated order.

Protect your back at all times.

And he fell into the darkness.

$\mathcal{P}$ANTALONE, emerging from behind the curtains, saw Scapino fall, and he saw the edges of the encampment blossom with the gaunt mercenaries. They came from every direction, emerging from the woods like demons from smoke. Eight. Nine. Ten.

The first to charge received a kick in his groin for his bravery. As soon as the second man came at him, Pantalone held his hand out before him, palm toward his face, so that the soldier was forced to see the ring. "You're in trouble now, my friend," he clucked. "Behold!"

He was not prepared for the reaction of the soldier, who seized his hand, bent it back until he heard the wrist snap, and then pried the ring from the dead finger. He saw, through the tears welling up in his eyes because of the pain, the other renegades advancing toward the wagon. He tried to move, to make some gesture to stop them, but agony seized his whole arm and immobilized him.

Then, from the interior of the wagon, came the loud, ferocious roar of a lion.

Good old Dottore. Pantalone smiled to himself.

"You, boy!" growled a gray-bearded mercenary. "What have you in there?"

"Can't you—hear?" groaned Pantalone through his pain. "Haven't you ever—heard a—Nubian lion before?"

"A Nubian lion?" Three or four soldiers, more desperate than the others, continued to move cautiously toward the wagon. "What are you doing with a lion?"

"He's a—pet." Pantalone smiled through clenched teeth. "That's why we—don't keep him caged." The men stopped and slowly backed away from the wagon.

"He's not caged?" quavered Graybeard.

Pantalone shook his head, and the concealed Dottore gave another pull on his roar maker.

One of the renegades, dirtier and more scarred than the others, shuffled closer to the wagon and began to sniff the air. Then he smiled and said to Graybeard, "A lioness, Captain. And it smells of roses." With that his hand snapped out and pulled back the heavy curtains. Colombina screamed. Dottore leaped on the renegade, knocking him to the ground. But in an instant the tall man disappeared under a barrage of kicking, pounding mercenaries.

Graybeard reached forward and seized Isabella by her wrist and attempted to pull her roughly from the wagon, but the young girl had been hiding a dagger behind her back, and now she lunged. Graybeard jerked back his bleeding hand with a curse. Two other mercenaries ran forward, but Isabella was on the ground, demonstrating the talents she had mastered in the Urbino court. Parry. Feint. Lunge. One soldier was disarmed, and the other had to switch his blade from his bleeding right arm to his left. But, like Scapino, she had forgotten the gray-bearded mercenary, who now moved quickly behind her, grabbed her wrist, and pressed until she dropped the dagger.

"Don't touch her!" shrieked Ruffiana, and she grabbed the man by his beard and pulled him away. Another mercenary moved toward her, but Ruffiana's thumbs sank into his eyes, and he collapsed to the ground screaming.

Graybeard had been forced to release Isabella to protect himself from Ruffiana, who now swung a heavy pike that had fallen from the fingers of the blinded renegade. It caught him full in the stomach, and he exploded with a violent curse, clutching his belly. Again the pike swung and caught another renegade under the chin, sending him wheeling back through the others.

Colombina and Isabella tried valiantly to assist Ruffiana, but the heavy folds of the Venetian dresses and the numerical strength of the mercenaries made them helpless.

Before he, too, had to surrender to blackness and pain, Pantalone saw Ruffiana bring the pike down on the head of one of a circle of renegades enfolding her. Then they were upon her, and Graybeard, snarling and cursing, shoved his way through them to look down on her. He reached down, grabbed Ruffiana by her hair, and lifted her head from the dirt. "Well, little Amazon, first we eat. Then we'll let you sing us to sleep." Still holding her hair wrapped tightly around his right fist, he brought his left back across her face with a violent blow that twisted her face to one side, and she was knocked unconscious.

*H*ARLEQUIN OPENED HIS EYES to suffering. He felt the sharp ache where the arrow had struck him in his back, and he tried to adjust his body to minimize the pain. He discovered that he was lashed to the front wheel of the guild wagon facing the encampment and the fire. He looked to his left, and after a moment, he recognized Dottore slumped forward, his face bloodied, lashed to the back wheel. He tasted foul water on his lips. He was conscious of a murmured silence, and he shook his head to clear his vision, but every movement caused the ache between his shoulders to worsen, and he soon sat still and tried to focus on what was before him.

What he saw was Colombina and Isabella tied together before

the fire, facing out, their hands lashed behind them. Graybeard squatted there ripping and tearing at some meat, pausing to take a deep draft from a bowl filled with wine. But his eyes never left Isabella.

Harlequin's anxiety was increased by the lack of bedlam and chaos. The renegade mercenaries had discovered the wine, but there was little sign of intoxication. By the fire, one of the wounded soldiers moaned and wailed, trying occasionally to lift himself on his arms to elevate his face from the dirt, but the deep slash across his back and shoulders prevented him. No one paid any attention to him, and one said to the wounded man, "You're dying. Be still."

The incident triggered a memory in Harlequin. He remembered strong and silent soldiers taking a city that had capitulated. The defenders had been promised that civilian life and property would not be violated. But within an hour the houses were aflame, and the mercenaries were carting away anything of value. Women and babies were screaming, and every pike and sword blade was bloodied.

And amid this desolation and destruction, the soldiers in the slashed-sleeve tunics and the soft caps moved with cold efficiency. They seldom spoke, did not roar in their blood lust. They moved with a cold and silent indifference as if they were apart from the ruin they were creating.

Landsknecht, Harlequin whispered to himself, mercenaries recruited from the peasants of the Tyrol. Professionals who were customarily paid eight hundred guilders for three months' service but, when the pay was late or considered inadequate, became a ruthless force of terror and pillage, disciplined even in their destruction. Brutal, strong, merciless men who signed a letter of articles that demanded that each man be responsible for his own weapons, his armor and his horse, that he would purchase food only from sutler women who traveled with the army, that he would obey his superiors without question.

Harlequin counted about ten or fifteen here, clearly composing a *rotten*, an appropriate name attached to a small subdivision of the five-hundred-man *Fahnlein*.

The renegades were passing around the canvases from the cart

without interest, as if their worth was questionable or of no importance. They scattered the contents around them as they evaluated
each item. One or two continued to eat, and some had collapsed
on the edges of the encampment and gone to sleep.

Where, Harlequin wondered, *are the others: Ruffiana, Pantalone, and
Scapino?*

A short, filthy mercenary with a scar that spanned the bridge of
his nose and right cheek crossed to Graybeard with one of the canvases unrolled before him. "Nothing but dresses, perfumes, some
statues. But look, Captain," he whispered. "A naked woman!
Look!"

Graybeard threw his stripped bone into the fire and then took
the canvas.

"It looks like the madonna there, doesn't it?" Scar Face grinned
as he gestured to Isabella.

Graybeard studied the painting for a while. "Yes," he muttered in
his hushed, rasping voice. "It looks like her." He smiled at Isabella
across the fire. "Is it you, madonna?" Isabella said nothing—which
Harlequin found encouraging.

Then Graybeard stood up and walked around the fire to where
Isabella was tied to Colombina. The once lovely Venetian dresses
had been ripped and shredded. "Is it you?" He leered at her. She
said nothing and tried to turn her head away, but he grabbed her
hair and jerked her face around to his. "Is it you?" he repeated, and
then his right hand grabbed her breast and began to knead it between his fingers. Isabella gave a small cry of pain and tried to kick
at her tormentor, but his left hand pulled her hair, and she
screamed.

He suddenly released her, took two steps back, and slowly drew
his dagger from its sheath. "Come," he growled, "let's see if it's
you." The other renegades had abandoned their methodical destruction to watch their captain, and one, a swarthy one-eyed man
hissed, "Yes. Let's see her!" Graybeard stepped toward her and began to slice through what little material remained on her bodice.

And suddenly Colombina grunted, "Hellfire and damnation!
What idiots!"

Only Colombina could have explained what she hoped to accomplish with her outburst, but it could not have been the reaction she received. Graybeard stared at her. The others stood like statues, quietly glaring at her through dead eyes. "You can't expect much from this fancy lady! She's ice and granite. You won't have much fun with her. Now if you really want a good show, just cut me loose and let me climb on that wagon. I'll give you something worth watching!"

The renegades continued to stare at her silently. Some who had been sleeping stirred and sat up. Graybeard grunted and gave no sign of understanding, but then, slowly, he passed the dagger from his right hand to his left, slipped it between Colombina's body and her arm, and cut the leather thongs binding her.

The cutting also freed Isabella, who slowly removed the rest of the leather from her wrists and backed away, carefully watching. Most of the others kept their attention fixed on Graybeard and Colombina, who forced a smile and moved slowly, suggestively, around the captain of the brigands, brushing against him in her own skillful manner. She walked seductively through the cluster of renegades to the ladder that led to the stage of the guild wagon. The mercenaries watched silently and sullenly, expressing nothing, even when she began a slow, rhythmic clapping. "Come on!" she commanded them. "I can't perform without music."

The men frowned, grumbled, did nothing, staring dumbly. But Graybeard and some others sat down to watch her, and then Colombina began to dance.

Oh no, Harlequin groaned to himself. *Don't do it.* He was further dismayed to see Graybeard suddenly reach up, seize Isabella roughly by a wrist, and pull her down on his lap.

It won't be long now, he thought.

*H*AD HE BEEN ABLE to turn himself around, or go to the opposite side of the wagon, Harlequin could have seen Scapino directly behind him, tied to the right front wheel of the wagon facing the dark woods.

Scapino's vision was dimmed by the dried and caked rivulets of blood from his reopened head wound. To his right, Pantalone was lashed to the remaining wheel, his broken wrist tied to the rim of the wheel making his pain much worse. Behind them, in the encampment, they had heard nothing for some time, and that silence was frightening in itself. But there had been no screaming, so they reasoned that the others were either dead or the renegades had temporarily abandoned their amusements.

They had realized the full extent of their danger when Harlequin was dragged, muddy and moaning, into the encampment from the marsh and tied to another wheel of their wagon. Scapino and Pantalone knew, in the lucid moments that the pain permitted them, that when the renegades had fed themselves, rested, and packed what valuables they could steal on the burros, they would kill all the survivors.

"When you hear the thunder, yell as loud as you can," came the dark voice from the woods.

Pantalone looked up to see who had spoken, but there was only darkness and shadows in the deep recesses between the trees. "What?" he whispered. "Who's there?"

"When you hear the thunder, yell as loud as you can," came the words once more, clear but hushed from the darkness. "And keep yelling as loud and as long as you can." There was a pause. "Do you understand me?" Pantalone nodded without understanding, and he glanced at Scapino, who indicated with a nod of his bloody head that he, too, heard and understood.

"Who are you?" whispered Pantalone.

But there was no reply.

*I*F THERE WAS ONE TECHNIQUE that Colombina had mastered, it was the "stall for time." She had no idea why she felt time was important. To the best of her knowledge, there was no one to come to their rescue, but if these hard-eyed men were desperate, so was she, and she continued dancing. Still, something inside her said, *Until the knife is at your throat, all is well.*

If Harlequin had convinced her that the prime ingredient to her art was loving it, her fear had dissolved any existing affection. Harlequin groaned to see that she was even worse than before. She tripped, nearly collapsed, staggered, tried to leap, and failed. But if the dance was awkward and embarrassing to Harlequin, it was totally fascinating to the *landsknecht* mercenaries. At first they stared in wonder at what she was attempting.

Was she having a seizure? Was this some sort of frenzied ritual when Italian women faced death? Was it a religious experience?

After a while their rapt attention degenerated into a clinical curiosity. Colombina had finally abandoned the shredded dress when she realized it served no purpose, and she hoped the sight of her total nakedness would hold their attention a little longer. She noted with some satisfaction that the bobbing of her bare breasts in the light of the torches seemed to work its own magic upon the men, though she shuddered to think that their response might have been a puzzled enchantment rather than seductive pleasure.

Graybeard was the first to recognize the absurdity of the situation. Whatever the portly naked woman was doing, it had little to do with his present agenda. Abruptly he shifted his attention to Isabella and bent the struggling girl back on the dirt, pushing her skirts about her waist and attempting to mount her. As if on signal, several mercenaries rose slowly and quietly climbed to the stage. Without a word or a sign, three quickly pinned Colombina to the wooden floor, and a fourth, the one-eyed man, worked his way between her legs.

When it came, the "thunder" surprised everyone, including Scapino and Pantalone, who were prepared for it.

The one-eyed mercenary on Colombina suddenly straightened, gasped, and fell to one side, his face a bloody smear of torn flesh. Scapino and Pantalone began to yell like demons, and they were surprised to hear echoing cries from the dark woods around them.

There was a cold confusion in the encampment. Graybeard rose quickly from Isabella and held his dagger before him, wheeling in circles, to confront his enemy. But the others, who had been resting, were still groggy from wine and weariness, and stumbled around in an attempt to locate the enemy or to find cover. Two or three began to slip silently into the safe blackness of the dark woods with their sacks of booty.

The second explosion came from a totally different direction, and Graybeard felt the sharp, stabbing, momentary pain as his face became shattered bone and flesh. Then he staggered like a great tree caught in a violent wind, and fell across the fire. His ragged clothing ignited and he burned like a torch, no movement apparent in the flaming body.

The other renegades were gone now, but occasionally there was a scream or an echoing thunder from the blackness that spoke of sudden death among the shadowed trees.

Isabella picked up Graybeard's knife and crossed to the wagon. She cut the bonds that held Harlequin to the wheel. "Damn," he muttered through his own pain as he tried to smile at her, "I can't leave you alone for a minute that you don't get into trouble!"

Together they released Dottore, Scapino, and Pantalone. Colombina found a cloak to cover her nakedness, and they all went in search of Ruffiana.

They found her in the space between the guild wagon and the trees. The *landsknecht* mercenaries had lashed her, naked, over a hogshead and coldly and objectively used her for their amusement. Her back and buttocks were a red blanket of small cuts designed to inflict pain, and all that was not scarlet was bruised and filthy. They stood silently for a moment, agonizing, and then Colombina quickly cut her lashings and, with no sense of self-consciousness, whipped away the cloak covering her own nakedness and tenderly wrapped it around the young girl. Scapino picked her up, and they brought her back into the clearing and laid her by the fire.

And Isabella, the self-sufficient, wept over her.

*I*T WAS A GREAT DEAL LATER, and Ruffiana had been washed and wrapped in warm blankets and placed in the bed of the wagon. A soft moan from the young girl gave them hope, and Colombina had forced a little water and some of the wine between her lips and had personally wrapped the abused body in wet linen strips.

Dottore had already worked minor miracles on Scapino's head and Pantalone's wrist, and was heating a knife in preparation for treating Harlequin's wound from the arrow, when Capitano Francesco Benevelli stumbled into the encampment.

In one hand he held a curious instrument: a long pipe mounted on a curved piece of wood and held by metal hoops or rings. A similar instrument was tucked into his belt. In his left hand he carried a bloody sword, and what little clothing he wore was splattered with blood and torn pieces of flesh. There was a small gash over his right eye, and he struggled for breath.

"*Scusi*"—he smiled at them—"but by any chance do you have a physician handy?"

He took one step and collapsed at Dottore's feet.

*O*N THE RIMINI ROAD, from Pergola to Fossombrone, the naked and mutilated bodies of men, women, and children littered the fields and the roadbed itself. Heads of young and old men were impaled on pikes along the roadway like kilometer markings, and the sky was dark with the black smoke from the burning houses and farms.

Michelotto Corella and Ugo da Moncado, mounted on great chargers, led their pike- and bow-men along the road.

Cesare's lesson had been taught.

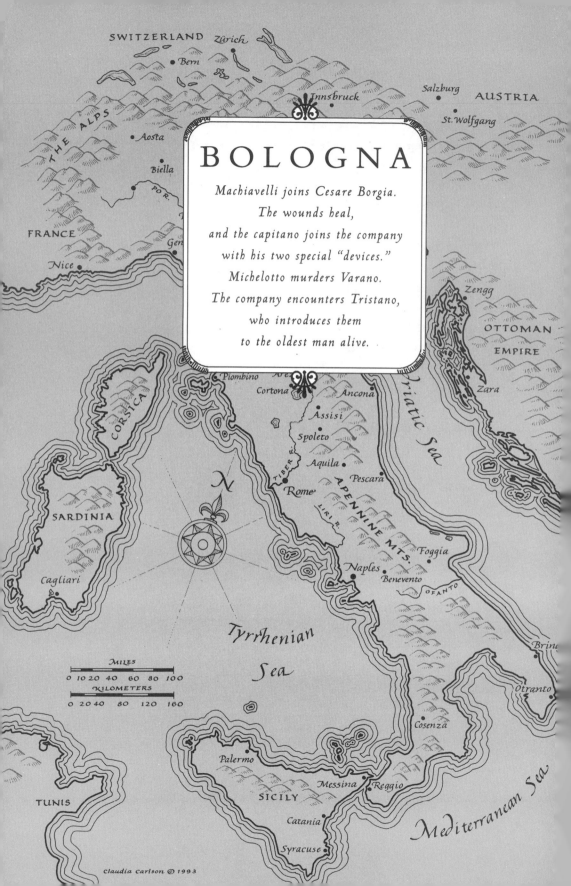

BOLOGNA

Machiavelli joins Cesare Borgia.
The wounds heal,
and the capitano joins the company
with his two special "devices."
Michelotto murders Varano.
The company encounters Tristano,
who introduces them
to the oldest man alive.

SWITZERLAND   Zürich

Bern

Innsbruck

Salzburg   AUSTRIA

St. Wolfgang

THE ALPS

Aosta

Biella

POR.

FRANCE

Gen.

Nice

OTTOMAN
EMPIRE

Zengg

Zara

Piombino   Are.

Cortona

Ancona

Adriatic Sea

CORSICA

Assisi

Spoleto

Aquila

TIBER

Rome

Pescara

APENNINE MTS.

SARDINIA

LIRI R.

Foggia

Naples

Benevento

OFANTO

Cagliari

Tyrrhenian
Sea

MILES
0 10 20 40 60 80 100
KILOMETERS
0 20 40 80 120 160

Brin

Otranto

Cosenza

Palermo

Messina   Reggio

TUNIS

SICILY

Catania

Syracuse

Mediterranean Sea

Claudia Carlson © 1993

Cesare Borgia received the Florentine ambassador in his private quarters at Imola in his customary black velvet doublet trimmed in silver brocade. He wore his familiar soft, black velvet cap with jeweled medallions representing both the bull *impresa* of the Borgia and the blue and white stripes of his French duchy, and a cross belt after the fashion of the Spanish with new Valencia boots. Both a sword and dagger dangled from his waist.

The ambassador, Niccolo Machiavelli, wore a long coat with a fur lining and slashed sleeves over a blouse with a heavy, jeweled collar, a short skirt, and high leather gaiters. A heavy gold pendant and chain of office was suspended from his shoulders and his long dark hair was topped with a soft, low-crowned hat after the Venetian fashion.

Cesare gestured Machiavelli to a chair beside his own, facing the fire, and signaled for wine to be brought.

"I trust you have been made comfortable, Signore Machiavelli."

The Florentine emissary nodded impatiently. "If it please Your Grace, I would like to perform my duties and return to Florence as soon as possible."

"Ah," sighed Cesare, accepting two chalices of wine from the servant and passing one to Machiavelli, "you are uncomfortable then. My apologies."

"No," replied the young ambassador, "it has nothing to do with my accommodations, Your Grace. I expected no more of a fortified encampment, but, well, the truth, my lord, is that I was recently married, and I only reluctantly parted from my young wife, Marietta, for this mission."

"A young wife," said Cesare with a smile. "I understand."

"I also am suffering from a severe palsy which I attribute to the climate, and—well—I am certain Your Grace is as impatient to finish our mutual business as I. Especially with the recent—difficulties—in the Romagna."

The smile vanished from Cesare's lips. "To which—difficulties—do you refer, signore?"

Machiavelli realized that the topic was not one to be discussed, but now that he had begun, he pressed on. "I am under the impression that your condottieri, Michelotto Corella and Ugo da Moncado, after ravaging Fossombrone, encountered the forces of Vitelli and Orsini. It is my understanding that your lances were defeated, and de Moncado captured."

There was a quiet moment while Cesare sipped his wine.

"The *Signoria* is well informed," he finally responded, and then he added, "To a point."

"I don't understand," said Machiavelli. "Was there no defeat?"

"There was a temporary—how do you say it?—a difficulty. But I have over five thousand foot soldiers in the Romagna, including six hundred Gascons and Germans, and soon I will add three thousand Swiss, two thousand French, and five hundred cavalry from Lombardy."

Machiavelli studied the young duke. "I also understand that Vitelli intends to march on Urbino and Oliveretto on Camerino. The *Signoria*'s agents report a plot against you is even now being prepared by your own condottieri."

"Really?" smiled Cesare. "Who precisely?"

"Petrucci and Paolo Orsini. Giovanni Bentivoglio."

"Ah." Cesare laughed. Suddenly he took a small silver bell from the table between the two chairs and rang it. A moment later the door swung open and a young man dressed in armor approached, his helmet cupped under one arm.

Cesare gestured toward the young man. "May I present Paolo Orsini? Paolo has a beautiful voice." The duke leaned toward Machiavelli. "And he has been singing for me all afternoon."

*I*T WAS HARLEQUIN WHO, following the raid, decided that the company needed a period of rest and recuperation, so the company had remained camped east of Modena near the Reno River, assessing damage, planning their future, and restoring themselves.

Two of the paintings had been destroyed beyond repair, and

one—the painting called *A Company of Wayward Saints*—was missing. Some of Isabella's gowns had been mangled and shredded, so these provided the linen and silk needed by Dottore for his repair work. Isabella's pouch of gems—of which only three remained—had not been discovered at the bottom of Salvation's feedbag, but Dottore's own pouch, which represented his pay for escorting Isabella, and which he had hidden within his blouse, had fallen victim to the *landsknecht* mercenaries and was not recovered.

Of the eleven men who attacked the camp, three died in the encampment and seven just inside the wooded area, all—presumably—killed by the capitano. Indeed, the capitano, on regaining consciousness, swore he had killed an additional six or more who had apparently crawled away to die unseen and unde tected. He had apparently fought with some degree of courage, picking off the fleeing renegades one by one as they ran in their panic through the woods. At least three must have turned to fight, for the capitano had been pierced twice in the chest and once in the right buttock. Fortunately none of the wounds were deep and seemed to have been delivered from defensive positions that, upon reflection, did not say a great deal for the capitano's skill with a blade.

He had awakened to the tender caress of Colombina bathing his head with cold cloths. He was stripped to the waist, which was not an unusual condition for his awakenings; but long strips of linen were bound around his chest and sides, which *was* unexpected. And to find an attractive, but fully clothed woman wiping his forehead was definitely a surprise. In his mild delirium, he gazed at the buxom woman through misty eyes and whispered softly and lovingly, "Annamarie."

Colombina continued to bathe his forehead. "Annamarie?" she said. "My, that name brings back memories. I knew a girl named Annamarie who married some guildsman and moved to Piacenza, but before that she was Annamarie Santini, although the boys called her 'Easy,' because she—well—you know—she was—generous. We grew up together, and it was Annamarie who taught me how to make a living—you know—when times are difficult."

Fortunately for his illusions of Annamarie's fidelity and his own peace of mind, Capitano had drifted back into a deep sleep after sounding the lady's name.

PANTALONE'S WRIST WAS now firmly locked between two slender slabs of light wood and mummified with linen. The young man wore the entire apparatus in a sling and, less than a week after the battle, watched the swelling evaporate. He was now able to pass a florin from finger to finger and back again—an exercise he practiced continuously.

Dottore had patiently explained to Pantalone that the wrist, being a joined area for interlocking bones, had only suffered a separation of those bones he was now immobilizing until they healed. This valuable information, he admitted, was a by-product of his observations on the dead subjects of Maestro Leonardo and from the anatomical studies da Vinci had sketched of the inside forearm and hand of a man. Dottore had studied the drawings and the dissected bodies in another attempt to divine the secret of da Vinci's art.

He abandoned the story that he acquired his medical knowledge from treating wounds caused by "a madman," and he had recounted his true history several times for the company around the evening fires. He also continued to tell another version of his life in which he was the illegitimate son of a Florentine lady and an Arabian bandit. His stories were second only to Harlequin's for romantic appeal, and only a little more plausible than Colombina's histories, in which she claimed to be the child of a Milanese lady and an Arabian stallion. The most astounding feat of legerdemain was Ruffiana's conviction that all her previous life had been an illusion, and that henceforth she was a virgin.

Indeed, the company had invented so many diverse histories and backgrounds, mixed occasionally with truth, that no one really knew anyone else save by their example and character.

Dottore's own wounds proved to be lacerations and large bruises that were healing and disappearing, and compared with the wounds inflicted in service to the maestro, they were more uncomfortable than disabling.

Scapino's head was now encased in a turban of Isabella's silks, which gave him a somewhat exotic appearance and permitted his scalp wounds to heal. Twice a day Isabella changed the linen pads and the poultice of leaves and herbs on his scalp, and then ceremoniously wrapped it again in silk. Dottore assured them that Scapino would suffer no ill effects from the reopened wound. He argued that the juggler's ridiculous behavior was normal for him, and he was no more insane than he was in Aosta.

The women had been comparatively unharmed physically by the attack. Ruffiana, who had been the most severely abused, had only a few visible bruises that gave testimony to the violence done to her. Her back and buttocks had been lacerated, but the purpose was to inflict pain and not to scar, and the wounds had healed quickly. Mentally her hard adolescence had provided a form of protection that kept her stable.

The change in the women since the attack was obvious. Ruffiana was no longer suspect, and her attempt to protect Isabella before she was overcome had endeared her to them. Colombina had come to see Ruffiana as herself ten years earlier, and Isabella finally realized that Ruffiana's relationship with Scapino, while complex and confusing to her, was not primarily sexual but familial.

Furthermore the young whore was revealed to have a quick wit and a tongue to match. She and Isabella occasionally engaged in verbal conflicts—totally free of malice—that amused and delighted the company. Ruffiana continually accused Isabella's upbringing of protecting her from the truths of life, and Isabella maintained Ruffiana's early life in the streets had given her a distorted concept of nobility and good manners.

It was Harlequin's wounds that proved most interesting to Dottore, for when he had stripped the man of his cloak of rags and shreds and cut away his rough undergarments, he discovered there was no wound from the arrow, only a large, purple bruise between his shoulders and minute lacerations of the skin. He then took a second look at the mantle of shreds and streamers, and saw that it was, indeed, the brigandine armor Pantalone had learned about in Piacenza.

The ragged and colorful cloak was actually a mantle of linen covered with thick metal scales about the size of a ducat. These scales were sewn to the outside of the cloak and then covered with an array of colorful rags that proved to be remnants of banners and flags. The cloak was actually quite heavy, but the armor had protected Harlequin from the arrow's point. The force of the blow had merely bent two of the scales, which, in turn, had bitten through the linen undercoat to lacerate and bruise the skin.

So Harlequin emerged as the least wounded of the men, and Dottore had promised to keep his discovery of the armor a secret between them.

He also did not mention to anyone that he had discovered a packet, wrapped in parchment and bound in a long strip of purple-and-silver linen, tucked into a hidden pocket of the cloak. After examining Harlequin's wounds, Dottore had quietly replaced the item without opening it.

But questions plagued Giacomo. Was Harlequin a Swiss mercenary? Was he a deserter? If he was no longer a mercenary, why did he wear brigandine armor? And what was the significance of the packet and the cloth wound around it?

*I*T WAS PROVIDENTIAL that the leader was the least incapacitated, for hard decisions had to be made and at once. If one of the renegades had escaped—which seemed to be the case—and if he told others of the paintings and the jewels, it was not unlikely that Harlequin and his band would be followed by a more disciplined, armed, and efficient force. With all roads to the north and Mantua closed and guarded by the Este mercenaries, should the wagon continue down the Via Emilia to the south toward Bologna, skirt the area by traveling north to Ferrara and Padua, and then cut quickly west to Verona so as to approach Mantua from the north? Should they consider continuing east from Bologna to Ravenna on the Adriatic and attempt a northern route by sea, perhaps from Venice? But Venice, of course, was out of the question since it would bring Isabella right back to the source of her troubles. Should they travel the byways and try to avoid being seen?

The most immediate problem now facing the company was sustenance. The renegades had devoured most of the food and wine, and the long rest period had fairly well exhausted the remainder.

All that remained of their communal wealth were three of Isabella's jewels, and the chance of exchanging them for money or supplies without attracting attention and suspicion was small indeed. The money changers of Bologna owed allegiance to the Bentivoglio, but Cesare had included that family in his list of "bankrupt rabble," so the *banchi di pegni* who loaned money on such items as jewels would be extremely cautious and suspicious of all strangers in that city.

So exchanging jewels for currency was out of the question.

The answer, like most answers in life, was forced upon them. Harlequin decided that since the company possessed a modified guild wagon, they might as well utilize it to make money to buy food. They had disguised the wagon by removing the two top corner poles and the cross beam and replacing them with lighter rods on which they strung the old curtain, now covered with patches and spare materials. This curtain was not some artistic background as the guildsmen employed it, but provided them with a place apart from the eyes of the viewers where they could exchange information, adjust clothing, and tune instruments.

They decided that they would attempt to pose as traveling mummers and entertain in the piazzas of Bologna. Colombina had recovered both her health and her confidence and improved to a point where her dancing was fascinating if not exciting, and Ruffiana had revealed a skill in innovative dance that was very exciting *and* fascinating.

Harlequin and Isabella could play the lute and sing, and Isabella was beautiful, which was reason enough to believe she might bring in a ducat or two just standing there in one of her Venetian gowns.

Pantalone's talent for mimicry had often reduced them to helpless laughter—especially when he imitated the aged. Like all youth, he saw old age as a ludicrous and a divine vengeance for having enjoyed oneself in the earlier years. So he created pantomimes of old men lusting for young wives they could never satisfy.

Scapino was now an expert acrobat, wire walker, and juggler. Taught by Harlequin, he had mastered how flying objects rested on the hands for only a scant second before being hurled away. So it was now simple for him to juggle fiery brands or sharp blades—which was exciting to watch—instead of the routine cups and balls.

Dottore's skill with wounds had proven invaluable, but his worth as an entertainer was limited to his ability to feign any language from a guttural German to a lisping French.

The company unanimously agreed that their immediate goal would be Bologna, and the quickest route to Bologna was the Via Emilia.

THE CAPITANO'S MYSTERIOUS WEAPONS fascinated Harlequin. They were revealed to be a form of "hand cannon" of a type the capitano called "wheel locks." The capitano said he had discovered them wrapped in a waterproof membrane and attached to the saddle of the "borrowed" war-horse, but he had first seen them in the Milanese court when they were presented to the duke as a gift from an armorer of Pistoia in Tuscany. The duke had christened them "pistols." The capitano had also seen them demonstrated—first in Milan and again later in the shop of Niccolo in Biella.

He explained the firing mechanism to Harlequin.

"Simply, gunpowder placed behind a projectile is ignited by this rough-edged wheel on a spring. When a curved trigger is pulled, the lock on the wheel is released. The spring causes the wheel to rotate rapidly against a piece of iron pyrite, which, in turn, causes sparks to ignite a small pan of powder to the side of the barrel. This powder passes a flame to a larger charge inside the barrel through a touch hole, and the resulting explosion of the gunpowder forces the projectile out the barrel at great speed and for a considerable distance."

Harlequin examined the powder. "Is this gunpowder the same used in cannon?"

Capitano nodded. "About one third saltpeter, sulfur, and charcoal. A little more saltpeter than the other two."

"Serpentine? That finely grained gunpowder?"

"No. The best way to prepare the powder is by corning: mix the three together when wet and then dry the mixture into a cake. Then crumble the cake, and each granule will contain just the right amount of all three. Much better than serpentine."

The capitano argued that these new pistols were a great improvement over the "matchlocks," which required a slow-burning match to ignite the powder and which had to be changed with every shot. Furthermore the pans on the new pistols swung out automatically to receive the next load of gunpowder, which made reloading faster.

"Never fast enough to please me," he continued. "I think these weapons can be used only once effectively, because it takes too long to reload them, and then, as the enemy charges, you have to revert to the dagger or the sword.

"Still," he added, "with pistols, a peasant is as good as a knight."

*T*HIS NORTHWESTERN APPROACH carried them through the fertile flatlands of the Emilia and proved an effortless passage, but as the cart and the wagon neared the city itself, the ancient Roman roadway began to flood with transients and farmers, church dignitaries, and nobles in great coaches or mounted on beautiful, caparisoned horses, and occasionally processions of penitents turning south on the Via Cassia to Florence.

There were also clusters of noisy, spirited students on their way to the university to begin or to continue their studies, wearing capes and cloaks that bore the crests of the noble families: the

Visconti, the Pepoli, and the ruling family of the Bentivoglio. These boisterous and worldly young men were in stark contrast to the young student clerics, quiet and withdrawn, of the College of St. Dominic, where Savonarola himself had studied. These were sons of the poorest of the poor who realized their only escape from their poverty was the Church or the military—depending upon their respective skills and character.

It was among these young clerics that Harlequin spotted the tall Dominican he had encountered in Pavia and Modena. Moved by a sudden compassion and a continual curiosity, Harlequin gestured the young priest and his traveling companion in Dominican white to eat with them at their encampment. "Come, Fathers," Harlequin called to them. "Share our humble meal."

Colombina whispered to him that food was in short supply, and if he didn't want to eat Death or Destruction within the next two days, he'd best ration his generosity. But there was something about the two pitifully thin monks that struck a chord of sympathy in everyone, and they made room for them at the fire.

As the clerics waited for the cold meat, cheese, and bread, Harlequin said to the taller of the two, "A small world, Father. How was the miracle of the sarcophagus in Mantua?"

"Alas," replied the tall priest, "all roads to Mantua are patrolled by Este mercenaries who seem to be looking for—something. Even the Cardinal of Modena, his Eminence Ferrari, had a small contingent of mercenaries—disguised as *landsknecht* renegades—searching for the—mysterious something."

The company exchanged glances. "Disguised as *landsknecht*?" Harlequin asked softly. "Why?"

The tall priest shrugged. "Who knows? Perhaps the cardinal didn't want to be identified with whatever it is that they seek." He accepted a bowl of food from Colombina. "The point is moot," he said quietly. "The cardinal is dead."

"Dead?"

"They say he—disappointed—the pope somehow, and the pontiff ordered him poisoned. His own secretary, Sebastiano Pinzon, performed the execution." The monk grimaced. "And that has made the pope even wealthier. Rumors are that the good cardinal had grown excessively rich in his lofty church position, so when he died, the pope confiscated all his possessions."

"So," Harlequin said quietly, "then I assume you are not going to—pursue—the Mantua miracle?"

The priest shook his head. "No, I will continue," he said. "But I and my followers have been invited to the College of St. Dominic, where I will teach the principles of Fra Savonarola, and—bide my time—in Bologna."

"Bide your time?"

"The political scene is—muddied. Francesco da Gonzaga of Mantua was recently awarded forty thousand ducats by the pope as a 'dowry' for a possible marriage between Cesare's infant daughter and a Gonzaga youth. That would indicate that the Gonzaga family is becoming allied to the Borgias. But the Borgias control Ercole d'Este and his mercenaries. I believe it may be only a brief time before Ercole is ordered to reopen the roads north to Gonzaga's Mantua. When he does, I and my companions will go there."

Harlequin considered this. "Then you advise patience? For a—visit—to Mantua?"

"Yes," mumbled the tall cleric through a mouthful of meat. "It is safer here for the time being. The pope placed an interdict on Bologna, but Giovanni Bentivoglio ordered the professors at the universities to tell the students—and their parents—to ignore the papal bull."

"Is that good?" asked Isabella.

"Oh yes." The smaller of the two smiled. "Giovanni's son Antonio was sent to Rome with a safe-conduct pass signed by Ercole d'Este and, after showing the Borgian pope how the Bolognese supported the Bentivoglio family, the pontiff gave in and signed an agreement with them. The safety of the city is now under a guarantee by the French king and the cities of Florence and Ferrara."

Colombina poured some wine for her two guests. "What of the duke?"

The tall priest laughed lightly. "The pope sent him six thousand ducats to pay his armies, but in return, Cesare had to agree to the alliance."

Harlequin poured some wine for himself. "And he agreed?"

"No." The tall cleric chuckled. "But he cannot do anything about it. He needs the French companies promised him, and the French king is a guarantor of the alliance."

The clerics and their hosts laughed. "An amusing sidelight," said the smaller, "is that the pope also needed to reassure the French of *his* loyalty, so he looked around, found his daughter-in-law, Sancia of Aragon, and had her imprisoned in the Castel Sant'Angelo."

"On what grounds?" asked Isabella.

He wiped his mouth on his sleeve. "The pope discovered that she was immoral. It appears he suffers from a spiritual myopia, because both Cesare and his brother Juan slept openly with her for years in the Vatican—and right under the nose of her Borgia husband, Jofre."

"So," said Harlequin, "what is the truth?"

"It is obvious," explained the tall priest. "The French and the Spanish are at war in the kingdom of Naples, so to prove where his allegiance rested, the pope looked around, found a daughter-in-law who is of the royal Spanish family of Aragon, and had her clapped away."

"She is safe enough," continued his companion. "When Cesare finds out that his mistress is imprisoned, the shriek will echo from Imola to Rome."

The gossip continued for the better part of an hour, and then the two monks finished their meal, rose, thanked and blessed their benefactors, and returned to the Via Emilia.

Only Harlequin noticed the giant mercenary with a mole on his cheek who had squatted patiently by the side of the roadway until the priests resumed their journey, and who now rose and followed after them.

$\mathcal{A}$s THE COMPANY PROCEEDED toward Bologna Harlequin sought some means of convincing the capitano to stay with them so they could have the added protection of his pistols, and mentioned in passing that Ruffiana had encountered a man in Modena who was looking for someone fitting the soldier's description. Later, when the capitano questioned Ruffiana herself, he realized that the man who was searching for him was his own adjutant, Cosimo the Sicilian, who now succeeded him as condottiere to the French marshal.

Consequently the capitano had his fears confirmed that he was now a fugitive from both the French and his own men. He had suspected as much in the weeks that he worked his way south from Piacenza, trading the armor of the war-horse for his own and occasionally disguising himself as a mendicant to hear what he could in the piazzas. As he saw it, there were now just two roads open to him. He could go south and offer his services as an experienced soldier to the Neapolitans or the Spanish, who were fighting the French, or he could stay in Bologna, hiding his identity, until he received further word from Bartolomeo Alviano.

Harlequin suggested another alternative once he felt the seed that he had planted in the soldier's mind had taken root: the capitano could help the company get Isabella safely to Mantua. On the first opportunity, Harlequin and Scapino pointed out that Cosimo and the French mercenaries would not look for a condottiere traveling with a troupe of mummers, and that his pistols could protect Isabella.

"If Isabella doesn't reach Mantua safely," Harlequin argued, "it might eventually mean marriage to a blackguard who would use her up like a fine horse until she died in marital harness before her time."

The capitano frowned. Harlequin whispered to Scapino, "When talking to the military, remember that horses are considerably more important than people." He turned to the capitano, and asked, "I'm curious about your background, Captain. How did the duke go about making a valiant soldier like you out of a poor, uneducated farmhand and—"

"No one made *me* into a soldier!" snapped Capitano.

"You mean it was something that grew on you—like a wart?" said the juggler.

"I mean no one took me from any farm! My father was a soldier! As was his father! I take after my father! We were a fighting family!"

"Mine, too," said Scapino. "You should have seen my mother take after my father! Why, one night—"

"Well, Captain," Harlequin interrupted, "you have to admit that if it wasn't for the support of the nobility, you wouldn't fare too well on your own."

The capitano feigned hysteria. "You're not serious? I can live off the land anywhere in the world! I can feed and clothe and shelter myself and defend what I have against anyone who tries to take it away! I'd like to see the Borgian duke alone in the middle of a wilderness or in the vast wastes of a desert! He wouldn't survive a day! No, no, my friends, it is the condottiere that makes the lord, not the lord that makes the condottiere!"

"If all this strength and self-sufficiency of yours can be bought for a few coins by any weak overlord, what good is it?" Harlequin replied softly.

The capitano continued to frown and visibly struggled to follow the reasoning. "You don't appreciate my position," he whined.

Scapino was about to reply when Harlequin suddenly emitted a loud, overly dramatic sigh and moaned, "Alas! The lost ballade!"

Everyone turned to him. "What?" asked the capitano.

"I was just sighing," said Harlequin, "over the loss of the great ballade that someone—a grateful admirer for example—might have written of a certain brave capitano who, let us say, spurned the wealth of the rich overlords and shook the banner of his own integrity in their faces!"

It was obvious from the look on the capitano's face that the bait had been delicious. "A—a ballade?" he whispered.

"I can hear it now!" declared Harlequin. "A march!" Everyone was watching him now, mouths agape, and he turned abruptly and nudged Scapino in the belly and repeated significantly, "I can hear it now!" The juggler, enlightened, began to beat a military tattoo on the side of the wagon with his hands.

There are moments in history when a great man, inspired by the loftiest sentiments of mankind, instantly creates a work of lasting value and universal appeal.

This was not one of those moments.

Nevertheless Harlequin began to sing to the music of a well-known, bawdy drinking song of Genoa.

> "The captain rode into town.
> Into the town rode he.
> A-searching for a noble cause
> And to find his destiny.
> A lord, a man of monied pow'r,
> Offered him rich pay,
> Commanding, 'Come and take my coins,
> And be my slave today!' "

Scapino, Dottore, and Pantalone quickly framed a little three-part harmony and repeated the coda. "And be my slave toda-a-a-a-ay!"

Harlequin slipped an arm around the capitano's shoulder and sang softly into his ear.

> "But then the captain turned away!
> They found his virtue strong!
> To sell his soul for foolish gold
> Would surely be a wrong!
> And thus the captain spake the lord,
> 'My lordship, list to me:
> Not wealth nor fame can buy my soul;
> For I am strong and free!' "

With that Scapino, Dottore, and Pantalone chimed in once again to echo the last line, "For strong and free is he-e-e-e-e!"

Harlequin instantly launched into the refrain, pounding his hands together in tempo; and the other three joined him half a measure behind, creating a curious echo effect, which gave the impression that only Harlequin knew the words.

> "For I am strong, and I am proud,
> And I am as good as you;
> So I will join some merry band
> That's happy, free, and true!"

And they joined together in a four-part passage that repeated, "That's happy, free, and tru-u-ue!"

When they were done, and the last strident chord still resounded on the night air, they turned to look at the capitano, who was staring at them with his mouth open in complete and total wonderment.

"Well?" said Harlequin, pleased with the response.

"That," uttered the capitano slowly, "that—is—the biggest pile of manure I've encountered since I was assigned to the Milanese stables as a young recruit." The others were silent before him. "You insult me, gentlemen!" roared the capitano, gaining momentum. "Did you really think I would be deceived by such a blatantly contrived farce and permit myself to be duped by a quartet of braying jackasses?!" He began to pace the area angrily. "You're like all civilians," he continued. "You think because the military indulges in a profession you personally find repugnant and incomprehensible, we must be idiots! Only when someone is hurling arrows at you, and you need someone to defend you, do you look upon the professional soldier as having any dignity or worth!"

"You're right." Harlequin nodded. "I apologize. It was a stupid trick."

"I didn't say that!" snapped the capitano. "It was clever. It is what I would have done. But your error was in assuming I was not bright enough to see it for what it was: an attempt to play upon my vanity. That was your basic mistake, you see. There isn't a vain bone in my whole magnificent body!"

Harlequin smiled and nodded again.

"But I see now that none of the women in this assembly are safe with men of such poor judgment and low, unethical behavior. I will, therefore, go with you to Mantua to protect the ladies!"

Harlequin's only reply was a wide grin that matched the capitano's.

"Now"—the condottiere laughed, placing his arm across Harlequin's shoulders—"how did that refrain go again?"

*I*N THE PUBLIC SQUARE of Pesaro, the giant strongman and principal condottiere of Cesare Borgia, Michelotto Corella, forced the young soldier to his knees. The townspeople who were ordered to the square watched with a cold silence both the execution and the mercenaries.

"Piero Varano," intoned the Spanish monk who had just administered the last rites to the condemned, "you have betrayed your lord, Cesare Borgia, Duke of Valentinois, Captain General, and Gonfalonier of the Holy Roman Catholic Church. Your sentence is death."

The young officer said nothing, head lowered as if he were memorizing the pattern of the cobbles. Michelotto drew the knotted silk scarf from his belt, wound it around both hands, and quickly threw it over Varano's shoulders. As he tightened the garrote and the young man struggled for breath, the giant whispered in his ear, "I performed the same kindness for your father."

Within minutes Varano's lifeless body was released from the strangulating embrace and fell to the cobbled square. Four mercenaries stepped forward and carried the corpse into the small church nearby to await burial, and the others dispersed the grumbling townspeople.

It was an hour later when a monk ran screaming from the church to the strongman's quarters. "He lives!" the frightened cleric shrieked. "A miracle!"

Michelotto rose quickly and crossed to the church with two of his mercenaries. They found the young officer breathing, eyes opened. Drawing his dagger, the condottiere leaned over the unfortunate soldier, smiled, and said quietly, "What was not done at lunch will be done at supper." With that he pushed the blade into the gasping young man's chest and twisted it.

And then he did it again. And again.

There is a story that the monk who had reported the "miracle" to Michelotto, and thus brought about the termination of the young man's life, was later recognized by someone at Cagli, who spread the word to the other townspeople.

They cornered the frightened cleric in a corner of the duomo and tore him, screaming, to pieces.

*I*SABELLA WAS DRESSED in one of her most elaborate frocks for their initial entry into the city, and with Capitano leading the small caravan on his great war-horse, looking for all the world like a toy cavalryman, the company's arrival in Bologna did attract a potential audience.

They made certain that their procession wound through the Piazza della Mercanzia, where it attracted the attention of the merchants and their customers. Then they proceeded past the Torre degli Asinelli and the Torre Garisenda on the Strada Maggiore and the palazzos of the Bevilacqua and the Podesta, in case the nobility might be interested. Finally they placed their wagon in the shadow of the brick Palazzo Comunale on the Piazza Maggiore near the corner tower clock.

Apart from watching the dances of Colombina and Ruffiana, the juggling and acrobatics of Scapino, and the singing of Harlequin and Isabella to their own accompaniment on the lute, there was really nothing for Dottore or Capitano to do. This proved somewhat convenient, because it freed the former to attend Zephyr, Salvation, Death, and Destruction. The soldier took a position atop the cart with his hand cannons, where he was available for instant retaliation if audience disapproval reached a frenzy.

The young student population was not averse to the charms of the women, and the young ladies of the Bentivoglio court occasionally showed their appreciation for Scapino's juggling and Harlequin's romantic ballads with a *zecchino* or two.

The company found, to their surprise, that their combined efforts provided enough for warm lodging within the city and an occasional feast at the inns. Since the cold hand of winter had fallen upon the Emilia and the roads to the north remained under the control of the Este mercenaries, they extended their stay in Bologna.

It was during the Christmas season—when the universities closed, and the city became crowded with competing troupes of mummers and minstrels for carnival—that the handsomest young man in Italy stopped by to watch the performance of Harlequin's company.

That cold afternoon Isabella had attracted a small crowd by just standing near the stage preparing to sing, when she—and her fellow players—became aware that she was the concentrated focus of one exceptionally gorgeous young man with dark hair, dimpled chin, and bright, searching eyes.

He was dressed in a rich, brocaded tunic with balloon sleeves that were considered fashionable for young nobility. A jeweled dagger and a sword were suspended from his wide leather belt, which was studded in silver. Around his neck he wore an enameled medallion depicting an eagle in flight. This was not, Harlequin noted, the crest of any of the ancient families, so he reasoned that it had been commissioned and designed to the standards of a newly rich, middle-class family. He decided the handsome youth was probably the son of a prosperous merchant who had invested in the right cargo of the right trading vessel at the right time.

These "new nobles," as the more aristocratic lords and ladies referred to them, constituted a new class of citizen: frequently possessing as much or more wealth than the old and highly respected families but with little or none of their sophistication. Nevertheless they were so far above the general population in wealth and power that they were "nobility by comparison." In addition to endowing private schools, the merchant class could afford mercenary armies to protect their goods and warehouses, so they had become a political power as well.

The handsome youth watched Colombina's dance with gracious admiration and threw her a florin. Scapino's acrobatic juggling of eight fire sticks drew vigorous applause, whistles, and two florins. Ruffiana's dance elicited a barbaric display of hoots and a *zecchino*. And Harlequin's songs were met with a quiet approval and two gold ducats. Isabella's song drew three ducats.

After the initial performance of the afternoon, Harlequin counted the money—most of which was directly attributable to the young gentleman—and was approached by that youth, who said simply, "Do more!"

"I beg your pardon?" said Harlequin.

"Do more!" he repeated. "Do it all!"

Dottore and Isabella joined Harlequin. "All?" he asked.

"The rest," insisted the young man. "You know, like the other mummers! Swallow fire! Dive through a ring of knives!" He tossed Harlequin another *zecchino*. "I have money!"

Harlequin fingered the coin. "That would be cheating you," he said. "Any flexible youth can leap through a ring of knives if the lady's husband is close behind him! Every drunken peasant swallows fire daily! My tricks are more elaborate. They are mystifying!" He leaned toward the youth and whispered, "I can make things disappear!"

"What things?"

"Like—*zecchinos*." Harlequin smiled as he flipped the coin to Scapino and roared, "Food!" The juggler instantly bolted up the side street to the merchants' stalls. "Thank you. Thank you," Harlequin said as he pretended to bow in all directions to the imaginary audience.

Instead of being offended, the youth simply grinned and turned to Isabella and Dottore. "What of these others?" he said. Then he pointed to Isabella. "I know she sings. What else does she do?"

Harlequin said softly, "What does she look like she might do?" Then he added quickly, "And you're probably wrong."

"I don't know," admitted the young man. "She looks like a lady."

"Precisely!" confirmed Harlequin. "She ladies!" He quickly wheeled on Isabella and called, "Lady something for the young gentleman."

"Do what?" said Isabella.

"Curtsy," said Harlequin.

"Curtsy?"

"Bow!"

"Bow?"

"Stop barking and curtsy!" snapped Harlequin. "Ladies curtsy, don't they? Curtsy!"

Whereupon Isabella drew her right foot back, and extending her elegant gown on either side, she executed a low curtsy to the young man, partially revealing in the process a suggestion of admirable breasts.

"Ah, very beautiful," mumbled the lad, "but, ah, hardly what I might—I mean—well, they—she is magnificent, but—that—is hardly, ah, spectacular."

"Ah, well," said Harlequin, dismissing Isabella with a wave of his hand, "like most women she ladies by day and spectaculars by night."

Isabella backed away and tried to hide her laughter with one delicate hand, and the young man turned his attention to Dottore. "What about him?" he asked.

"Yes!" responded Harlequin. "Isn't he? I'll bet you've never seen one of *them* before!"

"What is them? Are them? Those?" Exasperated, the youth whined, "What does *he* do?"

"What does he look as though he might do? And this time you're probably right."

"He looks like—I don't know—like my teacher at the university. He looks like—a scholar, perhaps."

"Magnificent!" Harlequin exploded. "What insight! You are an exceptional young man! Indeed he *is* a scholar! The prince of scholars!" He turned quickly to Dottore.

"Scholar the young gentleman something."

What Dottore produced was a directory of pithy Latin phrases suitable for funeral statuary beginning with *Solitudinem faciunt, pacem appellant* and ending with *Hic habitat felicitas!*

Harlequin looked surprised at the final quotation and whispered to Dottore, "Here dwells happiness?"

"I saw it above the door of a brothel in Bergamo," the doctor whispered.

Harlequin grinned and then turned to the young man. "Bravo! Isn't he worth the price of your gold all by himself?!"

"But—I don't understand," stammered the youth.

"No." Harlequin smiled. "*You* understand perfectly. *He's* the one who doesn't understand, but he pretends to! That's the jest, you see?"

"No, not exactly."

"Excellent!" Harlequin exclaimed as he pounded the young man on the back. "The difference between art and craft is the degree of understanding. The less you understand, the greater the art!"

"Ah." The youth beamed. "*Now* I see!"

"Oh, don't do that," groaned Harlequin as he again put an arm around the young man's shoulders and led him farther apart from the others. "The moment you see, you cease to be an audience and become a comedian."

The youth echoed, "Comedian?"

"That's our gift and our profession," added Harlequin. "We see everything! The hypocrisy behind the platitude! The treachery behind the smile and the outstretched hand! Everything!"

"Is that what you are? *Commediani?*"

"Did I say that?" Harlequin mused. Then he shrugged and said, "Well, why not?"

"What does that mean? Comedian?"

"What do you think it means?" replied Harlequin as Colombina crossed to them.

"Isn't he adorable?" Colombina smiled. "He has thousands of answers like that."

"Well," muttered the boy, "in the vulgar tongue—"

"Oooooo," squealed Ruffiana as she and the others joined the trio, "I adore a vulgar tongue!" The company laughed.

"In—the—vulgar tongue," continued the embarrassed youth as he looked around at what he now considered to be an array of escaped lunatics, "it means 'story.' So. I guess it means—you—do—stories?"

"Perfect!" cheered Harlequin. The others applauded.

The boy beamed at having been correct. "Then—tell me a funny story!"

"You're in the middle of one." Harlequin laughed. He gestured around the small circle. "We are all an illusion." He pointed to Dottore. "You don't really think this man is a scholar, do you? Observe the drooping nose, the eyes on loan from a dead fish. Does that face reflect mental alertness? Wisdom? Knowledge? No!" The others began to laugh, and Harlequin, encouraged, rambled on. "And yet!" he declared. "The supreme jest! He does speak Latin, Greek, and Polavian!"

The young man frowned. "I never heard of Polavian."

"Do you speak Greek?"

"No," murmured the young man.

"Then why should you be acquainted with Polavian? It's all Greek to you!" roared Harlequin.

"That," whispered Dottore, "is a very old joke."

"If I say he speaks Polavian, believe!" Harlequin rolled on. "He also speaks Marovich, Broko, Slamili, and Jogg!"

The youth slowly smiled. "You made that up!"

"Of course!" boomed Harlequin. "That's our art! We make up things!"

"*Commedia al'improviso!*" Dottore proclaimed.

Harlequin, relenting, then said quite calmly and evenly, "What's your name, son?"

"Tristano," the boy replied. "Tristano Remigio."

"Signore Remigio, you must forgive our little, innocent moment of hysteria just now. We have been performing all afternoon, and we are in need of food and drink, and while we appreciate your generous donations, our wealth is decidedly limited. So your rewards have made us giddy."

"Where are you going from here?" he asked.

"Mantua. As soon as the weather—and the Este—clear the way."

"Take me with you."

Harlequin studied Tristano for a moment. "Why?"

"Because I'm bored. Because I want to go somewhere else. Any-where." Then, after a moment, he spoke softly. "Everyone says there will soon be a conscription of all young males for the armies of the Bentivoglio. I am not militarily minded. Besides," he said brightly, "I want to be a comedian."

Harlequin sighed and put his hand on the boy's shoulder. "Tristano, my son, forgive me, but everything I just told you was a lie. Well, not totally a lie, but most certainly an imaginative embel-lishment of the truth." He softened his voice. "There is no such thing as a troupe of *commediani*. There is no such art such as the *commedia al'improviso*. We are not a group of individuals who go about the country making things up."

"But—but those terms? Those expressions?"

Harlequin became irritated. "I made them up!"

The young man beamed.

Harlequin laughed a little at the absurdity and then apologized. "I was having—a little jest—at your expense, I'm afraid, which is ungrateful of me. But you believed it, which is gullible of you. So, let us say, we gave you a small education in return for your gold."

Tristano looked at the assembly. "Well," he joked, "that's a better return than I'm getting at the university." He paused, and his grin widened. "As for your problem, I can get you all the food and drink you need: wine, cheeses, smoked meat, bread, everything. And flour and dried fish. Everything."

They moved closer to him then, and Harlequin said softly, "Now, lad, one poor jest does not deserve another. I told you our finances were—limited."

"I can get you all these things without any cost to you at all," said the boy.

Tristano disappeared in the middle of the encircling company as he explained the situation to them, and the twilight descended.

*T*RISTANO TOLD THEM about Signore Poliosco, the Mad Merchant of Bologna. Of the two hundred warehouses in or around the city, eighty-five were Poliosco's, and in these warehouses were everything that the company needed.

The merchant had wasted most of his youth making purchases and selling goods at considerable profit until—suddenly as it were—he was eighty. There had never been a woman in his life—which, he said, was the principal reason he had reached that venerable age with most of his wealth intact. But now he found himself a bearded, bent old man with no one to share all his lovely gold and jewels. He had begun to accept his own mortality, and considered that perhaps he should have been more generous with others. So now, Tristano told them, the mad merchant had looked around and settled on someone who would be his heir. Tristano, a nephew, was his choice.

From that day on, Tristano, himself the son of the wine merchant Remigio, was guaranteed an additional fortune upon the death of Signore Poliosco. As if that future wealth were not enough, anything Tristano wanted now, Poliosco provided. With this youth he was as generous and beneficent as he had been grasping, ruthless, and unscrupulous with others. And so Tristano promised to ask his patron to supply their needs as a personal favor to him, and took his leave of the company.

He sent word later that evening that the merchant had agreed, after some haggling, personally to oversee the transfer of goods. They should wait for the elderly gentleman that evening at the Via Due Madonne, near the Via Emilia.

*A*T THE APPOINTED TIME Harlequin, Dottore, Pantalone, and Scapino waited patiently for the old man to appear. Isabella and Colombina were at the reins of the wagon, and Ruffiana drove the cart. The capitano, excused from labor because of his wounds, but willingly serving as sentinel, sat astride Zephyr

Soon they heard a curious clip-clop and saw the flickering light of a torch coming toward them. They were not prepared for someone quite so old, so bent, so obviously near death's door. Signore Poliosco, in a fur and hooded cape to keep out the chill, looked to be a hundred and fifty. He did not so much walk as perform a jiggling trot, scissoring his legs a few centimeters forward at a time like a toy doll, without bending his knees. When he spoke, it was a rasping wheeze of an exhalation that reverberated through the air as though he were forcing each word through his blackened teeth and receding gums without parting his lips.

He was accompanied by a frightened young boy carrying a torch. "He is afraid," the old man explained, "of the *rascali*, Bologna's cutthroats, who operate in this vicinity. But I told him there were a great many of us, so he would be protected." He placed one wrinkled, gnarled hand on the boy's head and looked at the ragged leader of the company. "Are you the one called Harlequin?" he rasped.

Harlequin nodded. "Yes, I am, Signore Poliosco."

"You're confused!" the old man shouted. "*I* am Signore Poliosco! *You* must be Signore Harlequin!" He turned away, mumbling, "Ridiculous name. Well, Tristano has asked me to help you, and I cannot refuse that handsome young man anything. He is the son I never had. Yes. Yes. Well, follow me!" he wheezed. "Follow me!" And with that he creaked down a passageway barely wide enough for the wagon to follow.

"That man is too old," whispered Pantalone.

"For what?" Harlequin snapped.

"To be so old," Pantalone said.

The old man sets a vigorous pace for all his years, Harlequin thought, *or perhaps he is genuinely frightened of the* rascali *and wants to complete his business and retire for the evening.*

Following Signore Poliosco with their two vehicles, they soon came to a somewhat open area where a large storehouse was set back about two meters from the surrounding houses. A pair of large wooden doors, barred with a heavy log, guarded the entrance, and two armed mercenaries stood watching with curiosity and suspicion the small group approaching them. Harlequin noticed that they wore the crest of the hawk—an emblem also mounted above the large wooden doors.

"Open up! Open up!" called the old man as he ambled toward the mercenaries. "These good people need supplies, and I want to get home to bed!"

"Slowly, old man." One mercenary smiled.

Harlequin had never seen such a transformation.

"Old man? Old man!" screeched the merchant. "Is that the way to address your employer? This is what I get for hiring renegade ruffians to guard my storehouses! You've been drinking again, haven't you, you ignorant Neapolitan!" And suddenly Signore Poliosco flipped the heavy, silver-topped cane in his right hand and swung it, handle first, up between the mercenary's legs and into his crotch.

The poor soldier buckled over in pain and surprise, and the elderly merchant started toward the other mercenary, swinging the cane in vicious swipes that sent him fleeing up the passageway. "Stupid animals!" rasped Signore Poliosco. "If I didn't have so many storehouses, I'd be able to check them all now and again and see what kind of imbeciles my clerks hire as guards!" He turned and gestured to Pantalone. "Well, don't just stand there, you adolescent ape! Open up! Open up!" They quickly drew back the great log that barred the doors and swung them open. "Inside! Inside!" the old man urged the boy carrying his torch.

They lit other torches after entering the high-ceilinged room piled high with crates, hogsheads, barrels, casks, boxes, baskets, and huge logs of cheese and bologna and spiced meats. "This one!" the merchant snapped as he struck at a specific cask with his cane. "And this one!" And he struck another.

For the next quarter hour Harlequin, Capitano, Pantalone, Scapino, and Dottore were kept busy running back and forth with the stock until they had more than enough, and the old man was still striking an occasional crate and cackling, "This one!" After they convinced Signore Poliosco that they were satisfied, they extinguished the torches, and the old man dismissed the boy, saying,

"I'll ride back with these people! Now run quickly and go straight home!" And his helper bolted.

They were moving through the streets and small piazzas when suddenly the capitano galloped up beside the wagon and reported, "We're being followed."

"*Rascali!*" keened the merchant in terror. "*Rascali!*"

They broke into a small piazza and turned back to see a dozen strong young men running toward them, carrying torches, drawn swords, and daggers. Capitano wheeled Zephyr around and charged into the pack with his own sword raised high. As with most mercenaries who have nothing personally to gain by fighting and dying, the youths scattered around the piazza. Harlequin leaped to the cobbles and quickly executed a series of short turns that sent two attackers flying. He picked up the torch from one of the bandits and used it against another, who went screaming and flaming into the communal fountain.

He watched with pride as his principal protégé, Scapino, performed an awesome sequence of cartwheels, leaps, pivots, and smoothly effortless maneuvers—although he infrequently hit anyone. Pantalone, on the other hand, kicked, bit, and stomped until the enemy was strewn about the piazza mourning their cracked skulls and bleeding noses. Harlequin noted that even Dottore had defended himself quite capably with the old man's cane.

When he determined that the fight was gone from the *rascali,* Harlequin climbed back up beside his benefactor, who was smiling and nodding, and said, "It's safe now, Signore Poliosco. Where shall I take you?"

"Mantua," ordered the mad merchant of Bologna.

Then Harlequin stared in dumb astonishment as Signore Poliosco literally tore at his face until a handsome, much younger face appeared beneath the false beard and eyebrows and nose. "I suggest we hurry," said Tristano. "We have just robbed the main storehouse of my father, and he isn't going to be happy about the way you treated his servants."

"I told you he was too old to be that old!" Pantalone piped.

"But—the mad merchant, Signore Poliosco?" stammered Harlequin. "And—the *rascali?*"

"I made it all up! *Commedia al'improviso!*" shouted Tristano. "*Now* can I be a comedian?"

$\mathcal{T}$HEY RACED from Bologna down the east road to Budrio on the south bank of the Reno. The assembly now consisted of a mysterious vagabond who may or may not have been a Swiss mercenary; a frustrated dancer who imagined herself the personification of the Great Earth Mother; an occasional whore who spent most of her time trying to educate herself and end her physical relationship with Pantalone; a pretty purveyor of pornography—at least in the eyes of the hypocrite; an incompetent painter with a gift for healing; an ambitious and imaginative liar and thief who sometimes juggled; his lecherous bastard son on quest for the ultimate sexual experience; a disgraced warrior with a stolen horse and modern weapons; and the most handsome young man in Italy, who had just robbed his own father.

The communion of wayward saints was complete.

PART TWO

The Art

THE COMPANY ATTEMPTS TO
SOLVE THEIR DIFFICULTIES
AND CREATE A NEW THEATER OF
THE PEOPLE
THAT IS IRREVERENT,
BAWDY, SATIRIC,
ANTIMILITARY, ANTICLERICAL,
AND POPULAR.

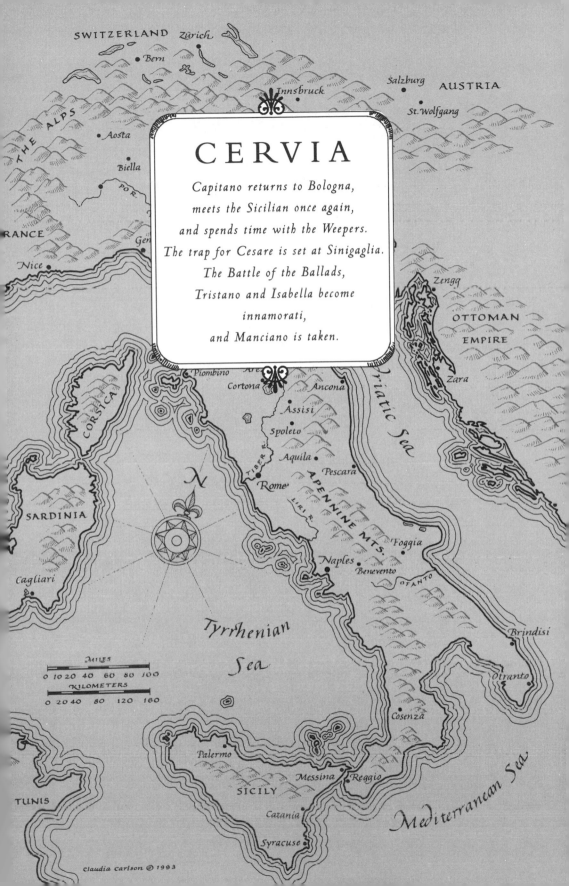

CERVIA

Capitano returns to Bologna,
meets the Sicilian once again,
and spends time with the Weepers.
The trap for Cesare is set at Sinigaglia.
The Battle of the Ballads,
Tristano and Isabella become
innamorati,
and Manciano is taken.

SWITZERLAND Zürich
Bern
THE ALPS
Aosta
Biella
Innsbruck
Salzburg AUSTRIA
St. Wolfgang
Zengg
OTTOMAN
EMPIRE
Zara
PO R.
RANCE
Nice
Ge
Piombino Are
Cortona Ancona
Assisi
Spoleto
Aquila
TIBER
Rome
Pescara
APENNINE MTS.
LIRI R.
Foggia
Naples
Benevento
OTANTO
Adriatic Sea
CORSICA
N
SARDINIA
Cagliari
Tyrrhenian
Sea
Brindisi
Otranto
MILES
0 10 20 40 60 80 100
KILOMETERS
0 20 40 80 120 160
Cosenza
Palermo
Messina Reggio
SICILY
Mediterranean Sea
TUNIS
Catania
Syracuse

claudia carlson © 1993

It was immediately evident that Tristano had presented the company with a mixed collection of items from his father's storehouse. In his disguise as Poliosco he actually had no idea what was contained in the numerous crates, barrels, boxes, and sacks he marked for removal; and as a result, the company now possessed a wide assortment of cheeses, smoked meats, and assorted wines, as well as forty eating knives, twelve basins, three sets of chain mail, a keg of nails, a hand loom, a churn, and a variety of half masks and grotesque costumes intended for the use of the guildsmen during carnival.

Their first campsite upon leaving Bologna was less than fifteen kilometers from the city. It was here that Harlequin informed the capitano that he was sending him back to the city to repay Tristano's father for raiding their storehouse.

"You want him to do *what*?" asked Tristano.

"To take these remaining gems to Bologna and try to get them to your father, for stealing from him," Harlequin explained patiently for the fourth time.

"But why?" complained the handsome young man. "My father has dozens of other storehouses. He can afford to lose a few items!"

"Because—despite appearances and our unfortunate tendency to acquire things that do not belong to us—we are not thieves."

"Speak for yourself!" snapped the capitano. "That's not my horse, and this is not my sword. These are not my pistols, and if I could have gotten the scabbard of the officer I killed to get it, I would have taken that, too!"

"You were struggling for your life. It was a question of survival."

"So is this!" said Isabella. "Those are the last of my gems!"

"We will survive."

"Easter will follow Christmas, too, but the time between can be an agony if we have no money," the capitano said as he paced alongside the wagons.

"Besides," argued Isabella, "the gems themselves were stolen from someone by the Sultan of Constantinople, you may swear to that. And even *that* someone had stolen them from someone else."

Scapino felt obligated to continue the debate. "The lords of Italy steal from the poor and from each other. The Church steals from the lords and from the poor, don't they—when they sell indulgences and dispensations and cardinals' hats?"

Dottore chimed in. "Historically the first man raped and pillaged the quiet earth to build himself shelters and keep himself warm. We are all thieves. We steal wood from the forest. Fish from the rivers. Time. We steal all we can."

Harlequin admired this rhetoric. "A splendid argument, Dottore. Worthy of the Curia. But it doesn't alter the truth. We took something belonging to another, and we must repay him."

The capitano studied the bizarrely dressed man for a moment, and then he smiled. "How do you know I won't take the gems and keep riding?"

Harlequin laughed. "Where? And why? You could have left us to die at the hands of the renegade mercenaries, but you didn't."

"I had considered it. Only an idiot charges on the first information he receives." He took their leader by the arm and led him apart from the others. "I had to study the situation, decide how my two pistols might work to maximum advantage." He smiled again. "But," he whispered, "by that time Colombina was totally naked and was performing what looked like some orgiastic ritual. The men were absolutely fascinated, so I thought I might as well watch for a while."

Harlequin returned the smile. "Capitano," he said, "for all your perversions, I think you have the stuff of heroes in you."

"Do you?" The capitano grinned. "Well, in the spirit of openness, let me tell you a secret: two of the dead renegades you found in the woods were not my work. Somebody else killed them."

Harlequin immediately became serious. "Three."

"You knew?"

He nodded. "They died by arrows. You had no crossbow. Someone else had to have killed them, so someone else must have been in the woods watching us."

The soldier agreed. "There were three or four of them. I wasn't aware of them until I fired the pistols and started the operation. Then, afterward, they disappeared as quickly as they came."

Harlequin placed a hand on his shoulder. "We know now that the renegades weren't *landsknecht* at all, but mercenaries of the Cardinal of Modena, so our rescuers might have been enemies of Ferrari."

"Perhaps," said the capitano. "We can also reason that they were really not interested in the paintings or the statues, yet they were obviously looking for *something*. What do you make of that?"

Harlequin shrugged. "I have no idea." Then he added softly, "Do you?"

"I don't make such decisions. I have all I can do to survive. And I always survive."

"So will we all," Harlequin said quietly.

They returned to the others, and Harlequin proposed to move the company farther east immediately. "We can't turn north to Mantua because there is some sort of small war going on just above us between the Este and the papacy. We can't go south because Cesare Borgia is in Imola just below us and waging war in the Romagna. And we can't go back to Bologna because Tristano's father must have surely brought the theft of his goods to the attention of his lord, the Bentivoglio. So it appears that we are in some small corridor of peace between warring factions, and the only road open to us is continually eastward. The capitano should be able to join us before we reach Lugo, since he is riding the fastest of our horses."

And so, within the hour, the capitano prepared to return to Bologna, but before he did, Dottore sought him out and pressed a small gift in his hands with hurried instructions. Later, when the capitano examined the items as Zephyr drank from the river, he found that his gifts included two blue-green vials and a heavy, curious ring containing a yellow powder.

"Aha," rejoiced the courier. "The mad physician strikes again."

*T*HE COMPANY CONTINUED EAST to Medicina and Lugo. Approaching Bagnacavallo, they soon learned that Tristano, in addition to his physical beauty, was an accomplished musician and poet. He appeared to have been trained in all the courtly skills without any of the ancestral history necessary to keep such graces in perspective.

In other words, he often appeared—to some—to be pompous and affected.

Save to Ruffiana, who lost her heart to his handsome profile almost at once.

And he, oddly enough, scorned the beautiful Isabella for the vitality and animality of the young wench and rode beside her whenever possible.

Pantalone, of course, did not take too kindly to this turn of events, since he still held Ruffiana to their "business" arrangement. There had been very few opportunities to demand compliance, because there was a quiet conspiracy among the company members to protect Ruffiana and to keep Pantalone too busy for sport. Nevertheless he kept an account ledger full of black marks—since he could not write—indicating the number of "favors" she owed him.

He was also disappointed that no one had believed him when he had instantly recognized a flaw in Tristano's portrait of the ancient Bolognese merchant.

The youngest member of the company dreamed of revenge.

Soon after departing Budrio, the company also discovered Tristano's excellent singing voice. The young man had begun to strum Colombina's lute and sing to Ruffiana, beside him in the wagon. It was a ballad of his own creation.

> "I sing of roses. One is red,
> The wanton of the flower bed.
> Her scarlet petals shower down
> On soft or hard or stony ground.
> All passing breezes kiss her blooms.
> Hers is the passion that consumes.
> I sing of roses. One is white.
> She only blossoms in my sight.
> Her special fragrance fills the air

When only I am standing there.
Another's touch decays and kills.
Hers is the passion that fulfills.
If red is Lilith, white is Eve.
If white is true, must red deceive?
Should Adam have to choose of two,
Which would he pick? And which would you?"

The song was met with bright response from Colombina, Dottore, and of course, Ruffiana. But shortly after, the sound of Scapino's raspy voice rose from the cart where he rode beside Isabella. His song was old and widely cherished among the denizens of tavern and inn when the Roman legions still ruled Italy.

"Oh Rosamarie, come lie with me
Beneath the shadowy linden tree,
Where not a single soul can see
How I do you or you do me.
Undo your blouse and let me sip
Of milky breast and honeyed lip.
Come lift your skirts and let me know
Those silky secrets kept below,
Above your knees, between your thighs,
And you may watch my manhood rise."

Isabella emitted a high-pitched cackle, and Scapino droned on happily.

"Come, let my ship drop anchor in
Your dark, secluded bay of sin,
And let the tidal ebb and flow
Of lust and laughter come and go.
Come, let the naughty nectars ooze
Down both our legs into our shoes,
Beneath our heels, between our toes,
While something strong between us grows."

"Disgusting." Ruffiana sniffed. Tristano agreed, and they began a second chorus of Tristano's ballad.

As if in reply, Isabella's voice joined Scapino's for a reprise of *their* song.

> "Oh, Rosamarie, come lie with me
> Beneath the shadowy linden tree,
> Where not a single soul can see
> How I do you or you do me."

"Well," muttered Harlequin, "they say music is the speech of angels." Then he smiled and added, "I assume that includes the fallen ones."

VITELLOZZO VITELLI, suffering the ravages of syphilis, leaned across the table and spoke softly but firmly to his fellow conspirators.

"I tell you, Cesare is in trouble. He has appealed to his father three times in one month to send him more money. He had to send to Venice for wheat, but Ramiro de Lorca, who is now with us, resold most of it." He gestured then to the unsmiling Spaniard seated beside him. "So Cesare cannot afford to feed his men. He is planning to dismiss three French companies and send them to Lombardy, which will leave him with only one hundred men. He believes we are loyal to him once again, and to show his faith in us, he has asked the Orsini and me to take Sinigaglia for him."

Oliveretto Eufreducci inquired, "Sinigaglia? Why Sinigaglia?"

"Because Sinigaglia is held by Giovanna da Montefeltro in the name of her son, Francesco Maria della Rovere, who is also Guidobaldo's nephew. With one blow, Cesare can strike at three enemies, and especially at the man he considers his principal enemy—Cardinal della Rovere."

He began to cough, and it took him some time to recover his breath. "But the point is this: Cesare has only a small force. We take Sinigaglia for him, but we send de Lorca to Cesare with the story that the defender, Andrea Doria, will only surrender the arsenal and supplies to him—personally. He will have to come, because he needs the grain and the weapons."

Vitelli moaned and adjusted himself in the plush chair. "The Orsini mercenaries and my own forces will encamp outside the town itself. Oliveretto here will keep his men within the citadel. We wait until Cesare is between us, and then we snap the trap on him."

There was a moment of silence, and the five conspirators looked at one another. Finally Oliveretto smiled and said, "Let's do it. Let's kill the Borgia bastard."

Vitelli watched as, one by one, the condottieri nodded approval. Then he turned to Ramiro de Lorca, seated beside him, and said, "Tell him. We'll await him in Sinigaglia."

*T*HE THIN, bleeding remnant of the young cleric hung suspended about four meters above the damp, earthern floor covered with blood-soaked rushes. His arms were drawn behind him, tied to a long rope that traced a path to the high ceiling, through a pulley, and back again. Two black-hooded men held him there, a broken man, his arms useless things no longer connected with his body.

Before this whimpering wreckage stood the ferret-faced cleric, Sebastiano, and beside him, the mercenary named Angelo.

"It was a method much prized during the French Inquisition," said Sebastiano, "first used, I am told, upon Jacques de Molay of the Knights Templar. Effective. After one or two falls, when the arms are torn from the sockets, a confession is always made."

"Was it necessary?" growled Angelo. "When you salted his old wounds, he told us everything he knew about Manciano."

"How can we be certain he told everything?" countered Sebastiano. "He confessed to a knowledge of the Savelli letters, and he admitted that they are being carried by a priest; but he has not told us whether that priest is the leader of the *piagnoni*, Manciano, or someone else."

"I believe he told us all he knows," persisted the mercenary.

"For one thing," Sebastiano continued, "I believe he knows who the third force in the Modena woods was. He could tell us who these others were that drove the cardinal's men from their encampment."

Angelo snorted. "You persist in linking the fugitives with the Savelli letters. But the mercenaries raided their encampment and found no letters."

"Then is it mere coincidence that Manciano appeared in three different cities at the same time as the fugitive caravan?" snapped Sebastiano. "Is it by chance that Manciano and this one shared a meal with the vagabonds outside Bologna? I tell you, someone in that fugitive group is linked to the *piagnoni*, and the *piagnoni* have control of the Savelli letters!" He gestured to the hooded torturers. "Well, we'll let him rest awhile, and then resume the questioning. He will tell us everything he remembers—before he dies."

The hooded men lowered the groaning, bloodied form to the floor and began to untie the ropes that bound him. Angelo watched them intently. "Why do they wear those hoods? Who can see them down here?"

The ferret-faced priest shrugged. "Who can tell? In these times even the wind entering through those small windows carries secrets. Besides," he said as the other men left the room, "their vow is to serve God, and to God only need their identities be known."

Angelo crossed to the side of the tortured priest and bent over him. "It also prevents reprisals," Sebastiano continued, "which is a continual hazard in their line of business."

In the dark corner of the room no one saw the thin blade of the stiletto slip silently and quickly into the man's heart, then Angelo rose slowly and turned to his companion, who was now seated behind a plain table in the opposite corner of the room. "You'll get no more from him, I'm afraid," said the mercenary. "He's dead."

"Dead?"

Angelo shrugged. "What does it matter? If you believe there is some sort of conspiracy here between these vagabonds and Manciano, why not just capture Manciano and find out?"

"Because the damned Dominican is smoke!" snapped Sebastiano. "I think I have him cornered in a church, and when my men enter, the place is empty! My agents see him on the street, and when they block off the passage, they turn the corner and no one is there! We only managed to catch this pitiful youth because he mistook one of my agents for a Weeper."

Angelo suggested, "It's possible the Weepers do have agents among your own. Perhaps that is how Manciano escapes you. He is warned by one of your own."

"It is possible. But it also works the other way. The duke has agents among the Weepers. One has to be very, very careful to whom we confide anything these days." The mercenary nodded and quietly slipped his stiletto back in its sheath unnoticed. "The point remains that the duke has entrusted us with the recovery of the letters before they reach his enemies, and that is what we will do," said Sebastiano. "Now go and get some men to see to the disposal of our young clerical friend."

Angelo left the room as the dark friar began to write upon a parchment at the table.

Sebastiano wrote in a quick scrawl, stopping only now and again to dip his pen into a vial of black ink. Finally he placed the pen aside and squinted to read the message by the flickering light of the candle.

To His Grace, Cesare Borgia, Duke of Valentinois.

We now have proof that the Savelli letters are being carried south by a priest—possibly to present them to the French or the Spanish in Naples, which would discredit the Borgias with the Catholic monarchies. There is also some mystery surrounding a group of travelers who seem to have had contact with Manciano. Reports seem to indicate that one of the group could be Isabella Zappachio of Venice. What are your instructions?

Your servant,
Alphonse Sebastiano.

He then placed the parchment to one side, selected a new sheet, and took up the pen again. First, he copied the salutation in fine, precise letters. Then he unrolled still another parchment and placed it beside the others. It contained six columns of letters, the first being a listing of letters in alphabetical order. He took up the first page and began to inscribe letters one by one above those in his original message. He concentrated upon the instructions he had been given about preparing coded messages.

The first line of your message will utilize the substitute letters of the second column. The second line of the message will use the letters of the third column, and so forth. Once transcribed in code, divide all the letters into blocks of six letters each. This will destroy any familiar word patterns, and also establish that you are using the six-column code.

It took Sebastiano half an hour to finish his coding, which he then transferred to the second parchment. Finally he folded the letter, dripped wax from the candle onto it, and turning the ring on his finger, sealed the document with the crest of the bull.

He carried the letter upstairs to the sacristy of the duomo and presented it to a young man waiting by the door. The young man mounted a black horse outside the church and directed the animal south.

At the village of Faenza, the messenger dismounted, climbed the steps of a small church, and handed the document to an ancient friar who waited there. The cleric took the parchment into a small room, where he slid the fine, narrow blade of a dagger under the wax and lifted it cleanly away from the parchment. He glanced at the contents, smiling at the apparently meaningless blocks of letters. He then took a piece of thin paper that he had been treating, rubbed it against the message, and removed it. The letters were now faintly traced in reverse on the special paper. The friar refolded the parchment, pinched a small piece of hot wax from the candle, rubbed it on the reverse of the seal, and pressed down tightly. Satisfied with his work after a quick examination, he returned the revealed document to the young man.

"In code?" asked the messenger.

"Barely. Letter substitution. Six-column format. Probably also a six-digit deviation between columns. It should take me about a quarter hour." The cleric chuckled. "Borgias are such children. Not like the old days when Paul the Second wrote in Greek, and we coded his messages using a numerical substitution that was spelled out in the *spaces* between meaningless symbols. Drove half the College of Cardinals insane."

The young man laughed, remounted the black horse, and headed north.

THE COMPANY HAD SKIRTED RAVENNA and approached the Adriatic with still no word of the capitano. They drifted into the small town of Cervia, where they decided they would wait, but the monotony and the gloomy premise that he might not return made them all agitated and fearful.

On their third day in the slumbering town, Harlequin's reaction to a proposal by Colombina was predictable.

"Sweet God in heaven, I shall drink myself into a quiet oblivion when I finally rid myself of this band of parasites." Harlequin sighed for the third time. "Haven't we enough trouble? Why can't we at least have peace among ourselves?"

Colombina pursued him around the wagon. "You say our best masquerade is to pose as a troupe of mummers, but half the company does nothing! Ruffiana and I can dance at least, and you sing and play instruments—"

"So do Tristano and Isabella," he countered, "and better than I do."

"Who needs so many musicians? We have only one lute, a tambourine, and the nakers that Pantalone picked up in Bologna. Scapino can juggle and do acrobatic tricks with Pantalone, and Dottore has about mastered that trick of breathing fire that Maestro Leonardo explained to him."

"Oh?" said Harlequin with surprise. "His tongue has healed, has it?"

Colombina sniffed. "It was only scorched." Harlequin grinned. "The point," she persisted, "is that our performance lacks romance. I say, let Tristano and Isabella try playing lovers in some sort of entertainment."

"What sort of entertainment? A play? Something religious? What?"

"Godsblood, we have enough of religion! Something romantic!" shrilled Colombina. "I tell you, people will pay to see them together! Two magnificent, beautiful young people in love! Everyone will be touched and delighted."

"They cannot stand one another," Harlequin reminded her.

"It doesn't matter what they *feel*." She waved his objection away. "They *look* like lovers! I imagine Abelard and Héloïse occasionally had problems—especially after he was castrated." Harlequin groaned. "Look," Colombina nagged. "Let them try. Make up something for them like you told Tristano you could do. Suggest a story, and let them improvise around it!"

"Sweet Jesus," muttered Harlequin, "why does that one ridiculous moment in my past keep resurrecting to haunt me? I told you there is no such art. Art demands discipline, and discipline requires written texts where language is sharpened with precision and order. God knows what would happen if performers were free to do and say anything they wanted to do. It would be bedlam!"

"It wasn't bedlam the night we did that St. George and the Dragon thing, and you know it! You were surprised how it made us laugh! It was funny!"

"It was silly!" snapped Harlequin. "Ridiculous! No!" He moved farther around the wagon, but was still pursued by Colombina. "All right!" he capitulated. "If you insist that they play lovers, then let us pick something from classical literature, write texts, and let them memorize their parts. Then we shall see."

She stopped in midattack. "Godsblood, must you *work* at everything? Romance can't be plotted! It just *is*! I see Tristano and Isabella as lovers! Not as Roman gods!"

Harlequin emitted one final, surrendering sigh. "All right," he repeated.

Colombina smiled and lightly patted his bearded cheek. "That's a love," she cooed.

Harlequin bit his thumb at her when she turned away from him and came around the opposite side of the wagon, where the company was seated by the fire, busily delousing one another. One by one the tiny vermin were searched out and removed from hair, skin, clothing, and more secret places and deposited in the several pots of hot water.

"Tristano! Isabella!" he called. "Come with me!"

They left the sides of their respective lovers and stepped forth. "Since traveling as a troupe of mummers seems an appropriate disguise for ourselves," he began softly, "I have decided to try—well—an improvisational piece as part of our entertainment." Then, very quickly, he added, "I would like you two—to pretend to be, ah, lovers."

Tristano looked as though he had been hit in the groin with a pike, and Isabella hooted. "Indulge me," Harlequin said. "I will give you a situation, and you make up your own words and actions, eh? Something—oh, I don't know—romantic—funny—or something."

Tristano whispered, "You're mad, you know."

Harlequin nodded quietly, "Yes, but do this one thing for me, and I promise not to bother you for the remainder of our journey. Eh?"

The young Bolognese looked at Isabella, who shrugged without interest. "All right," he agreed.

"Fine," Harlequin said. "Now, here is the situation. You are lovers. Clear?" They nodded. "But Isabella has discovered that you—Tristano—have been sleeping with—I don't know—a handmaid or someone."

"What kind of a handmaid?" asked Tristano.

"What kind?" snorted Harlequin. "How many kinds are there? Just a handmaid!"

"I mean, is she pretty or a little—you know—unattractive?" he asked.

"Idiot!" snapped Isabella. "I wouldn't have an unattractive handmaid!"

Tristano sniffed. "Certainly you would have unattractive hand-maids. They would make you look beautiful by comparison."

Isabella's eyes flashed. "I *am* beautiful! But I can't believe you'd be attracted to anything remotely resembling a woman. Perhaps a compliant sheep—if you had two or three shepherds to assist you."

Tristano made a deep curtsy to her. "I bow to an authority"—he smiled sweetly—"on shepherds—and sheepdogs."

Isabella's eyes flashed again. "Peasant bastard!"

The handsome young man clenched his teeth. "Aristocratic bitch."

The two "lovers" snarled at each other for a moment, and then Isabella hurled herself at Tristano, grabbed his curly hair, and attempted to wrestle him to the ground. He broke away by planting a heavy right to her midsection, and the air exploded from her lungs. Harlequin quickly moved between them.

"Bravo!" he said dryly. "Magnificent. True art. Now get the hell out of here!" He glanced at Colombina, watching from the shadows of the wagon, and walked to her. "Satisfied?" he asked her.

To his surprise, Colombina was delighted by the performance. "Now *that's* passion!" she cheered. "I just knew they'd be perfect together!"

THE CAPITANO FELT THE COLD, hard pressure of the blade at his throat, and he rose very slowly from his table in the tavern, being careful not to provoke or alarm the hand that held the knife.

"Lightly, Cosimo. Lightly," he whispered.

There was an eruption of laughter, and he felt himself turned violently around to face the big, scarred, grinning Sicilian.

"How did you know it was me?"

The capitano forced a smile to his face. "I'd recognize your pretty pointed tooth anywhere," he replied with the knife still at his throat.

He noted that two other mercenaries were taking positions just behind and to either side of the Sicilian. They did not wear the *impresa* of the Borgia, the bull, as Cosimo did, but the fleur-de-lis of France. All, however, were armed.

"What are you about, old friend?" murmured the capitano with the knife point pricking his chin. "Have you changed your allegiance?"

Cosimo laughed again and removed the knife from the capitano's throat. "I came alone when the duke sent word that you were in or around Imola, but the French were the ones who offered the bounty for your head, so they appointed these two to assist me." He sheathed the weapon. "Not that I needed them."

"Besides," said an eager young mercenary, "we are young and can always learn from the killing masters."

This one, said the capitano to himself, *could be dangerous.*

Cosimo signaled to the two mercenaries as he seated himself at the table directly opposite the capitano, and the men placed themselves on either side of the door.

"Where are these friends of yours I was told about, Captain?" asked the Sicilian.

"I have none," offered Capitano, "except—perhaps—you?"

"Always," swore Cosimo, then replied more seriously, "But this, you understand, is a matter of business. If I bring back your head, I receive one hundred golden ducats."

"Really?" the capitano marveled. "So much? Where will the duke get it?"

"What do you mean?"

The capitano leaned on the table. "I mean, the pope supports them as well he can, but the rumor is that Cesare hasn't enough money left in his entire treasury to feed the army he already has. You must know that he is preparing to dismiss three companies of French troops because he cannot feed them."

Cosimo glared. "He'll have enough to pay *me.*" He struck the table with his fist, and everyone in the tavern turned to look; but one glance at Cosimo's scarred and menacing countenance, and they quickly swiveled back to their own matters.

The capitano feigned indifference. "If you say so."

"I happen to know the duke bought thirty thousand bushels of wheat from the Venetians," the Sicilian pointed out.

"Then you must also know that it's gone. Disappeared," responded the capitano.

"He's lying," said one of the other mercenaries. "He's trying to trick you."

"You see?" Cosimo smiled. "I told you he was smart."

The mercenary glowered. "Cesare is smarter," he said scornfully.

Capitano nodded and muttered, *"Terribilita."*

Cosimo beamed. "Yes! Yes!" he roared. "That's it! Cesare has *terribilita!*" He leaned across the table and breathed garlic in the capitano's face. "And so have I."

"And I." The mercenary grinned.

Cosimo wheeled on him. "You?" His scowl silenced the guard. He waited a moment, and then turned back to his prisoner and apologized. "They don't know what it is to be a soldier," he said. "They come from the better families now. Breeding. Educated. Hoping to be a condottiere by noon tomorrow. They haven't seen what we've seen, eh? They don't know what we know!".

The capitano relaxed. "We know how to die, eh?" He smiled. "Oh yes. I know it's all over for me. But, well, do you suppose? I mean, let's share one last cup of wine in memory of the good times, then let it happen, eh?"

"Don't!" snarled the mercenary.

Cosimo glared at him again and then called, *"Vino!"* He gestured to the tavern wench for two goblets. "They'll never see the things we've seen, eh?" the Sicilian continued. "What do these beardless boys know about slitting a man's throat, eh? Before he himself even knows it! Scarlatti. Remember? He walked half a mile, I swear, before he realized he was dead. My knife went in and out so fast. And the girl—what was her name? In Padua?"

The capitano pretended to enjoy the memory. *Oh yes,* he said to himself, *you would remember that.*

"What was her name again?" Cosimo insisted.

"She—didn't have time—to tell us."

Cosimo roared with laughter. "That's right! We kept her busy, didn't we? The seven of us!" He laughed again. "But I remember her nipples. The big round nipples." He leaned across the table and whispered, "I kept them."

The capitano was relieved when the tavern wench brought the goblets of the dark wine. As his captor reached for one he suddenly waved his hands over the tops of the goblets and intoned a mock prayer, "O Lord of Warriors, bless this, the blood of the grapes of Italy, that when my own blood spills, it may return to the earth and the vine and the cup."

The Sicilian started to raise the goblet to lips, but the capitano grabbed his hand. "Wait!" he commanded. "Do you remember, Cosimo, how we used to gamble who was to have the best horse or the most plunder?"

"Or go first with the girls." Cosimo smiled.

"Yes, exactly," said the capitano. "You were a bold gambler in those days. Truly a man of *terribilita*." The Sicilian absolutely glowed under that most cherished of titles for Italian males. "Are you still the man you were, I wonder? We've grown a little fat, a little careless. Shall we, I wonder, have one last wager?"

Cosimo replaced the goblet on the table. "With what stakes?"

"The greatest. Life itself."

Cosimo studied the officer for a while. "Whose life?" he asked.

"Well, that's the question." The capitano smiled. "You see I have just poisoned one of these goblets of wine." He raised his hand so Cosimo could see the poison ring still on his finger, the cap open and revealing the empty space. "But the question is: which goblet? Even I'm not sure." He leaned back and smiled again at the fuming Sicilian. "You can take first choice, and if you're right, I die."

Cosimo growled. "You're going to die anyway," he said. "What do I get if I win?"

"Life," shouted the capitano. "That's the great wager! Life or death! And, if it matters, if I choose the wrong one, you can meet your Maker with one less murder on your conscience. And if you pick the wrong one, well, I'm sure these brave young warriors will send me on to join you immediately." He leaned across the table and muttered the word again. *"Terribilita?"*

Cosimo stiffened. He reached for one of the goblets and raised it to his eyes, studying the edge, the inside, the way the wine clung to the sides. He ran his finger around the rim and licked it lightly. Then he did the same with the other goblet. Finally he clutched one and announced, "This is my choice. That one is yours."

The capitano slowly reached out and took the remaining goblet. He glanced at Cosimo, who nodded once, and then they both put the goblets to their lips without hesitation or pause and swallowed deeply. The Sicilian replaced his goblet on the table and looked at his prisoner, who did the same with his goblet. "I feel fine." Cosimo grinned, and then, the smile fixed on his lips, he toppled across the table and knocked over his goblet.

Within a moment the two other mercenaries darted forward with their daggers drawn, and the capitano found his chin propped against another blade. "No more games," growled the guard, pulling Capitano to his feet by the point of the blade beneath his chin. He also reached over, seized Capitano's goblet, and downed the rest of its contents.

"Now," said the soldier, "the duke wants your head." But with that, the dagger fell from his fingers, and he looked down with amazement. Then he looked back up at the capitano and murmured, "Both poisoned? But how?" His knees bent, and he collapsed like a falling tree, landing at the capitano's feet. The remaining mercenary stood, mouth agape, staring at the capitano as if expecting him to fall, too, at any moment, but instead the seasoned soldier reached out and pulled the young man to him.

"Listen," he hissed at the youth. "Nothing can kill me. Do you understand that? I have power over death. Death serves my purposes." He slipped a small pouch into the mercenary's palm. "Go and tell that to your Borgian bastard! Is that clear?" The mercenary nodded frantically. "Move!"

With that the capitano hurled his remaining captor toward the front door, and the youth was gone in a moment. He then quickly removed a small vial from his belt, uncorked it with his teeth, and swallowed the contents. He had already swallowed the contents of the first vial when he first caught sight of Cosimo and his friends entering the tavern and blocking his retreat to the piazza beyond. He mentally repeated all the instructions given him by Dottore. *The poison is quick. You must drink the first vial to prepare your stomach for it, and then, five minutes after consuming the poison, you must drink the contents of the second vial. You will be ill for about two hours, but you will live.*

He felt cold and uncomfortable, and suddenly his vision blurred. The room seemed to be filled with white-robed men. "I'm—I'm going to sleep for a few hours," he mumbled, and with that, he drifted into the darkness.

WHEN HE AWOKE, it was in a hard bed in a cold and damp room. He turned his head and saw a young man in the white robes of the Dominicans.

"Where am I?" he asked. He felt as if his stomach had been removed, and his vision was still blurred.

The monk leaned forward. "You are in the monastery of Santo Michele in Bosco. You have been sleeping for two days."

Two days?

The cleric continued, "Once you can stand, you must get word to Bracciolini. Tell him—tell him they have Manciano."

FRA SEBASTIANO STOOD beside the inquisitor in the cold prison cell, looking at the bleeding and broken man. The tall Dominican, Manciano, had had the muscles of both arms ripped by the *strappado*, and his left arm had been deliberately and cruelly broken in three places.

252

"We don't dare do more," said the inquisitor softly. "Canon law will not permit anyone to try clerics without papal authorization." Sebastiano said nothing, but from his black robes he produced a parchment that he handed to the inquisitor. "What is that?" the torturer asked.

"A congratulatory bull from Rome, and a plenary indulgence for anyone who assists in forcing a confession from the Dominican."

The inquisitor glanced at the parchment. "I don't understand, Fra Sebastiano."

"I serve the pope directly," the ferret-faced cleric whispered. "I posed as a follower of Cardinal Ferrari in order to keep the pope informed." He raised his hand to permit the torturer to see the bull's-head ring. "But now the cardinal has been—removed, and I can drop my masquerade. His Holiness insists that you get this—heretic—to confess he was part of a conspiracy to defame the pontiff and destroy the stability of the Holy Roman Church. Make him tell us where he has hidden the Savelli letters. And His Holiness wants the names of every cardinal who assisted him in his conspiracy."

The inquisitor turned to face the weary Dominican, caked with sweat and blood. "I have received authority to continue your torments until you confess your conspiracy and give us the information we seek."

The broken figure managed to raise his eyes to face his torturer. "Authority from whom? From God?"

The inquisitor bristled. "I separate you from the church militant and from the church triumphant."

Manciano's blood-caked lips barely formed the words. "From—the militant only; the other—is not in your competence."

The inquisitor gestured quickly, and the ropes binding the priest's arms behind him were once again pulled tight. Now his battered body was jerked from the floor of the cell and lifted into the sky as the condemned Dominican screamed his pain.

"He will tell us," the inquisitor severely asserted.

"THE LADY'S MOTHER WANTS HER to go to the Pitti family in Florence at once."

The young monk who had been tending the capitano folded the parchment, dropped wax on it, and sealed it with his ring.

The soldier shook his head in bewilderment. "There seems to be a new breed of woman emerging these days."

"If you're referring to the daughter, perhaps. But if you are referring to the mother, she is indeed an exceptional woman. You must continue to protect her daughter." The cleric handed the sealed parchment to Capitano. "Give this to no one but Bracciolini."

The capitano was still trying to absorb this turn of events. "I find it difficult to believe that Isabella—"

The priest finished his sentence, "Isabella Zappachio of Venice is—of a somewhat—lofty station."

"How lofty?"

"Slightly lower than the courts of heaven."

"She is not a Zappachio?"

"Would the daughter of a painter—no matter how famous—be honored and educated in the courts of the doge and the della Roveres?"

"Then—who is she?"

"In due time you—and she—will know, but for the time being it is safer for everyone to know her only as the daughter of a Venetian painter." The monk moved his chair closer to the capitano's. "The thing is, you see, she could become a hostage in these familial wars. The doge has men searching for her. So, too, does the duke; and the Orsini have had agents posted from the time your band crossed into the Romagna." His eyes twinkled at the capitano's apparent amazement. "It was not by chance that we found you in that tavern."

The officer shook his head. "You have had men watching us?" The Dominican nodded. "Then it was your men I saw that night in the woods at Modena."

The priest shook his head negatively. "My dear captain, your little band of travelers have had armies on every side of you from the moment Isabella left Milan, but your friends that evening were not Weepers."

"Who then?"

"You'll find that answer in Florence. That is why you must go there directly. There are friends there much more powerful than we, and they will be waiting for you." He crossed to the wine table. "I have done as you instructed and sent a monk to Bologna with the gems. I must admit I am impressed at finding someone in these troubled times who is both honest and—apparently—fearless." He turned to face the capitano. "I am pleased that our organization has been able to be of some assistance to you. Does the knowledge that you were never alone make you feel more—secure?"

"Oh yes," said the capitano softly. "Like a bone between hungry dogs."

The Dominican laughed and poured him some wine.

*T*HE COMPANY AWAITED the capitano for two more days in Cervia before they felt they had begun to attract undue attention from the townspeople. Accordingly they turned south and approached the ancient stronghold of Cesena.

At the same time, in Carpineta to the south, Cesare Borgia announced to his French troops that he was preparing a great farewell feast to honor their release and their return to Lombardy.

And to do so, the entire force would be moving north the next day to his newly acquired storehouses.

To Cesena.

CESENA

Capitano happens upon a revolt
against the Borgias.
The ladies compare their loves,
and the company performs
a miracle play.
The pope and his son celebrate
the new year.

lthough the capitano was annoyed that Dottore's formula did not work within the prescribed time limits, he remembered the collapse of the Sicilian and the other mercenary, and he was satisfied. Besides, the miscalculation had provided him with the opportunity for a short rest with the *piagnoni* as well as information—and a message—concerning two members of the company.

Later he was to learn that the poison and its antidote had been a household secret of Lucrezia Borgia, who had passed it to her first husband, Giovanni Sforza, and subsequently it had traveled to the Sforza family, to the Moor, to the Maestro, and to Dottore—who had inscribed its dosage incorrectly.

Still, it is good to have a guardian angel, he thought, *even if he is occasionally incompetent.*

After leaving the monastery of Santo Michele in Bosco, he raced down the Via Emilia until he was stopped in the Piazza del Popolo at Faenza by a vast rabble intent, apparently, on destroying the fine statue of Pope Calixtus III that had been erected less than five years earlier. Long ropes had been looped around the marble pontiff, and columns of heavily muscled peasants stretched them taut and pulled. Unfortunately, as with most rapidly assembled and poorly organized mobs, the swarm on the left of the statue was working rhythmically against those on the right.

Discipline—what little there appeared of it—seemed to be generated by a group of white-robed friars who whispered instructions to the strongest and most menacing of the crowd. The friars themselves, however, did not participate in the attempted destruction of the statue.

Finally one or two shirtless barrel-chested men in leather aprons struggled up the marble pedestal and began to hammer at the pontiff with iron bars. One or two others seeking to assist this enterprise hurled huge rocks at the statue and succeeded in knocking one of the human barrels back into the arms of the mob.

Capitano was alternately dismayed and intrigued. It was an affront to his sense of military precision to see such raw force used with such total incompetence, but even more, he was surprised to see the people of a Borgian enclave wrecking an image of a former Borgian pope. He then noticed, on the edge of the piazza, a group of guildsmen silently watching the efforts of the mob. He reined Zephyr in beside them.

"What is happening here?" he asked.

They studied him momentarily without any sign of interest, in near insolence, and he considered then how he must look to them: an armed mounted knight without armor or crest. They silently and sullenly began to pull away from him when the soldier, with quiet control, tugged on the reins and the great war-horse obediently placed his right front hoof squarely down on the boot of a bearded guildsman, who screamed in pain.

"I didn't quite hear your answer to my question." Capitano smiled as he backed his horse off the injured man.

A young apprentice stepped forward and volunteered, "They are angry about the Borgian pope."

"Calixtus the Third?" asked the capitano quietly. "He's been dead for nearly fifty years!"

The guildsman who had come to the aid of their injured brother glared at him with even greater animosity, and one or two whispered unflattering remarks about the capitano and, what was worse, about his war-horse.

The officer was about to expand his instructional program in good manners when a great cry came from the mob's collective voice, and Zephyr reared on his hind legs in momentary fright. The capitano forced the great horse's head to the left, away from the sight and sound of the mob, to let the animal know his master was still in control.

The shout had been triggered by the hammering of the human barrels, who had finally succeeded in removing Calixtus's head from his body. The marble skull had tumbled into the piazza, where a brief battle erupted among the children for the prize.

During this diversion, the guildsmen had fled. Only the young apprentice remained.

"Now, boy," said the capitano, "I ask again. Why this outrage against a pope dead fifty years?"

The apprentice grinned. "They're not against this pope. They're against the pope in Rome now, Alexander. They feel he was responsible for the torture and murder of our young lord, Astorre Manfredi."

The officer knew of the rumors of the torture and murder of the young Manfredi, only eighteen years old, and that of his fifteen-year-old brother, by Cesare Borgia.

"The Manfredi brothers were murdered six months ago. Why this rage now?"

"You haven't heard? Where have you been?"

The capitano leaned from the saddle toward the boy's upturned face. "In the embrace of death," he intoned, "and you are likely to smell his stinking breath before noon if you don't answer my questions civilly and quickly."

"They say Cesare Borgia is in trouble," the apprentice replied civilly and quickly. "His own condottieri are rebelling, and there have been uprisings in many cities in the Romagna."

"Are you telling me that the Romagna is rebelling against the Borgias?"

"That is what they are saying. Even to the east. There is martial law in Florence!"

This was a new and interesting situation. As a military man, the capitano had been taught that Florence was impregnable: a walled city split by the Arno River, which became an additional fortress once the bridges were secured. Indeed, the Ponte Vecchio provided the Medici a covered retreat from the Pitti Palace to the Uffizi. In addition, the Florentines were famed for their citizen army, which arose at the ringing of the bells of the city. Should the city fall, theoretically a retreating army had only to fall back into the foothills of the Apennines, to the heights of the San Miniato al Monte.

If the city had really rebelled against Cesare Borgia, it could be a turning point in the duke's history. The capitano realized the company should know at once, and he urged his horse southeast to Forli.

*T*HE COMPANY SLOWLY MOVED into the courtyard of the Minorite Monastery of Santo Francesco near Cesena, and Harlequin announced that they would wait here for the return of Capitano. They had jointly decided earlier that they would not enter Cesena, because they knew it to be a Borgia stronghold and they had encountered villagers on the road who said the city was in rebellion. Further, the monastery contained one of the best humanist libraries in all of Italy. Harlequin, Isabella, and Dottore were eager to spend some time revitalizing their minds.

The time was also useful to Scapino and Pantalone, who repaired harnesses, and by all three women, who mended the clothing while exchanging the vicious little pleasantries that revealed their mutual respect and admiration. To a passing stranger, the sharp-tongued trio of darning women might have appeared to be mortal enemies, but women universally understand that the strongest animosity is expressed not in tirades but in total silence.

"Look at my skin," Isabella demanded as she viewed herself in a small mirror trimmed in silver. "The sun is destroying me."

"You look healthy for the first time in your life," protested Ruffiana.

"The color of cow dung might become you," Isabella countered, "but my complexion is normally alabaster and cream."

"Then die"—Ruffiana smiled—"and that lovely corpse color is yours forever."

Colombina snorted and bit the thread from her needle.

Isabella replaced the mirror in a small pack at her feet and returned to sewing. "You're jealous, because Scapino prefers snow to horse turds."

Colombina guffawed. "Where did a fine lady learn such language? What are tutors teaching the daughters of prosperous families these days?"

"I have no interest in Scapino," Ruffiana assured her as she exposed a little more of her ample breasts to the sun. "I'm content that Tristano, who is a man of quality, prefers hives of honey to small coils of bird shit."

"I'm content," purred Isabella, "that Scapino, who is a man with testicles, prefers *têtes* to teats."

Colombina glared at the girl. "I don't know what that means, but if it's French, it's probably filthy."

Ruffiana laughed and began to mend a tear in her lover's short cape. "Tristano wrote a new poem to me last night," she smugly announced after a brief silence.

"Ah, well," Isabella disdainfully returned. "You'd never find Scapino wasting our time like that."

Ruffiana looked up in surprise. "Wasting? Do you know how rare it is to find a man who cares enough about you, who respects and admires you enough, to write poems for you?"

Isabella stitched busily. "I do not wish to be admired. I'm not a statue. Nor do I especially want a man's respect. I'm not the queen mother." She stopped for a moment. "Do you know how rare it is to meet a man who wants you enough to wrestle you to the floor and rip off your clothes as soon as he gets you alone in the evening?"

"I know hundreds like that," bragged Ruffiana. "Thousands."

Isabella smiled sweetly. "And I know thousands who would waste my time reading me poems."

"I know three men who can read"—Colombina sighed—"but only one who can outwrestle me."

This brought another brief period of silence. "Tristano brings me flowers every day," said Ruffiana finally.

"Scapino brings me sheep intestines every night," boasted Isabella.

The other two stopped sewing and stared at her. "Sheep's intestines?" shrieked Colombina. "What the hell for?"

Isabella radiated all the self-assurance of the most knowing concubine. "He puts them over his . . ." She gestured how Scapino applied them, and then added brightly, "So we won't have unwanted babies. He cares about me."

Ruffiana shook her head and returned to her sewing. "In Piacenza they're called French sheaths, and all that Scapino cares about is himself and his appetites."

"Oh?" said Isabella quietly. "And what do you imagine would happen if you walked away one night when Tristano was reading you one of his love poems? He'd continue reading. It isn't you he's in love with. It's the sound of his own voice."

Ruffiana shrugged. "Well, better a man who is in love with his voice than a man in love with—his sheep's intestines."

Colombina chided both women. "Ladies, ladies," she said, "both your men are children compared to Harlequin."

Isabella and Ruffiana stopped to look at the older woman.

"Harlequin?" gaped Ruffiana. "But—he's *old.*"

Colombina bristled. "Old?"

"He's easily *thirty!*"

"Who *is* Harlequin anyway?" inquired Isabella. "Does anyone know? What does he want? What does he need?"

Colombina shrugged. "I don't know. Most of the time I don't even know what he's talking about."

Isabella laughed. "Neither does he. He makes things up. He's told us a hundred stories of his past, and I don't believe any of them."

Colombina put down her sewing. "I know. But I think there's something of the truth in all of them. He—he has—something in him so deep—he can't reach and grab it. Not yet." She resumed her stitching. "And I can't until he does."

Ruffiana nudged Colombina. "Has he slept with you?"

Colombina paused in her sewing. "No," she said quietly.

"Has he kissed you?" asked Isabella.

"No."

"Then how do you even know if he likes you?"

"I know," Colombina whispered. There was a pause, and she looked at them. "I know that when he is cut, I bleed; and when I weep, the tears are his."

There was a moment as the two women studied her. Then Ruffiana sighed, smiled, and resumed her own sewing. "Godsblood," she said, "I hope it isn't catching."

COLOMBINA, more than any of the others, had adopted an enthusiasm for the theatrical. Her initial experience with improvisation at Modena was enlightening, and she had taken to heart every word of Harlequin's absurd delineation of *commedia al'improviso* at Bologna. While debating the feasibility of undisciplined performers improvising a work, Harlequin had used words and expressions and quoted long-dead Greeks that Colombina had never heard of. He held low hopes of Colombina becoming an actress.

But, on her own, she had persuaded Dottore to read to her one of the manuscripts of *Abraham and Isaac* that they discovered tucked among the hogsheads of wine in the guild wagon. Dottore had patiently explained to her what a "cue" was, how an actor "takes a stage," and how a play was structured into "scenes."

"Where did you learn all this?" she asked.

"Where I learned most useless things." Dottore smiled. "At the court in Milan. The duke produced a play called *Il Paradiso,* written by a minor poet in honor of a wedding in the family. Maestro Leonardo designed the scenery, which was, as I recall, the entire top portion of a mountain that divided down the center, swung open like pages in a book, and revealed a 'heaven' of glittering stars and soft, vaporous, moving clouds."

"The Duke of Milan liked plays?"

"No. The Moor was less interested in theater production than in challenging the Este family of Ferrara, who, three years earlier, had not only mounted productions of Plautus's *Menaechmi* and *Amphitruo,* but had also commissioned *their* painter, Niccolo del Cogo, to paint three-dimensional backgrounds for them." He replaced the manuscript of *Abraham and Isaac* in its leather carrying case. "He also had his architect build a *theatrum* based on the writings and sketches of a Roman architect named Vitruvius. Furthermore, I heard somewhere that someone else built a *theatrum* in the Vatican itself."

Colombina began to dream, again, of dancing in a *theatrum,* in a great court, on a polished floor before painted vistas of mountains or marbled walls or streets stretching out to eternity like spokes on a wheel—all of which had been described to her by Dottore. He, in turn, had seen such marvels from pictures the maestro had used for reference when he was building the Moor's scenery. Sometimes Colombina heard herself speak in these dreams, but the words emerged in the vulgar tongue instead of the proper Latin, and the faceless audience turned hostile and laughed her from the stage.

*I*T WAS TWO DAYS AFTER their arrival in the monastery that the courtyard rang with the sounds of horses' hooves and the clang of armor and swords. Michelotto, the giant mercenary, swung down from his saddle and slowly encircled the wagon.

Finally the condottiere wheeled on the man in the bizarre cloak, who was watching quietly, and barked, "I was told you were here. You are mummers?"

Harlequin forced a smile and a mock bow. "We entertain, sire."

Michelotto removed his heavy leather gauntlets and motioned for a monk to attend him. "What do you do?"

"We sing. Play instruments. Juggle."

"No!" bellowed the mercenary, and then he turned to the monk, who backed away in fright. "Tell your abbot my men and I will take a meal here in your refectory. Five in all. I understand your cellars rival the Benedictines, so do not try to serve us some swill you maintain for transients." Suddenly the giant addressed Harlequin. "My lord, the Duke of Valentinois is weary of jugglers and wrestlers and ballad singers and acrobats. He wants to see a play. Prepare a play. When I return from my meal, you will present it for me."

"But, sire," Harlequin objected, "we—we have never before performed a play."

Michelotto glared. "This is not your guild wagon?"

Harlequin quickly reassured him that the wagon was, indeed, theirs.

"Is it? And your guild?"

"I beg your pardon?"

"What is the name of your guild? What do you do?"

"Ah—we are—bellmakers," said Harlequin.

"Bell makers?" queried the condottiere.

"How many guilds of bell makers have you ever encountered?" asked Harlequin.

"None," Michelotto said.

"It is an honorable profession," said Harlequin. "Someone has to make bells, don't they?"

"Ironsmiths, I thought," said Michelotto. "Or silversmiths."

"Well, sire, we are—the guild of—bellwrights. The Company of—" He thought, suddenly, of the destroyed painting of the dancing women and the half goats. "Wayward Saints! *I Santi Ostinati!*"

Michelotto snorted and turned away. "Then, as guildsmen, you perform *sacre rappresentazioni* on feast days. Play us whatever miracle play you performed on All Saints last month!" he started off. "My lord and his guests are assembled in the palazzo in Cesena. We are preparing a lavish feast to wish our French allies farewell. A miracle play would be just the thing for the French. When I return, prepare to show it to me."

And he and his four escorts disappeared through the archway and into the monastery.

The company, who had overheard the conversation, rushed to Harlequin. "What will we do?" asked Isabella.

"What choice have we?" reasoned Harlequin. "We cannot run. They'd catch us, and we'd have to confess that the wagon is stolen, and we are not guildsmen. Then they might search through our belongings and find Zappachio's paintings and your fine gowns and traveling cases, and then we'd really be in trouble. Apparently they haven't recognized you, Isabella, so we will keep you tucked away. We must—we *will*—perform a play." Then he gestured the others around him. "We have manuscripts of *Abraham and Isaac*, don't we? We'll try that!"

"Only some of us can read," Dottore pointed out, "and one of that number is a woman, who cannot appear in *sacre rappresentazioni*. We don't have enough actors."

"Who are the characters?" Harlequin asked.

"God!" Dottore snapped.

"I will play God," said Harlequin.

"Now, why doesn't that surprise me?" muttered Colombina.

"Since I am supposedly your leader," Harlequin persisted, "and yet I am consistently opposed, ignored, or barely tolerated, I see a striking parallel with the Almighty."

"Why can't I play God?" said Tristano, sulking.

"Because we are told we are made in God's image, and anyone can look at you and see that damned few men are made in *your* image." Tristano beamed, and that matter was settled.

There were no other objections.

"The angel," listed Dottore.

"As Tristano is the most angelic looking," said Harlequin, "he will play the angel."

"Abraham!" called Dottore.

Harlequin pointed at Dottore. "You're ideal, and since Abraham has most of the lines, and since you read, you can have the honor."

"Fine," said Dottore. "But what of the boy, Isaac?"

"Pantalone will play the boy."

"He cannot read."

"See if he can memorize. He picks up things quickly. He picked up Ruffiana, didn't he?"

"We won't have the time to teach him!"

Harlequin threw his hands in the air. "Then we'll let him just—respond—to what we say. Improvise! How far wrong could he possibly go?"

They were to find out within the hour.

*F*OLLOWING THE MEAL, the dark condottiere and his men drew stools into the courtyard facing the wagon stage and awaited the performance of *Abraham and Isaac*. Possessing only one script, Dottore and Harlequin had studied their lines first, and then passed the manuscript to Tristano, who had it less than a quarter hour.

Of them all, only Pantalone, who could not read the manuscript, was self-assured and relaxed. When he had been told that he was to play a child who discovers his father is going to kill him, he nodded, smiled, and intoned his credo.

"I can do that!"

We are in trouble, Harlequin thought.

Several crates and boxes and barrels were piled center stage to simulate both a mountain and the throne of God. "All right!" said Harlequin to his troupe. "Let's try it!"

Dottore announced the play, and Harlequin climbed unsteadily to the top of the weaving and slipping pile of crates and sat on a small box at the summit. "Now!" he whispered to those near him. "As it begins God—that's me—is in heaven and calls to His angel." He cleared his throat and suddenly bellowed, "My angel!"

Tristano, uncomfortable and only half interested in the entire proceedings, climbed the ladder to the stage and pretended to pivot and glide around the area, fanning his arms in the air. Colombina lost it at once and had to stifle her laughter in the walkway behind the mercenaries.

"What are you doing?" whispered Harlequin.

"I'm flying," replied Tristano. "Angels fly, don't they?"

"*This* one walks," snarled Harlequin between clenched teeth. "Now, just stand there!"

Tristano came to rest at the base of the mountain of crates.

Harlequin adopted what he took to be a God-like voice: booming, thunderous, oratorical. "My angel!" he roared. "Get thee to middle earth! I would try the goodness of Abraham's heart to see if he loves me!" Tristano nodded, genuflected, and started to leave. "Not yet," whispered Harlequin. "I have more." Tristano shrugged and returned to his previous location. "Tell him I command that he take his young son, Isaac, whom he loves so well, and make a blood sacrifice!" Tristano nodded and started to genuflect, but Harlequin roared impatiently, "Show him the way unto this hill, where his sacrifice shall be!" Again the youth nodded, genuflected, and was halfway across the stage when Harlequin bellowed, "And if he does this well . . ." Tristano raced back to his former position and stood at attention. ". . . all men will notice . . ." Tristano bowed and started off. ". . . and keep my commandments!" Harlequin shrieked.

As the angel, expecting more instruction, wheeled to get back into position, he slipped and slid into one of the bottom crates supporting the mountain, which trembled as if a volcano were inside, and Harlequin let out an involuntary yell. The mountain remained stable, however, and God let a sigh of relief escape him.

Tristano managed to get to his feet and stood rigidly at the foot of the mountain.

Michelotto and his mercenaries stared dumbly at the stage in both surprise and fascination.

There was a pause as Harlequin looked silently at Tristano, and the young man tried to see out of the corner of his eye if the Almighty was finished with that interminable speech. Finally Harlequin thundered, "Well, go!"

With that he threw up his arms and disappeared from sight as he toppled over backward and apparently fell down the back of the mountain, hitting every box, crate, and barrel along the way.

Tristano, alarmed, started to go to assist Harlequin, thought better of it, returned to his position, nodded, started off, ran back, genuflected, nodded, all the time peering to see if Harlequin would reappear around the side of the mountain. In watching, he walked backward and suddenly fell off of the wagon stage into the courtyard.

Colombina, doubled over, gasped for air. Isabella and Scapino were trying valiantly to stifle their laughter lest they disrupt the sacred play, but Ruffiana ran to her fallen lover and began to bring him back to reality. Dottore, in the meantime, had mounted the ladder and come to the center of the stage. "Oh, Father of Heaven," he began to intone solemnly, "who made everything, I come to pray to Thee again, and this day I will make Thee an offering."

Ruffiana had helped Tristano to his feet, and to his everlasting credit, the handsome young man climbed the ladder and again mounted the stage. At the same time Harlequin appeared on all fours around the opposite corner of the mountain and found himself falling off the edge of the stage into the shadows and the cobbled courtyard. As he fell he screamed.

So, too, did Colombina, who raced to his side, no longer laughing.

Dottore marched onward. "What manner of beast wouldst Thou like, Lord?" he implored the silent heavens. "It is my pleasure to do Thy will."

Ruffiana had also mounted the stage and was busily applying her own special form of medication to Tristano when Dottore glared in their direction and repeated. "It is my pleasure to do Thy will!"

Tristano quickly disengaged himself from Ruffiana's arms and took a step toward the center of the stage. Unfortunately his backward momentum also propelled Ruffiana backward, and she, too, went clattering over the edge of the wagon stage into the cobbles.

One mercenary leaned toward Michelotto. "What sort of miracle play is this?" he asked, but Michelotto, thoroughly caught up in the proceedings, simply shook his head from side to side.

"It is my pleasure to do Thy will!" roared Dottore for the third time as Tristano raced toward him and came to a halt directly before him.

"Abraham, Abraham," recited the young man quickly and without inflection as he kept glancing back to where Ruffiana had disappeared over the edge of the stage. "Our Lord commands—"

Dottore interrupted loudly, "I am of the true knowing. My Lord has but to command—"

"Yes." Tristano nodded, trying to hurry the proceedings along. "Well. The Lord commands—"

"And I shall do His will! For in all the world," he pontificated, "there is no servant more devoted to the true God than Abraham!"

"Bravo!" said Tristano. "Now! The Lord commands—"

"And so it is His province to command!" bellowed Dottore, on a roll. "For the Lord of all has but to command, and we must work His will!"

"Well said," muttered the youth, bobbing to peer into the shadows to see if Ruffiana had recovered. "Now the Lord wills—"

"And whatsoever He shall will me, it shall be done!"

"Magnificent."

"On earth . . ."

"Fine."

"As it is in heaven!"

Tristano stopped then and studied Dottore as if he were a strange being from another world. After a moment he opened his mouth to speak, but Dottore quickly blurted out, "Amen!"

They both stared at one another then for some time, and then Tristano began to talk as rapidly and as incomprehensibly as possible. "The Lord commands that thou shalt take thy young son, Isaac, and with his blood make sacrifice."

The response was magnificent. Suddenly Dottore's face took on the look of a man whose testicles were being ground under a mill wheel. His eyes filled with tears; and strange primal groans and tremors began to issue from his nose, his ears, his entire body. He trembled, quivered, weaved, staggered, shuddered, circled the playing area as if he were possessed by a one-legged demon, dragging his left foot, jerking spasmodically as if every muscle was diseased and every nerve shattered. He fell to his knees, on his face, rolled three times downstage and three times upstage, ripped his garments, made vague and violent gestures toward the sky, fell back, tried to rise, crashed with a sickening thud on the bare stage floor, moaned, roared, screamed, and cursed; and then, just as suddenly as he began, it was over. Dottore stopped in midgesture and recited quickly, "Oh no, Lord, no. Ask of me anything. The bull of my herd, the mother heifer, my sheep." Then, as an afterthought on the generosity of Abraham, he added, "One ram? Perhaps the black one with the broken left horn and the lame left leg?"

Harlequin, watching, groaned, and Colombina laughed. Ruffiana pulled herself to the front of the stage and watched, too, at the same time rubbing her bruised left ankle.

"But not Isaac," Dottore roared.

Tristano, who had stood, mouth agape, through most of these proceedings, now cleared his throat with a great vulgar noise and said quietly, "Are you quite finished?" Dottore glared at the young man and nodded. "Now," Tristano continued, "into the land of vision must thou goest and offerest thy childest—"

"Childest?" echoed Dottore.

"Thy child," Tristano corrected himself, "unto the Lord."

There was a pause during which Scapino whispered to Colombina, "He ought to see if God won't settle for his wife instead!" She went into renewed hysterics.

The angel exited the playing area to a rising crescendo of applause, which Ruffiana alone was doing.

Dottore came down to the edge of the wagon stage and called, "Isaac! Isaac!"

It is doubtful whether anyone was prepared for Pantalone's entrance as Isaac. He appeared as if he had been shot from a cannon somewhere in the dark recesses of the monastery beyond the arches. He landed nimbly on the stage, half hopped, half cartwheeled across the playing area, reciting in a loud, singsong voice, "I am here, Father, dearest, lovable old father of mine, who loves and worships me!"

Harlequin groaned again. Dottore stood as if someone had just struck him behind the head with a fence post. Finally he recovered enough to mutter, "We, ah, we must go make sacrifice to the Lord."

Again Pantalone erupted into a display of abnormal infancy. He hippity-hopped around the playing area, executed handstands and cartwheels, bounced on one foot, and shouted gleefully, "Oh goody-good, good, good, goody-good!" His final cartwheel hurled him into Dottore, who fell like a great tree toppling in the wind, and Pantalone ended sitting squarely on the poor man's ribs and chirping brightly, "Anything you say, old good-good father of mine, O keeper of the seal, protector of the poor and the helpless, guardian of the—"

"Get off my chest!" Dottore roared. Pantalone quickly obeyed and helped the older man to his feet. "Anything you say, old goody-good father of mine!"

Dottore looked as though he was considering personally sacrificing Isaac right there, but he gritted his teeth and ordered, "Pick up the wood and follow me!"

It is doubtful that any guild ever produced a scene like that which followed. Pantalone picked up an imaginary stick of wood, measured it with his hands, and sat it down at Dottore's feet. He then crossed the stage to the opposite side, measured another imaginary stick of wood, and finding it the right size, carried it across the stage, where he placed it with great exactitude precisely beside the other imaginary stick of wood. He crossed again, picked up a third imaginary piece of wood, measured it, bent it, found he had bent it too far in one direction and very carefully bent it back, measured it, looked perplexed, measured it a third time, and then walked across the stage to his "pile." There he measured both sticks with his hands, found the third stick wanting by three or four centimeters, and threw it away.

Dottore had stood watching this ritual for some time, but his patience was clearly reaching an end. He kicked Pantalone hard in the buttocks as he bent over to pick up a fourth imaginary piece of wood and roared, "Move!"

Pantalone mimed uncontrollable fright, then pretended to stack up seven or eight pieces of wood in a neat pile, tied it with an absurdly long piece of equally invisible cord, and finally hoisted it upon his shoulders.

Suddenly Dottore looked mournfully up to heaven and cried, "My heart breaks."

To which Pantalone replied, "My back isn't feeling too good either."

Dottore glared at the youth and began to walk around the playing area. Behind him, Pantalone mimed the exodus of the Hebrews through the desert. He staggered. He tripped on rocks. He caught one leg in a pool of quicksand. He pretended he had reached water and was swimming across it. He dog-paddled. He backstroked. He glided like a swan. He struggled with a water snake, and finally reached the opposite shore.

Dottore had no idea what was going on behind him. But the deadly silence emanating from Michelotto and the mercenaries was not reassuring. Further, it was in sharp contrast to the muffled but quite audible laughter of the watching members of the company—

and that of the monk community, which had begun to assemble on the walkways and under the archways to see the performance.

Finally Dottore began to climb the mountains of crates and barrels. Pantalone hopped along behind him, pretending to nearly fall and looking down with dismay and terror at the height. He then dropped to his belly and slithered the rest of the way behind Dottore like a snake.

Then the miracle: Michelotto chuckled.

Encouraged, Dottore turned and intoned, "Now, put the wood here, and I will begin the fire." Pantalone mimed dropping an enormous load of wood from his back. Judging from the area between his gaping arms and hands, the pile had grown from seven or eight sticks to four or five mighty trunks of trees. Dottore watched him perform this little ritual, drew an imaginary sword from his waist, and began to sharpen it on the side of the mountain.

Pantalone launched into a nonstop stream of words. "But, Father mine, what are we going to sacrifice? I mean, shall we catch a deer? Or a big fish? Or maybe even a little furry bunny—might—do." He began to look as though it had suddenly become clear to him what Dottore had in mind. He gulped, wiped his brow, struggled with words. "Ah—what—ah—what are you—looking at me that way for, Father dearest, patron of the arts, keeper of the keys, master of the world, guardian of the—"

Suddenly Dottore reached out and pinned Pantalone to the mountain with one hand on his throat and the other pretending to hold a sword to his belly. "Isaac," he roared, "I must kill thee!"

Pantalone just as abruptly brought his knee up into Dottore's groin, knocked his mimed sword away with one hand, and jabbed two fingers of the other in Dottore's eyes. The cries of pain echoed through the courtyard, and Harlequin was on his feet at once.

But Michelotto was definitely laughing now. And when he began to laugh, the mercenaries, the monks, and the watching members of the company, relieved, laughed loudly, too.

"Oh, bravo!" wailed Pantalone, breaking away. "Are you out of your mind? I'm just a child! A mere babe in arms! Look!" And with that he hurled himself into Dottore's arms, and they both collapsed in a heap on the stage floor.

To everyone's surprise, it was Dottore who got to his feet first, one hand clutching his crotch, and planted a foot squarely on the chest of Pantalone, who let out a great gasp of air and noise. Abraham snarled, "The Lord hath commanded that I sacrifice thee. It is the Lord's will, and I must do it"—he ground his foot into Isaac's chest—"because I am good at heart."

Pantalone then seized Dottore's leg and hurled him back and to the opposite side of the stage. He quickly bounded to his feet and faced the tall, thin man standing offstage in the courtyard. "Bravo for you!" growled Pantalone. "But I'm the one who's going to be filleted! What kind of a God is this who demands the death of a son?"

Dottore and Pantalone circled one another like fighting cocks, feeling each other out. "I will hear nothing against the Lord!" boomed Dottore.

"Well, think of this, old man," Pantalone cried. "You'll never get away with it. Lots of people saw both of us going up this hill. What are they going to think when only one of us comes down, eh? What are you going to tell them? 'The boy had a cramp and fell down the mountainside'? How will you hide the sword marks, eh? How about that? Murderer!"

Dottore finally broke. He stood straight up and yelled, "Harlequin!"

But Pantalone was not to be denied. With one flying leap he landed on the back of Dottore and began to box his ears as he exclaimed, "And when they catch you, it's the noose and gibbet for you, killer! This is an eye-for-an-eye society, butcher! They'll hang you higher than smoked venison."

Dottore wheeled around the stage with the boy riding his back and pounding his skull. "Harlequin!" he repeated urgently.

In bringing up his hands to protect his head, Dottore also cut off his vision. With a cry, he stumbled and both he and his burden toppled headfirst off the wagon and into their audience.

The mercenaries were instantly on their feet, hands on their sword hilts, when they noticed Michelotto rubbing his tearing eyes and shaking with laughter. "Now, *that's* a miracle play!" he exulted. "Cesare has never seen anything like this!" He turned abruptly to Harlequin, pressed a small leather pouch into his hand, and commanded, "Tonight! At the palazzo! Sunset!"

Two monks had brought the saddled horses into the courtyard, and the mercenaries mounted and galloped through the great arch and onto the roadway.

In a moment they had disappeared.

*I*N THE PAPAL APARTMENTS, the portly, hook-nosed pontiff slapped the parchment into the hands of his secretary, Francesco Troches, and grumbled, "It's from Cesare. I imagine he wants more money! He always needs more money!"

"What can we do?"

"I sent him six thousand ducats only ten days ago! What is he doing with it? I can't continue populating Italy with cardinals just to get enough money to keep him lord of the Romagna!"

Troches read the parchment as he followed his pacing employer. "He says his condottiere, Ramiro de Lorca, used the money to buy wheat and then resold it and kept the funds."

The pope wheeled on his secretary. "Then why doesn't he kill him and be done with it? Why come whining to me and demand more money?"

"He also says that de Lorca has been conspiring with other condottieri to entrap him, and he adds that his agents have captured Manciano, and the priest has confessed that two cardinals have been secretly supporting the rebels."

"Cardinals? Who?"

"Orsini and della Rovere."

"The bastards!"

"He says he will handle de Lorca and the two Orsini traveling with him, but he cannot proceed beyond a certain point until he knows that Cardinal Orsini and Cardinal della Rovere have been neutralized. He requests that you see to it."

The pontiff seated himself behind the small mahogany desk and fingered a silver-bladed dagger. "That—might—be possible," he said softly, "and profitable. If something should happen to Orsini and della Rovere, their properties—and wealth—could be seized by the Church. Yes." He took a quill from an inkstand and began to write upon another parchment. "Where is della Rovere? I haven't seen him in months."

"No one knows, but there is a rumor that he is in Florence."

"Why? What is he doing there?"

"I have no idea."

The pontiff wrote hurriedly. "Why do I pay agents to keep me informed of these things? Find out!" He quickly scrawled his name at the bottom of the parchment, folded and sealed it with wax, and impressed his ring on it. "Take this to Cardinal Orsini. It is an invitation to a feast during carnival. Tell him—discreetly—that we will have the most beautiful and amiable courtesans in Rome to celebrate with us, and—whisper this—I have arranged for an entertainment with those thirty priapus transvestites that he found so amusing at Easter."

The secretary smiled. "That will appeal to him."

"When he arrives, have him attend me in the Sala del Pappagallo. When he is inside, seal the doors and summon my guards to escort him to the Castel Sant'Angelo. Then see to it that my agents take immediate possession of his estates and property."

"The cardinal's old mother lives in one of his villas. What shall be done with her?"

"Why? Do you want her?"

Troches looked dismayed. "She is eighty years old, Holiness!"

"Eighty? Indeed? Then she has had a long and luxurious life and doubtless has a myriad of relatives and friends. Let her take up residence with them."

Troches genuflected. "Yes, Holiness," he said softly.

The pontiff stood to leave. "Oh yes," he said. "And serve the transvestites the new wine."

"The new wine is bitter, Holiness."

"We celebrate the new year, Francesco. Perhaps the wine will prove prophetic."

*T*HE COMPANY QUARRELED among themselves what to do next. Harlequin felt they had been lucky, but he was absolutely opposed to going to the palazzo and facing Cesare Borgia and the French mercenaries. Dottore argued that they had no choice, but they could leave Isabella, Colombina, and Ruffiana behind at the monastery with Scapino, Salvation, and the cart, only the four actors driving the guild wagon into the palazzo to perform the play.

There was some question whether they could do the same thing again before the duke and his condottiere, but after much consideration, they came to realize that their options were limited. The capitano had not yet returned. The women and the art would be safe in the monastery, and if the quartet of men failed to return, Scapino was to wait until the mercenaries had departed Cesena and the capitano returned, and then take the women to Mantua.

So sundown found the four men mounted on the wagon drawn by Death and Destruction, headed for the Piazza del Popolo. There they were met not by an escort of mercenaries but by a group of townspeople wailing and running around the piazza is terror and anxiety.

Then the performers saw it.

It was the head of Ramiro de Lorca impaled on a pike. His torso, still wearing the elaborate but bloodied suit and a purple mantle, was crumpled in the middle of the piazza. The great pool of blood seemed to well and grow in the scarlet light of the dying sun. Two other mercenaries, one apparently wounded and howling in pain, were scattered a short distance away.

"What—what happened here?" Harlequin asked one of the passersby as Dottore jumped from the wagon and went to the wounded soldier.

"There was some sort of a feast," breathed the townsman. "But suddenly the duke rose and shouted that this man, Ramiro de Lorca, had stolen his wheat and betrayed him to his enemies. He then grabbed the man by the hair, cut his throat, and threw him to his lieutenant, a dark giant of a man, who finished beheading the poor devil. Then they all came down here, mounted their horses, and rode away."

He gestured to Dottore's screaming patient. "Before they left, the dark giant drew his sword and ran through de Lorca's two soldiers."

"Where were the duke and his followers headed for?" asked Harlequin.

The man pointed to a frightened young girl, her head buried in the shoulders of a townswoman, weeping uncontrollably. "The wench over there says she overheard them say Sinigaglia."

"My God," muttered Harlequin. He suddenly caught a glimpse of something dangling from the third-floor window of the palazzo. He squinted against the glare of the setting sun and slowly the object came into focus.

It was Manciano, still wrapped in a bloodied Dominican robe. From the little finger of his broken and crushed right hand hung a light gray object that Harlequin could not identify at that distance.

Later he was to learn it was the dead man's tongue.

Dottore came toward them then and took Harlequin aside. "This one is dead, and this soldier is dying," he whispered to him. "There's nothing more I can do."

Harlequin nodded. "I understand," he said.

"He wants to be shriven," said Dottore. "He is afraid he will die in the state of sin and go to hell."

"Should I ride for a priest?" asked Pantalone as he approached them.

"He'll be dead before you return," replied Dottore.

Harlequin broke away from his friends. As he strode toward the small circle of people gathered around the dying man, he threw his hat to one side and began to slip his heavy, multicolored cloak over his head. This, too, he threw aside as he walked.

By the time he reached the others, he had begun to unwind what appeared to be a long, rolled-up linen sash. He stood above the dying mercenary, kissed a small blue cross embroidered halfway along the length of linen, and placed it around his shoulders.

"My name is Vittorio Bracciolini," he said quietly. "I am a priest."

*D*E LORCA, under torture before being decapitated, had enlightened Cesare on the plot to entrap him at Sinigaglia. The baited message came with the report that Sinigaglia had fallen, but the citadel would only be surrendered to Cesare himself. The Duke of Valentinois smiled, and agreed to come and accept the surrender. Then he secretly divided his ten thousand foot soldiers and three thousand cavalry into two "armies," each to travel to Sinigaglia by parallel march. He arrived, therefore, with an advance guard of only two hundred lancers. This gave the conspirators the impression that they outnumbered his forces.

But the two hundred lancers lined the only bridge over the canal from the old city, effectively cutting off any escape. Then, inviting the condottieri to celebrate the fall of the city in the Palazzo Bernardino, Cesare had both the front and back entrances bolted, and Michelotto set to work strangling Oliveretto Eufreducci and Vitellozzo Vitelli. Francesco and Paolo Orsini, and Paolo's son, were clapped into irons.

With their leaders either murdered or imprisoned, the separate armies were destroyed one by one.

The coup was hailed by Machiavelli, who reported to his Florentine superiors that the murdered men were also enemies of the city. Louis of France commended the audacity and boldness of his duke.

Cesare was the Caesar of the Romagna.

*A*T THE SAME TIME that Cesare was "entertaining" his condottieri at Sinigaglia, his father was sponsoring the carnival celebration in the Vatican.

The Roman "amusement" proved as propitious for the Borgias as the Sinigaglia celebration. Cardinal Giambattista Orsini was arrested with his relative, the Archbishop of Florence, and with Bernardino Alviano, brother of the Venetian condottiere. The cardinal's estates and monies were immediately confiscated and his aged mother was thrown into the streets.

No one dared to help her.

On receiving word of the cardinal's arrest, Cesare had the Orsinis strangled in the piazza at Sartiano.

It was a new—and promising—year.

FLORENCE

Harlequin tells his story at Terranova.
The Borgias attack the Orsini,
and Sebastiano becomes inquisitor.
Isabella meets her father,
and Harlequin is dispensed.

SWITZERLAND
Zürich
Bern
THE ALPS
Aosta
Biella
PO R.
Gen
Nice
RANCE

Innsbruck
Salzburg
AUSTRIA
St.Wolfgang

Zengg
OTTOMAN
EMPIRE
Zara

Piombino
Arez
Cortona
Ancona
riatic Sea
Assisi
Spoleto
TIBER R.
Aquilu
Pescara
Rome
APENNINE MTS.
LIRI R.
Foggia
Naples
Benevento
OFANTO
Brindisi
Otranto
Cosenza

CORSICA
N

SARDINIA

Cagliari

Tyrrhenian
Sea

MILES
0 10 20 40 60 80 100
KILOMETERS
0 20 40 80 120 160

Palermo
Messina
Reggio
SICILY
Catania
Syracuse
Mediterranean Sea

UNIS

Claudia Carlson © 1993

The events at Cesena had two immediate effects upon the Company of Wayward Saints, and the first was a change in destination.

The capitano caught up with the troupe a few kilometers south of Cesena and gave Harlequin the message that Isabella was not what she appeared, and that she should be taken immediately to Florence where "someone of importance" would protect her and take possession of the paintings and statues of Gentile Zappachio. They decided, then, to proceed south to Sarsina, to the Bagno di Romagna, through Settignano, and into the city from the west.

After cutting down the leader of the *piagnoni*, Manciano, the troupe took the body to the nearest Dominican abbey and then turned south toward Predappio on the road to Florence. At the same time, moving much faster, but further south and to the west, Cesare took Siena, passed Acquapendente, and Montefiascone, pillaged Viterbo, and started for Rome.

The second effect of the events at Cesena on the company was a heavy, uncomfortable feeling that descended like a suffocating blanket. The revelation that Harlequin was a priest seemed to inhibit the ensemble. Tristano's songs grew quasi-religious, and Ruffiana, to her astonishment, frequently heard herself compared to the Madonna rather than to the customary rose or a poplar tree. Scapino's bawdy ballads disappeared completely, and the ladies took pains to see that certain anatomical enticements were modestly tucked from sight when the familiar rainbow cloak appeared. There were no more bottoms pinched, lewd suggestions, or vulgar conversations, nor was there any crotch grabbing. Colombina sat apart from Harlequin now and looked for all the world as if self-destruction might be the only possible solution to her problems. Scapino and Isabella, as well as Tristano and Ruffiana, no longer openly kissed one another.

All in all, it was as if the presence of an acknowledged priest required a total denunciation of all that had previously been said or done. The reality of love was denied before the man who thought he served a god of love.

After Pantalone had pointedly referred to Harlequin as "Father," which made the leader wince and Scapino confused, Harlequin assembled the company in Sarsina.

"I have had about enough of this," he began. "I fail to understand how my presence has become such a problem for you when I am the same man I have always been. At worst, I am simply a member of a religious confraternity, but you treat me like a carrier of plague. Would one of you like explain this transformation?"

"Well," volunteered Scapino, "when we didn't know—you were—what you were—we thought you were—you—that is—ah—*human*, you see?"

"No!" shouted Harlequin. "I *am* human! Look! Two arms, two legs, one head—and all the other necessary appendages, I assure you!"

"Why are you screaming at me?" replied Scapino. "It's not my fault you're a priest!"

Colombina came to the rescue with a quiet suggestion. "I think we can resolve all this—if you—honestly—explained just what your—situation—is."

Harlequin was about to answer her with his customary absurdity when he stopped—it seemed as if for the first time—and looked at her, this somewhat faded, unhappy woman so full of love and tenderness, and then he quietly studied the others. *My God in heaven,* he said to himself, *I love them. I love them all. They have a right to know.*

"All right," he assented. "Tomorrow we take a slight detour to Terranova."

*T*HEY DID NOT KNOW where Harlequin was leading them, but by twilight on the third day, after traveling some distance south of Sarsina on a narrow, tree-lined, curving expanse of once paved road, they came to a large, elaborate villa, and Harlequin directed the caravan to halt near a grove of fruit trees.

He left them there and walked up a curving road that led to the main entrance of the villa, where he was stopped by two armed guards. After a brief conversation one of the guards entered the house, and a short time later emerged with a young man of about twenty years of age, dressed fashionably. The young man seemed pleased to see Harlequin, and after a moment he reentered the villa, and Harlequin returned to the company.

"Take the animals and the cart along this pathway behind the villa to the stables," he told Capitano, Scapino, and Pantalone. "Servants will take them from you. Then join the rest of us inside." He led Colombina, Isabella, Ruffiana, and Dottore up the roadway, and the three men rolled the carts around the side of the mansion.

"This," said Harlequin as he escorted the others toward the main entrance, "is Terranova. It is where I was born. My father built it and came here toward the end of his life with a young bride—my mother. He himself was born not far from here in a much less opulent but respectable dwelling."

"Who was the handsome young man who greeted you?" Ruffiana smiled.

"My nephew, Pico. And keep your lascivious hands away from him. He is young and impressionable."

"Does he live here alone?" asked Colombina.

"He serves as master of the estate, but several members of my—family—live here."

As they climbed the marble staircase to the large doors fronting the villa, the guards came to attention, which both startled and delighted the women. A single name was carved in the stone arch over the door.

Bracciolini.

Harlequin noticed them studying it. "There it is. The family name," he said softly. He motioned them into the villa, where they were met by servants who took them up a great staircase and into various rooms.

The room assigned the ladies was the largest and most comfortable. Tristano, who had fallen asleep in the wagon, was assigned to a room with Capitano and Dottore. Scapino and Pantalone were shown to the smallest room of the three, and Harlequin disappeared completely.

In each chamber a large iron tub was then filled with hot water, and the gentle suggestion was made that everyone—without exception—should bathe.

Long, plain gowns with slashed sleeves trimmed with tiny pearls and thin gold girdles were provided for the ladies. The men were given the formless robes, tights, and soft shoes in fashion in the better courts of Europe.

Soon they were summoned to dine.

They ate at a long table set parallel to another across a great hall and at right angles to a third mounted on a dais and linking the other two. The room was dominated by an open, circular stone hearth over which was suspended the roasting carcass of a deer. Cooks busied themselves in this area as servants hurried platters of cut meat and bread, cheeses, and other delicacies to and from the tables. Three great dogs padded between the tables and the legs of the diners and begged tidbits and scraps, which were, wisely, never withheld from them.

At the table opposite the company, richly garbed women and a small army of children talked among themselves, studied the company, and ate with forks—a device that was familiar only to Isabella, Tristano, and Dottore. Capitano, indicating he knew the function of the tined instrument but would not be a party to its use, ripped at his food with knife and hand, and most of the Wayward Saints followed his example.

The food was simple and abundant, and the wine was excellent.

Harlequin arrived later and was seated to the right of a lovely young woman at the main table. Her left hand was clutched tightly by Pico Bracciolini.

For once, the company saw their leader without his multicolored cloak. He was now dressed in tunic and hose, earth brown, trimmed in silver, with high boots and a silver medallion around his shoulders. *Somehow,* Colombina thought to herself, *this is the real man. This is what he is.* She would look up from time to time as she ate to see him silently staring at the opposite table or at the company. She noticed he ate sparingly and talked with Pico and the young woman exclusively, never with the older gentleman seated on his right. *But,* thought Colombina, *he is not happy.*

Following the meal, Pico addressed the diners and extended the hospitality of the villa to the company. He introduced Harlequin to some of the people at the opposite table, all of whom were Bracciolini or wives, husbands, or children of Bracciolini, and then Harlequin rose and gestured to his friends to come with him. He led them from the dining hall through a maze of torch-lit corridors and up a staircase until he stopped before a pair of large, carved doors. He opened one and invited them to follow him inside.

It was an incredible room: high-ceilinged, warm, and well illuminated by a blazing fireplace and numerous torches and lamps. The walls were packed with enormous leather-bound books and manuscripts. There were rolls of parchment in circular receptacles around the room, maps and scrolls, and animals stuffed and mounted in realistic poses.

Harlequin signaled the company to make themselves comfortable, and most of them, bloated and glutted from the abundance of food and drink after such a long period of austerity, sat or sprawled on the fur rugs and the richly upholstered chairs.

Dottore alone paced the full length of the room looking at everything. *Godsblood!* he thought. *It's the workroom of the maestro!*

Harlequin seated himself by a large worktable with his back to the fire and smiled at the others. "All right, children," he said. "I am prepared to tell you my history. Pay attention, take notes, and we will have a short examination on the important points at breakfast."

"MY FATHER," he began, "was Poggio Bracciolini. As I told you, he was born not far from here, in poverty, and so, when he became a young man, he wisely determined there were only two roads leading from his life of deprivation and squalor: the Church or the military. He weighed the two careers for some time. He coveted the adventure, booty, and the comradeship associated with the military life, but he also considered the fact that death rode with every regiment, and life was too precious to be risked in combat."

"I know the man," interjected Capitano.

"My father chose the Church and was ordained—fully determined, mind you, to combine the privileges of both professions with none of the responsibilities. He was clever, my father, and intelligent, so he learned quickly. His one weakness was in languages. His Greek and Latin were, at best, mediocre, a fact often mentioned by his enemies in future years—usually in Greek and Latin. Still, he wrote well, with a keen, satiric sense of humor, so he rose rapidly, becoming a member of the Curia under Pope Martin the Fifth.

"It was my father who arranged the little diversions in the evening for His Holiness and the cardinals. They would assemble in the Bugiale, the Chamber of Lies, and exchange tales and stories and, perhaps, dine or sample the best of the Vatican wine cellars. In time he wrote down some of these stories and tales in a book—"

"The *Facetiae*!" squealed Isabella.

Harlequin was pleased. "Oh, you're familiar with my father's book? Yes, he wrote the *Facetiae*. He also wrote a description of Rome, hundreds of pamphlets and letters, and a book against worldly monks and friars called *A Dialogue Against Hypocrites*—which was somewhat hypocritical in itself since my father lived openly with a mistress and fathered fourteen children during his priesthood."

"Fourteen?!" choked Colombina.

"He used to say that every man should have a hobby." Harlequin grinned. "And he often told my brothers that he was still more moral than the Vatican clergy, because he *knew* he was a hypocrite and openly acknowledged it."

"You mean that your father wrote an anticlerical book, the *Facetiae*, kept a mistress, and sired fourteen children without the pope knowing?" inquired Tristano.

"Oh, the pope knew," said Harlequin, "but my father used his sharp tongue and a quick pen to attack the pope's enemies such as Francesco Filelfo. As I recall, he labeled Filelfo a rancid goat, a horned monster, and the father of lies, and suggested that the only reason he still had any friends was due to the fact that they were sleeping with his wife. That delighted the Holy Father, so His Holiness indulged him."

"I imagine Filelfo did not think too highly of your father," Colombina pointed out.

"He did not," said Harlequin, "and neither did Filelfo's friends, who, unfortunately, included the Piccolomini, the Visconti, and the Sforzas.

"My father became an ardent humanist, a stoic, and an epicurean—whatever philosophy was most fashionable at the time and justified his behavior. He became friends with people like Salutati, Niccolo Niccolo, Alberti, and Manetti. But when Pope Martin died, he was replaced by Eugene the Fourth, whose family, as is often the case, hated the Colonnas; so my father's religious superiors became—well, they felt he should be a little more prudent in his personal life. My father's reaction to that was righteous anger, and he startled everyone by abandoning both the Vatican and his mistress and retiring to Terranova with a young girl of eighteen, whom he married.

"He was fifty-five, and through the intercession of friendly families, he was soon appointed chancellor of Florence. I was the last of his children, born when his wife was thirty-seven and he was seventy-four."

The men were awed, and Colombina's mouth dropped open in astonishment. "You said—seventy-four?"

Harlequin nodded. "The priest who christened me said it was a miracle, second only to the virgin birth; but my bastard half brothers and sisters suggested other possibilities, implying that my mother had expanded upon my father's hobby."

"Seventy-four," muttered Colombina.

"Poggio, on the other hand, gloated over my birth and proclaimed he would be fathering children at ninety."

"Seventy-four," whispered Colombina to herself, envisioning the elusive goal of motherhood as a new and distinct possibility.

"But, of course, I came into a somewhat hostile atmosphere. My numerous stepbrothers and sisters did not want Poggio fathering children at ninety—especially since that meant the estate would be divided into still smaller inheritances. Poggio knew it, so he devised a master plan for my future. I was to follow him into the Roman Church, but not until my education had fortified me with enough humanist principles and worldly knowledge to offset the ecclesiastical training that was to come."

Harlequin noticed that Pantalone had fallen asleep.

"When I was only five, my father died, but his wishes were honored, and I was quickly sent from Terranova to Padua to a school built on the principles of Vittorino da Feltre, whom he had admired. I was taught the required Latin and Greek—which my father had insisted upon—and classical literature from Aristotle and Plato through Cicero and Horace.

"Here I was taught that human life was sacred. That humanity shared a common brotherhood and was the highest form of creation. That if there existed a God to be known, He could best be known through a study of His masterwork, man. That the principles upon which a human life should be built were self-respect, dignity, freedom, and equality."

He noticed then that Ruffiana was also asleep.

"Eventually," he continued, "I was sent to Rome to study with John Argyropoulos, and still following my father's master plan, I was ordained at twenty. This presented me with a new set of convictions.

"The Church taught me that life had no meaning without a direct reference to God and my salvation. That man was, at best, imperfect and innately sinful. That the principles upon which a human life should be built were absolute faith, complete devotion to God and Church, and total dedication to the dogma. If that meant I must torture a woman, let us say, to get her to confess that she was a witch, I must do it, for the salvation of her own soul and to prevent others being contaminated by her."

Pantalone awakened only momentarily, fell completely out of his chair and at once returned to sleep, curled like a great dog on the fur rug before the fire.

"By that time Pope Sixtus the Fourth, Francesco della Rovere, had ascended the throne of Peter, and set about destroying the power built up by the preceding Barbo, Piccolomini, and Borgia popes. My teacher brought me to his attention. I wrote and read Latin and Greek, and French as well, so I was assigned to the Vatican library, which Sixtus had reopened.

"This was a most pleasant and beneficial assignment. It meant, of course, that I would not be called upon to torture anyone or, for that matter, hear confessions and give absolution. Here, too, I had access not only to the thousands of books by authors throughout the world, but also those which were kept locked away as suppressed or forbidden."

"Were there pictures in them?" asked Scapino.

"Some." Harlequin winked. "But when Sixtus died, the cardinals chose Innocent the Eighth, a Cibo, to succeed him. The Cibo were one of the families opposed to my father. As punishment for his sins, I was assigned to a parish to the north. My problem then, you see, was that I was working at my father's profession without my father's elastic conscience. I could not accept the cloak of priesthood without its obligations and responsibilities, and I gradually recognized the fact that I was never meant to be a priest. I lasted one year in that small parish. So one night I removed my robe, crossed the border into Switzerland, and became a mercenary. Or rather, I was trained to become a mercenary.

"But here I was taught that humanity only exists to be pawns for the acquisition of power and wealth. I was taught that the highest principles for a man to live by were bravery, cunning, deception—when it serves your honor—and a little theft on the side.

"I served with a mercenary regiment that was defeated in their very first battle—which was enough for me anyway, and then the Cibo pope, who did not take kindly to my departure from the punishing assignment of the parish, sent two priests—inquisitors—to seek me out. I told them I was—confused. I wished to have my priestly vows dispensed as so many others had been. They gave me to understand that in my case it was impossible. But three nights later a priest appeared, helped me to escape in my brigandine cloak, and gave me—something—that I was to take to Rome. Then"—he paused then to briefly smile at Colombina—"I encountered you.

"At Piacenza, I received instructions to go instead to Mantua, and since that was Isabella's destination, I naturally agreed to escort her. But the route was impossible, as you know, and we kept being pushed farther and farther east. Finally my contact, the Dominican known as Manciano, instructed me to go to Florence, where both Isabella and—my burden—would be lifted from me. I was given to understand that my father still had friends in the Curia whose families he had helped, and if I completed my assignment and passed my—burden—to someone in Florence who will identify himself to me, then it would be possible for me to get dispensed from my vows."

Colombina stood up. "Why didn't you tell us this before?"

"Who would have believed it?" countered Harlequin. "If God is the author of the dramas of life, He is hopelessly mediocre. His plots are filled with absurdities and implausibilities, and just when you think you can grasp the meaning, He changes the characters and introduces entirely new themes. He mixes His modes and styles, drops comic characters into melodramatic situations, dresses His performers in costumes that never match their personalities, and when your own scene is played out, you're still left bewildered, wondering if you were a major character or a supernumerary. Who would believe I am a priest, a son of a priest, a warrior who hates war? But—here is the proof—my father's study, his books, everything."

He came around to sit on the edge of the worktable. "So you see, I am weary to death of being treated like the beatific vision. I am just like you. There is no difference at all. Is that clear?"

They looked at one another. Colombina shrugged and started toward the bookcase. As she passed, Harlequin suddenly reached out and slapped her hard on the behind. "Clear?" he roared. Stunned, she turned and gaped at him, not knowing quite what to do. Then she slowly smiled, stuck her tongue out at him, and the others cheered.

In celebration, when they departed the following morning, they stole fourteen forks, two of the gowns, three robes, and a copy of the *Facetiae*.

Vittorio Bracciolini, who had led them to Terranova, was never seen again.

It was Harlequin who led them away—and later returned all they had stolen.

*M*ACHIAVELLI TOOK THE PARCHMENT from the courier and unrolled it. "Read it," said Cesare as he buttoned his black tunic and adjusted it to his broad chest.

The Florentine studied the message and said, "It is from your father. He congratulates you on your victories, deplores your attack on Viterbo, which, he reminds you, is church property, and he suggests you immediately launch an attack on Giangiordano Orsini at Bracciano castle."

"Ridiculous! How can I comply with that request? Giangiordano is subservient to the King of France and a knight. My own knighthood prohibits me from attacking a fellow knight."

Machiavelli chuckled knowingly. "Which means, of course, you do not choose to do it." Cesare smiled, and Machiavelli read further. "He also suggests that you attack Niccolo Orsini at Pitigliano."

Cesare buckled his sword around his waist. "God in heaven, has the old man gone mad? Has this vendetta against the Orsini disturbed his mind? Niccolo is a former general of the Church! And now he serves the Venetians! My father knows that Louis has formed an alliance with Florence, Siena, Lucca, and Bologna to—temper—my activities. I can't afford to offend Venice! I need them!" He crossed to the large mirror in one corner of the room. "If I could only locate this—alleged daughter—and return her to the doge, I could strengthen my alliance with Venice."

Machiavelli observed, "That is a becoming tunic, Your Grace."

"I like black," said Cesare, surveying the result in his mirror. "It raises the specter of death and elicits a feeling of despair—which are

potent weapons. Trim black with silver, as in the mantle of a cat-
afalque, and people tremble at the very sight of you."

Machiavelli placed the parchment on the duke's desk. "What will
you do about your father? He will not be happy that you refuse to
attack Bracciano and Pitigliano."

Cesare paused at the desk to study the map displayed there. He
bent over it, and after a moment he said quietly, "I will besiege
Ceri. It is under the command of Giulio Orsini." He stood and
smiled at the Florentine.

"That ought to keep the old bastard happy."

*U*PON LEAVING TERRANOVA, the company headed west
to the Bagno di Romagna and then crossed the Arno and continued westward until they reached the point where the roads fork—
south to Arezzo, west to Florence. They turned northwest through
Settignano until they could see the great city from a distance: the
vast sprawl of it set against gentle mountains, a city of earth colors
with multistory buildings, dominated by the domed duomo of Santa Maria del Fiore and the tower of the Palazzo Vecchio; the city
brought to glory by the Medici until the people rose against them
and expelled the family; the city Savonarola prayed might be spared
the wrath of God only to be executed by order of the Vicar of
Christ. Fickle Florence, divided by theologies and politics as the
Arno divided it geographically. From where they were, descending
the Via di Santo Leonardo, the company could see the four bridges
spanning the waters. The Ponte Vecchio dominated, the covered
bridge a small village in itself.

Harlequin, with Capitano sitting beside him, drove the wagon
toward the gate that opened into the walled city. Scapino followed
in the cart drawn by Zephyr, who, stripped of armor and harness,
was hitched to the cart as if he were a common workhorse; the stallion's great, strong head and back, however, denied the masquerade.
The women, cloaked in heavy shawls and dark clothing, were easily
acceptable as the reverent wives of guildsmen.

They were stopped at the Porta Santo Frediano by Florentine guards. Harlequin spoke for them.

"Kind gentlemen," he patiently explained, "we are members of the bellwrights guild, I Santi Ostinati, come to play *Abraham and Isaac* on the feast day."

"A play?" the guard asked, surprised. "On Ash Wednesday?"

"What better time for *sacre rappresentazioni?*"

"It seems a little inappropriate," said the guard. "It being the start of Lent and all. But if it's traditional . . ."

"Indeed it is," the Capitano declared with great enthusiasm. "What better and more inspiring work for Ash Wednesday than the story of the man ordered to reduce his son to ashes?"

The Florentine seemed stunned, but he managed to nod. "I never thought of it that way," he said, and told them to wait. He crossed to a small circle of other guards and whispered something to them. The delay seemed to stretch into hours before he again stepped forward and looked up at Harlequin on the seat of the guild wagon. "I suppose it will do no harm," he said. "Go directly down the Borgo Santo Frediano past Santa Maria del Carmine to the Via de Serragli. Turn left to the Ponte alla Carrara and continue on the Via del Moro to the Piazza Madonna. You can perform there."

"God love you, brother!" murmured Harlequin as he quickly urged Death and Destruction past the guard post. They proceeded as they were instructed, watched carefully along the route by armed men, and parked the wagon and the cart in the Piazza Madonna. Harlequin reminded them that Isabella was to be delivered to the mysterious "someone of power" in the Palazzo Pitti, which was on the south bank of the Arno. He instructed the company to wait and prepare the stage as if they were going to perform while he, the capitano, and Isabella went to the three-story palazzo.

There was some disturbance prior to their departure when Scapino suggested that he go with Isabella as a manservant, and Isabella insisted she didn't want to go at all. Then Dottore joined the debate and pointed out that as he was the man assigned the mission to bring Isabella to safety, he should see it through. But Harlequin assured them that this was merely a scouting mission, an attempt to

analyze the situation and decide what action to take. Isabella would not be compelled to stay where she did not wish to be.

At the Ponte Santa Trinita, the trio was stopped by still another group of soldiers uniformed in red and yellow. Their condottiere, whose back was turned to them, wore a magnificent suit of silvered armor. Harlequin testified that he and the capitano were guildsmen and Isabella was the captain's wife, and that they were going to the stalls of the merchants that line the approach to the Ponte Vecchio in order to purchase supplies for their brothers in the Piazza Madonna. One mercenary who barred their way turned to relate the story to the condottiere. The officer listened, nodded, and then faced the trio.

"Welcome to Florence, Father Bracciolini of the bellwrights." Angelo leered. "We've been expecting you."

*I*N THE SECOND FLOOR of the Palazzo Vecchio, Harlequin was hurled into a room furnished only with a long desk placed before the floor-to-ceiling windows that looked down into the Piazza della Signoria. Father Sebastiano sat behind the desk, guarded by mercenaries on either side, and Angelo, who stood apart watching them all, leaned against a wall.

"Ah, Father Vittorio," said Sebastiano. "It has been some time." He glanced at some papers before him on the desk. "But you may take comfort in the fact that our agents never lost sight of you once you surfaced in Biella."

Harlequin smiled. "You must congratulate them for me."

Sebastiano returned the smile. "I trust, Father Vittorio, you appreciate the serious position in which you find yourself."

"Of course I do," said Harlequin. "I'm standing. That's always a serious position—especially when the inquisitor is seated." He lowered his voice. "Or have you stopped torturing renegade priests?"

"Not at all," replied Sebastiano. "As you may well discover. But I will spare you the sermonizing."

"The best sermon I ever heard," said Harlequin, "was at an ordination performed by a Borgia cardinal. The bishop put his hand in the poor box and drew out a gold florin. Then he turned to the new priests and said, 'Go, and do likewise.' "

"Short and to the point," observed Sebastiano coldly.

"That's what I thought," said Harlequin.

The inquisitor studied his guest for some time, and then he said quietly, "Sit down, Father Bracciolini." Harlequin looked at him, shrugged, and sat down. "I, too, will come to the point," said Sebastiano dryly. "Where are the letters?"

"Letters?"

"Give us the Savelli letters," Sebastiano replied. "It is useless to pretend you don't know of them. We knew a priest was carrying them from Switzerland, but we thought it was the leader of the *piagnoni*, Manciano. But he—informed—us that you had them."

Harlequin stared at the ferret-faced cleric. "I know of no one by that name, but I assume, considering your particular talents, that he was subjected to torture. Anyone, under those conditions, would tell you anything you wanted to hear."

Sebastiano rose from behind his desk. "Be obstinate," he said, "and you are mine." He fingered the dagger. "You are, after all, a renegade priest. We have witnesses to heresy and blasphemy. We have people who will even swear to sacrilege. You have traveled with whores and murderers."

"I seem to recall a whore or two, but—murderers?"

Sebastiano returned to the desk and snapped open a scroll there. "A cutpurse sought by the lord of Savoy, an arsonist sought by the Bentivoglio, a runaway servant bonded to the Duke of Valentinois, a young whore wanted by a condottiere attached to the mercenary army of the Duke d'Este, a deserter who murdered—yes, murdered—an officer of the French, and a runaway student who pillaged his own father's storehouse." He looked up. "I am grateful that you have brought them all to us and—most importantly—the young woman sought by the Doge of Venice."

"My," said Harlequin, "I had no idea we were so popular."

"Oh yes," assured Sebastiano. "By capturing all of you, my lord, the Count of Valentinois can earn the respect and admiration of half of the noble families of Italy."

"My, hasn't destiny been kind to the former cardinal? And you serve Cesare, of course."

"Of course."

Harlequin sighed and studied the priest's face for a moment. "You said the Doge of Venice is seeking the young girl supposedly traveling with me?"

"You know her as Isabella Zappachio. But the lady is of much loftier parentage. The Doge of Venice has need of the girl's family. So if my master returns her to Venice, it will also solidify the bond between the Borgias and the Venetians."

Harlequin nodded. "Which means the Venetians will not interfere if Cesare decides to—extend his domain in the Romagna."

"His Holiness said you were intelligent," said Sebastiano. "That is why he has authorized me to—make you an offer."

"An offer?" Harlequin echoed softly.

"The holy father feels that you may have inherited the wit, practical wisdom, and cunning of your father. Therefore, if you give us the letters, His Holiness is prepared to give you a dispensation from your priestly vows—which you desperately want—as well as a position with the Church that will provide you with a substantial income, a palazzo, servants, and a title you may pass on to your children."

Harlequin slowly let the air escape from his lungs. "A dispensation, did you say?" Sebastiano nodded. Harlequin stood and walked to the windows, and Angelo shifted his weight as if he expected the bearded man to hurl himself through them into the piazza. "Now, that's what I call a temptation," said Harlequin. "St. Anthony would have a hard time with that one." He breathed deeply, relaxing, forcing himself to think, to concentrate. He turned to face Sebastiano. "And what happens to these—whores and murderers—if I am able to—locate—these letters for you?"

"The Milanese officer becomes what he has always been: a condottiere, a captain of mercenaries. Cesare Borgia has need of men like this Capitano."

"He needs murderers?"

"Soldiers!" snapped Sebastiano.

"Oh." Harlequin smiled. "I thought you just described him as a murderer." Then he quickly added, "And this—Isabella?"

"She will not be harmed. But she will have to be returned to Venice as—a guest, her future dependent on the behavior of—her family. As for the others"—the cleric shrugged—"the holy father will be benevolent, I'm certain, and extend his mercy to all of them, being Christians." He leaned across the desk to Harlequin and laughed lightly. "They are Christians, aren't they? You don't have a Turk or some Jews tucked away somewhere, have you?"

"I haven't checked lately." Harlequin grinned at him. "Now, let me see if I understand this properly. If I agree to—find and restore these—letters to Cesare Borgia, I will be dispensed from my vows and receive numerous blessings in wealth and prestige, and my companions will be—what shall we say? Absolved of their sins?"

"Yes," hissed Sebastiano.

"And if I don't?"

Silence.

"I see," Harlequin said softly. "I get burned alive, Isabella goes to Venice anyway, Dottore and Capitano go to the duke, Pantalone to the Bentivoglio, Scapino will be thrown into prison, and Colombina and Ruffiana will probably be given to your own mercenaries for whatever diversions amuse them. Tristano, I imagine, will be sent back to his father in Bologna—minus a little of his beauty."

Sebastiano leaned across the desk, still smiling. "Refuse the offer, Bracciolini. Please."

There was a long pause before Harlequin ordered, "Write it down."

"Write it down?"

"Every word, every promise," said Harlequin, "just as you told it to me." He leaned toward Sebastiano. "The word of the Borgia pope has been known to vacillate in the winds of change. I want a written carte blanche, a document with papal seal and signature, with everything noted."

Sebastiano sat for a moment without speaking. From beyond the windows the mass of monks and penitents could be heard singing a hymn in the piazza. "But why?" he asked coldly. "It would have to go to Rome anyway to be signed and sealed by His Holiness."

"*You* sign it," said Harlequin. "Sign it as a representative of the pope. You have that authority, don't you? You're his agent."

The priest studied the Vagabond for a moment and then shrugged. "If you wish." He took a parchment from a drawer and a small vial of ink, and he began to write.

Harlequin stood up and wandered over to the windows to watch the processions of monks leaving the piazza below. Behind him, he heard the scratching of the quill against the parchment stop, and he turned to find Sebastiano holding the document out to him. "Is this precise enough?"

Harlequin studied the neat, even handwriting. "You have not included all their names," he said quietly as he returned to his chair with the parchment.

"Mother of God, do you think I have a master list of every thief, whore, and murderer in Italy? Fill the other names in yourself."

Harlequin rose and returned the document. "You do it. I'll give you their names." He then recited the Christian names of everyone in the company as Sebastiano copied them into the body of the text. Then the cleric handed the parchment back to Harlequin, who examined it once more and again returned it to him. "The seal, please. The Borgia seal."

Sebastiano sighed, pinched wax from a candle, pressed it on the document, and then impressed the design from his ring—the Borgian bull—into it. He blew on the wax to cool it and gave the parchment to Harlequin. "There!" he announced.

Harlequin glanced at the seal, smiled, and placed the document on the edge of the desk.

"What is it now?" Sebastiano growled. "What do you want me to do with this?"

Harlequin bent close to him and said quietly, as if passing a secret between them, "I want you to take this document, with its Borgia seal, and roll it—very tightly—into a cylinder, and then shove it up your arse."

Sebastiano turned scarlet, but Harlequin continued, softer now and coldly. "I would sooner serve the devil himself than that ruthless, arrogant, malevolent horse turd who calls himself a father of the Church!"

The cleric stared at him, standing now, and then he suddenly snatched the parchment from the tabletop and held it to the flame of the candle. It instantly ignited.

"You do have a talent for fire," said Harlequin softly.

Without taking his eyes from his guest, Sebastiano shouted to Angelo. "This charade is finished! Bring in the others."

But as Angelo crossed to the doors of the chamber, they were suddenly hurled open and the room was filled with mercenaries— swords drawn, pikes and crossbows at the ready, wearing a crest that Harlequin immediately recognized. These soldiers, escorting Isabella and Capitano between them, formed a double file directly to Sebastiano's desk, and down this walkway strode a tall, white-haired man in the glorious scarlet raiment of a cardinal. He stopped before the desk.

"Ah, Father Sebastiano," he said in a booming voice. "At last we meet. I've read so much of your private correspondence over the past three years, I feel I've come to know you." The ferret-faced priest opened his mouth as if to speak, but the newcomer waved him to silence with a huge hand dominated by his cardinal's ring. "You know me, of course, but to clarify the situation: I am Cardinal Giuliano della Rovere of the Curia, and these—ecclesiastical prisoners—are now under my jurisdiction."

"But—" Sebastiano began.

Again the cardinal silenced him. "Of course I will commend your diligence in snaring these nefarious personalities when I meet with your lord, the Count of Valentinois. The Church is pleased that its militant arm is still effective and untiring." Sebastiano nodded dumbly. "I will, of course, assume complete responsibility," said della Rovere, and then he motioned to one of his soldiers. "Escort these—ecclesiastical prisoners—to the palazzo. They are to talk to no one, and no one is to talk to them. Understand?"

His condottiere saluted, and in an instant only two of the mercenaries and the cardinal remained in the room with Sebastiano and Angelo.

"You have done splendidly," said della Rovere. "Such fine work should merit you a station of more—opportunity. Have you ever thought of being a secretary to—oh—a monsignor, perhaps? Say, in Naples? Or Sicily?" Sebastiano turned pale, but the cardinal continued. "Ah, I see you haven't. Pity. A world of opportunity."

And with that he turned abruptly and strode from the room, followed by the remaining two mercenaries, and Sebastiano collapsed into his chair.

*H*ARLEQUIN, ISABELLA, AND CAPITANO were quickly ushered down the staircase and into a waiting carriage. Armed and mounted mercenaries stood guard around the carriage. Then, after the cardinal himself emerged from the palazzo and entered a second carriage behind the first, the entire entourage proceeded rapidly across the Ponte Vecchio to the Via de' Guicciardini and wheeled into the walled courtyard of the Palazzo Pitti. As the trio stepped from the carriage they were immediately escorted into the side door and up the stairs to the third-floor antechamber.

A moment later della Rovere came hurriedly into the room, where servants and mercenaries were carrying books and manuscripts, scrolls and parchments back and forth, stacking them in containers and crates. The cardinal himself continued examining a pile of papers as he talked to Harlequin, the capitano, and Isabella.

"Now listen carefully, because we do not have a great deal of time. The Pitti have permitted me the use of their palazzo, but I cannot remain in one place for any length of time. I will have to speak to you even as I prepare for my departure from Florence." He produced a sheet of parchment from several on his desk and handed it to Isabella. "Please, signorina. Sign this."

Isabella glanced at the page. "What is it?"

"An inventory of the paintings and statues of my friend and agent, Gentile Zappachio, that you were to bring to me. They will be safe with me, and the Venetians will never see them." He stopped to look at Isabella, and his voice softened. "I regret to inform you, signorina, that the man you called your father has been murdered in Venice and attempts have been made to suggest it was a suicide. I have evidence that it was not, but there is little that can be done about it." His voice softened even more. "He was not your real father, however. Nor was the kind and gracious lady you called mother your *real* mother." He smiled at her and said most gently, "But you have your mother's eyes."

Isabella looked up from signing the document. "Who—were my parents?"

The cardinal stared at her for what seemed an eternity before he delicately replied, "Your mother's identity must remain a secret— for the moment, but—I am your father."

Isabella stood motionless, her mouth open, looking deeply into the eyes of the man standing across the desk from her. "You? You're—my father?"

He nodded. "Your mother—well—she was betrothed at the time of our—romance—to a gentleman of another ancient and noble family. It was a marriage of alliances and power, which is vital to the maintenance of the nobility in Italy, so, understandably, as a member of the hierarchy, I could not acknowledge you without involving her. When you were born, I quietly arranged for you to be raised by the Zappachios, and your mother—married her nobleman."

He crossed and took her hand in both of his. "I want you to know that I have never deserted you. Never. Your mother and I love you very much, and we secretly have watched over you since your childhood.

"It was your mother who arranged for your education at Urbino. I saw to it that you were protected during your years in Venice, and I supplied Gentile with enough jewels and gold to keep you in comfort until—until word came to me that the doge suspected your true parentage and was about to use you as a weapon in his diplomatic alliances. I have made powerful enemies, my dear, and I do not apologize for that. The ferocity and cunning of my enemies is a testimonial to my own powers. But I could not have you become a pawn in my wars, so I had Gentile take you and his artifacts to Milan. At that time Cesare had no idea who you were, and I hoped, by playing upon Maestro Leonardo's allegiance to artistic freedom, he might convince the duke himself to provide an escort to bring you to Mantua."

"Why Mantua?"

"Let us say your mother has some influence in the courts of the Montefeltro and the Gonzaga. You also have friends among the Colonna and my own family, the della Roveres. All enemies to the Borgias. Somehow Cesare Borgia began to suspect your true parentage, and there was the distinct possibility that he would use you to control both myself and—and your mother."

"Can't you tell me who my mother is?"

"It is better you do not know, but you may discover the truth yourself. You have the *cassone* with your mother's crest upon the cover. My best agent reported that it was still in your possession at Pavia."

Harlequin approached the couple. "At Pavia? Then your agent was with the Swiss mercenaries at the crossroads?"

Della Rovere nodded. "And not far from you throughout your entire journey. He was—is—your shadow. It was my men who came to your rescue when the cardinal's mercenaries attacked you at Modena. This—special—agent saw them enter your encampment, but he had to ride back to the city to get assistance."

"And I'm never to know my mother?" Isabella asked.

"Certainly not now, my dear. There is still a great deal of danger involved. The Borgian pope has had Cardinal Orsini and three more of his family murdered. My family and I are next on his list, but for the moment he cannot find me, and he has nothing tangible to link me with the *piagnoni*." He patted Isabella's hand. "You will know your mother's name soon enough, but in these times, when

Cesare Borgia can change his alliances with each passing breeze, the less you know the better." He took the parchment from her and handed it to his steward. "Bring the paintings and the statues here," the cardinal commanded.

He turned then to address Harlequin. "It's fortunate you arrived when you did, so I could be of service to you." He bowed slightly. "As your father was of service to mine."

Isabella said nothing, but Harlequin noticed the tightening around her lips, and the capitano led her to a chair.

"But why—to kill my—to kill that poor old painter?" she stammered.

The cardinal nodded sympathetically. "Yes. My poor Gentile. Well, all I can tell you is that he died because Cesare Borgia wants to rule Italy. The new Caesar. He has already broken the power of the Riarios, the Malatestas, the Sforzas, the Manfredis, the Appianos, and the Varanos. He has murdered members of the Vitelli, Orsini, and the Este families. But he is intelligent enough to realize that he cannot kill us all. His real power rests with the Vatican, and Rodrigo cannot live forever. When the present pope dies, Cesare will need friends among the Curia to make certain that the new pontiff retains him as gonfalonier of the Church. That title is all that assures him that his murders carry the sanction of the Roman see. It legitimatizes his crimes. He was looking for some method to control my family and your mother's and, I suspect, Gentile kept our secret. When he could not confirm Cesare's suspicions, he was murdered." He paused. "I'm sorry. Cesare knows no morality. Machiavelli says he is dedicated to what the Florentine calls *virtù*. It is all very—Italian."

"*Terribilita*," mumbled Capitano.

"Precisely," the cardinal confirmed. "*Terribilita*." He returned his attention to the papers, some of which he discarded to his left and others to his right. "But the Borgias realize that no matter which family controls which province, it is the pope who controls Italy. When Rodrigo dies, there is a very strong possibility that I will be the one to succeed him on the throne of Peter, and then . . . !" His eyes flashed, and he smiled at Harlequin.

He paused then to look closely at Isabella. "I know this has all been shocking to you, my dear. But I have relied upon the blood of your mother—who is an exceptional woman—to sustain you. I have rejoiced in your courage and your intelligence. I have been delighted by the reports of your brave—and shocking—behavior at court. You have scandalized the pretentious and the pompous and alienated the common and the traditional. I'm very proud of you." He smiled gently at her. "But perhaps you would feel better, my dear, if you had some brandy and rested for a while." He turned to the capitano. "Would you escort the young lady into the reception chamber, Captain? There you will find an excellent brandy and a chaise. If you need anything more, call one of my servants."

The soldier helped Isabella to her feet, and they left the room. "All right," the cardinal announced to his workers, "see to the packing of the materials in the other rooms and get the carriages ready. Leave matters here for a while." The servants and mercenaries departed in a moment, quietly and almost, Harlequin thought, like magic. When the last had gone and the doors had been secured, the cardinal turned to Harlequin. "Now, Vittorio, the letters."

From his voluminous cloak Harlequin produced the packet, still wrapped in the linen stole of his priesthood. He opened it up and handed its contents to della Rovere. "What will you do with them?" he asked.

"Make copies," the cardinal replied. "Within a month every cardinal, every noble family in Italy will have a copy. The letters detail and document the crimes of Rodrigo and his bastard son. As long as Rodrigo is pope, the letters will have little effect. But when he dies, they will have a significant effect on the election of the new pope, and that will bring Cesare down." The letters disappeared into the clergyman's scarlet cloak. "Now, Vittorio," he said with concern, "you wish to be dispensed from your priestly vows. Why?"

"I—cannot bring myself—to judge others. It's all very fine to tell me that whose sins I shall forgive, they are forgiven, but—who am I to make such a decision?"

The cardinal smiled. "No one. Just a man in a box passing on the word from God. It is not vital that you *have* the authority. It is vital that the confessor *believes* you have the authority." He grew more serious. "You want a dispensation. With Rodrigo heading the Church, I'm afraid that's impossible."

Harlequin bristled. "Marriage vows, and even the vows of priesthood, are dispensed every day by the Borgia pope. He annulled the marriage of the French king and his own daughter! He dispensed Cesare from *his* vows."

"Technically Cesare was not a priest to begin with," noted the cardinal. "He was a subdeacon."

"He was made a cardinal!"

"So was I. Don't confuse politics with religion."

Harlequin paced about the room, angry and frustrated. "I was given to understand that I might find friends in Rome who could help me."

"Yes, they could," said della Rovere, sorting the papers once more, "but they will not. The insecurity of the times and the sense of impeding doom that hangs over the Vatican will prevent them. It is painfully clear that the Borgias will stop at nothing—and I mean *nothing*—to achieve their ends. As long as the Borgia pope is opposed to you—and you have just refused his offer—he will not dispense you."

"I have no hope then?"

"When a vow of marriage is annulled, it is theologically based on the conviction that the vows were taken either in bad faith or with inadequate knowledge of the total scope and nature of the promise. In other words, the Church is saying that a spiritual impediment existed from the beginning. Can you say, in conscience, that you did not take your vows in good faith?"

There was a pause before Harlequin replied softly, "No."

"Then can you say, in good conscience, that you were not aware at the time of your ordination of the responsibilities of your vocation or all that would be expected of you?"

"Yes."

"Then God has dispensed you. Here!" He took one of the

rolled parchments and threw it to Harlequin, who unrolled it and read it.

"This—this is a papal dispensation from holy orders! It carries the pope's signature and seal! And it bears my name!" Harlequin exclaimed.

The cardinal stopped in his sorting operations. "Yes. A beautiful job, isn't it? It comes from the same source as your forged carte blanche. When Bartolomeo Flores was arrested last October, we confiscated three thousand of them. Dispensations. Annulments. Titles to bishoprics. All manner of things."

Harlequin looked up. "Then it's a forgery."

The cardinal grinned. "I did not say so. And you may present it anywhere you wish, and it will be acknowledged as genuine. Any where."

Harlequin rolled the parchment. "But I wanted to . . ."

Della Rovere sighed and approached the tall man in the rainbow cloak. "I said God dispensed you, and I believe that. Now *you* must believe it. The promise you made, as with a marriage vow, is a very personal arrangement between you and God. It will make absolutely no difference if that lecherous reprobate on Peter's throne affirms it."

"But I—I don't know. I—I feel lost."

"Of course. But there is nothing I can do about that. God has the sharp eyes of a good shepherd. He sees and protects you. If you are not deceiving yourself, then go in peace—as a layman." He returned to the desk. "Your problem, Vittorio, is that you know now that God did not mean you to be a priest, and you know He did not mean you to be a warrior. So what then? Until you find your place, your own path to salvation, you will continue to feel lost, but it has nothing to do with a parchment containing the seal of Peter."

Harlequin approached suddenly, and impulsively dipped to one knee and kissed the cardinal's ring. Della Rovere smiled. "That's the first time in years that that gesture was made with no other motivation than respect." He lifted Harlequin to his feet. "Now listen carefully. Florence is not safe for you. Indeed, there is not much of Italy that *is* safe for you."

"Then what shall I do?"

"I have given that some thought. You already have your best possible disguise at hand. I would recommend that you continue to do what you have been doing. You have an unusual band of mountebanks with you. Take your mummers into the mountains. Avoid the large cities and make your living by doing what you did in Bologna. Entertain the people—not the wealthy lords and ladies, but the farmers and the smiths and the weavers. Stop at every monastery and abbey. They'll sustain you until the threat of Cesare Borgia has passed, and if you keep moving, you will have a modicum of safety. I, for my part, will keep Cesare so busy here and in Rome that he won't have much time to search for you."

He took a leather purse from the desk and tossed it to Harlequin. "This will sustain you for a while. Protect my daughter. Keep her anonymous if you can, but if you are genuinely in trouble, seek help from Isabella of Gonzaga. Cesare trusts her and corresponds with her, but that wily lady is even more cunning than he is. She is of the same mold as Isabella's mother, and she will be in the best position to help you. The girl's own mother, because of her marriage alliances, cannot assist her, but I, through my agents, will always know where you are."

Harlequin nodded.

"One other thing," della Rovere said softly. "Learn and remember the lesson of Savonarola. God has a history of leaving his saints and prophets to the mercies of the tyrant and the fool. Try to find a middle path between both the tyrant and the saint."

He turned back to his desk. "Now go! Before I feel compelled to take up a collection for that splendid sermon."

*H*ARLEQUIN, THE CAPITANO, AND ISABELLA departed nearly two hours later. Before entering his own carriage to begin his exodus from Florence, the cardinal told them, "Remember, I have been able to stand between you and your enemies for only a short time. They are still powerful, and you are still hunted. Leave Florence at once. Go to the mountains. And be careful!"

One by one they came to kiss his ring and receive his blessing, and then his caravan of carriages and carts snaked through the maze of narrow streets and disappeared.

*T*HE FUGITIVE TRIO MOVED as rapidly as possible toward the Piazza Madonna, but they had no sooner emerged from the side street than they knew that something was wrong. The wagon and the cart were gone, and they began to search.

They located the wagon a little later in a small piazza near the Ponte alla Carria surrounded by the chests and crates of Isabella's possessions. Death and Destruction were still in harness, but there was no sign of Salvation and the cart. Pantalone was stretched out on the floor of the wagon with Scapino holding his hands and Ruffiana sitting on his legs. Colombina was applying cold, wet cloths to the boy's face, which was swollen and cut, and Dottore was attempting to sew together the open wound on the boy's lower lip. This had obviously become a difficult endeavor, because Pantalone was definitely drunk and attempting to sing Scapino's most popular and irreverent air.

"Oh, Ros-a-marie, come sleep with me . . ."

As Dottore became conscious of Harlequin at his elbow, he said quietly, "To help ease the pain, we fed him our last bottle of brandy."

"What happened?" asked Harlequin as he watched the skilled hands at work. Then Pantalone decided that half the city was being denied the wonders of his voice, so he sang louder.

". . . between the shadow-y lin-den tree-e. . . ."

"Could you sew his lips together?" suggested Harlequin, but Dottore had finished his handiwork, cut the thread, and signaled Scapino and Ruffiana to release his patient. Ruffiana immediately cradled Pantalone's head in her lap and both consoled and silenced him with her bosom.

"Some mercenaries came," Colombina said as she walked to Harlequin's side. "They produced some sort of document and said they were going to take the paintings and the statues. Dottore said it was all in order, but Scapino insisted it was a trick and a forgery. He said the items belonged to Isabella, and he would defend them with his life. So—he attacked the mercenaries."

Harlequin sat on the edge of the communal fountain. "He did *what*?"

"You would have been proud of me," bragged Scapino as he leaped nimbly to the top of the fountain wall. "I kept my weight balanced properly, concentrated, kept my back against the cart so no one could attack me from behind! Oh, I was a fulcrum! I was!"

"Then what happened to you?"

Colombina concluded, "One of the mercenaries climbed on top of the cart and hit him on his head with the butt of a sword."

Scapino lowered his head to show Harlequin the sewn wound and the blood-matted hair. "Now tell me," he demanded, "how can a fulcrum guard his front, back, and top simultaneously?"

Harlequin sighed and placed his hand on the acrobat's shoulder. "My dear Scapino, I have one final lesson to teach you. There are times—most frequently—when the best fulcrum doesn't fight at all." He looked around the area. "And where is Tristano?"

Scapino sat beside Harlequin on the fountain. "He was fighting well when suddenly a guard struck him in the face and split his lip. It was nothing. A scratch at most. But he saw the blood, realized his beauty had been desecrated, and promptly fainted."

Colombina sat on the opposite side of their leader. "Not at all. He's just not accustomed to fighting. He only leaped into the battle when he saw you attacked. He was trying to protect you!"

"Me?"

"It was Pantalone who received the worst beating," inserted Dottore. "Probably because he was our best defender. He was everywhere, yelling, 'I can do that!' But there were too many."

Scapino glowed. "And do you know what he said when he charged in? He yelled, 'Leave my father alone!' That's what he said! 'My father,' he said."

Harlequin looked around at his battered comrades and suddenly the thought welled up in him, *My God, we* are *a family.*

"Well," he said quietly. "I'm proud of you, of course, but the document was genuine. Gentile Zappachio's art is safe with Cardinal della Rovere."

"And Harlequin is dispensed from his vows," Isabella whispered to Colombina.

"And our Isabella, it turns out, is the daughter of the cardinal and her mother is a married woman."

Scapino let out a wild shriek. "Really? That's wonderful! *You're* a bastard, too!"

Isabella laughed.

"But to anyone else who may be concerned, she remains a Zappachio," Harlequin was careful to add.

"Well"—Dottore sighed—"that ends my responsibility." He looked around at the others. "What do we do now? It seems to me the only hope for any of us is to stay together."

"We at least have each other," said the juggler. "And we're still alive."

Harlequin nodded. "With enough money and supplies for a month. And with only one wagon, a war-horse, and two burros."

"But we're still alive, aren't we?" Scapino persisted.

"Listen!" snapped Dottore. "All I've lost is a responsibility I never really wanted anyway. Now Isabella and I are both free. We did all we could." Suddenly he struck a mock-heroic pose, seized imaginary lapels with his two hands, and intoned in a deep, pontifical voice, *"Salvatione imper prohibis jus!"*

Harlequin was amused by the ridiculous posturing of the man. "And what does that mean, doctor?"

"It means," translated Dottore. "It means, 'In unity, there is a chance!' "

"Really?" Harlequin laughed. "In what language, pray?"

The reply came swiftly. "Gog."

Harlequin feigned surprise. "Why, doctor! I never knew you spoke gog!"

"Neither did gog." Dottore smiled, and then he added, "In mobbi, it means, 'It would be wise for us to move our behinds out of this city, and *then* make plans."

Colombina began to chortle. "A wise observation," she said.

He turned to her. "A talent induced in me by my cousin on my father's side," he said ponderously as though he were speaking some profound and hidden truth.

"Nobody was on his mother's side," added Ruffiana.

Scapino danced up beside him. "They were all on her belly." He grinned.

Dottore turned to Scapino and pretended to adopt a fencing pose. "Sir!" he roared. "You insult me!"

Scapino adopted a similar pose. "No! You insult me!" he shouted back. "It's your turn today."

Suddenly Dottore dropped the pose and the voice and became quite businesslike. "No, no, no," he said. "It's your turn to insult me. Remember? I insulted you yesterday when I said you had a face like a baboon's backside."

Scapino feigned shock. "That was an insult?" He turned to Harlequin. "It's the nicest thing he's said to me in years!"

Harlequin burst out laughing.

"I thought he was after my body," whined the juggler to Colombina.

They were all doubled over now, there, on the edge of the fountain wall: nine hunted people with little money and no direction; their only shelter a modified guild wagon; bruised, uncertain, and though unadmitted, afraid.

And they laughed as though they would die.

*T*HEY WERE SO CAUGHT UP in their banter that they did not notice the carriage that raced past them, across the Ponte alla

Carria and down the Via dei Serragli. It was not until the carriage was past the church of Santa Maria del Carmine that the occupant, Leonardo da Vinci, pondered what he had glimpsed at the fountain.

He turned his attention from the sheaf of designs and specifications for the ballistas, dummy guns, and catapults that Cesare Borgia awaited in Ceri and considered whether or not he had actually seen his bumbling assistant with a gang of mountebanks and mummers.

No, he reasoned. *It is some sort of curse he put upon me.*

And he returned to studying the designs.

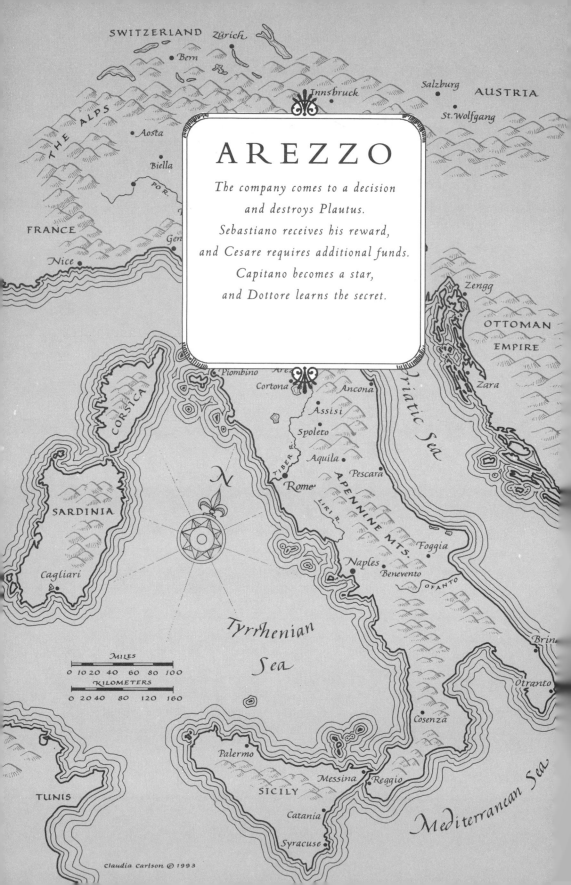

AREZZO

*The company comes to a decision
and destroys Plautus.
Sebastiano receives his reward,
and Cesare requires additional funds.
Capitano becomes a star,
and Dottore learns the secret.*

SWITZERLAND Zürich

Bern

THE ALPS

Innsbruck Salzburg AUSTRIA

St. Wolfgang

Aosta

Biella

PO R.

FRANCE

Gen

Nice

OTTOMAN

EMPIRE

Zengg

Zara

Piombino Are

Cortona Ancona

Adriatic Sea

Assisi

Spoleto

TIBER R.

Aquila

Rome Pescara

APENNINE MTS.

LIRI R.

Foggia

Naples

Benevento OFANTO

Brin

Otranto

Cosenza

CORSICA

N

SARDINIA

Cagliari

Tyrrhenian

Sea

MILES
0 10 20 40 60 80 100
KILOMETERS
0 20 40 80 120 160

Palermo

Messina Reggio

SICILY

Catania

Syracuse

TUNIS

Mediterranean Sea

Claudia Carlson © 1993

Before departing from Florence, Isabella's cart and Salvation were returned to the company with a hurried, scrawled note from the cardinal reading, *My men are agreeable to turning the other cheek—this time. May I suggest you inform your friends that pacifism is also a virtue?*

They went east into the mountains, and at Scttignano they felt safe enough to pause and consider what their future might be.

Harlequin presented the facts coldly. "Here we are, nine people without wealth, power, or a reliable source of income—with the possible exception of Tristano, who has a rich father—"

"Who, by now, has disinherited me."

"And Isabella who has family and friends of great prominence—"

"Who cannot acknowledge or help me," said Isabella.

"I am still, at least, a titular priest—"

"Sounds filthy," murmured Ruffiana.

"—who may or may not be dispensed from my vows, and the capitano is a soldier without an overlord. Dottore is an apprentice of everything, and a master of nothing."

"Mention that to me the next time your head needs repairing," grumbled Dottore.

"Pantalone and Scapino are cutpurses by vocation," Harlequin continued, "but have developed into adequate acrobats and jugglers."

"Adequate?" shrieked Pantalone. "I can do anything! Anything!"

"Except keep silent!" interjected Scapino.

"The cardinal says our principal threat comes from the Borgias, who wish to use Isabella as a pawn in negotiations with Venice. At the same time we may assume the Venetians have their own agents looking for her.

"Quite possibly the lords of Savoy have abandoned their search for Scapino and Pantalone, and it is reasonable to assume that Cesare Borgia and Leonardo de Vinci are far too busy waging war to give much consideration to a mercenary deserter and an indentured servant who has violated his contract.

"We can also assume that the Bentivoglio have forgiven Tristano since we paid for what we 'borrowed' from his father's ware-house—although it is doubtful that his family has forgiven him for abandoning his studies and disappearing with a group of mummers."

Ruffiana yelled, "There's a noble family in Pistoria who thinks very highly of *me*."

Harlequin paused as the others laughed again. "I'm sure there is," he said softly, "but the only friends we can truly trust are the della Roveres and the Orsini. But Cardinal della Rovere is playing a dangerous game with Cesare Borgia, and the Orsini are being obliterated one by one."

Colombina gave a great sigh and called, "What is your point, Harlequin?"

"The situation, as the cardinal outlined it, is this. It isn't safe for any of us to show our faces in the major cities. It occurs to me that it might make it more difficult for our enemies, however, if we disbanded and made our individual way in different directions."

The laughter died, and an oppressive silence descended on them. Finally Scapino whispered, "It—makes sense."

"Absolutely," grumbled Pantalone.

"A band of rabble like us—attracts attention," agreed Colombina.

Isabella stood up angrily. "Well, I am suffocating on the audacity and barbarism of these 'noble' families. We saw the bulging ware-houses of the Bentivoglio while just outside children were begging alms. The man I always knew as my father was murdered by the 'noble' families. I have been passed from city to city and hand to hand like a valued possession, and I'm tired of it! I'm tired of these arrogant wars of the Colonnas and the Orsini and the Este and the Borgias and—yes—the della Roveres! At Urbino I was taught that the nobility had the right to rule, because they were better educated and wiser and stronger. Well, I think Ruffiana and Scapino are better educated! They could survive where the noble lords and ladies would starve! And Harlequin and Dottore are wiser than all the scholars I met in Venice, because they openly admit they do not know everything! And the captain is stronger than all the condottieri I've encountered, because he at least knows he is only a pawn in a game played by the selfish and the cowardly and fights only when he must!" She paused then and looked at the others. Then she asked softly, "No matter what my father, the illustrious cardinal, wishes, I do not choose to return to the life at the courts of the nobility. With you, I have found a family that cares about me. I have found that I have some worth beyond that of a marriageable pawn to still another dissolute duke or count! I'm not returning to Urbino or Florence or Rome—unless we go together!"

Scapino moved beside her. "Listen. Wherever you choose to go, I am with you. If I have to return to thieving, at least it will be for someone I love and not for myself."

"A moment!" roared Dottore. He crossed to Isabella. "I've been with you from the beginning, haven't I? My friend, Gentile, gave you into my care, didn't he? The fact that you are not his daughter doesn't alter my promise to look after you. Wherever you go, I go, too."

Ruffiana stood. "I can't let you travel with those renegades. It would be indecent for a lady to travel with two men. Besides, as you said, your court training wouldn't serve you well on the back streets. I, ah, I'd better go with you."

"Well, I came for the adventure, and so far it has been the best time of my life!" declared Tristano. "Besides, I'm just as unhappy with the 'new nobility' as Isabella is with the old. I've watched my father work day and night, shortchange friends, make deals that brought others to ruin, and ignore his family." Then he looked at Ruffiana. "And—well—to tell the truth, I've grown accustomed to—well—I can't let you go anywhere without me." And he moved to her side.

"You're not going with *her* without *me*!" thundered Pantalone as he moved to the opposite side of Ruffiana. "We have an agreement!" He then smiled at Scapino. "And someone has to look after my papa."

"Well," grumbled the capitano, "I could find employment anywhere. These are good days for professional soldiers, but to tell the truth, I'm a little weary of swords and pistols and obeying orders from idiots who play for power with my life." He crossed to stand beside Scapino. "You'll need my pistols to keep the enemy at bay—at least until you finish your fulcrum training."

"And who will cook for this small army if you leave me behind?" wailed Colombina. "Godsblood, I wager not one of you knows enough to boil the potatoes before you put them in a peasant pie. You'll starve without me." She looked at Harlequin. "I let two husbands walk out on me. It's *my* turn to walk."

Suddenly they realized that they were all grouped together around Isabella, facing Harlequin, alone, across the campfire. He smiled at them. "Yes," he said quietly, "well, I thought it would be too good to be true." He came around the fire. "That leads us to the alternative. We have to earn our bread. The cardinal suggested we continue as mummers, but there must be hundreds of acrobats and minstrels out there, and you saw Tristano's reaction when he saw us in Bologna. He wanted more: fire-eating, leaping through rings of knife blades."

"I still want more," teased Tristano as he slipped an arm around Ruffiana.

"I was surprised to see that collectively we seem to possess some wit and—an outrageous and apparently boundless imagination, and we *are* traveling with a portable stage." There was a pause. "I've been thinking of something—different. Performing—*real*—plays."

"Like the *sacre reappresentazioni*?" asked Isabella.

"No!" Harlequin said firmly. "Definitely *not* like the *sacra rappresentazioni*."

"Consider what we did to *Abraham and Isaac*," recalled Dottore, "I think that is a prudent suggestion."

"I'm thinking of secular plays. Comedies. Perhaps Plautus and Terence. These plays have been performed in the courts of the nobility for years, but no one performs such amusements for the people. Dottore, Isabella, and I have seen plays performed at Milan and Urbino and even in the Vatican; so, although the Church frowns on theater, they privately endorse it."

Harlequin surveyed their faces. They were so obviously determined to stay together—at least for the time being—that he could see them grasping at the possibility. "All right," he announced, "we'll prepare something for Arezzo." Then he muttered, "And may God have mercy on our souls."

THE COMPANY of Wayward Saints wound their way into the mountains to the fortress city of Arezzo, which perched on the slope of a hill in the middle of a beautiful and fertile region of Tuscany. They slowly circled the crest of a hill that dropped off to their left. They passed through two of the four quarters that divided the city, past the old duomo. They turned south and began their descent down the sloping street toward the Piazza Grande and the Church of Pieve di Santa Maria. Around them in the tilted, irregular piazza were multistoried houses with broad-eaved roofs favored by the Tuscans. The houses had small wooden balconies from which unsmiling wives and daughters watched the wagon and the cart pass.

As the procession wound its way past the ancient church with three tiers of loggias and a remarkable campanile, a group of masons and apprentices stopped working on the main portal of a new building modeled on Venetian lines opposite the church. The workers said nothing, did not smile, and soon returned to their work.

They skirted the Palazzo Pretorio on the Corso Italia and the Palazzo della Fraternita dei Laici, which had been built during the time of Francis of Assisi. On the Via dell'Orto, they noted the small house where Petrarch was born, and they were watched by small bands of armed men along the Passegio del Prato, the pretty little park that separated the church from the palace.

Colombina noticed a frown on Harlequin. "What's wrong?"

"I'm not sure," said Harlequin softly. "But the *impresa* on that man's tunic is the same as that worn by Sebastiano."

O N   T H E   C A R P E T of the second-floor reception room of the Palazzo Vecchio in Florence, Father Sebastiano sprawled on his back, eyes wide and looking frantically at the high ceiling as if wondering who had plunged the stiletto in his throat. Into his line of vision, a swarthy, black-bearded face appeared and looked down at him. The man was cleaning the blade of his stiletto on the dying monk's robe and silently watching the cleric struggling to breathe through the rivulets of blood choking him.

"He said you must know why you die, or he will not be totally satisfied," whispered the assassin. "He said to make it clear to you." Sebastiano made a low, choking sound and began to move his body from side to side in an attempt to relieve his mouth and throat from the blood; but his assailant brutally placed a foot on his chest.

"Not yet. You can't die until I tell you everything." He pressed harder with his foot, and the dying priest gave a great gasp of air that momentarily cleared the passage and permitted him to breathe again. "By good fortune, the woman His Grace needed to help him form his alliances fell right into your hands—along with the Savelli letters." He removed his foot from his chest. "And you permitted that cardinal to bluff you and walk away with everything!"

The dying man no longer moved. The wide, staring eyes were open and still.

"The duke hates incompetence," whispered Blackbeard. "He won't abide it. He can do nothing—for the moment—about della Rovere, but you are another matter." He straightened up and replaced the stiletto in its sheath. "Now," he murmured, "I have been commanded to take up the pursuit again, and Cesare dislikes delay as much as he hates incompetence."

He wiped the blood from his hands on a silk handkerchief, and then dropped it on the dead man's chest.

"He said to commend you for the work you did in tracking the girl and the letters, but with the escape, your organization became expendable."

He smiled at the lifeless form. "And so did you."

He turned and swept from the room, and it was minutes before the great curtains before the floor-to-ceiling windows fluttered and were pushed aside.

Angelo looked down at the lifeless body. Then he wheeled, looked quickly in each direction at the door, and was gone.

"I DON'T THINK WE'RE WELCOME," whispered Colombina as she noted the cold hostility of the townspeople as they drove through the Porto Crucifera.

"They are wary of strangers," Harlequin replied. "I can't say I blame them. Arezzo has an unhappy history of always siding with the losers of wars and suffering the consequences of their bad choices. In Roman days they backed Marius against Sulla, then Pompey against Caesar. That Medici palazzo was built by Bishop Tarlati, who led the Ghibellines into defeat at the battles of Lucignano and Rondine. In gratitude, they buried him in their cold and unattractive duomo."

"That would explain why they are glaring so hard at Capitano," Colombina said.

And, indeed, the most scornful looks seemed to be lavished on the military figure on the great war-horse that preceded them down the street.

They considered putting the wagon and the cart in a small piazza in the southern part of the town, but the square dropped so severely that they could not block the wheels satisfactorily. They continued down the hill, past the church of St. Bernardo, and found themselves at the stately ruins of an old Roman amphitheater.

They brought their vehicles into the ancient theater and stopped on a small but level area behind the false proscenium. Harlequin dismounted and wandered alone onto the circular playing area strewn with rubble and looked up at the rows of curving stone seats that faced him. "This amphitheater once held eight thousand people," he said.

"We will play here."

*H*ARLEQUIN AND DOTTORE had spent much of the time from Settignano to Arezzo trying to piece together a working script of Plautus's *Menaechmi.* Harlequin recalled reading a copy in the Vatican library as a youth, and Dottore had seen a copy of the playscript that had been prepared by scribes. The duke, at the time, was considering a production of his own to rival that of a recent production by the Este family.

Both men remembered that the plot vaguely concerned identical-twin brothers who were separated as children and had grown to young manhood in two rival cities. Each brother was unaware of his twin's existence. Harlequin remembered that the twin brothers had identical twin servants, and Dottore seemed to recall twin wives to the young men. This surplus of identical twins was considered highly improbable, so they eliminated the twin wives as stretching the limits of the audience's credibility.

Dottore pointed out that even with the elimination of the wives—or at least one wife—there were two other female roles: a slave girl and a procurer.

"Who shall pay the slave girl?" he asked. "Pantalone?"

"No. I think not."

"You're probably right. Tristano would be more attractive."

"Ruffiana will play the slave girl."

Dottore's reaction was immediate. He blew a mouthful of wine across the campfire. "But—but she's a woman! You can't put a woman on the stage!"

"Why not?"

"Because it has never been done. Female roles have *always* been performed by men—even in the classical era. You'd be breaking with tradition!"

Harlequin shrugged. "We're breaking with tradition by performing secular plays! Why shouldn't a woman perform female roles?"

Dottore was indignant. "It's—it's scandalous! Immoral! It's degrading!"

"If it doesn't degrade a man to perform a female role on stage, why should it degrade a woman?" pointed out Colombina.

"Because the audience *knows* he is a man, and they suspend belief! If they know it's a woman up there, they think she *really* is what she is playing!"

Harlequin frowned. "Are you telling me the audience can't separate the actress from the role? That a woman playing a prostitute really *is* a prostitute?"

"Exactly!"

Colombina laughed. "Then what do they believe of a man who plays female roles?"

"They believe he is an artist!"

Harlequin threw up his hands. "Your logic confounds me, but it is a moot point, because we have too many roles for just the men in the company. We also need a money lender and a quasi-military ruler of the city-state."

"And it seems to me," said Dottore, "that there were also two or three officials, a cook and—"

"I don't remember so many people," Harlequin argued. "Perhaps the duke's version was an improvement of his scribes, or perhaps you are confusing *The Twins* with some other classical comedy."

"How many do you think I've read?" Dottore fumed.

Casting the male roles also presented problems.

Harlequin felt that he and Scapino should play the two comic servants, because these poor characters had to be beaten on several occasions and, he reasoned, it required seasoned acrobats to pretend to be beaten and thrown around the playing area without actually getting hurt.

Pantalone, on the other hand, felt he was as good an acrobat as Scapino—and maybe even as good as Harlequin. "Anything you can do, I can do!" he declared.

Harlequin then pointed out that he had hoped to cast Tristano and Pantalone as the identical-twin masters, because they were the younger members of the company and almost identical in height—which was essential to the plot. But Pantalone argued that Dottore was also the same height as Tristano, and both could read and so learn the vast number of necessary lines. Harlequin agreed, and assigned Tristano and Dottore the roles of the twin brothers.

Then Pantalone decided he would play the miserly money lender.

"But he's an old man," argued Harlequin.

"Or course!" snapped Pantalone.

"Why should you, the youngest member of the company, play the most ancient character?"

"Because I see age for what it is," Pantalone replied. "You would sentimentalize it. So would Dottore. To you, age implies wisdom and experience, because you *are* old and you want to put it in the best light. But to me it is only wrinkled skin and failing memory, poor eyesight and aches and—"

"All right," said Harlequin. "You can play the money lender."

"Old men always make idiots of themselves chasing after young girls," the boy continued, gesturing at Tristano, who walked from the campfire with his arm around Ruffiana's waist.

"Fine," muttered Harlequin.

"And they're always trying to do things they did years ago when they were younger, and they always end up making fools of themselves," said Pantalone.

"I see your point," grumbled Harlequin, remembering the fall he had taken yesterday practicing a cartwheel.

"And they keep trying to look younger than they are—"

Harlequin grabbed him by his collar. "One more word," he growled, "and you're going to age rapidly."

Pantalone shrugged and disengaged himself.

Colombina seemed right to play the procurer, and Isabella was picked to play the wife of Dottore. When Ruffiana objected to this, Harlequin pointed out that role of the wife required more lines, and Isabella could read. So Ruffiana became the slave girl with very few lines, but as Harlequin reminded her, she looked like someone a man—like Tristano—would want, so she was satisfied.

Character names were another problem. Harlequin and Dottore

agreed that someone in the play was called Dormio or Dromio; and they decided that the twin brothers should be called Dormio of Ephesus and Dormio of Syracuse, because the names of these places sounded remotely classical.

But Colombina argued that the names were too unfamiliar to a local audience, and the Aretines would have no idea how distant the cities were from one another. "Why not call one man Dormio of—I don't know—Bergamo. And the other Dormio of—Rimini. Everyone knows how far apart those towns are."

They agreed, but then the servants' names were hotly disputed, and the coauthors compromised on Asclepius, which Dottore associated with the inventor of medicine. They also decided to limit the other characters to a Signora Dormio of Bergamo, a slave girl, a female procurer, a money lender, and the military officer.

Finally they developed a script between them that owed more to faulty memories, a dozen sources other than Plautus, and the availability of talent.

The play, as they envisioned it, would begin with Dormio of Rimini and his servant, Asclepius of Rimini, arriving in Bergamo. The adaptors agreed that the appeal of the piece was in the confusion of the twin brothers with their respective servants, so immediately Dormio R. would send Asclepius R. off to find a slave girl for sale and would give him a pouch of gold with which to make the purchase.

The second sequence would have Dormio of Bergamo sending *his* servant, Asclepius of Bergamo, off to pay a debt owed the money lender and also to prepare a dinner for his master. Asclepius B. also receives a pouch of gold.

Asclepius of Rimini, however, returns to Dormio of Bergamo, mistaking the twin for his own master, and the result is a conversation between the two in which Asclepius thinks they are discussing slave girls, and Dormio thinks they are discussing the dinner. When Dormio discovers Asclepius has given his money to a procurer, he beats him off the stage.

The reverse situation between Dormio of Rimini and Asclepius of Bergamo brings the same result, a beating of the servant, when Dormio R. discovers that Asclepius B. has given *his* money to a money lender.

These opening sequences were to be followed by a scene between Dormio R. and the procurer and the slave girl that is interrupted by the arrival of the wife of Dormio B., and an equally confusing conflict between Asclepius R. and the money lender.

The comic quality of the scenes are based on mistaken identity, and the play is resolved when the twins confront one another for the first time and explain the situation to everyone's satisfaction.

The problems inherent in the script became obvious the next few days. First, when Harlequin tried to explain the story to Scapino, Pantalone, Colombina, and Ruffiana, who were permitted to improvise their lines within the strict outline of the plot, no one could follow the action without confusion. Second, the cast was so large, everyone had to play something: so the capitano, who could read, found himself playing the military ruler of Bergamo, who had no lines.

The major problem was the suggestion of identical twins.

They pondered the question for some time, and it was Colombina who dragged one of the barrels from the cart and brought it before the assembly. She removed the top to reveal the Venetian carnival masks and accessories that were part of the bounty extracted from the Bologna warehouse. "Tristano didn't know what these were when he ordered us to take them, remember? Well, now they can serve a useful purpose."

Impulsively Harlequin kissed her on the cheek. "Perfect!" he cried. "Two sets of identical masks to suggest identical twins! And it is just what we need to hide our identity from anyone who may be in the audience and looking for us!"

The half masks chosen for Tristano and Dottore were pale, mustachioed, and not very attractive. Tristano objected loudly, but eventually he submitted to the collective approval of the company and the singular persuasion of Ruffiana.

The half masks chosen for Harlequin and Scapino were black, suggesting both Moorish ancestry and a link with the deposed

Duke of Milan. The masks were also hook-nosed for comic effect. Capitano, as the governor, was permitted to pick his own mask, but no one saw it prior to his entrance in the play.

The women protested against wearing masks, and the company decided, after allowing that the women themselves were attractive and could probably be more entertaining that way, that they would be spared the half masks but would wear loupes or dominoes.

Harlequin also saw in the use of these masks a return to the conventions of the classical Greco-Roman theater, and the coincidence that they were to perform a Roman farce on a Roman stage was considered an omen that boded well for the production.

There was no time to rehearse the work, other than what they called a "line run" in the evening preceding the performance, because, by day, Harlequin planned to send the company throughout the city to provide small amusements of juggling, acrobatics, and dancing to entice the populace to the amphitheater in the afternoon. The "line run" proved somewhat disconcerting, because the illiterates improvised totally different lines every time they attempted to rehearse.

Harlequin was somewhat dismayed when only a handful of peasants, guildsmen, maids, and children followed Ruffiana and Tristano back to the stone seats of the amphitheater. "What did you expect?" asked Colombina. "These are working people. They can't just stop their labors to come watch a group of mummers playing."

Harlequin and Colombina had painted and hung a remnant of material between two pillars on either side of the proscenium on which was printed—in uneven letters and in the vulgar tongue— *The Company of Wayward Saints.*

Among the few people, Harlequin also noted one or two clerics wearing both the brown of the Franciscans and the white of the Dominicans. This worried him a little, because he knew from bitter experience that what one sanctioned, the other was compelled to condemn.

There was no sign of nobility, which did not surprise Harlequin. The lords would naturally assume that if the entertainers were professional, they would first present themselves at their palazzi for proper endorsements and—hopefully—subsidies. Performing for the general multitude marked them as "vulgar entertainment" and not worth the attention of the aristocracy.

But, on signal, the play began.

*H*ARLEQUIN, wearing his flamboyant cloak of bright rags and patches and the ridiculous beaked hat, entered with a lute and sang an introductory song in which he gave due credit to Plautus and announced the title in the original Latin.

"What's it called?" one corpulent wife asked her friend, both of whom continued shelling peas in the upper seats.

"The *Men Et My.*"

"The men et my what?"

"I don't know." The other woman shrugged. "Listen and find out!"

Harlequin had gone on to explain that there were two sets of twins separated in infancy and raised in alien cities. He then jigged out of sight of the audience as Tristano entered and summoned him into the playing area again by the name of "Asclepius"—which caused some little confusion. Quickly they established that they were servant and master, and that they were now in Bergamo.

The audience became stone with the seats of the theater. Three began to eat, and one or two commented on his surrounding neighbors, "What kind of a guild play is this? Which is God?"

On stage Tristano sent Harlequin out to purchase a slave girl, and then both exited to be replaced by Dottore and Scapino. They were immediately confused with Harlequin and Tristano, and it took some time for Dottore to communicate the basic fact that he was the other twin, and that he lived in Rimini. To underscore the identity of the twins, however, he decided at the last minute to mention his birthplace. Unfortunately playing Abraham when intoxicated was a far cry from facing a silent and presumably hostile audience as Dormio.

He couldn't remember his birthplace.

So he said, "Montevarchi."

And the laughter began.

"Of course," Harlequin whispered to Colombina backstage, "they consider him a pompous pain in the arse. Where else would he originate but from their rival town?"

Dottore then ordered Scapino to go to the house of the money lender, repay the debt owed, and then make preparations for the master's dinner, spending a great deal of time explaining to Scapino what he wanted: "Fresh fruit, three roasted pigeons, and a wheel of the local cheese, which is foul smelling but delicious." Scapino nodded and went off one side of the stage as Harlequin, in the identical mask, entered from the opposite side.

There was a small burst of laughter indicating that some of the audience, at least, realized they were seeing the other servant and not a remarkable demonstration of bi-location. Now, stunned at the sudden appearance of Harlequin, Dottore began his inquisition.

"Is the fruit fresh?" he demanded.

Harlequin looked confused, scratched his chin under his half mask, then, enlightened, replied, "Fruit? Oh, the fruit! Oh yes, master," he cooed with a lecherous grin, "the fruit is very fresh. Lovely and spirited." He nudged Dottore. "Eighteen years old."

Dottore removed the beaked hat and hit Harlequin with it. "Fresh? At eighteen years? That fruit isn't spirited, it's *fermented*!" He hit Harlequin again, who bobbed in front of his master. "Is there nothing less ancient, blockhead?"

Harlequin looked totally confused. "Ancient? At eighteen?" He performed a half-turn comic walk, which made the audience laugh again. "Well, would fifteen years be more to your taste?"

Dottore again swept Harlequin's hat off his head and beat him with it. "Fifteen years? Are you mocking me, knave? Fifteen?"

Harlequin began to wail. "Twelve years, signore? Ten? Surely not under nine!"

Dottore growled. "I want something picked just this morning, you imbecile!"

Harlequin moaned. "I *did* pick her this morning!"

Dottore hit him again. "You were not to make the selection, you horse's arse! Bring me a selection, and I will choose what I want to eat."

Harlequin nodded stupidly. "To—eat?"

"Precisely, you farting toad!"

Then enlightenment. "Of course." Harlequin leered. "I understand!" He swept down to the front seats and mock-whispered to the audience. "A passionate old rascal, eh?"

The audience laughed with him. A few viewers shouted obscenities—which aroused more laughter—and from the corner of his eye, Harlequin noted more people appearing at the top of the amphitheater, apparently drawn by the sounds and their own curiosity.

Dottore pulled Harlequin back into the playing area. "Now, about the flesh. It's plump, I trust?"

Harlequin looked astounded. "Why—no, signore. I thought your taste ran to something—trim and lean."

Dottore hit him again. "Plump, I say! I want something I can grab and get my teeth into!"

Harlequin grinned lecherously. "Oh yes, master, she's well endowed. There's plenty to grab and get your teeth into."

"Three of them, naturally?"

The audience howled even before Harlequin began his characteristic comic walk. "Three of them?"

Dottore grabbed him roughly by his cloak. "Did I not order three, idiot?"

Harlequin shrugged and whined, "I thought they only came in pairs!" Then he added quickly, "I could get one with the customary two, and there is an unfortunate one who suffered an accident with a scythe and has only one remaining. Should I bring these two—with three between them?"

Dottore caught him and began to pummel him with his hands, and Harlequin, while cartwheeling, saw more people coming into the arena and taking seats. "Not two!" roared Dottore. "Three! Three!"

Harlequin, now on his knees, began to wail and weep. "Yes, master. Of course."

"Now," continued Dottore, "about the rest . . ."

Harlequin began to walk on his knees in supplication. "The—the rest?"

Dottore leaned over the hapless servant. "It stinks, doesn't it?"

Harlequin began to climb up Dottore's body until he had his feet under him again. "Oh no, master! Not at all! I wouldn't dream of bringing you one that stinks!"

Dottore cuffed him again. "Moron! I insisted that it stink! It is the stink that indicates it is ripe and full of the richest milk!"

Harlequin wailed again, "I had no idea!"

Dottore paused in the beating. "Didn't I explain this to you before?"

"Not quite as clearly."

"Go back and get precisely what I ordered!" screamed Dottore. "Repeat my instructions so I know you have them!"

Harlequin quickly recited, "Extremely young, but with three instead of two, and she must stink."

Dottore beamed and patted Harlequin on the back approvingly. "Excellent! That's perfect! Now go!"

Harlequin galloped down to the audience again, then mock-whispered, "He's mad, you know."

By this time the audience had gone a little mad themselves, and the laughter could be heard at the crest of the hill, where Blackbeard and three mercenaries rode into the Piazza Grande.

*L*ATE DURING THE SECOND SCENE, two fashionably dressed men and their ladies appeared, probably attracted by the noises. Upon hearing the performers speaking the vulgar tongue instead of Latin, they withdrew as quickly as they came.

But the audience had obviously grown. Here and there were guildsmen and tradeswomen. An apprentice or two had snuck away from his chores to see what was going on in the amphitheater. Farmers from the outlying districts who had just delivered their goods to the merchant stalls paused to watch.

The laughter of the audience generally continued through the sequence where Scapino announced to Tristano, who was expecting a slave girl, that he had arranged for "young, fleshy creatures, stuffed with grapes and bread pieces, each hot and crusty."

And he added, ". . . and one of the most foul-smelling pieces I could find."

The beating of Scapino was more spectacular, because with every blow, Scapino would cartwheel backward across the playing area and land in a heap with, apparently, every bone in his body shattered into a thousand pieces.

From that moment on, however, the laughter began to ebb, and Harlequin was considering other possible alternatives for the company.

Then the capitano entered.

He had stuffed a pillow beneath his blouse and was wearing a half mask that incorporated an enormous pair of spectacles and thick mustaches that curled up on either side of his face. His cloak was far too big, and his mock sword was apparently sheathed in a six-foot-long cylinder that dangled from his side and occasionally between his legs in a bizarre suggestion of an erect and unwieldy penis. He constantly tripped over his own feet, the cloak, and the slightest crack in the stony playing area. He managed to impale everyone around him at least once with the absurdly long sword.

The audience roared.

Three times he bent to recover a dropped item and ran his sword and sheath up the skirts and between the legs of Isabella and Colombina, both of whom then proceeded to beat him around the head as he whimpered with cowardice.

The audience hooted and whistled and shouted comments.

On the topmost tier of seats, Blackbeard and his three assassins, dressed in somewhat elegant fashion without a visible crest or *impressa*, entered and watched.

The capitano, although he had no words assigned to him, began to expound on the glories of war and battle; and the deep, pompous, affected tones were delivered in a grotesque parody of a French accent. When he began a long and complex testimony on the beauties of eating snails and the legs of frogs, the mob whistled, shouted, and pounded their feet on the floor of the curving stone area.

And, even better, they rained small coins on the strutting, pretentious caricature marching absurdly around the area.

Harlequin, watching from behind a pillar, was both delighted and shocked. "He's struck a chord with the Aretines," he whispered excitedly to Dottore. "They've seen so many conquerors and suffered so much at the hands of the military, they delight in seeing them ridiculed. And the capitano has drawn upon his own experience to ridicule every pompous, arrogant officer and commander he was ever forced to serve under." He stopped and looked at Dottore. "Do you realize what we have here?"

Dottore grimaced, watching the coins strike the stone surface around the capitano's feet. "Yes indeed," he whispered dryly. "Another actor."

"THAT'S THE GIRL, Poli," Blackbeard whispered to one of his confederates at the top of the amphitheater. Poli placed one hand on the hilt of his dagger, but the leader placed his own hand over his. "We are Venetians in a Florentine stronghold, idiot. We can't do anything here. Any disturbance and we'd all be hung from a tree in the Passegio del Prato with no questions asked."

"What should we do then?" asked Poli.

"You ride to our agent in Montevarchi and have them send word that we've located the girl," replied Blackbeard. "The rest of us will watch—and wait."

Poli rose and made his way back to where the horses were tied to an iron ring in the wall. He was so intent on loosening the reins that it is doubtful that he was aware of the presence behind him until the thin wire was cutting into the flesh of his throat and he crumbled to the earth. The presence then lifted the body and threw it over the saddle of the horse and led both the horse and the dead assassin through the Piazza Grande and past the Church of Santa Maria della Pieve.

*T*HE WIRE CUT into the soft throat of the young man, and after a brief and futile struggle, he fell to the cold floor beside his dead brother. The strangler, Michelotto the giant, unwound the bloody wire and threw it into a corner of the room and turned to face Cesare, who was seated on the high-backed chair between the tall windows.

"Efficient as usual, Michelotto," said the duke, studing the bodies of the young nobles. "I imagine their family will want them buried with their father and brothers in Camerino."

Michelotto admitted, "I don't know which Varano to notify, sire. I don't think there are any left."

"Is that correct? Let me see. Giulio, the old bastard who refused to pay tribute to my father—"

"Dead. Strangled in Pergola."

"His son, Piero?"

"Strangled in the main square at Camerino. Did it myself. When he recovered in the church, I finished the job with my knife."

The duke smiled and glanced at Machiavelli, standing by the windows and looking down into the gardens at Cattolica. "Yes," he said. Then he rose and crossed to the bodies of the murdered men and kicked them lightly. "And here we have Venanzio and Annibale. That leaves—let me see—Gianmaria?"

He looked at Michelotto, who shrugged. "Of no consequence," said Cesare, now turning to Machiavelli. "Did we send the small Venus of the Montefeltro to Signora Isabella of Mantua?"

"Yes, Your Grace," replied the Florentine. "And the Cupid she requested from the spoils of Urbino." He smiled. "She said it was of classical origin."

"Only if Michelangelo is an Attic Greek." The duke laughed as he ascended once more to the throne. "But it's a small price to pay for her support. She has ties to every ruling family in Italy and Spain. An Este, daughter of Leonora of Aragon, married to a Gonzaga, and sister-in-law to a Sforza and my own sister, Lucrezia." He sat and surveyed the cold room. "Did she ever send me those hunting dogs she promised?"

"Yes, Your Grace," Machiavelli replied.

"An incredible woman. She lives by that motto of hers: 'Neither hope nor fear.' "

"I don't trust her," growled Michelotto.

"Very wise of you, Michelotto." The duke continued speaking to Machiavelli. "Any word from my father?"

The Florentine studied a parchment that he took from his waist. "He has created nine new cardinals at one hundred and thirty thousand ducats a hat."

"Bravo!" Cesare stroked his beard. "Was his secretary, Francesco Troches, among them?"

Machiavelli consulted the parchment. "He is not listed."

"That will prove bothersome. He was certain that he would be honored with the scarlet cap this time. Have Father keep an eye on him. He knows too much about everything. What else?"

"Your father is grateful for the list of *marranos* Michelotto sent him, because, since they are secret Jews, he can tax them heavily. And—oh yes—it seems that the Venetian cardinal, Giovanni Michieli, was suddenly taken ill and died."

"The green powder?"

Michelotto laughed and Machiavelli shrugged. "Your father immediately confiscated one hundred and fifty thousand ducats from his estate."

Cesare smiled broadly. "Did he? Well, send him my congratulations, Niccolo, and add that I could use one hundred thousand of those ducats for new uniforms for five hundred members of my army. Red and yellow with my name embroidered on both the front and the back. In return I will parade them in front of the Vatican for his amusement—and as a warning to his enemies."

Machiavelli crossed to the desk, took a quill pen, and inscribed something on the parchment. "Only one hundred thousand?"

"You're right. Ask for two hundred thousand," said the duke as he started from the room.

"After all, it's for the glory of the Church, isn't it?"

COLOMBINA AND RUFFIANA COUNTED the money thrown to the company following the performance. Ruffiana was expert in determining which coins were genuine, and Colombina's talent was in judging what goods could and should be bought with their profits. The number of coins was limited by the poverty of the community, and most were of small denomination, but with a florin from the purse donated by Cardinal della Rovere, there was enough to send Dottore to search out merchant stalls and purchase food.

This assignment fell to him because Capitano, Pantalone, Tristano, and Scapino disappeared immediately following the production; and Harlequin and Isabella, head to head, began a spirited analysis of the performance while Colombina and Ruffiana were busily preparing the evening meal from their dwindling supply of goods.

Dottore took this as an opportunity to leave the wagons and wander through the piazzas and byways of the city alone. He plodded slowly up the steep Via Cavour toward the brick Church of St. Francis, where something—he could never explain what precisely—stopped him and drew him inside.

The interior of the church was vast, single-aisled, with a high ceiling. Though it was illuminated by hanging oil lamps and candles, shadows clung together in the corners of the old and chilly building. An Aretine wife knelt before a large ceramic statue of the Madonna, and Dottore remembered that Arezzo was, at one time, noted for such ceramics.

He took a few more steps into the church, which held the faint aroma of incense. He was trying to identify the scent when he turned to his left and saw something. The enormity and brilliance of it, even by candlelight, took his breath away.

It was a huge fresco that depicted the events and the circumstances surrounding the loss—and ultimate restoration—of the true cross. It began with the death of Adam, since from his grave grew the tree that would provide the wood for the cross. Scenes fell upon scenes in the sprawling work, and event flowed into event, forcing

Dottore to realize that time, too, is never still, but flows endlessly, like a river.

But what surprised and delighted him most was the luminosity and clarity of the colors. There were no shadows whatsoever in the fresco, as if the entire work had come into being in one magnificent moment at midday. The colors were clean and fresh, as if they had been applied only that afternoon.

"Do you like it?" came a low, soft voice beside him, and Dottore turned to discover a tall, white-bearded man who stepped forward out of the shadowed corner.

"Yes," Dottore murmured. "Very much."

"I painted it," the man said quietly, without pride or apology. "A long time ago."

"It is beautiful," Dottore said as he turned to look at it again.

"And bright, isn't it?" said the old man.

"Yes." Dottore nodded. "As you can see—"

"I cannot see," the man said. "Which is why I ask. Which is why I come here, now and again, waiting for the sound of footsteps, the pause which lengthens as I know someone is looking at it. Then, as now, I ask the same question: 'Is it bright?' "

Dottore studied the bent-nosed face with the heavy, white brows that shadowed the sightless eyes. The man was extremely tall, un-bent by age, straight as a poplar tree. Everything about him said, Here is a proud—perhaps an arrogant—man.

"The colors are as bright and clear as you painted them," Dottore confirmed.

"Good. Good." The painter sighed. "I supposed what I really come for is to make certain that the fresco is still here, that they haven't tried to remove it or deface it."

"They?" Dottore asked.

"The shadow lovers," murmured the tall artist. He paused and then apologized, "I'm sorry. I did not introduce myself. I am called Piero—Piero of the French Mother."

Della Francesca! Dottore remembered that he had seen some other examples of this bright, clear style of painting in the Vatican when Verrocchio had taken four apprentices to the holy city to study the frescoes and architecture. He told the painter, "I have seen some of your work in Rome."

"Have you? When was that?" asked the old man, obviously pleased.

"More than ten years ago," Dottore responded, surprised at the vast amount of time that had passed since his apprenticeship.

"And I painted them a good ten years before you saw them! Makes me ancient, doesn't it?" The blind man sensed the surprise in Dottore. He beamed and stated proudly, "I am past seventy." Before Dottore could reply, della Francesca took him firmly by the elbow and said, "Come, walk with me a little. I am accustomed to speaking loudly—as a man of these mountains must. This forced whispering hurts my throat."

They stepped back into the cold twilight, and the old painter drew his cloak around him. Dottore felt the chill only in his legs, but as they soon began to walk in long, loping strides up the steep hill toward the Piazza Grande, the blood warmed.

The streets were empty except for an occasional soldier-at-arms wearing the Medici crest who watched with suspicious curiosity. No attempt was made to detain or approach them.

"My home is in Sansepolcro, not far from here." The blind man spoke in a surprisingly deep, booming voice. "Tomorrow I will go home. Higher into the mountains. Then—very soon I think—I will die."

The cold, unemotional manner in which the statement was made both fascinated and depressed Dottore. "Any man who has survived so many wars could live to be over a hundred," he said.

"Wars or no, as I said: I am past seventy, and there is not much time left for me. Besides, becoming blind enhanced my other senses, and I hear the light tread of death behind me and to my left. Soon I'll feel the warm breath on the back of my neck, and turn into that waiting embrace. Soon."

They walked awhile together in silence.

Dottore wanted to speak, but the words did not come, which surprised him. But finally he told the artist of his apprenticeship, his years with da Vinci, the hurt that he had not been trusted with the "secret."

Della Francesca laughed. "Shall I tell you the secret of making art?" Dottore felt his heart stop. Was he finally to be initiated into the society of Leonardo and Gentile? "You say you once thought the secret was the light, and you painted a goat girl by twilight, but it left you unsatisfied. Describe her to me."

Dottore launched into a detailed analysis of his former model. The dark hair, shoulder length. The deep brown eyes and the curvature of the lip. He outlined her figure, the length of her legs, the roundness of her breasts. Della Francesca listened intently and then said, "That's all very fine. But describe the girl."

"I just did," said Dottore.

"No, you did not," snapped the artist. "You described the *appearance* of the girl, which is like saying that della Francesca is a tall, old, white-bearded man. I am not what you *see*. What you see is a lie, or, at best, an artificiality. If you were to show the goat girl your painting—or, better still, her reflection in a mirror, and if you were to ask her, 'Is this you?,' she would most certainly say no—or lie."

He stopped and clutched Dottore's arm. "Before you paint the subject, you must *know* the subjct. And that has little do with what you see. Remember. This is a blind man speaking." Della Francesca coughed. "But I see now with a deeper sight than my eyes ever provided. If I could still see the easel, determine the shades and hues or my colors, I could still paint the truth." He smiled and resumed walking. "That is the secret of making art, my friend. Simply show the truth."

"What is true for you may not be true for me."

The painter stopped again. "Then it is not true for either of us. Great art is timeless, because truth is eternal. The artist shows the wound. The viewer bleeds."

They walked on again in silence for some time. As they reached the narrow street that led to the Piazza Grande, della Francesca stopped again and asked, "When you saw my frescoes in the Vatican, were they in favor with the pope?"

"I don't know. I know one or two cardinals at that time were critical. They objected to your shadowless light. They said you rendered your subjects flat and stark."

"They meant I had painted them as they were. I placed the subjects in the hot and unmerciful light of God's sun, and I painted the truth. There are some—many—who will never like that. It makes them uncomfortable. They love the shadows." The older painter snorted. "Be warned, my friend, they are both numerous and powerful, the shadow lovers. The uniformed murderer who calls his slaughter patriotism. The priest who sells hope by quaratines. The teacher whose pride and arrogance makes him disseminate knowledge as if it were God's word. The rich and famous who wallow in self-indulgence and perversion because they believe they are superior. The artist who prostitutes his gift by measuring success by wealth and public attention." The blind man shook his head. "There are so many, so many. And those who do not romanticize or justify their vices, they destroy. They must." He coughed again, and then, recovering, he rasped, "Or live in the blinding glare of the light of the truth that damns them."

They had reached the Piazza Grande and stood now in the light of the torches erected outside the palazzo that now housed the Confraternity of the Misericordia. "Listen," della Francesca said as they stopped for the last time outside the palazzo, "if you wish to be an artist, work with truth. Let it rest on your palette with your colors and dip your brush in it before every stroke. Turn the light on them: the corrupt, the wicked, the pretentious. Turn the light on them."

Dottore nodded and grasped the old man's hand in both of his. "Thank you. I think I see how you have survived for so long."

Della Francesca smiled. "Can you? Young gentleman—and my age entitles me to call you that—it is not very complicated." He sighed and spoke in a softer, less demanding voice. "I lived because I refused to die. But now, well—over my shoulder I have glimpsed the face of death, and she is a very beautiful young girl. She has invited me to her home. I would be less than a gentleman if I didn't give serious consideration to her offer."

Dottore laughed with the blind painter, and then he said good-bye and turned to go down the road to the amphitheater. He had only gone a few steps when he heard della Francesca call after him, his booming voice echoing down the narrow street, "Turn the light on them! They cannot stand the light!"

*T*HE TWINS PROVED so popular that the company remained in Arezzo for two weeks, and in that interval, Cesare employed the new war machines of Leonardo da Vinci at Ceri. These included new catapults and dummy weapons that drew the enemy fire, and a huge sloping platform that enabled his forces to ascend the walls and overcome the defenders.

With the advent of spring, Ceri fell.

Then, early one morning, as soon as light streaked the sky above the mountains, the company departed and worked their way still farther into the Apennines.

And, as the sun climbed directly overhead, three mounted riders, armed and well dressed, followed after them.

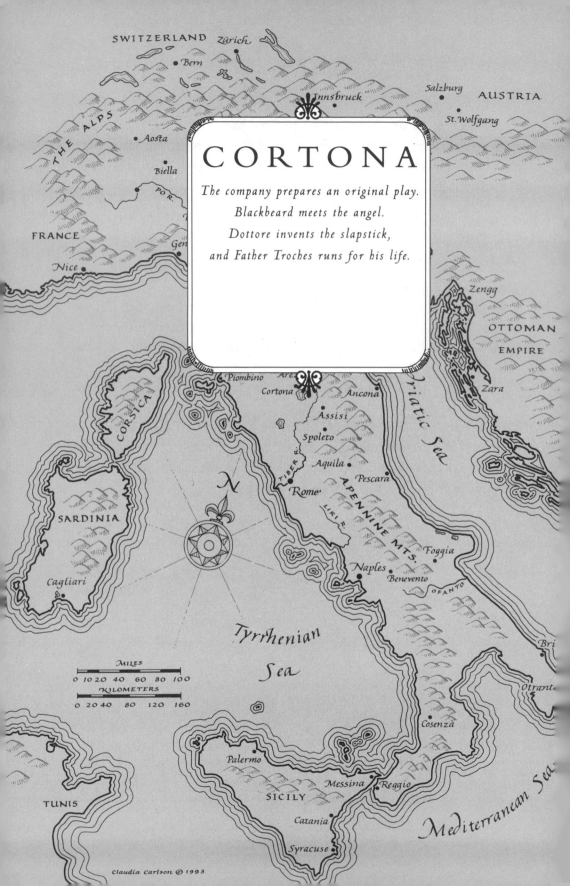

CORTONA

The company prepares an original play.
Blackbeard meets the angel.
Dottore invents the slapstick,
and Father Troches runs for his life.

Claudia Carlson © 1993

Cortona is located halfway between Perugia and Assisi, not far from Lake Trasimene near the Umbrian border, and embedded in hills. The city was ancient at the time of Hannibal. The huge foundation stones that were used to construct the walls of the city, formerly twenty-six hundred meters long, were quarried by Etruscans; and the road was off the main routes. Not being one of the most well-traveled roadways in Italy, it had been gutted and reduced by time and the elements to little more than occasional mud flats and short stretches of cobbled street.

Salvation and the burros pulling the wagon and the cart found the steep ascent to Cortona almost impossible. The entire company walked beside or behind the vehicles, and during one particularly difficult passage, Capitano permitted Zephyr to be harnessed with Death and Destruction.

Being off the customary routes, the people of Cortona were surprised and delighted by the arrival of the troupe, and the children especially erupted in a communal excitement of squeals and laughter, dancing beside the wagon and the players as the company pushed and pulled themselves past the impressive Fortezza Medicea, built on the ruins of the Etruscan wall, and past the busy workers building the Cathedral of Santa Maria on the site of another church. The vehicles crawled along the Porta Santa Maria and the Porta Colonia, through the busy Piazza del Mercato, and through the shadows of the Palazzo Pretorio, three stories tall and dominated by an ancient watchtower. They rattled their way near the Sanctuary of Santa Margherita and finally came to rest in a beautiful, triangular piazza before the Church of San Cristofero, who, Harlequin noted, was the patron saint of travelers.

"And lepers," added Isabella.

The church itself was four hundred years old, but the piazza was lined with beautiful chestnut trees beginning to bud in the warm spring sun.

"It looks as though entertainment doesn't pass through here often," commented Colombina.

"Not likely," agreed Scapino. "For amusement these people pay a visit to the duomo and watch the body of Santa Margherita da Cortona fight against corruption."

"Who?" asked Ruffiana.

"Santa Margherita da Cortona," Isabella repeated. "She had prophetic visions and was allegedly the cause of many miracles."

"She went about in rags," continued Dottore.

"And cared for the poor and orphaned," said Isabella.

"While her own children had to shift for themselves," Dottore noted.

"We will hear nothing against the good Saint Margaret," said Harlequin. "After all, we are guests in her village, and who are we to judge the woman beneath the saint's mask?"

*T*HEY QUICKLY ESTABLISHED their encampment and held a meeting to discuss their next production.

"The women should not have to wear masks," insisted Isabella. "Our own faces are an attraction, and besides, we are not like Scapino or Pantalone. We are not *zanni*."

"I agreed to that in Arezzo," Harlequin reminded her.

"Then I should not have to wear a mask," argued Tristano. "My face is as pretty as hers!" This caused a slight conflict between Isabella and Tristano, with most of the company taking sides until Harlequin whistled them to silence.

"The point is not whether all the pretty members of the troupe should wear masks or not, it is a question of ease and comfort. I will accept the argument that the *innamorati* must, of necessity, play face-to-face on most occasions, and the masks would be an awkward hindrance. Tristano then, too, may dispense with his mask. The masks will be worn only by the *zanni*: Scapino, Pantalone, Capitano, Dottore, and myself.

"Now," he continued before anyone else could interrupt with some objection, "I have come to the conclusion that the weakest element at Arezzo was the age of the script. What do Aretines—or Cortonans—know of, or care about, classical Rome? We are a theater for the people, speaking in Italian — as Plutarch wrote. So let us play something that is universal. Something that is relatively common to everyday people."

Dottore, standing by the wagon with a curious-looking wooden paddle he called a *batte*, spoke. "Poverty?"

"Love," volunteered Colombina.

"Sex," corrected Pantalone.

"Both," Ruffiana smiled, then added, "Adultery."

"What?" asked Dottore.

"Adultery," repeated Ruffiana. "Listen. Stop by any communal well in any town or village anywhere in the world, and what will be the center of the gossip? Adultery. Who is sleeping with whose wife or husband. It's—what did you say? Universal."

"I protest!" roared Dottore. "Universal or not, is adultery appropriate material for theater? I mean, who finds adultery amusing?"

"Not adultery," she countered. "The adulterer! Haven't you ever noticed the man obsessed with sex?" She smiled at Pantalone. "*There* is a ridiculous figure! Honest men turn to thievery and deception. Clerics become satyrs. Misers lavish their wealth without a second thought. Intelligent men act like imbeciles!"

Harlequin smiled at her. "You may have a point there. Anyone obsessed with anything can become a proper subject for ridicule, whether the obession is sex or wealth or—yes—even piety."

Dottore was not convinced. "But adultery is a sin. That is the heart of the matter. It seems to me that treating the matter lightly in a comedy diminishes the offense. The sin becomes merely a social abnormality!"

Harlequin nodded. "Perhaps. But all the laudable efforts of religion to dissuade mankind from adultery, or greed, seem to have had small success over the years. Perhaps ridicule will produce better results."

Dottore shook his head. "That has not been my experience."

"Which?" asked Ruffiana. "Ridicule or adultery?"

The company laughed at Dottore's discomfort, and Harlequin quieted them. "I think Ruffiana has a point. Why not a story in which Pantalone is married to a woman who is neglected and abused and having a romance with—Scapino. Now, the fun is the seduction must take place right before the eyes of the old man. He must be thought so stupid by the audience that they can laugh at him."

"And nudge one another and say, 'It's old Giovanni!'" Colombina laughed.

"Further, the old man, too, must be at least thinking of being unfaithful so we can excuse his wife of betrayal," suggested Pantalone.

"Excellent!" exclaimed Harlequin. "Then we can have him cuckolded twice: once by his wife and once by his mistress!"

"He must be so vain," continued the boy, "that he is easily duped by both the women so we can see that his stupidity is due to a lack of wisdom and virtue, and not to any lack of intelligence."

The company began to take up the thin threads of the story and weave them into a pattern of entrances and exits. They exchanged comments and compliments on certain pieces of stage business that had appeared at Arezzo, and they decided that this *lazzi*—a small comic diversion—was to be the sole property of the creator who would be permitted to use it at any time the laughter seemed to be diminishing or the mood drifted into pathos or drama.

"It has begun," Harlequin whispered to Colombina as he watched the company excitedly attack the project.

"Now, how do you stop it?" she whispered back.

*A*T THE TAVERN off the Piazza del Mercato, Blackbeard finished his wine, rubbed his mouth against his sleeve, and looked around the crowded room.

Now where did those idiots go? he thought to himself. *I simply asked them to check the horses, and they've been gone a quarter hour.*

"They're dead."

He was startled from his reverie by the knife that seemed to come from nowhere and stuck in the tabletop, tightly wedged between two open fingers of his right hand. Then the knife grew a hand and the hand turned into a black-sleeved arm and Angelo quickly dropped into the empty chair across the table from the assassin.

Confused, Blackbeard withdrew his hand from the tabletop and stared at the huge mercenary, who had a dark mole on his chin. "They're dead," the giant repeated. "All of them."

Quickly Blackbeard reached for his own dagger sheathed at his waist, but Angelo's blade was wrenched from the table and now pricked a small red spot at Blackbeard's throat.

"Who—who are you?" whispered Blackbeard.

"An angel," said Angelo. "Guarding saints. And unless you listen carefully and understand what I am telling you, I am the angel of your death. Do you understand this much?" Blackbeard nodded, carefully, lest he inadvertently impale his chin on the dagger's point. "Good," murmured the giant. "The mercenary you sent from Arezzo never left the city. He is buried by a roadside shrine outside the city. Your other two companions sleep the eternal sleep in the stables next door, and you will share their condition if you don't do exactly as I tell you. Do you still understand?"

Blackbeard swallowed and nodded again.

"You are to go back to Florence and report to your superiors that you have lost the trail of the fugitives. Somehow, in these mountainous regions, they simply—disappeared—along with your companions. You alone survived to bring the message to the Borgia agents."

"I—I can't do that. They'd kill me. The duke would have me killed as he had Father Sebastiano."

"If you don't do as I say, your death here and now is certain. If you do as I command, you may find you have friends in Florence who will protect you."

"Friends? Who?"

Suddenly Angelo withdrew the dagger from Blackbeard's throat and cut into the tabletop. Quickly he carved a suggestion of a tree. "You recognize this sign?" he asked. Blackbeard nodded. "Then look for it."

The giant mercenary rose quickly and sheathed his dagger.

"Now ride as fast and as far from here as you can. Deliver the message, and then look for your friends." He leaned across the table until their noses nearly touched. "If I ever see your ugly face again, it will be the day of your death."

He turned and disappeared into the crowded tavern and a moment later watched silently from the shadows of the palazzo as Blackbeard saddled his gelding and raced from the city toward Florence.

Angelo smiled and reentered the tavern.

Even angels get thirsty, he thought.

"Now watch," commanded Dottore. "And listen." And with that he swung the *batte* and caught Pantalone on his buttocks. The sound, however, suggested that he had fractured every bone in the boy's lower body.

"God preserve us!" muttered Harlequin.

"Did it hurt?" Dottore asked Pantalone.

"No more than a kick from a wild horse," the boy replied.

"He's lying," Dottore smiled. "It hurts less than a regular *batte*, and the noise is louder than one of Capitano's pistols." Harlequin took the *batte* and examined it. It was only two slender strips of wood, bound together at the handle, but separated just below the handle by a small wooden dowel. "You see," Dottore explained, "when you hit someone with it, one board slaps against the other with a loud noise. The surprise of it will delight everyone and add to the amusement."

Harlequin beamed. "Your years with Leonardo weren't wasted. You're a genuine artist."

"I know," Dottore agreed.

"What shall we call it?"

"I thought—a slapstick."

"Nice," Pantalone commented dryly. "Now invent something to make the arse incapable of feeling pain."

"We have it." Dottore grinned. "It not only dulls the seat but petrifies the brain as well. It's called 'watching Pantalone for an hour.' "

The boy grabbed the slapstick from Harlequin and chased Dottore around the wagon. "I like it." Harlequin smiled. "Make it part of your *lazzi*."

*T*HE CLEVER WIFE drew every man, woman, and child in Cortona. They pressed tightly against each other in the piazza in the warm spring air, thus creating an even warmer sense of companionship among the members of the audience. Children who were too small to see over the heads of the adults were placed in front of everyone, and directly behind them, mothers and whatever nobility the town could afford sat on crates, boxes, barrels, and large decorated rocks. They had come following the parade of the juggling, dancing, singing, acrobatic members of the company through the streets of the town.

Now Harlequin appeared on the very edge of the wagon stage and strummed Colombina's lute. He began to sing of love and marriage and how one often ruins the other, which instantly evoked knowing laughter from the audience.

He set the scene, placing the action on a known street in Cortona, which also delighted his listeners. He explained the affair between Colombina and Scapino, both of Cortona, and how Pantalone—of Florence—was being cuckolded.

The attendees especially roared at that.

And then Harlequin was gone.

Colombina raced on stage, shrieking with false alarm and gathering her skirts around her waist as she was pursued by Scapino. Bare-legged and codpieced, he chased her over the chairs, over the table, under the table, finally catching her against the table and bending her over it.

There was the sound of the menacing offstage footsteps.

"Damn, my husband!" she cried.

"I thought your husband's name was Pantalone," said Scapino.

Colombina broke from his embrace. "Quick!" she hissed at him. "You must hide!"

"Where?" Scapino asked. "Besides," he said, strutting like a peacock and flipping his *batte* obscenely between his legs, "I'm not afraid of your husband! He's old and bent and weak and—"

"Master of the sword." Colombina moaned.

"I'll hide someplace," Scapino agreed quickly.

The two adulterous lovers began to search all over the stage for a suitable hiding place as the crowd laughed. "Get in the chest!" someone shouted from the audience.

And for what seemed to be an eternity, Colombina tried to stuff Scapino into a small chest obviously insufficient for his size. Finally she grabbed him and plopped him down hard on an upstage chair near the back curtain.

"Sit," she commanded.

"But my breeches," wailed Scapino. "I'm nearly naked!"

"Were did you leave them?"

"Out back by the hay mound."

The footsteps grew louder.

"We'll get them later," she whispered. "Sit down!" And with that she slammed the poor *zanno* into the chair, straddled him and covered his legs with her wide skirt, and threw a shawl over both his head and her own, tying it under her chin. Suddenly she looked startled and gave a small jump. "What's the matter with you?" she snapped. "We haven't time for that now!"

Scapino's muffled voice came from under the shawl. "I can't help it. I think I love you."

She glanced heavenward with a deep sigh as the approaching footsteps grew still louder and more insistent. She muttered, "All right. All right." With that she flipped her skirts up in the back and sat down once more, spreading the folds out to hide Scapino's legs. "But be quiet!" Again there was a little bump, and she was nearly sent hurtling off the stage. "This won't work," she groaned. "I will have to grab the back of the chair to keep from falling."

"All right," came Scapino's muffled voice. "You hold on to the back of the chair, and I'll slip my arms under yours like this." His bare arms appeared on either side of Colombina and made elaborate gestures in the air. The footsteps were enormously loud now.

"This is insane," she breathed, and at that moment Pantalone entered, tripping over his own feet and falling onto the center of the stage.

"Sweet Lord in heaven, that's a long staircase," he wheezed, and the audience applauded and laughed.

"Ohhhh," moaned Colombina, obviously in ecstacy.

"Oh what?" asked Pantalone, turning upstage to face her.

"Ohh," she groaned, "how nice—it is—to see—you!"

He scratched his head in bewilderment. "Is it? Then why aren't you on your feet to greet your husband like a dutiful and respectful wife?"

Colombina was bumped once again and clung to the chair as Scapino's hands fluttered about her face and neck. "I am—weak from the sight of you." She sighed.

Pantalone pondered that for a moment and turned to the audience. "Is that a compliment?" he asked a young woman seated behind the row of children. He wheeled suddenly to find Scapino's hands fondling Colombina's breasts. "What are you doing there?"

The hands began to posture and primp, adjusting the knot of the scarf under Colombina's chin, smoothing the skirt. "I was—just—admiring you," said Colombina.

"Admiring me?" Pantalone frowned. "Admiring what? The back of my head?"

At that Colombina jumped again and half screeched, "Yes!"

"What?" asked the puzzled Pantalone.

"You—have a—magnificent—head—from the—back. A truly astounding—seductive head. Just—turn and let me—see it again."

Pantalone, with an amazed expression, looked at the audience, who roared. He stood with his back to Colombina and muttered, "This is ridiculous." Again Scapino's hand flew to Colombina's breasts, and she inadvertently gave a little shriek. Pantalone wheeled at once. "Are you all right?" he asked.

"Nearly."

"What?" snapped Pantalone, losing patience.

"Yes! Yes!" She smiled. "It's just—that the—sight—of the back—of your head is so—so . . ."

Pantalone turned to the audience and shrugged. "I can't understand this at all."

"Imbecile!" someone shouted, and everyone laughed again.

"Florentine!" someone else yelled, and the listeners laughed all the more.

Pantalone wheeled back to face Colombina. "The back of my head, you say?"

"I know it sounds foolish," cooed Colombina as Scapino's hands lightly brushed her breasts, her throat, and her thighs, "but—I have heard—women in the marketplace—look at the back of your head—and say—things."

"Things? What sort of things?"

"Things like 'Oh, that Pantalone! The back of his head is so wonderful! The way his sparse hair bobs when he runs!' They all melt for you. There isn't a dry thigh in the town!"

"The back of my head?" he repeated.

"Especially—when—you run," panted Colombina.

"I rarely run," he snorted.

Colombina began to bounce about. "Well—it also happens—when you—bob—up and down—as you—walk." She moaned. "It makes—the hair—curling over your collar—go up and down—up and down—up and down."

Suddenly she let out a bloodcurdling scream and shouted, "Oh, my sweet lamb!"

Pantalone nearly fell off the stage in fright and awe. "You haven't called me your sweet lamb in years!" He approached her carefully as she ceased to move, and he studied her closely as she wet her lips with her tongue. "It really does that much for you then? This view from the back veranda, as it were?"

"Oh yes," Colombina insisted, wiggling on Scapino's lap. "Oh yes, yes, yes, yes."

"Gad, what vehemence!" Pantalone told the hysterical crowd. Then he winked and did a little jig. "Perhaps Pantalone will ride tonight, eh?" The audience howled. "I'll just give her another little jolt." He grinned, and he quickly turned his back on Colombina and hopped.

Colombina's eyes widened as something was happening to her under her skirts. She gasped, "Oh!"

Pantalone grinned. "My goodness, what power! And from the back of my head!" He hopped again.

"Oh!" screeched Colombina, and she resumed her up-and-down bouncing on Scapino's lap.

Pantalone absolutely beamed. "Why wasn't I aware of this years ago?" he inquired of the audience. He hopped again.

Colombina's motions were getting violent. "Faster!" she screamed.

Downstage, Pantalone frowned. "Faster?" he muttered. "I didn't think speed was essential. Oh well, all right." And he hopped three or four times quickly.

"Faster! Faster!" she shrieked.

He began to hop like a scared rabbit with one foot caught in a snare. "I'm—a—little too old for—much—of this," he wheezed.

At that moment, as Colombina's bouncing reached a crescendo and Pantalone was hopping and the audience was laughing until tears began to pour down their cheeks, Dottore entered. "What is this?" he murmured in amazement at the sight before him.

Pantalone stopped hopping. "Oh, it's you, doctor," he said. "What do you want?"

Dottore drew himself up proudly and intoned, *"Nobis pro ratio studiorum!"*

Pantalone waved him away and came down to the edge of the stage. "Well," he muttered, "I can't afford that. What other diseases are you peddling today?"

Dottore crossed to the right of Colombina's chair. "I have come," he pompously announced, "to examine your wife—as I do every month." He quietly dropped one hand on Colombina's breast, and Scapino's hand promptly slapped it.

"Why do you examine my wife?" snarled Pantalone. "For that matter, why do you examine every wife in the village once a month, and every man only once a year? And why are you always taking the women out to the hay mound behind the house for your examination? Are we in danger of an epidemic?"

"It is best for women to be examined monthly to prevent disease from occurring." Dottore smiled. "Disease strikes at odd times and in strange places. And I take the women out to the hay mounds to preserve their modesty." He grinned broadly as he placed one hand on Colombina's thigh. Again Scapino delivered a sharp rap with his knuckles. "Ow!" yelped the doctor, staring at Colombina.

"You never examine the strange places," growled Pantalone. "Only the overly familiar ones."

The doctor lunged for Colombina's breast, only to be met in midair in a hand lock with Scapino. For a moment the two wrestled silently behind Pantalone, who was busily brushing the hair on the back of his head. Colombina's husband confided, "I have just discovered the source of my charm and fascination over women, and I was about to bring my wife to the point where—" He suddenly wheeled, and the two hands disengaged. "Why am I telling you all this? Get to your business! It's bad enough you feel and fondle and pat my wife, but I must pay you exorbitantly for your time in the bargain! So, go on! Go on!"

Dottore bowed to Colombina. "Shall we retire out back to the hay mound—as customary, my dear?"

"No," she said sweetly. "Not today, doctor. I have a headache."

"That's—unusual," muttered Dottore.

"That shows how much you know about illness," snapped Pantalone. "She's had that same headache every night for the past six months."

"I—I am more comfortable here." Colombina smiled. "Near my loving husband." Suddenly she gave another gasp and said, "Oh!"

"What is it, my dear?" inquired Pantalone.

"Was it a pain?" asked Dottore, peering closely at her.

"Yes," said Colombina.

"Sharp?" asked Pantalone.

"As a knife," she replied.

"Where did it attack you?" asked Dottore.

"I am embarrassed to say."

"I am a doctor. You can tell me everything."

"No. I can't."

Dottore stood stunned for a moment. "Well," he declared, "we must examine those embarrassing areas especially." And with that, he suddenly flipped up Colombina's skirts and exposed Scapino's bare legs.

"Isn't that unusual, that growth of hair, doctor?" asked Pantalone.

Dottore glared at Colombina. "Not as unusual as that tattoo of a heart that has 'Mother' inscribed on it."

"I don't remember a tattoo," said Pantalone directly to the audience. "But then again, she always undresses for bed in the dark."

"There is more to this than meets the eye," grumbled Dottore.

"And let it remain so!" snapped Colombina as she quickly snatched her skirts from Dottore's hand and lowered them to the floor again.

"But, my dear Pantalone," Dottore said, "this may be something fatal—something catching. I think it demands examination in the hay mound."

"Catching?" gulped Pantalone. He wheeled on Colombina. "Modesty be damned, my dear. You must do what the doctor says."

And Colombina began to bounce up and down again. "But," she insisted, "I have my own relief, husband. I just—do—this—and I feel—ah—better."

"Bouncing like that?"

"That's right. Just—bouncing up and down, up and down . . ."

"And that relieves the attacks?" asked Pantalone.

"Yes!" shrieked Scapino.

"What?"

"I—have—a chest cold," said Colombina, hastily.

"Then we must examine the chest," insisted Dottore as he began to undo the ties of her bodice. Instantly there was another hand-wrestling match between Scapino's hands and those of the doctor's. Suddenly the bodice was undone, and Scapino slipped his hand inside Colombina's blouse and fondled her breast. "No, dear." Dottore smiled, trying to remove the hand. "I can do that."

Scapino's hand slapped Dottore's. "I prefer to do it myself, doctor," cooed Colombina, and the juggler again inserted his hand into her blouse. "Just tell me what I'm looking for."

"How modest!" exclaimed Pantalone.

"How unusual," repeated Dottore.

With that Ruffiana entered carrying a small basket of berries. "I brought Colombina the berries for . . ." She noticed the bouncing and approached the chair suspiciously. "What is this?"

"The doctor is examing my wife," said Pantalone, and he placed his arm around Dottore's shoulder and led him far downstage right. "Doctor," he asked confidentially, "do you think she should be bled?"

Dottore shook his head. "I do not agree with those physicians who bleed the ill over every little thing. I prefer to render my bill and then watch them bleed."

Behind them Ruffiana had suddenly whipped away the shawl to reveal Scapino's head behind Colombina's. "Aha!" she snarled at him in a whisper. "So this is why you've been too tired to make love with me lately!"

"Wife, darling," moaned Scapino. "I can explain everything!"

Downstage, Dottore was slipping his arms around the shoulders of Pantalone. "You have nothing to worry about, Signore Pantalone," he said. "I cannot explain the pain, but I naturally have the cure."

Behind them Ruffiana told Colombina, "I see your problem—it is the chair!" And with that she suddenly pulled Colombina off Scapino's lap. "Let me try it!" And she flipped her skirt in the back, took Colombina's place on Scapino's lap, and covered his bare legs with her skirt. Colombina quickly wrapped her shawl around Ruffiana's head and so hid Scapino's.

"How can you have a cure when you do not know the disease?" Pantalone asked Dottore.

"Because—I am a physician," said Dottore, "and *mea culpa, mea culpa, mea* maxima *culpa!*"

Pantalone's eyes widened and he quickly came down to the edge of the stage. "That's certainly true, isn't it? I mean, you can't argue with that!" The audience howled, and there were more cries of "Florentine!"

Pantalone turned to see Colombina standing behind the table, and Ruffiana bouncing with great vehemence and angry determination in the chair. "Here! Here!" he cried. "What is this then?"

Ruffiana replied, "I think it is this chair that caused—all your—wife's—problems." She began to bounce even faster. "So I'm trying to see—if—it—is—yes!" She gave one shriek and then seemed to collapse. "It's definitely the chair," she said with a smile.

Suddenly Dottore was behind Colombina. "That may be very well, but I must examine the patient to see if there are any after-effects." With that he bent Colombina over the table and flipped her skirts above her shoulders.

"What is this?" screamed Pantalone. "I eat off that table!"

"It's all right," assured Colombina. "I am accustomed to this form of examination. Why don't you—take my mind—off this unpleasant—but vital—probing—by—showing me the back of your head again?"

Pantalone frowned. "Wellll, are you sure? I don't want to waste the power."

Colombina groaned from the "examination" being conducted by Dottore, unseen behind the mountain of skirt. "I would like it very much," she breathed. "And I am certain that Ruffiana would like to see it, too. Wouldn't you, my dear?"

Ruffiana, resuming her bouncing, shouted, "Yes! Yes!"

Pantalone recoiled from the passion behind the cry, and came down to talk to the audience again. "Godsblood! What a fever, eh?" He beamed. "How can I refuse?" And with that he turned his back to Colombina and Ruffiana and began to hop on one foot and then the other.

"Yes!" screamed Ruffiana.

"Oh, my God!" cried Colombina.

Pantalone grinned at the listeners. "Isn't this wonderful?" He hopped faster. "Truly remarkable. And to think—I—never—knew—I had—such—power!"

Suddenly Ruffiana rose and adjusted her skirts. Scapino dashed out and came back with his breeches, and Dottore collapsed on the table, which permitted Colombina to stand and adjust her own dress. Out of breath, Pantalone slowly turned to face them. "Scapino," he said, "what are you doing here?"

Scapino struggled frantically to dress himself as Ruffiana tried to hide part of him with her skirts. "I—ah—I just—walked—in," he said.

"You look like you *ran* in," noted Pantalone. "You're panting like a winded dray horse."

"I—I had an exhausting morning."

"Well," said Pantalone, "I don't—" Suddenly he pretended to see something off to the right. He quickly grabbed the weary Dottore and pulled him far downstage, where he whispered, "It's Isabella. My beautiful Isabella. She's coming here."

"What?" asked the doctor.

"She's approaching! The one woman I desire more than life itself!" He lowered his voice. Listen, doctor," he said softly, "I now know the power I have over women, and I must use it while I have it. Could you—please—take my wife somewhere else and continue your examination? Like a good fellow?" He slapped a small leather pouch into Dottore's hand, and it jingled and clicked.

"But of course, Pantalone. I understand perfectly." Dottore crossed back to where Ruffiana, Scapino, and Colombina were gathered, and whispered to them. Then, in a much louder voice, he declared, "Come, Colombina! We must probe more deeply—into the seat of your difficulties."

"Could be amusing," she acquiesced.

"So let us depart to the hay mound and leave our Pantalone here to have a moment's peace." They all laughed and giggled together and nodded their agreement, and left by the up-left doorway. Pantalone was now the only actor onstage.

Instantly Isabella came in from the right, and he rushed to greet her. "Isabella! Isabella!" Pantalone turned his back on her. "My—

hair! Does it look all right to you—from the back, that is?" And the foolish old man began to bob up and down again.

Isabella's moved center, still behind Pantalone, looked at his hair, shrugged to the audience, and asked. "Are you feeling well, Signore Pantalone?"

He continued to bob and hop and wiggle. "Do not resist, my darling," he half crooned. "There is no shame in admitting that my power is too much for you."

"The power? What power?"

"The power of me!" Pantalone caroled with obvious relish and glee. "The magic of—the head!"

Isabella looked directly at the audience and shrugged again. Then Tristano appeared onstage, entering from the right, led by Ruffiana, Scapino, Dottore, Colombina, and Capitano. They gestured to Isabella for silence and prodded Tristano forward into Isabella's arms.

Downstage, Pantalone continued bobbing, but it was evident that he was weakening.

"Do you feel it yet? Can you feel the magic of it?" he called.

Tristano kissed Isabella, and she smiled and cried out, "Oh yes! I feel it! It's—overwhelming!"

Pantalone jigged with more vigor, rubbing his sweating palms together in anticipation. "Perhaps a little more," he whispered to the audience, "just to make certain I have her." They roared.

Upstage, Tristano whispered to Isabella, "My heart beats faster and faster when I behold your beautiful face!"

Isabella looked deeply into Tristano's eyes and murmured, "Oh yes. My own heart beats faster."

"What, my dearest?" cried Pantalone. "I can't hear you. The blood is rushing to my ears from all this bobbing and hopping. What did you say?"

"Faster!" said Isabella.

Pantalone gasped. "You, too?" He looked at the audience. "Why is speed such an essential?" But he began to move as fast as he was able. "I can't take much more of this," he confided to the house.

Tristano hugged Isabella. "Tighter," she said.

"Tighter?" echoed Pantalone. "How does one hop tighter?"

Tristano stroked Isabella's breast. "Gently." She sighed.

"Oh, thank God," murmured Pantalone as he slowed his pace and gasped for air. "I hope I haven't overdone it," he whined to the audience.

Behind him the company snickered and giggled and left the stage. Pantalone wheezed and choked for three minutes, and then said, "Are you ready, Isabella?" Receiving no reply, he looked at the audience with fright. "I hope it didn't prove too much for her. A little of me is sufficient for delicate natures." The crowd laughed louder. "Are you ready, darling Isabella?" he called. Again there was no reply. Cautiously he turned. There was no one there, of course, and he picked his way to where Isabella had been but a few moments earlier. He then proceeded to peek under the table, in the chest, on the ceiling, growing more frantic with every disappointment. "Godsblood," he exclaimed. "It was too much. She melted away from the heat of her passion." He began to cry with great exaggeration. The more he cried and howled, the more his listeners howled themselves. "I've killed her!" he wailed. "I don't know how to control this incredible power!"

At that, Colombina entered and came down to her grieving husband. "What have you done? I warned you it was a very powerful charm you possessed!" Pantalone wept loudly. "Now you must make restitution, my darling," said Colombina.

"Restitution?"

"For releasing your full force upon the hapless girl. Now you must promise me you will never again use this talent against another woman."

"I promise."

"And you must keep this seductive power of yours for me alone—as your lawful wife."

Pantalone groaned quietly to the audience, "Where's the fun in that?" Then, louder, he declared, "I promise."

"And whenever I choose—such as when I am being examined by the good doctor or visited by some other—friends," continued Colombina, "you must do as I say and turn your back on us and hop—just for me."

"I promise," he muttered.

"Then our life together will be gaiety and happiness as long as we both live," cried Colombina. She beat her tambourine once, and the stage exploded with dancing, playing, cavorting players in a bright *saltarello*.

It rained coins.

*T*HE GNARLED AND WRINKLED HAND of the boat captain closed around the golden florins. "We sail for Corsica within the hour," he growled. "Be on time or I go without you."

Father Francesco Troches, mantled and hooded in black, nodded and returned to the waiting courtesan seated in his carriage on the waterfront. "We leave soon, my darling," he whispered to the beautiful woman in the darkness. "As soon as we get to Corsica, there is another boat waiting to take us to Genoa, where the French king will have his emissaries waiting for us."

"I don't understand any of this, Francesco." The courtesan pouted. "Why don't we just remain here in Rome and wait. I'm sure the pope will make you a cardinal soon."

"Yes," he wryly replied, "when I can find two hundred thousand ducats to feed his purse! No. I can be rewarded with that much, and more, when I tell the French king that Cesare is planning to make a separate alliance with his Spanish enemies and show Louis this correspondence between the duke and Gonsalvo de Cordoba!" He produced a cylindrical leather case from under his cloak. "Who knows? The French might even make *me* a duke! After all, I have more information and documentation about the abuses and crimes of the Vatican than any man alive."

"That can be changed," said the low voice behind him.

The priest had no opportunity to turn and see his assassin. The thin blade of the stiletto pierced the cloak and the tunic beneath it and plunged directly into his heart. Francesco wheezed and stood on his toes for a minute as if he were about to dance, but then the

lifeless body seemed to shrink as it slid forward off the tilted blade and onto the worn wooden planks of the dock.

"Thank you, madonna," said Michelotto as he bent and wiped the blood from his stiletto on the dead cleric's cloak. Then he turned the body over and took the leather case from the stiffening fingers. He opened the door to the carriage and climbed into the darkened interior. "Now, Signorina Fiammetta," the dark giant cooed softly, "how do you propose we pass the long hours on our return to Rome?"

The coachman snapped his whip, and the six horses and the black carriage became one with the shadows of the night.

*A*s THE PERFORMERS CAME DOWN the steps from the wagon stage, they were met by a Harlequin who was smiling but somehow different. He calmly asked them to assemble behind the wagon, because he had something to say.

When they had gathered together, Harlequin looked at the sky as the dark clouds formed. "A little rain is coming," he said.

Colombina nodded. "Not very good news for a troupe who have no roof on their stage."

Harlequin glanced to where Scapino, Dottore, and Isabella were checking their wealth. "A man came to me after the performance," he said. "A farmer. He said there was an old building farther up—on the other side of Assisi—that has been abandoned. An old church, he says." He turned to Colombina. "How do you feel about turning it into a *theatrum*—just for the rainy season? While we sharpen our skills a little?"

Colombina's heart jumped. A *theatrum*. Her dream. She smiled and nodded happily.

Harlequin kissed her lightly on the forehead and turned to the others. "Then that is what we will do. We're safe from our enemies here in the mountains, and we can work at our leisure, performing now and again to make enough money to keep us going. A *theatrum* base will provide us with an opportunity to work at our art. We can sharpen that art the way a warrior sharpens his blade, and we may be better prepared for the coming battle."

They looked at one another. "Not another battle," complained Scapino. "My head hasn't recovered from the last one!"

"I have come to realize," said Harlequin, "that we lose so many battles because we have always given our enemies the choice of weapons and the battlefields. Any soldier knows that is a poor way to conduct a campaign."

The capitano snorted. "But what a triumph if you still win the day."

"Yes," Harlequin agreed, "but we haven't been winning. Now, let us spend this rainy period in and around this secluded *theatrum*, preparing our weapons, sharpening our skills, and refining our *lazzi*. Then we can go down and face our enemies. Not in their courts or battlefields, but in the hard and honest sunshine of the piazzas."

Colombina studied him. "Come down where? To Florence?"

"To Perugia! Orvieto! Terni! Viterbo! Rieti! Wherever there is a piazza filled with people or a communal fair or a carnival or a celebration!"

The company began to whisper and laugh among themselves, but there were no objections voiced and no quarrels. "What will we do there, in Terni and Viterbo?" asked Colombina.

Harlequin crossed to her and clasped her hands. "We are going to give the poor an opportunity to be rich—for an hour," he said softly. "We are going to let the lame walk and the dumb not only speak—but sing! We are going to work miracles with time and space and conditions! Create a communion of saints! And then . . ." His voice grew more hushed, and his eyes began to twinkle. "And then," he repeated, "we go to Rome."

The company grew silent. "To Rome?" said Colombina softly.

"But—the pope . . ." growled the capitano.

"We have our own pope. He is old and degenerate and afraid. We call him Pantalone. Cesare Borgia himself struts and growls and snarls among us. We call him the capitano. Who is Ruffiana if not Lucrezia? Let us show them to the people. Not as they pretend to be, but as they are: pompous and frightened and wicked and noble and ambitious and lazy. Let the people see them eat and drink and deceive one another—and us."

There was a general silence, and then finally Scapino did a forward somersault and landed in front of the group. "Why not?" he said. "What's the point of being a fulcrum, if you never have a chance to fulc?"

*T*HE NOTE WAS PASSED to him by a young boy just as he was about to mount the seat of the wagon for the company's departure for Assisi. Harlequin took it, gave the boy a coin, and unfolded it. He read it, and then he read it again.

"What is it?" asked Colombina.

"I'm not sure," said Harlequin, and he looked around to see if anyone was watching him. Seeing nothing unusual in the piazza, he passed the note to Colombina. "Test your newly acquired knowledge." He smiled "What does it say?"

Colombina focused on the words and pronounced them carefully. "You—are—safe," she read. Then she looked up at Harlequin. "What does that mean?" she asked.

Harlequin shrugged. "I have no idea," he said as he urged the burros forward, "but God—and cardinals—work in strange ways, their miracles to perform."

Colombina shrugged, too, and then she inched herself closer to Harlequin and wrapped her arm through his as the wagon and the cart and great war-horse rode under the archway and into the sheltering mountains.

ASSISI

The omens of the rondine and the owl.
The celebration feast in the vineyard,
and Cesare goes for the gold.
Fra Lorenzo explains it all,
and the Romagna begins to unravel.

SWITZERLAND Zürich

Bern

THE ALPS Aosta

Innsbruck

Salzburg AUSTRIA

St. Wolfgang

Biella

POR.

RANCE

Gen

Nice

Zengg

OTTOMAN
EMPIRE

Zara

Piombino Are

Cortona Ancona

Assisi

CORSICA

Spoleto

TIBER R.

Aquila

N

Rome

Pescara

Adriatic Sea

SARDINIA

APENNINE MTS.

LIRI R.

Foggia

Cagliari

Naples

Benevento

OFANTO

Brindisi

*Tyrrhenian
Sea*

MILES

0 10 20 40   60 80 100
KILOMETERS
0 20 40   80   120 160

Otranto

Cosenza

Palermo

Messina Reggio

SICILY

Mediterranean Sea

Catania

UNIS

Syracuse

Claudia Carlson © 1993

The road to Assisi took the company south and east, in the shadow of the umbrella pines, cypress, and myrtles that are landmarks of the Umbrian countryside. They decided to bypass the large city of Perugia and found themselves on a bad road north of the city. The ancient Roman roads were dust, loose stones, and ruts that were transformed into muddy streams in the wet weather that now afflicted the area. On sunnier days the company ran the gauntlet of the provincial farmers selling their goods along the roadside to avoid having to pay the city toll on their produce.

They also skirted the hilltop towns and castles, which were rumored to be infested with bandits.

On the way, they performed at Pretola and again south in Bastia, where they planted the wagon stage in the shadow of the medieval town wall. They stopped for a free meal at a Benedictine abbey that had been erected on the ruins of an ancient fortress and then proceeded southeast to Assisi.

The skies above the mountains were shadows of the mountains themselves: gray, massive, cutting off the light and chilling the souls of the company as the rains chilled their bodies. The Assisi road, however, was not as steep as the road that had led them into Cortona; but when they arrived in the pink city of Subiaco stone, their mood of depression was deeper than at any other time in their journey.

Part of this overall depression was due to the sight of Assisi itself on the slope of Monte Subasio. In the gray, cold light of the rain-filled sky, the natural coral tones of the buildings were washed away, and the two churches, one above another, seemed less imposing, the soaring arches that form the artificial base for the major building transformed into dark eyes peering down on them from the slopes.

Inside the city, the streets were steep and stepped in some places, and even the curious diamond-shaped designs woven into the paving was less a delight than a puzzle. They crawled past the ancient Roman amphitheater at the Porta Perlici and noted, with some dismay, that the majority of the windows in the houses were barred and that each house was marked with the *porti dei morti*—the "dead man's doors"—little more than narrow slits that denied entrance to more than one person at a time. The bars and the narrow doorways were defenses against attack, of course, but to the company who caught only glimpses of faces peeking from the shadows of the houses, the precautions not only served to keep intruders out, they also seemed to keep the inhabitants in.

Still, the view from Assisi was awesome: the broad Umbrian plain, the olive groves, the smaller towns of Trevi and Montefalco, Spello and Foligno far below and beyond.

The company also noted the great masses of swallows, called *rondini*, that glided and circled over the towers of the basilicas.

"There's an omen," said Dottore softly.

*I*N THE VATICAN, Pope Alexander VI looked down on the parade of the red-and-yellow-uniformed elite corps of Cesare.

"The boy is proving difficult," grumbled the rotund pontiff. "I've done everything for him. Everything. Inundated him with wealth and position, and how does he repay me?" He turned to face the tall cardinal who was his chamberlain. "I ask him to attack Bracciano and kill Giangiordano Orsini. He refused! I said, 'Then move against Niccolo Orsini at Pitigliano!' He refused again! Finally he lays siege to Ceri, and when it falls, what does he do with Giulio Orsini? He brings him here to me! To Rome! And I have to swallow my bile and treat the bastard like some noble gentleman!"

The chamberlain said nothing, knowing nothing was expected of him.

"Doesn't he see that our mutual enemies are the Orsini and the della Roveres? They will stop at nothing to destroy both of us! Why doesn't he do what I ask of him?"

This time the pope paused and glared at his chamberlain, and the tall cleric knew he had to offer support. "The duke says that prudence and gentility may be more in order at this point than armed conflict. He feels he must mend some bridges, placate some old enemies, in order to consolidate his victories in the Romagna."

The pontiff glared. "Placate?" he roared. "He is leaving enemies alive! He has never done that before! It will be taken as a sign of weakness and, most assuredly, these villainous cardinals will rise up against both of us—led by della Rovere and the Orsini family!" He turned back to look out the window. "What can I do, Casanova? What can I do about this rebellious young lord?"

The chamberlain slowly walked toward the pontiff and whispered in his ear. "You could do what the French request. Send him off to fight against the Spanish. Stuart d'Aubigny was defeated in Calabria, and the Duke of Nemours has surrendered the Castel Nuova in Naples. Louis is frightened of losing the Neapolitan kingdom, and you are bound by treaty with the French to supply him with men and arms. He wants Cesare and Cesare's troops. Give them to him."

The pontiff turned and studied his chamberlain. "Very good, Casanova. Very good. It might teach the boy a little humility. Louis is forming a new army under La Trémoille to attack Fuenterrabía. I think it is about time Cesare honored his commitments."

He stepped back suddenly as a dark figure darted through the window, dashed in terror and confusion against the stone walls, and then fell at the pontiff's feet. The brown owl fluttered once or twice and died.

Rodrigo Borgia's eyes were wide and frightened.

"An omen!" he whispered. "A bad omen!"

*I*N ASSISI the company wound their way through the Piazza del Comune, which contained the bleak ruins of a Roman temple to Minerva and the oppressive, towering Torre Communale.

As they passed through the piazza, they came upon a sight even more horrendous and depressing: masses of humanity, crippled, diseased, some lacking limbs or with gaping wounds, crowded a makeshift shelter in the piazza. They looked upon the passing wagon and the great war-horse with almost no interest and less cordiality.

The narrow street led them to the Piazza Santo Francesco and to the Via del Seminario and the Via Portica beyond. They enumerated the string of palazzi—Giacobetti, Bindangoli, del Podesta, dei Priori—as the company approached the piazza before the Church of Santa Maria Maggiore.

The caravan continued through the piazza. They entered the Via Fontebella, which led them to the entrance of the Basilica of St. Frances of Assisi. The basilica was enormous, constructed on two levels, and served as a seminary as well as a church. As they approached, a short, rotund, brown-robed monk came rushing down the steps as fast as he could. Harlequin reined Death and Destruction to a stop.

"Fra Lorenzo?" Harlequin asked.

"You must be the comedians Signore Robelli talked about. Well, well. It will be nice to have comedians as neighbors." And he chuckled with such apparent and sincere amusement that the company took encouragement from him.

"We weren't sure you would feel that way," said Harlequin, stepping down from the guild wagon. "There was hardly anyone in the streets—except for the—sick and wounded in the piazza."

Fra Lorenzo blessed himself. "The poor unfortunates. Homeless. Refugees. But there are also a number of soldiers here, too. Wounded. Abandoned." He shrugged. "We do what we can, but . . ." He shrugged again.

"Why are they here?" asked Colombina. "Shouldn't they be in—institutions—hospitals—something like that?"

The fat little monk smiled. "Of course. My very words to them. But they come—of course—expecting the miracles."

"Miracles?"

"Well, who can say? Something happens. Often. Oh yes. Very often." He motioned them into the basilica. "Come inside, and we will see what we can feed you, eh?"

They followed him inside, and he waddled ahead of them down stairs and around corridors until they came to the refectory, where three or four brown-robed seminarians were eating at long tables. He had the company seat themselves as he gestured to the young nuns to serve the guests. The nuns neither spoke nor looked at them, hurrying the food to the table and then disappearing through an archway.

"They are from the Order of Clarissa, the poor Clares," explained Fra Lorenzo. "Santa Chiari is buried at the opposite end of the town in a pretty, somewhat smaller basilica surrounded by orchards and with that unique square-topped campanile which you must have noticed as you came into Assisi."

Harlequin had to admit that he had not.

"Well"—the monk smiled—"it is of no consequence. There are much more interesting relics here—other than me, that is."

Within minutes the table before the company was stocked with fresh fruit, roasted meat and fresh bread, bowls of uncooked carrots and celery, lettuce and olives, and earthenware pitchers brimming with a rich, dark wine.

"Eat! Eat!" commanded their jovial host.

*T*HE FOOD WAS ELABORATELY PREPARED and abundant in the vineyard of Cardinal Adriano Castellesi da Corneto on the warm evening. The cardinal bustled around, seeing to every dish placed before his guests: Cesare Borgia, his father the Pontiff of Rome, and his portly brother Jofre.

The dining table had been placed under an immense *baldacchino* in case the weather turned inclement and was covered with an embroidered cloth that contained the coat of arms of the newly appointed cardinal. The napkins of silk were folded in the shape of arches and columns, and the sparkling glassware glinted and flashed in the scarlet light of the setting sun.

On the portico of the palazzo itself a group of musicians filled the cooling, early-evening air with soft music.

"I trust you will find the salad to your satisfaction," gushed da

Corneto. "I personally saw to its preparation. Turnips and lemons with slices of sweet ham, caviar, capers, fresh fruit, and olives."

"I must have only a small portion." The pope sighed. "I'm getting much too obese, and this is an unhappy time for fat men. It seems there has been a never-ending parade of funeral corteges under my window lately—and all fat men."

"Nonsense." Cesare smiled as a servant filled his glass with wine. "It has nothing to do with obesity. It is the malaria."

"Let's not speak of unpleasant matters," urged Jofre. "The evening air is cool, and the food and company are excellent. We are here to celebrate the appointment of our new cardinal host, and to delay the departure of our brother Cesare one more day; so let us enjoy the moment."

Cesare laughed and sipped the wine. "I endorse the thought, brother. Any day that keeps me from joining the French in their untidy little war against the Spanish is a day to celebrate! I drink to that!"

The host beamed with good feeling, and the guests promptly emptied their wineglasses and then threw them against the poles supporting the canopy.

My God! da Corneto screamed internally. *That's Venetian glass!*

*A*T THE CONCLUSION of the good refectory meal, the company followed the little monk down the corridors, and Colombina said, "You mentioned miracles."

"Well," said the cleric, "see for yourself." He gestured to the side chapels that lined the lower level of the basilica. It was actually a crypt, low-ceilinged, columned, and vaulted, but each small chapel was filled with hand-carved crutches, bloodstained sheets, wheeled chairs and narrow couches.

"I don't understand," said Colombina.

"I didn't make them myself." Fra Lorenzo laughed with a shrug.

Scapino pushed his way toward him. "Are you telling me these—things—were left behind by—cripples?"

"By *people*," Fra Lorenzo corrected. "They came with diseases, with wounds, perhaps unable to walk or stand, but as I told you, something happened, and they walked away with clear skins and healing sores." He paused and amended his statement. "Some do. Some do not." He turned and continued through the crypt.

"Do you believe these were miracles?" asked Scapino.

The little Franciscan stopped again and smiled gently. "I believe some were cured." He made that characteristic small shrug again. "Italy is a land of miracles. Here in the mountain towns especially you can visit any church and see a bloodstained piece of cloth and hear the story of how a humble priest questioned the real presence of Christ in the Eucharist, only to have the wafer turn to blood at the Consecration. Or how another priest placed a communion wafer in his breviary as he went to visit a dying man, and when he opened the book to recover it, the pages were wet with blood. In that particular case, a page from the breviary held to the light will reveal an image that suggests the Christus."

"I've heard such stories all my life," said Scapino, "but—"

"You question them," said the cleric. "I understand you. And the stories are numerous. A levitation here. A stigmata there. It must appear to the Europeans that one reason there is so much decadence and violence throughout the world is that God is busily creating miracles in Italy."

"And you . . .?"

"Oh, here we believe in miracles," said Fra Lorenzo, "but we also bind the wounds and clean the running sores. We pray for a miracle and do what we can."

"WE NEED A MIRACLE," said the aged priest. "I have done what I can, but the holy father remains feverish and is coughing up bile. I bled him again yesterday, thirteen ounces, but to no avail."

"Thirteen ounces?" roared the tall, thin cardinal-chamberlain Casanova. "God in heaven, the man is seventy-two years old!"

"It is prescribed procedure," argued the priest as he poured the contents of a vial into a crystal decanter of clear liquid. "I did not submit him to the more—shocking—practice of plunging the sick man into a receptable of ice water to remove the outer skin. The duke submitted to the procedure, and he is vomiting less, but he still complains of the stomach pains."

The chamberlain crossed the window. "The Spanish envoy says you ordered the duke dipped into the warm entrails of a disemboweled mule. Is that customary?"

The priest paused in his chemical tinkering to peer over his glasses at the cardinal. "That is a ridiculous rumor. The Spanish envoy is a disemboweled mule."

"There are other rumors. Many." Casanova turned to face the priest again. "Is it. . . ? I mean, has there been an investigation for the possibility of—poison?"

The aged priest shook a small vial of greenish liquid and studied it against the flame of a candle. "I understand that there has been some questioning of Cardinal da Corneto, since he insisted the food was prepared under his close supervision. But no charges have been made."

The chamberlain crossed to the priest and whispered, "There is a rumor that the duke provided da Corneto with some of the Borgian poison, *contarella*, in an attempt to murder his father."

"Nonsense! The duke, da Corneto, and three others were also afflicted, but to a lesser degree. Would the duke consume poison himself?"

"Perhaps—a mistake?"

The old priest snorted. "Perhaps it was an evil spell." He snorted again. "Nonsense! Unscientific bilge! I feel it may be more a matter of obese gentlemen badly digesting the rich food served them—combined with malaria."

"You blame everything these days on malaria, you old fraud," jeered the chamberlain. "I know for a fact that the Bishop of Chiusi died of syphilis, and you said it was malaria!"

The priest angrily poured the contents of the vial back into the carafe. "I had no idea you were such a specialist in medicine," he growled. "And I did not say the bishop died of malaria. I said he died of fright. And that he did—when he learned that the duke's armies were marching on his city!"

The chamberlain was not to be deterred. "You say it was a matter of indigestion by fat men. May I point out that the Duke of Valentinois is not obese? Far from it. How do you account for that?"

"He ate less."

The cardinal sighed. "Well, it's useless arguing with you." He started toward the archway. "Has the holy father requested my presence? There are matters of state that—"

"He has asked for no one. Neither Cesare or Lucrezia nor any other relative. He told me to summon only the Bishop of Carinola and have him at hand—in case."

"The Bishop of Carinola?"

"His confessor," murmured the old priest as he seized the decanter and shuffled through the archway.

"We need a miracle!" he called from the darkness.

*H*ARLEQUIN AND FRA LORENZO ENTERED the lower church from the Piazza delle Logge, and the little monk gestured to the chapel of St. Sebastian on their left, the chapel of St. Anthony, and the entrance to the monk's cemetery. They passed the chapel of St. Catherine, and Fra Lorenzo drew Harlequin's attention to the frescoes depicting events in the life of St. Francis.

Finally they stood in the transept before the high altar with the vaulted ceilings and the frescoes of Giotto.

"This is—quite a church," Harlequin said softly.

Their host replied, "It is very big and very elaborate. Not down here, of course, but upstairs. I have grown accustomed to it, but I'm afraid I am in the camp of Brother Leone."

"What do you mean?"

The Franciscan grimaced wryly. "Oh, you do not know the story of this basilica?" He leaned forward and lowered his voice. "St. Francis, you see, was very explicit in his instructions to the order. He stressed personal poverty, a nomadic way of life, going from place to place and preaching the word of God as we share the lives of the people. He was not given to great basilicas, or shows of pomp or authority. But when he died, the order immediately began to build a basilica for his body. The order split into two camps. A certain Brother Elia insisted on the building, and Brother Leone insisted that such ostentatiousness was contrary to the teachings of Francis." He shrugged and gestured to the walls. "Well. Here it is. The Elias of this world always seem to win."

Harlequin smiled at the little monk. "Well, not always."

"Later, I will show you the cross of St. Damiano," said Fra Lorenzo, and leaned nearer Harlequin and whispered, "It is supposed to have spoken to St. Francis at one time."

"The cross *spoke*?"

"Perhaps. It is reported to have said, 'Go forth and build my church.' That's the legend." He looked around at the huge basilica. "I believe Brother Elia took the commandment literally."

Harlequin laughed, and the little monk smiled.

"And later, perhaps," added Fra Lorenzo, "you will find time for me to show you the Piazza del Vescovado—where St. Francis rejected his father's wealth."

"*H*E'S DEAD?" came the whisper from the sickbed. "You're sure?"

Michelotto nodded and leaned closer to the ill Duke of Valentinois. "Your father passed away last night. His—his face became all black—and swollen. His tongue—his tongue just—grew and grew—until it dangled from his mouth—and they couldn't—push it back in again."

Cesare groaned.

"They—they had his body lying in state in the Sala del Papagallo, and then—the attending priest ran out of the room and screamed that a—a monkey—had scrambled into the room, leaped on the body, and tried to pull the tongue from the dead man's mouth."

The giant mercenary gasped for air, and his face was covered with a cold sweat. "But—when they went in, there was no one there, but—but they say—the body seemed to be—to be—well—boiling. There was foam pouring from the mouth, and—well—they couldn't find anyone to stay with the body. No prayers were said. No vigils. Nothing."

There was silence for a long while, and the giant was about to rise and depart when Cesare put out a hand and grabbed his sleeve. "Listen, Michelotto. This is more important! Seize that chamberlain! What's his name? Casanova! Hold him and make him give you the keys to my father's closets. You'll find two chests inside. There should be about two hundred thousand ducats in jewels and silver in one and another hundred thousand in gold in the other. Bring them here! Go!"

As ill as he was, the duke nearly hurled the mercenary away from the bed, and in a moment Michelotto was racing to the quarters of the chamberlain.

FRA LORENZO SMILED at them. "But let us talk of you. You will perform for us, yes? By that I mean, you will perform for our poor penitents in the Piazza Communale?"

Harlequin looked around the table at the others and, after a minute, said to the cleric, "We would like to perform, of course, but there is a question as to what we might do."

"Do what you did in Cortona. Signore Robelli said it was very very funny."

"It was funny for Cortona," murmured Harlequin, "but we have found that the production must be tailored to the audience. In Arezzo, for example, what was most popular was an attack on the military. The Aretines, because they have had enough of wars and battles, responded. In Cortona, we did a little something based on—ah—on adultery."

"Well, here you will find people who are tired of war, as you will find adulterers," said the monk. "I must be about my other duties, but I'm certain you will perform magnificently. I will see to it that quarters are found for you. The men can sleep here, and the women in the convent of Santa Chiari, and soon—eh?—we will have the play."

Harlequin stood and nodded dumbly, and before he could say anything further, Fra Lorenzo was gone. "Well," said Harlequin, turning to the company, "Has anyone a suggestion on what we should play for people awaiting a miracle?"

*T*HE GENERAL CONSENSUS WAS that this production should definitely eliminate some of the customary bawdiness and sexual subject matter so as not to offend the good clerics.

"Many of these people are sick or wounded, and they have abandoned physicians to come here and seek a miracle," said Harlequin. "That would seem to suggest something in which we can strike a few blows against doctors and their methods of bleeding and dosing. In other words, let's pit Dottore against Pantalone, who is dying."

"No," Scapino insisted. "There's not much that is funny about dying. Let Pantalone *think* he's dying when actually he's strong as a Borgian bull. *That's* funny!"

The others agreed, and an outline quickly evolved in which Pantalone is convinced by his scheming wife, his greedy daughter, her arrogant betrothed, and a clever servant that he is dying. They are attempting to force him into revealing how his estate should be divided upon his death. Enter Dottore, bribed by the family to assist in the plot, and he prescribes outlandish medicines and treatments that make the old man feel genuinely ill. Then Scapino, as the wily servant, changes sides and tells his master of the plot, and Pantalone feigns death. The family instantly exposes their greediness and deception and their callousness toward the old man, who recovers before their eyes.

The production ends with Pantalone leaving all his wealth to Scapino, philosophizing, "I can't take it with me when I go."

The *soggetto* offered Scapino an opportunity to develop a *lazzo* he had been thinking about in which Pantalone, drugged into sleep, is carried around the stage and deposited one place only to pop up in another seconds later.

The company set to work with a new enthusiasm, and Harlequin wandered out of the refectory, up the staircase, and into the upper church.

It was elaborate. Tiled. A cross-vaulted ceiling with innumerable frescoes detailing the life of the saint. More than a hundred and fifty years old, the paintings did not pay tribute to the good saint's poverty or his miracles, but instead concentrated on depicting his service to Pope Gregory.

"Ah, Brother Elia," whispered Harlequin to himself, "the world was too much with you."

*T*HE SIX BURLY MEN carried the body of the dead pontiff into the small room of the Capello delle Febbre and placed it unceremoniously on a table. The body was dressed in the ceremonial robes of the Pope of Rome, including the miter, but when the porters dumped the lifeless form on the flat surface, the headdress fell to the floor and was kicked aside.

"We better work fast," said one. "In this heat, he'll stink before long."

Two carpenters came into the room with a plain wooden coffin, but it was obvious at once that the receptacle was too small for the obese body.

"Didn't you take measurements?" snapped the head carpenter to his assistant.

"When would I have time?" the other whined. "He died only yesterday! I thought he was much—smaller."

The eight men considered the problem, and the head carpenter pointed out that it was too late to consider building a new coffin.

"The way I see it," whispered a porter, "the Curia wants it over and done with."

The head carpenter nodded. "He's got to be underground to-day."

They decided then to strip away the vestments, hoping this might buy them a few spare inches, but even when the portly body was stripped and covered with a white sheet, it was plain that it would not fit the dimensions of the wooden casket.

"It has to be done," the head porter said to the carpenter, and the woodworker nodded his agreement.

So there in the candleless room, without a choir or incense, the corpulent carcass of Rodrigo Borgia, Pope Alexander VI, Bishop of Rome, Vicar of Christ, Supreme Pontiff of the Universal Church, Grand Patriarch and Primate of Italy—fleshly lips, bald crown, hook nose, and all—was dumped into the wooden frame and pummeled and pushed and beaten until, like soft dough, it filled the wooden frame, and the lid was nailed down.

*A*s IF to grace the production, the sun broke through the heavy rain clouds the following afternoon just as Harlequin entered to sing his prologue. But the change in the climate did not seem to have an effect on the audience, who watched with blank eyes, not smiling or giving any indication of pleasure or pain. They simply watched—and listened.

The reaction on the company was evident. Ruffiana began a *lazzo* based on eating grapes in which she would pop one into her mouth, throw another up and snatch at it with her teeth, peel still another, and then insert a stalk of a dozen or more grapes in her mouth and pull out an absolutely empty stalk.

Normally the sequence provoked laughter, but now there was such a stillness that Ruffiana momentarily lost her composure. One of the grapes went into her eye. Another flew with such force into the back of her mouth that she choked on it. When the *lazzo* was complete and she left the stage, she was nearly in tears.

Pantalone had some little success. He created a small catalog of pains and aches and disturbances that he audibly inventoried in loving detail, and by the end of the sequence, most of the audience was chortling or, at very least, smiling.

But it wasn't until Dottore entered, administered a sleeping potion to Pantalone that instantly rendered him unconscious, and Scapino began to try to get his master from a chair, right, to a small cot, left, that the laughter really blossomed throughout the audience.

It was a physical-comedy sequence. Scapino would labor to bring Pantalone to his feet, but it seemed as though the old man's body had completely turned to gelatin. His legs would not support his torso, and his neck refused to uphold his head. His legs were flung about like thick pieces of spaghetti. There was not one single bone in his entire body.

Scapino propped the old man against his chair and quickly ran across the stage to bring the bed to him. But when he was only halfway across, Pantalone's body began to sag and dissolve, and Scapino had to dash back and try to prop him up again. Once or twice he reached the bed and managed to move it an inch or two in the general direction of the old man. Finally Scapino got Pantalone on the cot, but when he turned his back, Pantalone, with incredible physical skill, slipped completely under the cot, where he instantly coiled into a peaceful fetal position, thumb in mouth.

Scapino, of course, could not find his master.

And so began a search that became more and more frantic, compounded by entrances of Colombina, Dottore, Capitano, Isabella, and Tristano—all demanding to see Pantalone or they would beat the servant in retribution. To save himself, Scapino sent the searchers off in different directions while he resumed his desperate search for Pantalone's body.

Harlequin, watching from the front of the wagon, noticed Fra Lorenzo. The little monk was looking intently at the stage, almost studying it, and then he would look at the laughing audience, but not once did the monk laugh. Finally Harlequin worked his way closer to him and whispered, "Don't you think it's funny, brother?"

The little monk wheeled as though he had been caught in the act of doing something forbidden. Then his eyes softened and he whispered, "Incredible. This is an incredible power you have here." Harlequin watched him as his eyes devoured every moment, every pose. Then the cleric continued, "Imagine. To make them laugh like this. When they have so little to laugh about. So much hurt. So much unhappiness. Yet you make them laugh." He turned then and looked straight at Harlequin. "This," he said softly but intently, "is a sacramental art."

Harlequin wanted to laugh at the monk's intensity, but something kept him from it, and he remained silent.

"It is," insisted the man with great solemnity and awe. "Your little art leaves a mark on us—an indelible mark that we can never completely erase or forget; and, like a sacrament, it marks us all as one common humanity." He led Harlequin to one side as the audience exploded over a new *lazzo* Colombina had just created involving a reckless method of plucking a chicken.

"Listen," Fra Lorenzo explained. "This is quite remarkable. We are accustomed to plays where the heroes are angels or saints or knights. Here you show us servants as heroes. They are the cunning and the intelligent ones, and then we realize that this is truth we are watching, isn't it? I mean, without his servants, the noble master of the house couldn't find his own clothes or prepare a meal for himself. This—this is truth."

He paused for breath. "And we see ourselves up there. Each of us. We all know in our hearts that we all cheat. We all lie—at least sometimes. We get caught, too. We feel guilty then—like Scapino when he realizes what a bad trick he is pulling on poor Pantalone. But we laugh at Pantalone, too, because we see in him what we are as well. We hoard material things and justify our greed. We eat too much. We think too much. We do not think at all. We belch. We stammer. We break wind." Suddenly his eyes brightened, and he tapped Harlequin hard against his chest. "Yes! That's it! We do! We *all* break wind!"

His voice dropped again. "There are some who actually deny that they break wind. You can see them in the frescoes upstairs. King. Cardinals. Popes. Men and women of power and wealth. Fine ladies. These are above breaking wind. It is as though they merely hire servants to break wind for them." He grinned. "But then you show them to us, and we have to laugh because we realize the truth. We all break wind! The cardinal, the count, and the cook are one!"

He began to laugh, his eyes creased at the corners, and his pudgy face screwed into such an expression that Harlequin wondered if he was really laughing or about to cry.

"What did you call it?" whispered Harlequin. "A sacramental art?"

The cleric nodded and continued to laugh so hard that tears did well within his eyes. "Yes, yes."

"But," Harlequin pointed out, "only a priest can administer a sacrament."

The little monk gasped for breath and then, wiping his eyes, he responded, "But that's the point. When you recognize Pantalone's foolishness in yourself, and forgive it, are you not absolving both yourself and him of the sin? If the cardinal and the cripple are one, are we not all priests?"

*D*ESPITE THE SLOW START and Ruffiana's discontent with herself, the performance was highly successful. The audience whistled. They beat on the ground with their sticks or canes or crutches. They clapped their hands or—those who had only one hand—slapped their thighs. There were even a few *scudi* thrown to show their appreciation.

The Wayward Saints performed again the following day, and the next, and at the end of the week a courier appeared at the basilica with a message for Harlequin.

It was short and to the point.

Come to the henhouse, it read. *The fox is dead.*

DESPITE THE URGENCY IMPLIED in the message, they left Assisi sometime later in the bright light of the warming sun. There was the bittersweet scent of autumn in the air, and a few of the myrtles and oaks were beginning to adorn themselves in pale yellow and scarlet.

Fra Lorenzo saw them to the wagon and the cart and apologized for the lack of monks and nuns for this farewell. "You understand why our young seminarians cannot be dismissed now. There are many things to be done. Harvest. Preparations for All Saints and the Nativity. So much to be done."

"I understand." Harlequin nodded.

"It was very kind of you to come to us at this time and bring such a wonderful gift to these poor unfortunates who have so little."

Harlequin regarded the good, holy little man before him and smiled. "It was nothing," he whispered, "compared with the gift you have given us."

Then he turned and mounted the wagon, motioning Death and Destruction to follow the tracks of Capitano and Zephyr. The wagon lurched once and slowly creaked forward on the gutted and descending road into the valley and the path to Rome.

IN HIS APARTMENTS, Cesare paced the floor and coldly conducted the inquisition of the assembled condottieri and cardinals.

"What of the Romagna?"

Michelotto, still in his dusty and damaged armor, sat sprawled over a chaise, quaffing wine from a silver chalice. "The vultures are gathering. In Perugio and Urbino the people are circulating pamphlets against you and your father. The treacherous Venetians have supplied Guidobaldo with troops, and their damned condottiere, Alviano, has replaced Malatesta on the throne of Rimini. The Florentines and Giampaolo Baglioni have driven our forces out of

Magione and Camerino. They say that Alviano and Baglioni have sworn a blood oath to find and kill you. The Orsini are behind that, of course, and the cowardly bastards are rushing to reclaim their estates. I set fire to Monte Giordano to remind them we still exist, but Savelli is back in his palazzo and opened the prisons. The Orsini control the Porta San Pancrazio and Prospero Colonna is just outside the city." The dark mercenary smiled at Jofre. "With your wife."

Cesare wheeled. "What?"

Jofre shrugged. "Prospero freed Sancia from the Castel Sant'Angelo. He has promised her safe passage to Naples."

Cesare bit his lip and said nothing for a moment. Then he turned to another in the assembly. "And what do the College of Cardinals want of me?"

"They want you out of Rome," Casanova said boldly, "at least until after the election of the new pope."

"Did you tell them I am still too ill to travel?"

"They were unimpressed. They give you until the second of September. The Sacred College will meet in enclave to elect the new pope, and they want no interference from the nobility."

Cesare crossed to his desk and sat in the ornate chair behind it. "What are my chances of retaining the title of gonfalonier?"

"It's done," assured Casanova. "The cardinals met and confirmed you in your office. You are responsible for public security."

Cesare toyed with a dagger. "That's good," he said thoughtfully. "That gives me some power. My men can control Rome under the pretext of maintaining order."

"You will have to tread softly," said Jofre. "Cardinal Sforza has returned and—Giuliano della Rovere."

Cesare slammed the dagger down on the desk. "Della Rovere? So the treacherous dog has surfaced after all this time, has he?" He stood behind the desk. "Where the hell has he been hiding?"

Casanova remained unruffled. "He says he was not hiding at all. He spent some time in France and Spain, was the guest of the Gonzaga in Mantua for a while and the Pitti in Florence. He said he was just conducting a survey of the population to determine

how the Church could best serve them, and now he has returned for the good of Italy."

Michelotto finished his wine and toyed with his chalice. "Why don't you let me handle della Rovere?"

Cesare crossed quickly to the giant. "No!" he snapped. "That is exactly what you must *not* do! Another assassination and the entire College of Cardinals would turn against me! We have power over the eleven Spanish cardinals, and Louis has assured me of the support of the Cardinals d'Amboise and Sforza. If we can maintain our control of, say, just nine or ten of the Italians, we could see to it that the new pope is someone amiable to our family."

"Giuliano della Rovere is campaigning for the throne of Peter," Casanova pointed out.

"Let him! D'Amboise carries as much weight." The duke resumed his place behind the desk.

"If della Rovere wants a confrontation with me," he said softly. "Let it begin now."

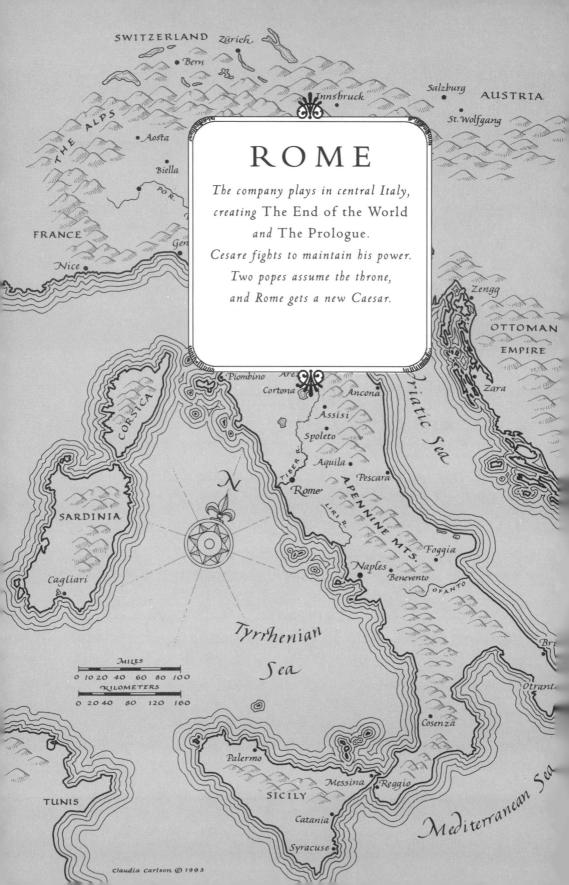

ROME

The company plays in central Italy,
creating The End of the World
and The Prologue.
Cesare fights to maintain his power.
Two popes assume the throne,
and Rome gets a new Caesar.

SWITZERLAND *Zürich*

Bern

AUSTRIA

Salzburg

St. Wolfgang

Innsbruck

THE ALPS

Aosta

Biella

POR.

FRANCE

Gen.

Nice

Zengg

OTTOMAN

EMPIRE

Zara

CORSICA

Piombino

Arez.

Cortona

Ancona

Assisi

Spoleto

Aquila

TIBER R.

Rome

Pescara

Adriatic Sea

N

SARDINIA

APENNINE MTS.

LIRI R.

Foggia

Cagliari

Naples

Benevento

OFANTO

Bri

MILES

0 10 20 40 60 80 100

KILOMETERS

0 20 40 80 120 160

Tyrrhenian

Sea

Otrant.

Cosenza

TUNIS

Palermo

Messina

Reggio

SICILY

Catania

Mediterranean Sea

Syracuse

Claudia Carlson © 1993

Despite the advice from della Rovere to "come to the henhouse," Harlequin and the troupe agreed to take time to work and refine, to embellish and experiment with improvisational farce—wedded to a soft satire—until they could unanimously decide that they could live up to Fra Lorenzo's vision as a "sacramental art."

After leaving Assisi, they played *The Dying Pantalone* for the villagers of Eremo near the Porta dei Cappuccini in a wooded area where, legends say, St. Francis used to meditate. In the Piazza Maggiore in Spello they offered *The Clever Wife* and were invited to reprise the production two days later in Sassovivo.

Descending into the broad, flat plain approaching Foligno, they were intercepted by a courier of the Trinci family who issued an invitation for the company to play *The Clever Wife* in their palazzo during the Giostra della Quintana, an equestrian festival performed on the second Sunday in September. The company agreed to come only if they could put the wagon stage in the Piazza Comunale and play for the common people as well. The Trinci agreed, and the troupe stayed a week as guests in the palazzo and performed in the afternoons to wide approval and reward.

In Trevi, they performed in the piazza outside the new town hall and had to compete with the masons and carpenters still erecting the duomo that had broken ground more than a century earlier.

They took a brief rest at Castel Ritaldi, played nearby La Pieve, and then moved south to Spoleto, where they performed twice: once in the Piazza del Duomo for the workers and townspeople and once in the courtyard of the grim fortress with its six towers perched above the oak trees on Montelucco Hill. Here they played *Abraham and Isaac* for the Orsini mercenaries who had reclaimed the beautiful town once governed by Lucrezia Borgia.

It was an Orsini condottiere that brought them the news that the College of Cardinals had elected Francesco Piccolomini pope.

The fox still prowled the farmyard.

"WHO?" asked Cesare of the papal courier.

The young man kneeling before the duke raised his head to answer. "Francesco Cardinal Piccolomini. He has chosen the title Pius the Third."

Cesare glowed with the news and turned to Michelotto. "Piccolomini! Imagine! While della Rovere and D'Amboise fought for the throne of Peter, this aged gentleman sneaked by and grabbed the miter! Wonderful!" He turned to face the papal courier. "What other news?"

"His Holiness wishes me to convey to you his gratitude for the support of the Spanish cardinals."

"As he damned well should!"

"And he wishes to inform you that you are free to return to Rome and once again assume the duties of gonfalonier to the Church."

Cesare wheeled and clapped a hand on Michelotto's shoulder. "Ha! I'm not finished after all! Della Rovere must be having cramps in his agony of frustration!" He crossed quickly to his desk and gestured to Michelotto. "Give him something! A gold florin! No! Two florins!"

The giant condottiere pressed the coins into the young man's hand, and the courier thanked him and bowed from the room.

"Now can I handle the matter of della Rovere?" Michelotto inquired.

"Not yet," said the duke as he continued scratching the quill against the parchment at his desk. "We still hold Cesena, but Giovanni Sforza is in Pesaro and Malatesta in Rimini. We can count on the five hundred foot soldiers and the one hundred and fifty horsemen still with me, but I desperately need more men and money if I am to pull out of this alive and in command of the Romagna."

"Where will we find the men?" demanded the mercenary. "The French and the Florentines are cold toward you, and our allies are deserting everywhere."

"That's why I think it may be time to change the color of my coat." Cesare laughed as he finished the epistle, sprinkled drying powder on it, and then sealed it with wax and his signet ring. "I am writing to Gonsalvo de Cordoba, offering my allegiance to the Spanish cause against the French. There is a large Spanish army in Rome, and I have another twelve thousand men I can command in the Borgo. If Spain will assist me, the French may have to come to terms with me."

"What about the pope? How will he react to his gonfalonier switching loyalties to the Spanish?"

"The French are being beaten in Naples. The Spanish king and queen are as Catholic as Louis. The old man will go where I lead, and then . . ."

Michelotto took the parchment. "Then?"

The duke came and whispered in the ear of the condottiere.

"Della Rovere is yours."

*T*HE COMPANY DECIDED to take their time, await further word from della Rovere, and perform in the cities controlled by the Orsini and the Colonnas. Nevertheless they avoided major towns like Cascia to play the more remote hill towns such as Roccaporena, Monteleone, and Ferentillo. In Arrone they performed *The Clever Wife* in an old fortress in the Terra quarter.

On approaching Terni from the east, they saw the crest of the town depicted in stone on a road marker and noted that it was a depiction of St. George slaying the dragon, so they decided to perform their version of that legend. Then word reached them that the town was besieged by malaria. Later they came to learn that this disease, common to the area, was known as "the dragon's breath."

For reasons beyond fear of quarantine, they now felt the need to perform before a more urban, hopefully cosmopolitan audience. Rural audiences responded more to the physical and regional humor than to the satirical elements that they considered their forte. The pratfalls and acrobatics of *Dying Pantalone* brought gales of laughter, but the mistaken identity base for *The Twins* often confused their peasant attendees.

So they reversed their route and turned north to the major city of Orvieto, despite the fact that this city was under the direct protection of the pope and had been the refuge of pontiffs since Pope Urban IV. Because of a rivalry between the Monaldeschi, Filippeschi, and Alberici families, the Saints remained in Orvieto for more than two weeks, performing in the palazzo of one family and then in the palazzo of another. The rest of the time they performed in the afternoons in the Piazza del Duomo.

They took time to visit the Cappella dei Corporale, where Fra Lorenzo had told them that the bloodstained cloth of the "miracle of Bolsena" was enshrined. During the visit, they stood stunned before the newly painted fresco of Luca Signorelli depicting the end of the world.

Most of the actors were stunned by the painting. Pantalone, however, was inspired for a new farce in which the old miser is convinced by a monk that the end of the world is at hand and that he can buy his way into heaven if he leaves everything to the Church. Dottore, knowing Pantalone is in no danger of dying, conveys the news to Pantalone's wife, Colombina, and the two devise a trick to teach the old man a lesson.

Soon the house is besieged by Dottore, disguised as a cardinal, and Tristano, Capitano, Scapino, and Harlequin disguised as monks. They have come to take possession of the promised items, because they don't want "to wait until the last minute." Scapino, Harlequin, and Dottore take the furniture, the paintings, the hoarded coins, and the jewels, but Tristano walks away with Pantalone's mistress, who, they argue, has "always been treated like a possession," while Capitano carries off Colombina.

The farce ends with Pantalone, destitute and alone, wailing and waiting for the promised end of the world, not realizing that his world—which consisted of possessions and wealth—has already ended.

They turned south to Viterbo and Ronciglione and played *The End of the World* to enthusiastic applause and a shower of coins.

They played Narni and Rieti and L'Aquila, Avezzano, and Sulmona; and then, to see if there would be a difference in response, they backtracked to L'Aquila a second time to find that they were eagerly greeted, audiences pouring from the surrounding countryside on hearing, "I Santi Ostinati are returning."

The troupe began to amass, along with their skill and experience, some little fame throughout central Italy. They had created and developed a repertory of short and long sequences including *The Prologue*, *The Liar*, and *The Woman Who Cooked Her Dog*. Each had created and refined personal *lazzi* that included catching a fly and eating it as if it were a roast pig and walking in tandem when Scapino's blouse gets caught in Pantalone's waistband. The most popular *lazzo* for Capitano was the one in which he cannot get his sword back into his scabbard and demolishes half the furniture and half the cast, ending with the fat officer dancing blithely off with the sword clutched to his bosom as if it were a much-loved beautiful damsel.

They also had a repertory of biblical sketches that were always popular on the eves of the great feasts. Knowing that the following day the guilds would be offering a much more dignified and ritualistic version, the Saints delighted in performing a satiric version that would make it difficult to watch the real thing with a straight face.

Fearful at first that they might bring the power of the local church authorities down on them, they attempted *Abraham and Isaac* under very particular conditions. But when they found, upon reaching a town or village, that the local parish priest often requested just such a work, they began to play the biblical stories with more self-assurance.

St. George and the Dragon was a favorite of everyone, especially since it now featured Capitano as St. George and Harlequin and Scapino together as the dragon, and Isabella, of course, as the fair maiden.

The Saints' version ended with the dragon devouring St. George after deceiving him into thinking he wasn't a dragon at all, but a malformed and cursed St. Bernard dog.

They marveled at the fact that many of the stories and sketches simply did not make sense. Absurdity seemed to be the keynote for their material, embellished with sharp and incisive character satire. They also learned that there was a precise, effective pace at which the material must be played, and that if they allowed themselves to lag, the audience had time to recognize the ridiculous nature of the plot and was less attentive.

Conversely, if the pace was too fast, or if the troupe became too involved with each other or with technical devices, the audience was left confused and unhappy.

The secret, of course, was to start at a moderate tempo with some degree of sanity and reality to the sequence, and then to move faster and faster, playing the sequences without having to think about them. This left the performer free to grasp quickly a change of mood in the audience or to capitalize on a comment hurled at the stage or to abandon his or her lines entirely and break into a song.

The sequences were never the same. Never. And some guildsmen who saw the Saints perform in Orvieto were surprised to see the same sequence in Narni later and find it totally different, although it retained the same basic plot line.

They resumed a route toward the Holy City, playing Stroncone, and then entering the area of the Sabine Hills to play Rieti. It took a better part of a day to reach and play Parfa Sabina and Palombara Sabina, then Vicovaro and Tivoli.

Finally, they felt they were ready. Although they heard nothing more from della Rovere, they voted to enter Rome.

*C*ESARE BORGIA PACED the floor of the narrow ante-chamber in the Castel Sant'Angelo and, in a sudden eruption of rage, swept the quill and inkstand from the small corner table. "The bastard!" he roared. "The ungrateful, arrogant Spanish bastard!" He wheeled to face Michelotto, dirty and worn and panting like a horse that had just been raced to near death. "Where did he go?"

The mercenary tried to catch his breath. "I can't be sure. Probably to join the other Spanish fighting the French near Naples." The condottiere crossed to the sideboard and poured himself some wine. "It's all part of the conspiracy between the Orsini and that damned Gonsalvo de Cordoba! When he forbade the Spanish to serve under our banner, we lost half of our fighting force. It was only a matter of time before de Moncada deserted us."

"I gave that bastard honors and wealth! I let him and his men pillage towns throughout the Romagna! When my father screamed for his head after the massacre at Pergola, who saved him? When the damned Orsini took him prisoner at Calmazzo, I rescued him!"

"If we meet again, I'll strangle him on the spot," promised the dark giant.

Cesare strode to the window and looked into the piazza. "How bad is it? Are we in danger here? Should I send the children away? Rodrigo, Giovanni, Girolamo, and Camilla are with me." He turned to face the condottiere. "I have two hundred thousand ducats in reserve in Genoa. Should I send them there?"

Michelotti considered the situation. "You are still gonfalonier of the Church, and that makes you responsible for the security of Rome. The Orsini know that, and I think I can push them back across the Sant'Angelo bridge. As long as you carry the authorization of the pope, any resistance is criminal. We are in the right."

"Jesu Christi!" Cesare bellowed. "The right? Guidobaldo was in the right in Urbino! And Sforza in Milan and Pesaro! That didn't stop me! The Orsini will pay no more attention to the 'right' than I did!"

"There is no real danger to us—yet. I'll secure the bridge, and then, perhaps, we should ask the Piccolomini pope for more power. A papal bull demanding the Orsini back out of the city perhaps."

"Yes. Yes. I'll try that." Cesare paced again. "Where is della Rovere?"

"No one knows. He's like smoke. Just when you think you have him, he dissolves in the evening breeze. Some say he is a constant companion to the pope."

The duke grew calm and handed his exhausted condottiere a

goblet of wine. "You've been loyal to me through all of this, Michelotto. I could always rely on you. I will never forget that."

The giant raised the chalice to his lips and smiled. "Unfortunately," he said, "neither will the Orsini."

*T*HEY CHOSE TO APPROACH the Holy City from the northeast, through Sette Bagni and Prima Porta, using a route recommended in the *Descriptio Urbis Romae*, written by Harlequin's father.

Word of their presence in the area reached Cesare even as the company paraded toward the Tiber, and he wrote an order for Michelotto to take the troupe captive.

"I have one more hope," he said. "The Venetians want the girl. If I can form an alliance by giving her to them, the Florentines and Urbino might negotiate."

As usual, Capitano, in full costume with false red nose and enormous belly, rode Zephyr. He was followed by Scapino and Pantalone, in tights and jackets, wearing the half masks of their characters, performing acrobatic tricks or juggling or doing handstands and cartwheels. Harlequin was usually included in their small band, playing a reed pipe or a lute, with Colombina not far behind, dancing and twirling and pounding her tambourine. Dottore drove the wagon, with Isabella perched prettily upon it and waving to her admirers. Ruffiana and Tristano brought up the end of the procession with Tristano playing an instrument and singing and Ruffiana dancing.

The city had obviously heard of the Saints and were ready for them. Cheering groups of people laughed and waved to the players as they wound their way through the streets and piazzas. Even the normally quiet clerics, monks, and nuns waved and shouted an occasional "bravo!"

Small children, naturally, dogged the trail of the company and imitated the *zanni*, and virile young men, gathered together in small groups, summoned enough collective courage to whistle at Isabella and Ruffiana and to make obscene gestures that the latter sometimes returned.

As they approached the river the company heard the rumble and thunder of hooves. Two columns of mounted mercenaries bearing the papal insignia entered the piazza and surrounded them. Capitano pulled Zephyr back to the side of the wagon, and Harlequin stepped forward to address the leader of the mounted troop.

Michelotto smiled down at the masked, bizarre man in the absurd hat and whispered. "I thought you'd never get here, Bracciolini." Then, much louder, in a voice that echoed from the houses surrounding the piazza, he intoned, "By order of Cesare Borgia, Duke of Valentinois and Gonfalonier of the Holy Roman Catholic Church . . ."

Harlequin then heard another flurry of hooves and was aware that something was happening beyond the ring of the red-and-yellow-uniformed horsemen, but not being mounted, he could not see over or around them. There was a muffled argument to his left, and a clatter and clang of armor and sword behind him; then, after a moment in which Michelotto himself wheeled his mount around to see the cause of the clamor, the circle opened, and four mounted knights forced the Borgia horsemen back. Through this widening gap Harlequin could see a splendid coach pull up just beyond the surrounding horsemen, and from it stepped Cardinal della Rovere.

He strode vigorously toward Harlequin, his arms extended in an embrace. Harlequin accepted the embrace and dropped to one knee to kiss the cardinal's ring.

Michelotto moved his horse closer to the cardinal. "You are preventing us from obeying the orders of the gonfalonier," he snapped.

"Indeed I am." The cardinal smiled. "Because, at the moment, the Church has no gonfalonier."

He gestured to Angelo, now in full raiment and bearing the tree *impresa* of the della Rovere, and the condottiere nudged his gelding forward and handed Michelotto a sealed scroll.

The dark giant took the scroll, examined its seal, broke it open, and read the contents. Harlequin saw his gloved hand tremble and nearly crumble the parchment, and a slow exhalation of air escaped through his clenched teeth. "How is it possible?"

The cardinal gestured to the scroll. "He was a very old man, you know." He held out his hand for the return of the parchment, and Michelotto slapped it into his glove. "He contracted a fever and was bled. Unhappily his health continued to decline, and two hours ago His Holiness Pius the Third died. The power of the Church now resides with the Sacred College of Cardinals, and that august body has granted this troupe of mummers permission to perform in Rome."

Michelotto's mount neighed and nervously darted to the left. The mercenary swung him around and said irritably, "The pope reigned only twenty-seven days!"

"Yes," said della Rovere softly. "But he died naturally—unlike others."

Michelotto seemed about to trample the cardinal when Angelo maneuvered his own gelding between them and forced the Borgia captain back. The mercenary glared, wheeled, and galloped his horse through an opening in the encircling cavalry. Without a command, the remainder of the mounted Borgian supporters turned and followed their leader out of the piazza.

Harlequin saw, then, that the cardinal had brought his own mounted knights, who had, in turn, encircled the Borgia forces. "I had to be certain the hot-blooded assassin didn't forget himself and act on his own," explained della Rovere. He handed the scroll to Harlequin, who opened it and read: *The Sacred College of Cardinals of the Holy Roman Catholic Church do, by this proclamation, declare that the bearer is authorized to present comedies within the boundaries of the city of Rome for the Feast of All Saints' Day and should not be subject to any interference or hazard that would prevent the prompt dispatch of this authorization under pain of mortal sin or possible excommunication from the body of the faithful.*

Harlequin looked at the tall, thin prelate, who continued to smile. "The tides have shifted dramatically. An enclave will be held immediately to select a new pontiff, and I have enough cardinals in my pocket to assure election." He led Harlequin back toward the coach. "I have even notified the goldsmith to have the Ring of the Fisherman engraved with my name, and an army of my friends are prepared to post my arms on every corner in Rome." He stopped at the foot of the small steps leading to the coach. "The point is: Cesare's days are numbered, and he knows it. You are safe."

Harlequin grinned and passed the parchment to the capitano, who handed it to the other members of the troupe. At that moment Isabella broke through the group of performers, genuflected, and kissed the cardinal's ring. The prelate leaned and gently lifted her to her feet. Then he produced a small scroll from the voluminous sleeves of his robes.

"My dear," he whispered. "On this parchment is inscribed the name of your mother. If you take it, you will be free to go to her and take possession of your heritage. Her husband, knowing my power, will acknowledge you as legitimate." He leaned closer to her. "What shall I do with it?" he asked.

Isabella looked at the sealed document and then at Scapino. "Your Eminence," she said softly. "Bastards are more comfortable among their own." She returned the scroll. "Burn it."

"So like your mother," said della Rovere admiringly. He turned then to Harlequin. "You may rely on a more formal dispensation from your vows, Vittorio. I have heard of your success, and I think you may have found your vocation after all. Your performance, by the way, is in the Piazza Adriana outside the Castel Sant'Angelo. I wanted it to be convenient to—the new pontiff—if he should choose to come and watch you, as I am certain he will." He lowered his voice. "Of course this is dependent upon an enclave that moves swiftly to elect the new Vicar of Christ."

Harlequin, speechless, simply nodded.

"I have made all the necessary arrangements for two performances," the cardinal continued, "and if you should choose to stay in Rome longer and perform, simply go to the authorities and say I am your sponsor, and no one will interfere with you."

He turned then and climbed back into his carriage. When he was settled inside, he leaned from the window and blessed the genuflecting troupe. "Is there anything else I can do for you, Vittorio?" he asked.

"I think you have done quite enough, Your Eminence," replied Harlequin with a laugh. He glanced around at his performers. "Unless you have some way of preventing nobility from sitting on our stage and making comments while we work. They've done that in three or four cities we've played."

"Or if you can stop them from throwing nuts or fruits at us when we're bad," added Scapino. "That has happened, too."

The cardinal suddenly remembered something. "Oh! I think, if you have the time and opportunity, that you might wander to the east, near the Church of Santa Maria Maggiore. There's a small piazza there, called the Four Fountains. I think you'll be interested in what is there."

He leaned back into the shadows of the coach and the driver whipped the horses forward. Eight of his mercenaries moved in front of the coach as it turned to leave the piazza, and the remainder took up positions behind it. Within minutes, the troupe was surrounded by hordes of the curious Romans, who pressed toward them to find out what had happened. Harlequin took the reed pipe from Colombina and played a bright little *saltarello*.

"Come!" cried Scapino. "To the Piazza Adriana! The famed comedians, Santi Ostinati, will play on the eve of All Saints!"

C ESARE BORGIA SAT MOTIONLESS behind the small desk in the Castel Sant'Angelo and listened to the report of his condottiere. Finally he said quietly, "So. The arrogant bastard has finally made it."

Michelotto nodded. "He thinks he has. He has made separate arrangements with some of the Spanish cardinals, but D'Amboise still controls seven or eight."

There was a moment before Cesare began to smile, and then he laughed. "Incredible," he roared, and gasped for air. "Damme! This della Rovere is incredible! What would I have to give, do you think, to win him to my side?"

"He is getting it for himself," Michelotto murmured. "The Throne of Peter."

The dark duke paused in his laughing. "Yes, yes. And the amusing fact is that this one may well prove worse than my own father. He is a lecher and blood hungry. His whores inflicted him with the French disease, and his reign will be one of revenge and warfare. I wanted to be Duke of the Romagna. Della Rovere wants to be Emperor of Italy. Well"—he smiled—"this is a lesson to me in not permitting my enemies to live. Still, we can't kill everyone, can we?"

He rose and came around the desk. "I have heard a great deal about these comedians, and you say their version of *Abraham and Isaac* was amusing. Let's have a look at them." He crossed to the windows. "Tell Machiavelli he will have to put aside his intrigues for a hour or so and accompany us. I've never seen him laugh, and it might prove a remarkable experience."

Michelotto nodded and walked to the great doors of the office. "I suppose Cardinal della Rovere will be enclosed with the Sacred College and far too busy to see the performance. A pity. I understand these mountebacks are irreverent and shocking. Should his trained monkeys decide to take a few swipes at him, it might be interesting to see how their sponsor might respond."

O N T H E E V E of All Saints, the new pope had not been elected, and the company decided to play *The Prologue*—a sequence they created at Avezanno ridiculing the sponsor who had invited the troupe to perform. Now they decided that they would pretend that they were in Rome at the invitation of the gonfalonier, Cesare Borgia himself, directing their satire at him.

The capitano was the only dissenter. "It is one thing to enter the bull's arena with courage and faith. But it is another to pull his tail."

As the masses of humanity poured into the Piazza Adriana, Scapino was already amusing the crowd with his juggling, and Pantalone, without his mask and robes of the old miser, was telling outrageous lies to a small knot of young women on the edge of the audience. Children, as usual, sat close down front or perched on the edges of fountains and walls, and some tall fathers carried their smallest offspring on their shoulders.

Harlequin did not see the duke and his entourage, but the square was filled with local priests, monks, and nuns, young seminarians with the "shaving bowl" hat common to the Spanish, and flocks of Roman working men and washerwomen. The cardinals were locked in enclave, so there was a notable lack of purple or scarlet among the viewers.

Then he noticed the three hooded clerics in black who were standing on a raised area to his right. What separated them from the others in similar robes was the fact that they were surrounded by a small circle of armed men in red and yellow who discreetly formed a barrier between the trio and the rest of the crowd. The other thing that caught his eye was the flash of gold on the breast of one of the monks.

Finally it was time to begin. Harlequin stepped forward, strummed his lute, and started to sing. He sang of the glories of Rome and the power of the Church, and then Scapino entered and pushed him aside and began a series of absurd comments about Romans and their habits that soon had the audience laughing.

Suddenly Scapino broke off his narrative to set the sequence known as *The Prologue*. "Listen," he told the crowd. "We are going to do a play for you today, and the other actors are preparing it now. Me, I can't read, so I will not appear. The play will feature Dottore, that enormous windbag from Bologna." The audience roared and applauded. "And that pompous ass, Tristano, from Venice, of course." Again the audience responded to the insults of the enemy cities. "And here comes Dottore now," he whispered. "I'll hide up here inside the basket and let the old idiot make a fool of himself."

With that, he dashed upstage and leaped gracefully into a huge hamper. As he did so Dottore entered down left holding a scroll from which he was memorizing his lines.

"I have but an hour to live," Dottore intoned pompously.

Scapino stuck his head out of the hamper. "Which is unfortunate for him but fortunate for you, since he dies in the middle of the first act." And he ducked his head again.

Dottore pretended to look around for the speaker, but seeing no one, he shrugged and continued reading. "I have here a list of the many, many things wrong with me. My heart carries the final rhythms of my life."

"Diddle-li-dee, diddle-li-doo, diddle-li-dildo," sang Scapino from inside the hamper.

Again Dottore glanced around. Again he shrugged and read his scroll. "Something is very wrong inside me. . . ."

Scapino's head popped up again. "His umbilical cord became entangled with his small intestine, so throughout his life, his waste has been recycled. Consequently now, in age, he is full of—"

He was stopped by Dottore suddenly wheeling around, but Scapino was too quick and disappeared inside the hamper.

Tristano now entered from down right with a similar scroll. He, too, was memorizing his lines. He paid no attention to Dottore. "Ah, my beloved," he began, "my heart is . . ."

". . . rapidly deteriorating," read Dottore, "and my lungs are filled with . . ."

". . . the scent of your incomparable . . ."

". . . gases," finished Dottore.

Tristano, annoyed, bellowed even louder, "I die . . ."

". . . within the hour," continued Dottore. "Look how my warts resemble . . ."

". . . the breasts of Venus," extolled Tristano. "Your eyes are like . . ."

". . . twin bedpans," groaned Dottore.

Suddenly Scapino popped up behind the two actors and pulled a resined chord through one of Dottore's bull-roarers, but the sound emitted this time was closer to a flatulent discharge. He instantly disappeared again as Dottore glanced at Tristano, sniffed the air, and then moved a few steps farther away from him.

"Your gentle mouth," Tristano recited, "is like . . ."

". . . a sinkhole of corruption!" snapped Dottore.

Scapino reappeared with a small tube through which he blew a pea at the back of Tristano's neck. He disappeared again as the young lover slapped at his neck and then glared at Dottore. "Don't do that!" he commanded.

"Do what?" asked Dottore.

"Just don't do it!" Tristano repeated, and he resumed his reciting. "Flower of my soul, I shall water you with . . ."

". . . my poor urine," said Dottore.

Again Scapino popped up with his peashooter and fired a missile against the back of Dottore's neck. As he bobbed back into the hamper Dottore glared at Tristano. "You're not amusing."

"I'm not supposed to be," said Tristano, puzzled. "I'm the lover."

Dottore swept across the stage at Tristano. "Don't pretend innocence!" he roared.

"I *must!*" cried Tristano. "I'm the *lover!*"

At that, Harlequin entered quickly and yelled, "Ruffiana! Pantalone! Capitano!"

And Scapino leaped from the hamper yelling, "Cheese! Melon! Two eggs!" And as Dottore approached him he added, "Ham!"

Harlequin waved a scroll in the air as the company gathered around him. "His Grace, the gonfalonier of Rome, has just given me something!"

"The French disease!" Scapino announced.

Some of the audience gasped. Some laughed.

"If you will keep your mouth closed . . ." said Colombina to the juggler.

"You'll have fewer holes in your teeth," observed Ruffiana.

Harlequin continued. "His Grace has given us an invitation to perform in Rome for all the good people!"

"But I don't see any cardinals out here. Why aren't the cardinals watching us?" Scapino frowned.

"They are in enclave," said Harlequin. "And show a little respect for the gonfalonier. He serves the Church—"

"Not to mention Lucrezia, Juan, Jofre . . ." Scapino counted on his fingertips.

This time the laughter swelled.

"He was once a father of the Church!" declared Harlequin.

"And of Rodrigo and Giovanni and Girolamo and Camilla—and possibly Isabella, Francesca, Roberto, Angelo—" Scapino continued enumerating the children.

"That will be enough!" interrupted Harlequin.

"Precisely what their mothers said," Colombina sagely murmured.

The laughter was now unanimous.

Capitano, who was on the fringe of the company, had an opportunity at this point to glance over at the three monks that Harlequin had singled out earlier. The monk with the gold medallion, Capitano reasoned, must be Cesare. He noticed that two of the other monks were arguing with one another, but the gold medallion was shaking rapidly.

"Godsblood," Capitano whispered to himself. "The bastard is laughing!"

*T*HE PERFORMANCE PROCEEDED SMOOTHLY: the audience had laughed constantly from *The Prologue* through the capitano's final dance with his naked sword. Now Harlequin appeared again, strumming his lute, and spoke the closing lines.

"Remember." He smiled. "As surely as there is a communion of saints, there is also a congress of fools—and it's the same company." They laughed. "Be warned, therefore, noble Romans," he intoned, "and especially you, signore, with your hand up the skirt of your companion." Another volley of laughter. "And you, signora, with your lips tightly pressed together in recrimination—as a barrier, I suppose, against an impudent tongue." Another eruption of laughter. "And especially you, good monks . . ."

Harlequin was pointing at the three black-robed men, and many turned to look, but the raised platform was empty and the mercenaries gone.

Harlequin shrugged and continued. "You who lack only a mirror to identify the fool you have been laughing at, all of you, be warned! You are human. You are vulnerable. And when next the Santi Ostinati come before you, the mask I wear may be *your* face."

The crowd began to hoot and whistle.

"But remember!" Harlequin raised his voice to dominate the crowd. "Remember! Life is full of deception and cruelty! The world is made of laws and rules and restrictions that apply only to the poor and the helpless! Be warned! Magistrates and nobles and clerics and knights are around every corner waiting to seize you at any moment and without provocation! If you speak the truth, no one will believe you! If you lie, everyone will be your friend! But take a lesson from Harlequin! Always run as fast as you can! Scheme and plot and seize what falls your way!"

He smiled, strummed a final chord, and almost whispered, "Every fool has to win—sometime."

He began to perform a little dance, when someone shouted from the rear of the crowd.

"They did it! We have elected a new pope! It is Cardinal della Rovere!"

*F*OLLOWING THE PERFORMANCE, when it became obvious that no one was going to come after them and haul them before an ecclesiastical court, the company celebrated and counted the wealth collected from the audience.

Among the coins was a heavy gold medallion bearing the image of a bull surrounded by tongues of fire.

"What name did he choose?" Harlequin asked.

"Julius. Pope Julius the Second."

"The Second?" said Harlequin. "I don't remember. Who was Julius the First?"

Dottore laughed lightly. "It's of no concern," he said. "He didn't choose it to honor the first Julius. He took the name of the first Roman emperor."

Harlequin smiled. "You mean, he took the name of Julius. . . ?"

Dottore nodded. "We have another Caesar."

O N THE FOLLOWING MORNING, the Feast of All Saints, they moved their wagon to the Piazza del Popolo for the second performance requested by Cardinal della Rovere.

As the remainder of the company went out into the city to announce the afternoon performance, Harlequin, as suggested by della Rovere, went alone to the Church of Santa Maria Maggiore, and as he came around the corner of the structure into the Piazza of the Four, he stopped in surprise.

There in the piazza was a small wagon, not half as high as the guild wagon, but otherwise remarkably similar. There was a pale blue curtain at the back of the stage area suspended from a rod hung between two tall, forked shafts. A small crowd of children, wives, and guildsmen had gathered in front of the wagon and were intently watching—Harlequin.

It was undeniably himself upon the stage. The armored cloak of rags and patches had been transformed into a cape of many shaped patches, and this motif was carried through the blouse and tights of the performer in the black half mask playing the lute and singing. The hat was unmistakably his own. Enormous, beaked, with an impudent peacock feather stabbed into the brim, it was instantly recognized as Harlequin's.

The song itself was unfamiliar, but the performer had no sooner ended it than a comely, somewhat plump woman entered in the earth-brown skirt and red petticoats of Colombina! A dialogue occurred about who should do the marketing, and the two characters addressed each other as "Arlecchino" and "Colombina."

There was Pantalone in the long robe and the jingling purse at his waist. And Dottore with the half mask and the black cloak. They were there! All the members of the Santi Ostinati!

Harlequin stayed well within the shadows and watched the performance. It was, he was certain, *The Clever Wife*, but with variations. Then he noticed the banner that hung above the wagon, just below the stage level. It read *I Confidenti*.

He watched only a little more, determining precisely what *lazzi* this impudent troupe of imitators had stolen from his company. He was angry. He was considering the possibility of assembling the Saints and then returning and wrecking this wagon of thieves.

Then he heard the laughter, and his anger turned to a quiet sadness. Who was he to claim the exclusive ownership of the characters and the *lazzi*? Hadn't he argued from the beginning that the troupe was only a temporary communion of Wayward Saints? And wasn't this imitation a supreme compliment? And, above all, weren't both troupes performing the same small miracle of bringing laughter to dark places?

He remembered, then, what Dottore had told him of della Francesca's cry in Arezzo: "Turn the light on them! They cannot stand the light!"

He watched a little more as the *innamorati*, called Maria and Gregorio, made a comic shambles of a love scene. *Yes,* he told himself, *it is all as much theirs as ours.*

He turned and went back into the shadows of the church to the Piazza del Popolo, where he told the others of the second *commedia* company he had seen.

"Where did they get our material?" asked Pantalone.

"They probably saw us perform somewhere—or one or more of them did," said Harlequin. "And seeing how popular we were, they decided to try it themselves."

"Why don't they make their own theatrical style?" snapped Isabella.

"It *is* their own," said Harlequin. "It is us—passed through them, through their own experience and skills."

It was time for the company's performance to begin, but as Har-

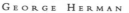
lequin started to strum his lute prior to his entrance, he stopped at the sound of a heavy staff striking the floor of the stage. He looked out and saw a courier in the livery of the della Rovere standing between two armed knights and reading from a scroll to the audience.

"By order of His Holiness, Giuliano Cardinal della Rovere, Julius the Second, Vicar of Christ, a punishment of fines, stripes, or imprisonment shall be rendered to such persons who sit upon the stage, stand in front of the actors, make unseemly noises, or throw apples, nuts, or garbage at the comedians."

The members of the company looked at one another, and two or three well-dressed members of the nobility who had seated themselves up on the stage stood and left it. There was derisive laughter from the crowd, and someone yelled, "*Commedia! Bravissimo, Commedia dell'arte!*"

Harlequin was stunned, but somehow he entered and began the introduction. Through the entire afternoon, the cry of that spectator echoed in the hearts and minds of every member of the troupe.

Dell'arte!

Professionals.

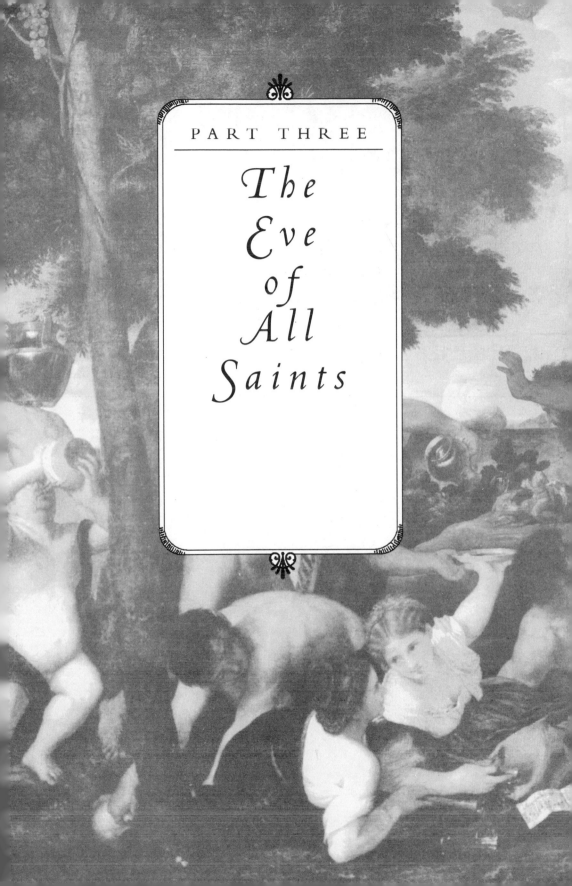

PART THREE

*The
Eve
of
All
Saints*

NAPLES

On reviewing the situation.

SWITZERLAND Zürich

Bern

Innsbruck Salzburg AUSTRIA

St.Wolfgang

THE ALPS Aosta

Biella

POR.

FRANCE Gen.

Nice

OTTOMAN

Zengg

EMPIRE

Zara

Piombino Arez.

Cortona Ancona

Assisi Adriatic Sea

CORSICA Spoleto

TIBER R. Aquila

Rome Pescara

APENNINE MTS.

LIRI R.

SARDINIA Foggia

Naples

Benevento

OFANTO

Cagliari

Tyrrhenian

Sea Brindisi

MILES Otranto

0 10 20 40 60 80 100

KILOMETERS

0 20 40 80 120 160 Cosenza

Palermo

Messina Reggio

TUNIS SICILY

Catania Mediterranean Sea

Syracuse

Claudia Carlson © 1993

On April 12, 1523, in the city of Naples, Vittorio Bracciolini, more widely known throughout Europe as *Harlequin*, died at the age of fifty-five, and the Santi Ostinati was disbanded.

Seventeen years earlier, in the Church of San Gregorio in Modena, Vittorio had been united in marriage to *Colombina Fortini*. The ceremony was performed by the bishop of the province, who had been a poor parish priest in the village of San Lucia until he became a participant in a miracle that brought him to the attention of the wagon makers' guild and ultimately to the superiors of the Church. The miracle itself was attributed by the good bishop to San Gregorio, his patron, who immediately became the patron of the wagon makers as well.

Nine years later, in 1515, the Santi Ostinati returned to play in Florence and were well received—especially by a young, handsome painter named Buonarroti who painted the troupe in action. Unfortunately the young man engaged in an artistic rivalry with Dottore's old mentor, Leonardo da Vinci, into whose hands the painting subsequently fell and by whom it was, apparently, destroyed.

Dottore (Giacomo Martinelli) did not renew his acquaintance with Leonardo at this time, but they did meet again in Milan in 1515 when the artist-inventor served the invading Francis I. Now, at fifty-four, Dottore finally discovered the "secret" that had separated him from the glories attributed to his master: he had no talent as a painter. Instead he was a gifted writer—a fact affirmed for him when Leonardo was permitted to read a history of the Santi Ostinati that Dottore had compiled. The maestro praised the manuscript highly and insisted on taking it to Rome when he entered the service of Leo X. Unfortunately Leo was a Medici, and feeling his family was not treated well in the manuscript, the holy father gave it to the Vatican library. Naturally it was never seen again, although the title once appeared, in the eighteenth century, on the Index of Forbidden Books.

When Harlequin died, his widow, Colombina, then fifty-four, saw to it that her husband had the last rites, just to be absolutely

certain of salvation, and then she gave the body over to Pico Bracciolini, Harlequin's nephew, who took it back with him to
Terranova for family interment.

Colombina then joined with *Scapino Petrucci* or Biondo or
Torrigiano, forty-eight, and *Isabella Zappachio*, forty-three, and they
all retired to Milan, where they were able to purchase a small estate
from a modest fortune given to Isabella by her family, provided that
she never acknowledge her relationship to them.

This was partly due to the fact that Isabella was now an actress,
which was a disreputable vocation, and partly because she lived
openly with Scapino without the blessing of the Church. The reason for this lack of sacramental protection was that Scapino was
vague about possible precedent marriages, and Isabella, while she
had no qualms about living in adultery, was morally opposed to
bigamy.

There were no children of this union, possibly a result of
Scapino's proficiency with sections of sheep intestines.

In 1515, the French invaders under Frances I commandeered the
estate for the regimental officers, and Scapino, Isabella, and
Colombina made them so comfortable that they stayed an extra
three days and failed to rendezvous as scheduled with the main
force—thus losing the battle. The result was that the three old
troupers were honored as Italian folk heroes, and Isabella's family
once more acknowledged the lovely lady as a limb on their family
tree.

Which proved fortunate two years later when a plague swept Milan and the surrounding countryside, killing Scapino and
Colombina within two days of each other. They were buried side
by side in an olive grove and received the last rites—principally due
to Isabella's lie that Scapino was the illegitimate grandson of the
current pope.

She then went to live her remaining days with her mother's relatives in Mantua. She survived the War of the Holy Alliance and
the War of Illicit Federation and died, finally, at eighty-one, remembered by descendants of the della Rovere and Gonzaga families
as a "wonderful story teller" and "a venerable, wicked old woman

who used to pinch the backsides of the handsome young male servants."

By a direct bribe to the archbishop, Isabella, too, made a death bed confession and received Extreme Unction, though according to some, she kept running her hand under the young prelate's cassock while he chanted the final blessing.

With the disbanding of the Santi Ostinati, *Capitano Francesco Benevelli,* fifty-seven and frightened to death of becoming sixty, was "converted" to a life of meditation and quiet devotion, retiring to a monastery at Pavia. In 1525, however, the capitano—who was then known as Brother Pax—and his fellow monks found their monastery in the center of a battlefield with the French forces on one side and the Italians on the other. The temptation was too great, and he ran leaping from his robes directly into the heart of the conflict.

Unhappily he helped defeat the French but suffered fatal wounds, dying two days later under the loving care of his brother monks, who forgave him his moment of violence. At the end he hallucinated and died crying, "Zephyr! The *rascali*! To arms!"

He died not knowing that a young French officer dying at his very feet was the elder son of the marshal whose war-horse he had stolen decades earlier.

The capitano died not knowing as well that in addition to some other offspring, he had fathered two sons who were to figure prominently in Italian history.

By Louisa, the daughter of the armorer Niccolo of Biella, he sired Giuliano, named, supposedly, after Pope Julius II. And this young gentleman became an armorer himself, eventually refining the crude "pistols" of his father's day into light, portable hand weapons that eventually proved superior to any developed by the French or Germans. He died very wealthy, having allied himself with the most nonparticipatory element of warfare.

By Annamarie Masaccio, the ever-faithful, and the wife of the grand master of the clothmakers' guild in Piacenza, the capitano fathered Filippo, who was named, wisely if inappropriately, after his mother's husband. He, too, became a cloth merchant and dealt directly with the Turks in Constantinople, becoming a close friend and adviser to Selim, who eventually rose against *his* father, Sultan Bajazet, and massacred his kinsmen. Whereupon Filippo *fils* found himself in something of a monopolistic advantage and became very wealthy, too. He supported and shared his income with his mother, Annamarie, who was by that time an attractive, still-young widow. She married again and outlived three additional husbands—and, according to rumors, more than a dozen close friends—before she herself died in 1533.

Tristano Remigio was forty-three when Harlequin died. He was instantly asked to work in another *commedia* troupe being formed in Florence, and he traveled with them for one year playing the capitano's role. Although still handsome, he rejected the *innamorato* role because it bored him. His brief appearance as Poliosco years earlier had struck a spark in him to play character roles.

With him went *Alphonso Rossi*—which was the real name of *Pantalone*, revealed by his errant mother some years later when the Wayward Saints had achieved some degree of fame and popularity and were once again playing Vercelli. At thirty-six, Alphonso was too old for Pantalone roles, which were, by now, always being played by the youngest male of the *commedia* troupes. So he became Dottore, incorporating much of the *lazzi* invented by Giacomo.

Ruffiana went with Tristano, but did not play *commedia* again. When she contracted a terminal illness in 1524, Tristano married her on her sickbed, and she died in the good graces of the Church—even to the point of being buried in sanctified ground, an honor denied to the man who later took the *commedia* techniques and incorporated them into high farce, Molière.

Tristano then left the troupe, unhappy and bored, and returned to Bologna, where he sued his brothers for a share of his dead father's estate and won the case, principally because Pantalone became his "advocate" and confounded the duke's magistrates with phrases in obscure languages and references to wholly imaginary precedents of the law. Tristano lived only three years longer, dying comfortably—but bored—on his estate outside Bologna. His funeral was attended, according to some, by one hundred and fifty-two women of all ages, who wept as though they themselves were at the point of death.

Alphonso continued with the troupe as Dottore until a great many years later. He died attempting a backward cartwheel as new *lazzo* for this character. He had married a young woman of the troupe, named Isabella Traviotti, who played one of the *innamorati*, and they had four sons, each of whom, in turn, played Pantalone using their father's old *lazzi*, and each of whom founded their own *commedia* companies as well.

Soon after his election as Pope Julius II, *Giuliano della Rovere* started a campaign to make the Romagna a papal domain by cannon and cunning, driving *Cesare Borgia* into oblivion with exceptional skill—despite the fact that to assure his election, the cardinal made a deal with Cesare promising to keep him as gonfalonier.

He did not.

When confronted about this broken promise, Pope Julius II argued, "We do not consider that our promises to Cesare Borgia went beyond the security of his life and his stolen money and goods—most of which has already been dissipated."

Cesare and his few remaining condottiere were arrested, and *Michelotto Corella* was tortured under orders from the Vatican. Nevertheless, the loyal giant disclosed nothing and was imprisoned for three years while della Rovere seized all Cesare's assets and demanded that he reimburse Guidobaldo of Urbino, the Riarios, and the city of Florence for the Romagna wars.

In 1506, Michelotto was released and became condottiere to the Florentines.

As for the Duke of Valentinois, *Cesare Borgia*, he was imprisoned by the pope, then released under an agreement with the Spanish. He fled first to Naples, where he had a brief encounter with his brother Jofre and Jofre's wife, Sancia, who now maintained a separate residence from her husband. Then he was imprisoned again, this time by a betrayal on the part of the Spanish, who had apparently studied and mastered the techniques of Cesare's *virtù*.

Upon release he fled to Spain, was imprisoned again, tried to escape, and was transferred to a more secure prison, the castle of La Mota in Castile. He escaped from this prison and ran to friends in Villalon who saw him safely to Pamplona. Then the King of Navarre appointed Cesare captain-general of his troops fighting Luis de Beaumonte with the Spanish forces.

Alone and surrounded by twenty knights, Cesare was unhorsed and stabbed to death. The Spanish stripped him of his weapons and armor and left his body on the field.

Lucrezia Borgia had two more ardent romances, the first with Pietro Bembo, a Venetian poet whom she met, it is said, at a ball given in the Ferrara palace of Ercole Strozzi. The second was with Francesco da Gonzaga, her brother-in-law, who was rumored to have been rendered sterile by the French disease. A catalyst for intrigue, these romances resulted in the murder of Ercole Strozzi by persons unknown, the appointment of Bembo as private secretary to Pope Leo X on the death of Julius, and the naming of Francesco as gonfalonier, Cesare's prized position. Having already provided four sons and one daughter for her husband, Alfonso, Lucrezia became the guardian of both Cesare's and her own children.

Finally, after years of intrigue and deception. She turned to piety, wore a hairshirt under her gowns, and became a member of the Third Order of St. Francis. On June 24, 1519, she died as the result of her eleventh pregnancy, having received Holy Communion and a plenary indulgence from the pope.

Her husband immediately found comfort with his mistress, Laura Dianti of Ferrara.

*A*NGELO PERELLI, giant condottiere of della Rovere and the guardian of the Saints, died of syphilis in a remote corner of the Romagna in 1512. No priest was available, and he died unshriven.

The *French disease*, which was given that title during the Renaissance, received a formal name in 1530 when a physician of Verona wrote a Latin poem commemorating a shepherd named Syphilius, who was allegedly its first victim. In 1520, it became an international epidemic throughout North Africa, Asia, and India.

The Italians always maintained it was the French who brought the disease to Italy. The French continued to claim they first caught it from Spanish women in Naples when they invaded Italy. The Spanish argued that they first encountered it in the "natives" brought back to Spain by their great navigators, including Columbus.

The "miracle cure" of Cesare's physician, Gaspare Torrella, was never recorded, although some have said it was an ointment laced with mercury.

Scapino's "sheep's intestines" were to attain some glory as the best prevention to acquiring the disease. Casanova was to refine them, but it is generally believed that the modern condom was created by the English in the early eighteenth century.

There is a nationalistic moral in that somewhere.

*T*HE BURROS, *Death* and *Destruction*, were grazed on the estate purchased by Colombina, Scapino, and Isabella. Destruction, who was female, produced a single foal, who was promptly named Survival.

Salvation was sold to a Savoy farmer when the Saints departed Italy to play a one-year engagement in France, and apparently died in old age of natural causes.

Zephyr, the war-horse, followed his master to the monastery and became a stud for the monks' growing herd.

*T*HE DEATH of the *commedia* itself came late in the seventeenth century when more and more distinguished crowned heads invited the Italian comedians to play their courts but requested copies of the *soggetto* in advance.

With the death of improvisation as an art form, the Theatre of the Actor passed into memory to be replaced by the Theatre of the

Playwright, and then by the Theatre of the Impressario, who cannot write, act, take a fall, do a handstand, juggle, swallow fire, walk a tightrope, sing a ballad, dance a *saltarello*, play a musical instrument, make a four-minute *lazzo* out of catching a fly, or understand those who could do these things.

They also do not break wind.

ABOUT THE AUTHOR

In his sixty-four years of life *George Herman* has been a steelworker, a hat salesman, a trade-paper editor, printer's devil, a pizza maker, a radio deejay, a cartoonist, a published poet and short-story writer, an award-winning playwright, a public-relations specialist, a photographer, a professional actor and director, a theater critic (for the *Honolulu Advertiser*) and columnist (*Honolulu* magazine), a university professor, composer, ballet librettist, father, and parent (not necessarily in that order).

Thirty-three years ago, while associate professor of theater at Villanova University, he began a play about a run-down troupe of *commedia dell'arte* actors. Four years later this work, *A Company of Wayward Saints*, won the McKnight Foundation Humanities Award, premiered at the University of Minnesota, and was published by Samuel French. Since that time the play has had productions in every state, in more than thirty American universities, and in four foreign countries. In *Carnival of Saints*, his first novel, he has returned to the Italy of the Renaissance and to his nine favorite actors.

Born in Virginia but raised in Maryland, Herman has resided in Boston, Washington, D.C., Iowa, Pennsylvania, Minnesota, Montana, and Hawaii. He is presently a resident of Portland, Oregon.